EVERY YEAR I AM HERE

JOANNA BERESFORD

For my dad, Alex

PART I

A kind person with no children would like to adopt baby; small premium. Alice, Post Office, Valley.

— ADVERTISEMENT IN THE
QUEENSLANDER, 1891

CHAPTER 1

DUTTON PARK, BRISBANE, AUSTRALIA, NOVEMBER 1891

*L*illian heard the woman before she spied her. A primitive groan carried on the breeze, causing her to lower the paintbrush in her right hand. She scanned the scrub one hundred yards to her left. There a figure crouched, partly hidden behind a thicket of stringy-bark and banksia, with skirt and petticoat pulled up to reveal slender thighs.

Lillian sucked in a breath of tangy eucalyptus and tried to slink out of sight; she already had enough troubles of her own. However, her unwieldy corset prevented such a measure. There was nothing to do except remain upright. Besides, curiosity exceeded her usual sense of decorum as she watched the woman writhe on the ground.

Over the past hour, Dutton Park had become deserted. Not a picnicker or ferryman appeared to be about for Lillian to summon any help. It was unusual for a Sunday afternoon. Until that moment, she had been glad of the peace and quiet, painting her watercolour and pretending to be the fine lady she was not... yet. How had the stranger managed to escape her notice?

The seconds turned into excruciating minutes. In the branches, currawongs called to each other, piercing whistles soaring above a cicada chorus. A quick rustle beneath the leaf litter sent a thrill of alarm up her spine. The half-finished watercolour puckered on the open sketchbook and Lillian's dream of being able to pull herself out of a miserable domestic position slid farther away. Green ants scurried by her boots. In that fugitive state, aware any movement might alert the struggler to her presence, at last relief was granted.

The woman's long mane swung as she lurched then sank against peeling bark. Lillian watched her drag an olive-green shawl from her shoulders to wipe the sweat away from her face and neck. The stranger then dropped the wrap on to the ground and fiddled with it. Finally, she rearranged her skirt and petticoat and staggered back on to her feet.

The poor waif was simply dressed in a grey skirt and white cotton blouse still buttoned up to her throat. Even from that distance, Lillian could see the ordeal had left dirt smudged all over her cuffs and elbows. There was no way to get a good look at her face.

Still unsteady, the stranger weaved through the adjoining cemetery's headstones and headed in the direction of small cottages marking the park's perimeter.

Lillian waited until she had vanished from sight before rising to stretch her legs. They prickled all over with pins and needles as blood flow was restored, forcing her to hop from one foot to the other for relief. She bent down to snap the paintbox lid shut and packed it into her basket along with the brush. With the sketchbook tucked firmly into the crook of her arm, she wandered over to where the woman had struggled.

The infant was silent, wrapped tightly in the knitted shawl and nestled on a bed of leaves and twigs. Flies and ants had already begun to infest the puddled afterbirth lying nearby. A couple of larger insects crawled over the baby's slick hair to suckle at sealed eyes. Lillian wished she could say she was surprised to see the sorry sight but she had witnessed each of her sister's labours. The moment she'd laid eyes on the stranger, it was clear birth was imminent.

She darted another look at the cottages and shivered. Were they concealing witnesses to her conundrum? What on earth was she going to do? She'd specially chosen Dutton Park – a good mile's walk from West End – because she had been craving some solitude. The shameful stray had usurped the last of her precious time. Why else would a mother have left her baby behind unless it was illegitimate?

Lillian thought again of her sister and her worries intensified. Patricia would be fretting about why she hadn't yet returned from her walk, not because she was worried about her but because she wanted extra help with the children. Lillian felt frozen with indecision. She had a plan to change her life. It was possible to do such a thing in the colony – her mother had always said so, even if her own dream had shrivelled the moment her foot had stepped ashore.

Lillian finally stooped to bat the flies away from the newborn's twitching nose. The gesture proved futile; the insects immediately returned to continue their scavenging. She crouched on her haunches and tugged the woollen wrap from the little one's body to discover its sex. It was a boy and a healthy-looking one at that. The umbilical cord had roughly been severed; by scissors, a knife or teeth, Lillian couldn't tell. His mother had at least had enough sense to tie it off tightly with a small piece of twine.

The baby's fair-skinned belly rose and fell. Every part of him appeared to be located where it should, except for a large wine-coloured birthmark discolouring his right thigh. Lillian traced her finger around its irregular circumference. He wriggled in response, screwing his face up until he resembled a grumpy old man. She smiled and picked up a corner of the shawl that remained unmarred by dirt to wipe the muck out of his eyes and mouth. He was ugly in the squashed-up way newborns always were yet also quite adorable, especially the way he blinked up at her with old-soul eyes and began to squawk. She was already beginning to fall in love with him and the thought depressed her. Before his tiny siren could gain traction, she quickly wrapped his plump body up nice and secure again. As she tucked in the last corner, a piece of paper slipped from the layers. Lillian unfolded and discovered it to be a promissory note, to the value of one pound. She refolded it and slid it between her top two blouse buttons to lodge it safely between her breasts.

A crunching step on dry bark and a small movement flashed at the corner of her eye. Scared, Lillian glanced around her yet couldn't see anything out of the ordinary. She gently laid her hands on the newborn and felt his warmth emanate from the yarn. There was the sound again. Instinctively, Lillian pulled her own shawl up over her mouth and her bonnet down and twisted back toward where she had been painting. Another girl, younger than herself, stood like an apparition. A buzz filled Lillian's ears. The cicadas' cacophony re-entered her consciousness. She snatched the baby from where he was resting and began to run. Her shawl flapped against her face as she neared the girl, who instinctively held her arms out in self-defence.

'Please, you must take him,' Lillian murmured, thrusting the precious bundle straight into them.

Without looking back, she hurried out to Gladstone Road – the thread to stitch her back to the safety of the West End and her sister. Unfortunately, the baby was of no use to Lillian, even though she missed him already. She'd never be allowed to keep him.

CHAPTER 2

GOOD DECISIONS

*W*ith lungs on fire, Lillian raced along Gladstone Road, drawing ever closer to Patricia's house. Her heart pounded as she put a mile between herself and Dutton Park. The younger girl had screamed with outrage the moment she found herself clutching the baby. Lillian imagined her finger pointing towards the city like a compass. Any Good Samaritan emerging from the cottages to see what the matter was would easily be convinced to set chase after the culprit who had committed such a callous deed. They would drag her straight to the police station if they caught her. Lillian shuddered at the idea of having to defend herself against charges of child abandonment. The fact she'd not been the slightest bit pregnant that morning did nothing to quell her distress. She was a worrier. Patricia always teased her for blowing situations with a justifiable explanation out of proportion. At that moment, Lillian's nervousness knew no bounds but, despite her panic, she forced herself to throw a glance back over her shoulder. Nobody was coming.

She pulled the shawl fringe from her mouth, slowed to a trot and began to feel foolish. It was such a relief finally to reach Musgrave Park, so close to home, and stop for a moment on a park bench to take a rest.

Sweat beaded on her forehead and under her arms, soaking into her cotton blouse. Whether because of shifting the problem on to another girl or knowing how her brother-in-law would react if she'd brought the baby home, her stomach was churning. She collapsed on to a bench beneath a sprawling Moreton Bay fig tree until her heartbeat returned to normal and she felt well enough again to complete the last leg of the journey.

≈

Lillian found her sister in the kitchen, head bent, darning a sock.

Patricia looked up and frowned before resuming stitching more vigorously than the task required. 'Where have you been? You said you would only be gone for two hours. Why did you bother coming home at all if you weren't going to spend any time with us?'

Lillian contemplated a pile of unwashed clothes in a wicker basket, cooking utensils scattered across the table, and her younger nephew, Thomas, kneeling on the floor rolling a toy train. She scooped him up and pulled him on to her hip. He clutched his train with his left hand and entwined the pudgy fingers of his right around the strands of hair at her nape.

'Ow! Be gentle, little chum,' she murmured against his apricot ear.

Lillian took a seat at the table and manoeuvred the small boy so he faced his mother. She tickled him until he erupted with laughter. The ploy to lighten her sister's mood worked somewhat. Patricia set her darning down, licked her thumb and smeared it across her son's cheek.

Still sitting, Lillian craned her neck to see into the adjoining parlour. 'What've you done with Peter?'

Patricia studied Thomas's face for signs of more grime. 'Alf took him to the wharf to watch the sailboats. The yacht club's holding a regatta today.'

'Isn't that nice of him?' Lillian couldn't hide her sarcasm any better than her sister knew how to suppress her irritation. She was sorry Patricia had ended up married to an oaf. At least from observing them she knew what not to accept from a future suitor. Hers would be a marriage of the heart *and* the purse.

'He's doing his best,' Patricia snapped. 'You can keep your judgement to yourself, thank you very much.'

'Oh, so it's all right for you to say mean things about him but not me? I see how it is.' Lillian paused before trying to cajole another smile from her sister. 'Very well, I'm sorry. I didn't want to be out for so long.' She meant what she said, even though none of it had been her fault.

Patricia pushed her sleeves all the way up past her elbows, revealing forearms browned by the summer sun. Long, delicate fingers that would have been far better suited to piano playing – if only they'd grown up in a different world – resumed flying rhythmically as she turned her attention back to the sock.

In a final effort to placate, before she'd have to admit the whole afternoon was a complete disaster, Lillian decided to confess the reason for her tardiness. Her conscience needed soothing. It was impossible to decide on her own whether the decision to pass the baby to a girl even younger than herself had been the right one or not. It certainly didn't feel right. She didn't need to be a mother herself to know that. The image of her unsuspecting saviour rose sharply in her mind. The girl wore an embroidered dress and hat, a mother-of-pearl comb pinned back her rich brown wavy hair and a pair of gold drops hung from her ears. A split-second glance had told Lillian everything she needed to know – the baby would be safe. The girl no doubt had a wealthy, respectable mother who would know what to do, not a poor, dead one like hers and Patricia's.

For her sister, Lillian loosened the truth: the other girl had offered to carry the baby boy off to the Diamantina Orphanage, which conveniently sat across the road from the cemetery in Dutton Park. Her breath hitched, torn between choosing that ending instead of a much nicer one, where the girl took the baby to her mother instead, to adopt him instantly into the bosom of their luxurious home. In the end, Lillian felt it best to keep her explanation realistic. Even after sharing her contrivance, Lillian found the burden on her conscience only slightly allayed and it disappointed her.

'Goodness! Poor little chap,' Patricia said. 'What a fright for you. Lucky somebody else was on hand to help. I suppose The Diam really is the best place for the child if his mother can't care for him but doesn't it only take babies when families can't afford to keep them? What would a married woman be doing in the middle of a park giving birth by herself?'

Lillian raised an eyebrow.

Patricia tilted her head to one side and rolled her eyes. 'Yes, well, it's still unfortunate. I hope a nurse took him in. It's hardly the baby's fault.'

Lillian pointed to a slab of bread sitting on a wooden board at the far end of the table. 'Can I have a piece?'

Patricia nodded. 'Yes, do. I saved the last of the butter for you as well. After you've eaten, would you be a dear and bring in the dry washing so I can hang out the next lot? If you can fold it as well, that would be lovely.'

Lillian felt glad to be able to conclude the visit on a happy note. Easing Thomas back to the floor to continue playing with his train, she descended the three wooden steps beyond the back door and collected napkins from the line of wire strung up between two leaning posts. The honeysuckle climbing the side of the outhouse in the far left corner of the yard released a pleasant scent. Patricia's vegetable patch was flourishing along the fence. Her sister had a successful green thumb, which was fortunate because her lazy husband wasn't good at providing very much at all those days. At least Alfred's industrious father had had the grim foresight to bestow on his son a deposit for the cottage as a wedding gift.

With his miserly approach to spending on his family, despite the fact Alfred had been out of work for eight weeks, he hadn't yet felt the pinch like many others living in the West End. Lillian suspected Alfred also had other nefarious ways and means to make a pound, ways she hadn't yet uncovered. To her disgust, she knew – indeed had seen with her own eyes – how he'd begun to enjoy the extra idle hours... by spending her own hard-earned money at the Terminus Hotel over on Melbourne Street.

The screen door slammed against the outside wall as she unclipped the last sun-warmed napkin.

'Lillian. There you are.'

Alfred swayed on the top step. His voice grated. It was just as well there wasn't another hour to spare to have to listen to him prattle on.

'Alfred.' She acknowledged him through gritted teeth and did her best to keep her expression neutral. 'Did you enjoy watching the race with Peter?'

Patricia hovered behind her husband's shoulder, her nostrils flaring. Lillian kept her own sharp tongue on a leash. What had happened to the determined person she used to turn to for advice? Who was this quivering ghost in the shape of her sister? It was a crying shame.

'Yes, but unfortunately Peter tripped over his own feet and fell over. I had to bring him straight home to his mother because he wouldn't bloody stop crying.' Alfred looked down at his son with disappointment. 'Would ya, boy?'

Lillian watched her elder nephew whimper behind his father's legs. Fell or pushed? Alfred's temper didn't flare only at Patricia.

'I really must be heading back,' she said. Anything to avoid being caught up in his avalanche of self-pity.

Despite his injury, Peter burst past his father into the yard. 'Aunt Lillie, I don't want you to go!'

'Sorry, Peter, but I must. I promise to come back next weekend like I always do.' Despite his pleas, she urgently wished to rid herself of all of them.

'Have you given Patricia your wages yet?' Alfred asked.

Lillian grabbed her nephew's small dimpled hands and swooped him around in wide circles. The promissory note scratched against her skin as she swung him back to happiness and disguised her scowl. 'Yes I did.' Well, most of it, except for two small coins well hidden under her bed. They were an investment in her future, one without the hateful Alfred in it. At the current rate, she feared she'd be a wrinkly old spinster by the time the plan could be put in motion.

'Good girl.'

Lillian slowed and deposited Peter unsteadily back to earth. It was time to retrieve her basket and go. Loading her arms up with clean napkins, she walked to the back steps.

Alfred did not attempt to move.

'Excuse me please, Alf. I have to say goodbye to Patricia.'

'She's busy.'

'Alfred, please. She asked me to fold the napkins before I

leave.' Lillian was careful not to let a whine creep into her voice.

'Listen to you. Haven't you learned a few airs and graces working in that fancy house? Don't forget I was the one who found you that position.' His glare dared her to protest but she would not grant him the satisfaction of an argument.

'See you next Sunday, Patricia!' she called out instead, depositing the napkins on the step at Alfred's feet. She crouched in front of Peter and pulled him into a hug. 'Be a very good boy for me, won't you? Do you understand?'

The little boy nodded.

'Look after your mother.'

She pecked his cheek and straightened, pretending not to see the way Alfred warily watched them.

'Aren't you going to give your brother a kiss goodbye, too?'

She ignored him and hurried to the side of the house, rushing up the space between the wall and fence while Alfred's derisive laughter trailed after her. Angry, she strode up on to the veranda, flung the front door open and flew up the narrow hall to snatch her basket.

Patricia looked aghast. Lillian quickly blew her a kiss as Alfred spun on the back step, knocked the clean napkins into the dirt, and lunged at her. Too quick for his grasp, she ducked back up the hall out of harm's way.

'Oi, get back here!' Alfred shouted.

Mrs Lin, from the market garden further up the road, was wandering past the front gate. The elderly woman swung a startled glance between Alfred and Lillian as they erupted from the cottage. Her expression swiftly descended into disapproval. The whole street would soon know their sorry business.

Lillian scuttled past and curtly nodded a greeting, still expecting Alfred's hand on her shoulder at any moment. Risking a quick glance back, she saw the front porch remained empty. He'd obviously been chastened by the presence of a witness and retreated, deciding she wasn't worth the bother of a public chase. She knew he would not forgive nor forget her impertinence yet euphoria set in at having foiled him. Each instance where she managed to evade his authority held a hollow victory. However, a needle of discomfit pricked at her. Patricia would be the one to bear the brunt of his chagrin that evening. Lillian chided herself for being selfish but there were so precious few other outlets available to be able to express her frustration.

After such an eventful afternoon, with two lucky escapes, it was a relief to head back to her own lodgings. It had initially infuriated her when Alfred secured her a position at Rose-mead. Before Alfred was dismissed, when his boss, Mr Shaw, had mentioned he was in need of reliable domestic staff, he'd wasted no time offering her up. Lillian had watched her brother-in-law sit at the kitchen table to fabricate a reference before sealing it in an envelope. He'd given her instructions to hand it over on arrival at the stately Kangaroo Point address.

She would not be indebted to Alfred. She would not! He was her sister's first poor decision, not hers. Rounding the corner, Lillian paused to whisper a curse upon his head.

Brisbane River forged beneath Victoria Bridge as she crossed it, sidestepping hand-swinging promenaders and the Sunday devout. She decided to take advantage, before the light faded, to detour through Queen's Park. Alfred's hold began to weaken as the greenery pressed in on her senses. The injustice of being unable to kiss her sister goodbye abated. The scent of gardenias wafted across the late afternoon air, evoking memories of their mother's favourite perfume; a large bottle had always sat on the tiny oak dressing table in their room. Lillian remembered watching her carefully squeeze a spray behind each ear as she readied for an evening of entertaining.

Rather than producing sadness at the memory, the scent comforted.

Up ahead, the Edward Street ferry pulled into the wharf, which served to set Lillian's spirits right once and for all. No dawdling, simply a step aboard for the final leg of the trip. It would not do to be late.

As she turned into Shafston Road, the Shaws' immaculate mansion loomed up ahead. The large brick house decorated with lacy balustrade was set back into a sprawling front lawn and separated from the street by a white picket fence. Even as shadows began to fall across the grass court stretching alongside the property, Mrs Shaw and her daughter, Olivia, continued to play a tennis match. With a sigh, Lillian stepped over the property's threshold and braced herself for another week of domestic drudgery.

A rush of wind overhead frightened her. She batted her hands in the air and looked up in time to see a black-and-white blur materialise into a magpie. The fiend alighted in the branches of a large elm planted inside the gate and stared down. Not wishing to receive another dive-bombing, Lillian raced to the back porch. Except for a cursory glance to see what the fuss had been about, the players ignored her, as was their custom. She would have received a greater shock if Mrs Shaw and Olivia had rushed over to try with their rackets to save her from the bird.

Still perturbed, Lillian entered the house and traipsed up two flights of stairs to the stuffy attic she shared with Catherine. Her roommate was a Scotswoman who spoke with a thick Glaswegian brogue and, other than her sister, was the only friend Lillian felt she had. With Patricia so busy with Alfred, her children, and keeping up the cottage, it had been a relief to find another ally. At three years older, Catherine always seemed to have a word of wisdom to help keep her spirits up.

For the moment though, the room was empty. In fact, the whole house seemed far too quiet. Mrs Menzies, who doubled both as cook and housekeeper, would be outside collecting herbs or feeding scraps to the chickens. In her hurry to get inside, Lillian hadn't had time to look around the garden. She didn't know when Catherine would return from visiting her friends. It couldn't be much longer; dinner needed to be prepared and ready to serve by six o'clock.

Lillian unbuttoned her boots and slipped them off her stockinged feet. They had gathered plenty of dust from the roads that afternoon. She dipped her handkerchief into the pitcher sitting on the washstand. It still held some water from her morning wash. She'd been in too much of a rush to finish her chores and leave for Patricia's to bother emptying it. Picking up a boot and dotting two eyes and a slip of a smile on to the leather, she then reached over to the dresser and retrieved a polish kit. Mrs Shaw might not worry herself about saving a servant from an avian attacker but she would notice immediately if Lillian dared serve her dinner up while looking the slightest bit shabby.

Beyond the closed door, the floorboards emitted a steady squeaking. Catherine must have returned. Lillian expectantly waited to greet her but Donald Shaw poked his head around the door instead. His face broke into a grin. From the hopeful look, he obviously believed she was happy to see him.

She clutched her quilt and froze. He'd never been so brazen.

'Hello, Lillian.'

'Hello,' she murmured back.

Donald slid inside the room and sauntered over, taking one of the bedstead's brass domes into his palm to caress it. Seizing an uninvited seat, he took in the meagre decorations around the room: a portrait of Catherine's brothers hanging on the wall, a silver candlestick on the nightstand that had been Lillian's mother's, and a cast-off embroidered hand towel hanging off the washstand. Donald's silk waistcoat and the gleaming gold watch chain hanging from his breast pocket made a mockery of the sparseness.

'Did you have a pleasant time at your sister's this afternoon?'

'Yes, I did. Thank you for asking.'

'I'm glad to hear it.' He smoothed the worn pattern on her quilt with his long, well-manicured fingers.

Donald was Mr and Mrs Shaw's younger son. At twenty, he was a full year older than she was. Lord knew her mother and Patricia had drummed in the message of abstinence the moment her monthly blood began to flow. It was unfair of him to dangle himself in front of her like a carrot on a string before a goat. She could have screamed. She could have run right out the door. The path was clear.

Lillian didn't want to do either. After all, Donald had been the secret object of her desire since the moment he'd strolled, cock-sure, into the kitchen while she'd been working and stolen a thick slice of ham off a serving platter. He'd put a finger to his lips and winked at her right as Mrs Menzies – cantankerous woman that she was – turned around and caught him red-handed.

Lillian had struggled to contain her laughter.

'Get away, you scallywag!' Mrs Menzies had shouted.

The cold cut was intended for him anyway. It was of no consequence to Donald whether he took it by stealth or had it served up to him alongside the rest of the family. He'd simply bowed his head with mock contrition at the cook's tirade and retreated to the dining room.

They were lucky, Mrs Menzies, Catherine and herself. Donald possessed a naturally sunny disposition. The trouble for Mrs Menzies was she had known him since he was a rambunctious child. Now he'd grown into manhood, he was well within his rights to order them all about, and yet he refrained. His spoilt little sister, Olivia, on the other hand, was a churlish, sly witch of a girl who took every opportunity to remind all of them of their proper station within the house.

Lillian felt light-headed with Donald sitting on her bed cheekily beckoning her to come sit a little closer. Did he forget she was the one who had the task of emptying his chamber pot each morning? She knew more about his bowel habits than he did, yet being the recipient of such unsavoury knowledge did nothing to discourage her affection for him.

She had a ridiculous urge to confess what had happened at Dutton Park that afternoon. Perhaps her callousness would shock him enough to leave her alone for good? What did he care about women's private matters? He might even report her. She couldn't risk losing such a bright flame in an otherwise dull existence.

Donald, who rode a strong mare and had been born with a cricket bat in his hands, would never understand the desperation that drove a young woman to discard her own flesh and blood. Lillian could scarcely make sense of the woman's actions herself. Would he shudder if she pulled back the curtain on the reality life held for lesser mortals? All those very same reasons were precisely why she found him so attractive. Donald understood how to enjoy his privilege and made no apologies for it. He lent her a glimmer of hope that one day – if she made very good decisions – it would be possible to be able to do the same, despite their beginnings in life being so unequal.

Undeterred by her reluctance, Donald edged closer and slowly connected the tips of their fingers. She held her breath and kept her eyes firmly fixed on his. He did not make personal resolutions easy to keep.

'I missed seeing your friendly face about the house today,' he said.

'I –'

His lips were upon hers quickly and hungrily. She pressed into his hands that were pawing at her blouse.

A steady thumping of boots shook them both immediately to their feet before Catherine entered the small space.

'Och, no!' The Scotswoman scanned the scene before her and, deciding no harm had yet been done, barged past to plonk down on her own bed. 'Get out of here, Donald. Yer cannae get Lillian and me into trouble.'

He raised his palms to show the moment between them was well and truly dispelled and exited without objection. Lillian wished he wouldn't let Catherine push him around; she was only a servant.

'For Christ's sake, Lil. Cannae ye at least be locking the door?' Catherine lay back, flung an arm across her eyes and loudly yawned.

'I didn't invite him in.'

'I dinnae care whit yer do but at least be careful, hen. Why yer'd want to spend any time with that cheeky bastard is completely beyond me.'

'He's not! Donald works very hard and has impeccable manners.'

'If his manners are so impeccable, whit's he doing in a room he shouldnae be with a maid whose reputation is the only thing of value she has?'

Lillian poked out her tongue and fetched her apron and cap from where they hung on a hook on the back of the door. Catherine had an answer for everything.

As her infuriating friend's eyes were concealed, Lillian retrieved with some difficulty the bank note from where it had slipped down inside her corset. She crouched beside her bed and rummaged under the mattress to find a slit she had created months ago. The note slid between her other treasures: a cherished illustrated copy of her childhood favourite, *Pinocchio*, the only photograph ever taken of herself and a small cloth bag filled with hard-saved coins. She would need to find a better long-term solution for all these items but for now there was no time. She rose and finished tying her apron strings about her waist before securing the cap to her hair with several hairpins.

'Catherine, aren't you going to come down and help?'

'Aye, in a wee bit. By the way, I'd be putting those paints back from where they came before anybody discovers yer've been thieving.'

Lillian's basket and its paraphernalia jutted halfway out from beneath the bed, where she'd hastily kicked it as Donald entered.

She blushed. 'I was only borrowing them.'

'I won't tell Mrs Shaw yer a crook if yer dinnae tell her I was taking a wee nap instead of getting ready to work.' Catherine slowly lifted her arm and winked. 'By the way, if I'd wanted to steal yer things I'd have done it a long time ago. Yer far too suspicious.'

So Catherine knew about her hiding place after all? Lillian sheepishly plucked the paint box from the basket. She quickly rinsed the brushes but left them and the sketchbook behind. She'd managed to save for the latter by withholding two measly pennies a week from Alfred and Patricia.

Heading down one flight of stairs to the first floor, Lillian ventured on to the landing and paused to make sure nobody else was about. The dull and steady rhythmic thwacking of a tennis ball on catgut strings satisfied her the ladies of the house were still busy playing tennis, despite there being scarcely any light left to see by. She continued along to Olivia's room, carefully turned the brass doorknob to avoid squeaking and entered.

Shut safely inside the cavernous and rather luxuriously appointed room, Lillian crept over to the cherrywood writing desk stationed beneath the tall sash window. She pulled open the lid and slid the paintbox back on to a little shelf where it had been sitting that morning.

She never feared being caught; she was quite adept at arranging items so the owner never noticed a thing missing. Pickpocketing clients who had imbibed one too many glasses of Madame Claudette's finest brandy was a skill all the children she had grown up with had quickly honed, even if Patricia liked to pretend she'd been above such dishonesty. Even if the men who frequented the bawdy house realised they'd been robbed, they were unlikely to report the petty crime to a constable. For her own part, how else was she going to further her education and interests if she wasn't prepared to make use of the available equipment needed to be able to do so? A lady should be well-versed in literature and art and that was precisely what Lillian intended to be one day; a lady, and a sophisticated one at that. She didn't know quite how just yet, but it was certainly going to happen. It infuriated her to see expensive materials go to waste when there was an opportunity to make some money from them. If she could demonstrate her artistic ability to the owners of one of the exclusive shops, perhaps the offer of an apprenticeship would be forthcoming. The cinders in her belly stoked into flames at the thought.

It had been obvious to all of Rosemead's occupants that Olivia's foray into watercolours was going to be brief. The spiteful girl had furiously balled up a failed landscape in front of her father when he'd dared to compliment her and thrown the offending page straight into the lit drawing-room fireplace. While Mr Shaw was a very successful and formidable solicitor, it appeared he was no match for his spoilt sixteen-year-old daughter. Lillian felt quite certain Olivia had long forgotten she even owned the paintbox. Still, she hoped Catherine wouldn't use the knowledge of her misconduct to hold her to ransom later. It was true the Scot had never given any reason for Lillian to doubt her but one could never be too careful.

Shuffling steps sounded out on the landing. Lillian held her breath lest she was about to be caught without even a cloth in her hand for dusting. There should be no other reason at that time of the evening for her to be entering Olivia's bedroom. Catherine was the one who took care of the linen and bed-making, not her. The fear of punishment made her shiver. Whoever it was passed by, much to her relief. She hastily exited and hurried down the final flight of stairs into the safety of the kitchen.

Mrs Menzies had reappeared and was busy setting a pie on the table next to a freshly picked bunch of parsley that needed chopping.

'There you are, Lillian! Where have you been? And where's Catherine?'

Mrs Menzies never seemed pleased to see either girl. Lillian supposed the chore of coordinating cooked meals for ten mouths every single night was enough of a reason for the woman's prickly demeanour. The cook used the same accusing tone as Patricia had earlier. Unlike Patricia, Mrs Menzies would not relent for an embroidered excuse. Lillian wisely kept her mouth shut and did her best to look contrite.

'Here. The family will be inside shortly for their tea. Go set the silver. Once you've done that, come back and start cutting up those herbs.' Mrs Menzies wiped her hands on her apron and pointed at the parsley.

Lillian did as she was told.

When the family had assembled around the mahogany

table, their patriarch, Mr Henry Shaw, closed his eyes and delivered grace with his usual aplomb. Lillian suppressed a laugh at Donald's irreverent glances as his father's tightly closed eyes sent bushy eyebrows dancing. It was frivolity on her part to think Donald might hold sincere affection toward her. Surely he thought of her as no more than a toy? Play with her he certainly had those past few months.

Even the sight of Fergus, Donald's older brother, also still a bachelor – with his immaculately pomaded hair and handkerchief peeping from his breast pocket – failed to amuse her that evening. Ordinarily she found Fergus a source of fascination. He courted a carousel of women, being eligible with inheritable wealth and a position at his father's firm. He also enjoyed horsing about with Alfred and the other chaps they'd attended school with more than ten years ago. That evening, though, her thoughts continued to be clouded by the baby she'd been forced to leave in the park.

'Whit're yer doing?'

The carpet came into focus and Lillian realised she'd been caught head down in a stupor. Catherine had slipped up behind her and she hadn't even noticed.

'Nothing.'

'Olivia's been staring daggers at yer, waiting for her glass to be refilled.'

Lillian glanced across the table and saw the sour girl scowling back. She hurried over with the decanter.

'Best be getting yerself back to the kitchen before Cook throws a right wee fit,' said Catherine as Lillian returned to her side.

She clutched at Catherine's sleeve. 'I've done a terrible thing.'

'Well whitever it is, hen, surely it cannae be as bad as holding up the dinner service. Come on now.'

Lillian dutifully followed her back to the kitchen and refilled the decanter as Catherine retrieved a large dish of roasted vegetables from the sideboard. Despite the steaming aroma tantalising her nostrils, Lillian's appetite had completely disappeared.

Outside, darkness descended the same way it had inside her.

CHAPTER 3

KANGAROO POINT

*L*illian awoke to find herself twisted up inside her
sheets with her nightgown sticking to her back. She'd
been dreaming of ants crawling all over her skin and
found herself still clawing away at the imaginary creatures on
her arms. A peek under the curtain revealed a still-black sky.

She couldn't rightly leave in the middle of the night to go
and make sure the poor baby had indeed been taken out of the
park, but she wanted to very much. She could have left that
baby on the steps of the Methodist church or the Anglican
cathedral or the Diamantina herself. Had her hasty actions
doomed her as an accomplice to murder? Surely the wretched
mother was lying in her own bed somewhere and praying
someone had used the pound note to feed, clothe and love her
son? The other younger witness had looked so helpless when
Lillian had shirked responsibility like a morbid game of pass the
parcel.

She wrenched the bedclothes from her limbs and drifted
back into an uneasy sleep.

Catherine shook her by the shoulders and peered down at her with concern. 'Hey, yer were talking in your sleep.'

Lillian rubbed her puffy eyes. 'What did I say?'

Catherine slid her arms inside her shirt sleeves. 'I couldn't tell whit yer were blethering on about. Must have been something to do with that terrible thing yer did.'

'Pardon?' Lillian struggled to sit up, startled.

Catherine laughed. 'I'm only teasing, hen. Remember? Yer said as much last night but didnae mention whit it was you'd done.'

'I did, didn't I?'

'Whit was it then, the terrible thing yer did?' Catherine's face was lit up with mischief as she finished buttoning her shirt.

Lillian racked her brain. 'I... I let Donald put his hand underneath my skirt and touch my knee.' The excuse sounded weak, even to her.

Catherine playfully squashed Lillian's cheeks between her warm palms. 'Scandalous. As if I didnae know about that already. For a wee moment I thought yer'd done something criminal.'

Lillian gulped. 'Of course not.'

'Whitever it is, yer'll keep. I'll get yer secret out of yer one way or another.' Catherine retreated to her own bed. She reached for her boots, put them on and hurriedly laced them up. 'See yer in the kitchen. Yer'd better hurry up.'

Catherine left as Lillian reluctantly rose, feeling weary from her disrupted night's sleep. She filled the washstand bowl with water from the jug her bedfellow had already retrieved from the well and washed her face and body to get rid of the stale perspiration that had left her feeling sticky all over. Today marked one year since her arrival at Rosemead. The anniversary was an unpleasant reminder there were several months of stultifying heat ahead to endure in the poky attic. The thought did not cause much distress: she was used to being uncomfortable. She wiped herself down with a rough towel, patted at her eyes and got dressed. The temperature lowered by several degrees as she plodded downstairs.

As Lillian entered the kitchen a loud squeal shattered the morning quiet and immediately roused her from her fugue.

Mrs Menzies turned to Catherine. 'Now who on earth do you think that could be?'

'Maybe Olivia found a wee cockroach in her bed.'

'We can only hope,' said Lillian.

'That's enough from you two.' Cook whipped a dishcloth at them. 'Whoever it is, they're somewhere out the front.'

The shrieking and shouting intensified, which spurred all three of them to hurry down the hall and burst out on to the wide veranda beside Mrs Shaw and Olivia, who were holding their hands to their mouths. The sight in front of them was worse than Lillian could have imagined.

Beyond the gate, an exquisitely dressed young woman was clutching her left ear with fright. The same magpie that had bothered Lillian yesterday afternoon was in the middle of a repeat bombardment on its newest victim. On its next descent, the bird succeeded in knocking the woman's bonnet to a crazy angle. The lady had already fallen from her bicycle, which now lay twisted on the ground. Her efforts to retrieve it one-handed while attempting to ward off her attacker were proving ineffectual.

What made the spectacle truly disastrous was the moment Donald pushed through the onlooking huddle clutching a tennis racket and taking aim at the marauder. His bravado gave the victim time to seek shelter behind his hastily tucked-in shirt. Satisfied the bird was temporarily warded off, Donald bent to retrieve the bicycle and set it upright. He then offered his arm to the poor woman. She gratefully tucked her gloved hand into the crook of his elbow and held on for dear life.

Something about the sight of them standing together, Donald's face etched with concern while keeping a wary look-out, made Lillian feel truly sick to her stomach. He wheeled the bicycle up the front path and leant it against the balustrading before ushering his prize past her. His mother and sister hurried anxiously inside after them. As the young lady had passed, Lillian noticed the pristine white gloves held to her ear had bright bloodstains seeping into them. The wheels were responsible, of course. While that naughty magpie had swooped at Lillian's head the previous night, the gesture had merely been a warning. It was the passing carts, bicycles and dogs the creature detested above all else.

Mrs Shaw dispatched her to retrieve iodine and cotton wool from the medicine cabinet. Lillian returned to the draw-ing-room in time to see the visitor being gently guided to the ottoman. The young woman found herself immediately flanked on the seat by Olivia and Mrs Shaw. Lillian slunk into a corner and listened as the stranger told them both in faintly clipped English tones that her Christian name was Mary and that she and her family, the Forsyths, lived not far from the Observatory at Spring Hill.

Mrs Shaw launched a polite but steady stream of questions to ascertain that Miss Mary was the daughter of the respected doctor, Joseph Forsyth. As if her father's esteemed position weren't enough to pique interest, the guest went on to explain that her mother, Mrs Elizabeth Forsyth, was an active supporter of the Society of the Prevention of Cruelty as well as local suffragist activities.

'A progressive lady indeed,' Mrs Shaw exclaimed. 'I myself am a longstanding member of the Diamantina Orphanage

Ladies' Committee; since its inception, actually. I should think your mother and I might have quite a bit to talk about if we were to meet. Tell me, dear Mary, which church does your family attend?'

'All Saints on Wickham Terrace. It's Anglican. You may have already been able to tell I'm English by my accent.' Mary covered her self-effacing smile with her glove before remembering it was soiled with blood. Embarrassed, she quickly lowered her hand back to her lap and tried to cover it with the less affected one.

'Yes, of course.' This news served to puff Mrs Shaw up with further pleasure. 'Here, Mary, I can get one of the girls to wash that spot right out for you.' She raised her hand and beckoned Lillian from her corner. 'Come and take Miss Forsyth's glove. Olivia dear, perhaps you would be so kind as to let Mary have a spare pair of your own to borrow for the meantime?'

Olivia stood immediately and left the room with swift steps to retrieve a set from her dresser.

Mrs Shaw plumped her skirt. 'Olivia and I would be happy to venture over and return your glove tomorrow when it's back to its original condition.'

'Oh yes, please do. Mother will be delighted to meet you, especially after I tell her how you came to my aid this morning,' Mary said. She flicked a shy look at Donald who had seated himself by the window. 'You've been most gracious.'

He grinned with delight. It had not escaped Lillian's notice that Donald appeared to be intently hanging on to every word coming from Mary's blush-coloured lips.

Indeed, it was easy enough to see why he would be intrigued, Lillian thought. Mary was a "bonny wee lass", as Catherine would say. Her blonde hair – despite its recent ruffling – still held the remnants of careful styling. The wisps about her temple and cheeks kindly framed enviably high cheekbones. She was a girl who was obviously careful to wear her hat outdoors to protect such alabaster skin from burning beneath the hot Queensland sun. Lillian's fingers fluttered to her freckled face with dismay.

Mary slowly removed her gloves, daintily plucking at each cloth finger, and handed them over. Lillian remained poised as was expected of her, despite the unsavouriness of the task, and took the offering down to the laundry to attend to the stains. By the time she returned from scrubbing them with lye and leaving them to soak in a bucket of lukewarm water, Olivia had retrieved clean gloves and Catherine had wheeled in the tea trolley.

'Do have a cup, dear. It will help settle your nerves. You've had a huge shock. The magpies are appalling around here. You'd think they'd be long finished their nesting by now.' Mrs Shaw gave Catherine a nod to proceed to pour without waiting for Mary's response. 'I shall have to see what can be done to get it moved on.'

Lillian shuddered. She knew what that meant.

'Thank you, everyone, for your kindness,' Mary said, politely receiving the cup and saucer.

'Do you take milk or sugar?' Mrs Shaw asked.

'A little milk, thank you. No sugar.'

Catherine obliged the request and handed it to Mary before pouring a cup for Lillian to give Donald, all the while glancing out of the corner of her eye with obvious amusement.

Lillian conveyed the beverage across the room where Donald received it with a cursory thank you, never taking his eyes from Mary's face. She returned to her original position and tried not to let despondency seep in, otherwise Catherine would never let her hear the end of it.

'I really must be on my way. I'm meant to be meeting my friends at Mowbray Park at nine o'clock.' Mary replaced her empty cup to its saucer. The tea had done the trick – she seemed much brighter. 'We're going rowing on the river.'

'That sounds lovely!' Olivia clapped her hands. 'I wish I could come.'

How lovely, Lillian thought resentfully, to have time on a weekday for a trip on the water.

Mary remained decorous at the hint. 'Well, if you would like to, I know there is enough room for one more.'

'Mother!' Olivia almost leapt off her seat. 'May I?'

Her mother shook her head with regret. 'I am afraid not, my dear. You have school to attend. It's almost nine. If you don't hurry, I shall have to write a note to explain your lateness.'

Lillian felt a pang of joy watching as Olivia's chest sagged with disappointment. However, it went no way at all toward alleviating the distress she felt watching Donald being so enchanted by their guest.

Mary reached out and lightly touched Olivia's hand. 'Another time perhaps?'

Olivia gazed back at her, mildly appeased. 'Oh yes, absolutely. I would love that.'

Mary glanced at the grandfather clock standing sentry by the window and looked concerned. 'Goodness. Is that really the time?'

'Donald could take you across to Mowbray Park in the trap. You wouldn't mind, would you, dear?' Mrs Shaw asked.

Pointedly, Lillian thought.

Donald immediately stood, cleared his throat and adjusted his cufflinks. 'Of course. It would be my pleasure.'

Lillian bit her upper lip with chagrin. Mowbray Park lay in the opposite direction to his office in the city. The detour would lengthen his journey to work by a further twenty minutes. Wasn't his job far more important than making sure Mary had a row on the river?

'Are you quite sure? I wouldn't want to cause any more trouble.' Mary hesitated and Lillian wondered if the girl was torn between accepting an unchaperoned lift with an eligible and – in her own opinion – handsome young man or, missing out on a day with her friends.

It seemed clear to Lillian that despite a difficult start to Mary's day, the outlook had become significantly brighter for her with each passing moment. While hers, on the other hand, had withered right before her very eyes.

Mary smiled coyly and accepted Donald's offer.

Concealed behind the drawing-room's heavy lace curtains, Lillian watched their departure. She cried out as though in pain when Donald held out a chivalrous hand to assist Mary as she climbed up and took her place on the buggy seat above. He looked very dapper, now fully dressed in his well-cut charcoal morning coat and a bowler atop his crown, as he effortlessly mounted alongside his charge. She wondered why Mary struggled to look him in the eye. The silly girl had hardly seemed able to take her eyes from the carpet the entire time she'd sat on the ottoman. On the occasions Lillian herself had stolen a moment with Donald, she'd taken pride in never flinching from his gaze, which up until that point he had bestowed on her pleasingly often.

Despite their unequal social standing, the realisation their attraction was mutual had become clear the moment she'd encountered him coming in from the stable not long after arriving at Rosemead. Until that point, she'd admired him from afar and felt certain her feelings were one-sided. That morning, all those months ago, she'd stood on the gravel, carrying a basket of wet laundry to hang out on the line. Shocking pleasure had passed like an electric current from her throat to her groin when he'd purposely brushed past her. It couldn't have been an accident; there had been more than enough space for him to go around.

Their first kiss had been a hurried encounter. The following afternoon, he'd tugged her into the upstairs bathroom while she'd been on the landing trying to dust a portrait of his grandfather. As he pulled her into his arms, the brush of his short beard had tickled her face and his tongue had probed delightfully between her lips. In the next breath she'd found herself ejected out of the small room with a light slap on her rear, wondering if anything had really happened at all.

Lillian lived for those chance meetings yet never managed to summon enough courage to instigate one herself. Why, only last week Donald had charmed her by presenting a small pink rose picked fresh from the garden. It still lay decaying against the wall beneath her bed. Mrs Shaw would have a fit if she saw it. At night, though, she retrieved it from its hiding place and inhaled the remnants of its scent. Catherine thought she was absolutely ridiculous. 'Are yer trying to make potpourri?' she taunted.

The only bit of satisfaction gleaned from Mary's unwelcome appearance was the sight of Miss Olivia standing forlornly on the gravel beside her mother, waving Donald and his damsel off down the street, obviously resentful at having to attend her regular classes at school. Lillian wondered what Mrs Forsyth might have to say about her daughter's lack of a chaperone but knew without having to look that Mrs Shaw was almost beside herself with glee.

She mournfully continued to gaze out and sigh as Catherine began to tidy up the empty cups and saucers. 'Please don't say I told you so.'

Catherine handed her a damp cloth. 'Why wouldnae I do

that when I can see yer poor wee heart's been smashed to smithereens?'

'No it hasn't.' Lillian listlessly swiped at a large glass bell displaying a pair of stuffed galahs. Their black glass eyes followed her. She detested that room, with its gloomy green Chinoiserie wallpaper, dried flower arrangements and dead birds. It felt like a mausoleum. Indeed, it was where Donald's affection for her had been snuffed out.

'Very well. If yer say so.' Catherine picked up the tray, leaving her to dwell on the unfortunate turn of events for as long as she liked, or at least until Mrs Shaw returned to the house and gave her yet another chore to do.

CHAPTER 4

AMBITION

*A*fter the morning's excitement had died down, any faint hopes Lillian held about wretched Mary's presence being a one-time occurrence foundered. The rest of November passed in a boring blur as she wistfully watched Donald's frequent comings and goings from the house. Sadly, he appeared to revel in his new status as a rescuing hero. Mary had gladly handed over a calling card with her address printed in smart cursive as she left so Mrs Shaw and Olivia would know where to deliver her salvaged gloves – the same gloves Lillian had to hang out to dry and carefully iron. She'd petulantly turned one of them inside out and snipped a tiny thread inside one of the fingers, using a pair of nail scissors she found on Mrs Shaw's dressing table. The ends satisfactorily sprang apart. It would take several wears for the deed to have its desired effect and Lillian was confident by then she wouldn't be suspected as a saboteur.

Mrs Shaw was distracted by the mounting events in her social calendar. 'I feel as though the silly season has come early this year,' Lillian heard her say to her husband over breakfast.

Mr Shaw studiously hacked at the top of his boiled egg as his wife moaned about all there was to do, and said, "Hmm,' in all the right places.

Taking the buggy out with Olivia to pay Mary and her mother the expected visit heralded yet another invitation for Mrs Shaw to squeeze in. Mary's mother Elizabeth asked Mrs Shaw whether she and Olivia would like to attend a fundraising luncheon for the Society of the Prevention of Cruelty. It would be taking place the following Wednesday at their home. Mrs Forsyth explained it was the least she could do in exchange for the kindness they'd shown Mary.

Lillian learned those details at dinner that evening as Mrs Shaw and Olivia gossiped excitedly about the Forsyths' crystal chandelier and fine carpets.

'Oh, they've got six housemaids, Henry. Six!'

Mr Shaw took his time raising his napkin to wipe the edges of his mouth. 'We're not getting any more maids, Edith.'

Mrs Shaw wouldn't allow her husband's lack of enthusiasm curb her own. 'Two of them are Aborigines and one's a young apprentice from the Diamantina. The Forsyths are very altruistic, you know.'

'So it would seem,' was his curt reply. 'However, altruism doesn't pay wages. We have more than enough help.'

Lillian shrank against the wall as Mrs Shaw threw a disdainful glance in her direction and sighed.

'Yes, I know that well enough, Henry, but dear, you should have seen the place. It was...' Mrs Shaw waved her hands about, trying to settle on a grand enough word. 'Magnificent.' She glared across the table at her youngest son. 'Donald, I do hope you will invest some time in thinking of original ways to entertain Mary when you call on her. She's accustomed to such fine things.'

'Yes, Mother.' Donald hastily shoved a fork filled with roast beef into his mouth to thwart further talk on the subject.

As Lillian offered him some gravy for his meat, she was quite sure she didn't want to know what he really thought. It was very clear he did not wish to engage in an argument over his mother's unwelcome prying into his personal affairs, not because he felt it was none of her business but because her observations were correct: Mary had experienced only the best kind of quality the colony had to offer. Besides, a grown man did not need his mother's advice on courtship.

Lillian's feelings were hurt when Donald impatiently waved the gravy boat away and sat brooding over his dinner.

'Now, Edith, leave the boy alone.' Mr Shaw shot his wife a warning look.

Mrs Shaw reluctantly switched to the more mundane matter of her desire to order a lovely new dress fabric she had seen in a store that morning.

If it weren't for Catherine's irreverent pranks and humour, Lillian doubted she could continue much longer with the monotony of her work and the added agony of watching Donald and Mary's courtship blossom. That was the problem with owning more than an ounce of intelligence. Like the gold-miner's pan, the mind always sifted for interesting ideas to polish. Dusting, washing and serving gave her thoughts far too much space to roam.

As Sunday morning dawned, Lillian wondered what state of affairs would greet her at Patricia's place when she arrived. It never occurred to her not to go to her sister, despite Alfred's vicious temper. Patricia relied on both her help and the bulk of her wages. Lillian simply did not have the heart to refuse, regardless of Catherine's regular invitations to go spend an afternoon with her and her Scottish pals instead.

At noon, she made her way along the riverbank, following

the same path as always; boarding the Edward Street ferry, zigzagging through the streets to reach Queen, crossing Victoria Bridge and continuing until the familiar cottage on Montague Road appeared over a rise. Lillian always approached cautiously, keeping an eye out for Alfred. What a wonderful Christmas gift it would be if he suddenly disappeared altogether. As she stepped on to the front porch, Patricia swung the door wide open. Her sister must already have been watching her arrival from one of the bedroom windows.

Lillian drew back with fright at the sight of her. 'What happened?'

A swollen magenta bruise framed Patricia's left eye and four angry scratches traversed down the side of her neck.

'Did he do this to you?'

'Don't fuss. It looks far worse than it feels.'

'Have you actually looked in a mirror?'

'It was an accident. He didn't mean to. He came home late last night and tripped over. I was in the way, that's all. Quickly, come inside.' Patricia furtively looked left and right before pulling Lillian inside by her sleeve. With the door firmly shut behind them, her sister led the way down the short passage into the kitchen and headed over to the stove. Peter jumped down from a chair to hug her, burying his head in her skirt.

She squeezed him back, stooping to kiss the soft hair on his head. Her older nephew was such a serious soul.

'Leave Aunt Lillie be.' Patricia herded him into the parlour. 'Play with Thomas while I get your food ready.'

Lillian tried to stay calm and quiet so as not to alarm the boys. 'Where is the bastard?'

'He's not here.'

She struggled to contain her rage. 'Alfred's a gutless prick, that's what he is! When he gets home, I'll take that bloody poker over there and shove it right up his arse.'

'Arse!' Thomas shouted from behind the door.

Patricia winced. 'Really? Unfortunately, you won't get the pleasure. He's taken the train up north this morning to go and see a man about some work. I don't know when he'll be back.' Her tone soured. 'We had a fight. He didn't bother to tell me exactly where he was going.'

The economic slump had squeezed the farmers even more tightly than the manufacturers and everybody knew it. Alfred had the smooth hands of an office worker, not weathered labourer's calluses. Even if the farmers wanted someone with legal experience to help them plead their cases against bank foreclosures, it was impossible. Half the banks had already shut their doors. He was on a fool's errand, as far as Lillian was concerned.

'What does he think he's going to achieve up there? He'd make a lousy station hand. I read the papers Mr Shaw leaves lying about. The farmers don't have any money to pay wages.' She folded her arms. 'I hope a bull kicks him in the head.'

Patricia grabbed her. 'Listen to me, Lillian. I swear he didn't do this on purpose. He came back from the hotel a little worse for wear and tripped on the hall runner. I tried to keep him upright but I ended up falling too. I hit my face on the doorframe.'

'Right, and those scratches miraculously appeared on your neck as well. Don't lie to me, Patricia.' Lillian put her hands on her hips and assessed her sister's injuries more closely. 'He shouldn't drink so much. That money is for feeding the children. I work hard all week and he wastes it. Why shouldn't I be cross with him?'

Patricia's shoulders slumped as she released her. 'What on earth am I going to do, Lillian?'

Lillian wrapped her arms about her sister's waist. 'I'm glad he's not going to be here for a while. You'll think of something, Patricia. You always were the resourceful one, like Ma.'

'She's the one who made the mistake of sailing halfway around the world to this godforsaken place,' Patricia said, sulking.

'What makes you think we'd be any better off in England if she hadn't?' Lillian pulled her handkerchief from her sleeve and offered it. 'I know you do miss her. Here, dry your eyes. You don't want the children to see you upset.'

Patricia sniffed, dabbed at her cheeks and managed a small smile. 'And we also don't need them to hear any more cursing from you. Here I was starting to think how fine you were sounding these days, mixing with the gentry and rounding out your vowels.'

Lillian grinned back. She rummaged through her basket and retrieved an envelope. 'I do try. Look, here are my wages. At least you'll have enough money to buy something nice for the children to eat this week now you don't have Alfred guzzling it all down at the hotel with his cronies.'

She wished she'd brought along something extra from Rosemead's pantry but Mrs Menzies had been bustling about in the kitchen making pastry when she'd left. Still secretly tucked away in its temporary hiding place was the pound note and she had yet to come up with a better solution for it. It worried away in the back of her mind. What if somebody went and rifled through her belongings? If Donald was audacious enough to climb the second staircase, what was stopping Olivia from getting bored and snooping about up there, too? Lillian hadn't really stopped to consider what to buy with the sum. That was the thing about money; the more she had, the more she wanted. Perhaps it was better to have nothing at all? Despite Patricia's straitened circumstances, Lillian wasn't ready to surrender the note for mundane goods. Surely she did enough for the little family already?

Patricia picked up a tin bowl filled with dirty dishwater and headed for the back door to water her vegetable garden with it. 'I'm glad you've come early, Lil. Would you be able to mind the children for half an hour after we've eaten? I have an errand to run this afternoon.'

Lillian followed her outside, curious. 'Would you rather I go and do it instead?'

It seemed as if Patricia scarcely left the house those days. What could possibly be so important?

'No, it's fine. I need to go over to the Hamilton place.' Patricia paused. 'It seems I do have something of value to offer, after all. I've been asked to be a nurse.'

Lillian snorted. 'A nurse? What do you mean? And what's Mrs Hamilton going to think about your abilities when she gets a look at your face?'

Patricia gingerly raised her fingers to check the abrasion. 'I'll have to cover it with powder. Anyhow, I don't mean a medical nurse. Mrs Hamilton needs a wet nurse. If there's one thing I do know how to do, it's feed babies. Mrs Hamilton came by early yesterday,' she added, pointing at her cheek, 'before this happened. She knocked on the door and told me the midwife, Mrs Carter, had referred her. Mrs Hamilton also said she was willing to pay me a premium if I'd agree to take care of her grandson, as well as a further eight shillings every week to continue his maintenance for as long as was needed. So, Lillian, you can roll your tongue back inside your mouth and shut it. I welcomed her inside, took that poor baby straight out of her arms and set to nursing him immediately. I would have kept him right then and there but Mrs Hamilton insisted on taking him home to gather a few of his things together and to let the family say their farewells. She hadn't wanted to set her hopes too high in case I didn't agree to the arrangement. It's fair to say she was extremely grateful when I told her I would. The truth is, Lillian, she told me that the very sound of the baby's crying at night compounds his father's own suffering. It's rather tragic. Mrs Hamilton thinks it best if the newborn is cared for at another home for the immediate future.'

Lillian peered into the parlour where Peter and Thomas were squabbling over the toy train. 'Haven't you already got enough children on your hands as it is?'

Patricia shook her head. 'I can do this one thing for that poor family, Lillian. They buried poor Molly only a fortnight ago. They're grieving badly so close to Christmas. If you'd seen the poor little mite you wouldn't be so sceptical; he was positively starving. Even a blind person could see he's not thriving on any of the alternatives. A newborn needs more than pap and sugar water to live on. He was pitiful to look at. I told Mrs Hamilton I would come up to the house myself to collect him when you got here.'

Lillian sat in the rocking chair and pitched it backwards and forwards. Despite Patricia's unwillingness to admit it, her sister had certainly inherited her resourcefulness from their mother. Patricia could wrap her new position as a wet nurse up as charity if it made her feel better but Lillian doubted she would be quite as generous giving her milk to somebody else's baby for free. The jolting reminder of the tough times in which they found themselves was oddly reassuring and worked to absolve her own guilt. She had been wise not to bring the abandoned baby home. A pound would be enough to maintain his care for only a few weeks. Then what?

The wind picked up and swept around the house's timber boards. It blustered through every crack and rattled loose windowpanes when Patricia brought Molly Hamilton's baby back. Even after applying powder to her face, it was impossible to disguise the swelling on her cheek completely. Lillian wondered if Mrs Hamilton chose not to notice, grateful instead that her most pressing concern was going to be taken care of.

There was no point in continuing to judge Patricia any more than she already had. Peter and Thomas swarmed excitedly about their mother's skirts as her sister plunked the little bundle down on the kitchen table and unwrapped the delicate white blanket he came wrapped in to reveal spindly arms and legs.

'I think it's ugly,' Peter announced and turned away.

The baby boy lay on the table like one of the turtles Lillian had seen in the pond at the Botanic Gardens, with a flat, round middle and a neck feebly arching up to try and take in his new surroundings. His little feet drew up and rotated as though he was treading water. He was much skinnier than the one she had found at the park. A squall of protest quickly rose from his lungs after Thomas reached out from his vantage point on a chair and poked and prodded at his face.

'Baby.' He looked up at his mother. 'Mine.'

'He's not a toy,' Patricia said, lifting her younger son from the chair and taking a seat.

'Here,' she instructed Lillian, 'Take this.'

She deposited a small bottle with a rubber teat attached, still half-full of milk, into Lillian's hands .

The contents felt cool to the touch. She wasn't sure what her sister expected her to do with it.

She stared at the infant. 'Should I?'

'No, it's cow's milk. He won't drink it and you can hardly blame him. I don't know why Mrs Hamilton insisted I take a bottle when she's paying me to feed him in the first place. Tip it out.'

Patricia unbuttoned her shirt and released her left breast from confinement. She raised the infant to it. He hungrily gulped down the sustenance he needed, choking as the milk made rivulets down his chin. It was clear enough to see the poor mite was starving. Patricia grimaced at his vigorous tugging but otherwise settled into the task.

'What about Thomas?' Lillian glanced at her nephew.

Patricia scoffed. 'Look at me. I have more than enough for both.'

Lillian felt silly for worrying the tiny usurper might threaten the very safety of their home. He couldn't weigh more than six and a half pounds at most.

'Don't stand there gawking.' Patricia pointed at the food on the table.

Lillian set about cutting up the loaf of bread and stirring the stew Patricia had set cooking on the stove.

When the baby had taken his fill, he lay back in a stupor.

Patricia's voice held a note of triumph. 'Eight shillings a week. Can you believe that?'

Lillian didn't wish to dampen her optimism. Even coupled with her measly wages, the amount would barely cover the mortgage and food and they both knew it.

Why Patricia had settled on Alfred as the one to marry, Lillian thought she would never fully understand. He was far too full of bluster. The privilege he enjoyed was entirely due to his industrious brick-making father putting him through Brisbane Grammar, where he'd been able to mix with boys from the upper echelon. Alfred's enduring friendship over the years with Donald's older brother, Fergus, had helped secure him a clerk's position at Shaw and Wheatley. The appointment was certainly not a result of the mediocre marks he'd gained during his years at university in Sydney.

It was no accident he'd been one of the first to lose his job when the partners had to make cuts. It was clear to Lillian the delight Alfred took in drinking spirits each close of business further leached his tolerance for the drag of long working hours. She wondered if the reason she had never seen Alfred's father smile during the short time she'd known him was due to disappointment in his son. It boiled her blood to know the worthless sod had gone north and left Patricia, not leaving even a penny to care for his children. Even unemployed, Alfred considered the factory his father had helped build too far beneath him. When he'd come home and made such a prepos-terous announcement Lillian stopped accepting herself as a hindrance. She could cook and clean as well as any other woman on that street and would continue to do so for as long as her sister needed her help. Maybe she took after their mother as much as Patricia did, after all. Although she did secretly wish Sundays with her little family would grant her a reprieve from the relentless chores at Rosemead. It never turned out that way.

She stroked the baby's dark, downy hair. 'Where will he sleep?'

'I'll tuck him into the dresser.'

It was as good a place as any and warm, too – close to the stove that perpetually heated the room. She picked up a rag and wiped curdled milk off her sister's shoulder where the baby had hiccupped.

'What's his name?'

Patricia stroked his rosy cheek with her thumb. 'Molly named him Stephen.'

Lillian had seen Molly from afar a few times. She'd been an apprentice in the Hamiltons' fabric store over on Stanley Street before their son fell in love with her. The couple had married in June only the year before. Stephen was to have been Molly's first child before the dreaded fever had taken her. It had happened very quickly.

'Do you think he looks like her?'

Patricia peered at Stephen. 'I don't know. All newborns look the same.'

'Yours didn't.'

'That's because they're mine.'

Lillian was amused. Alfred and Patricia's children had a hint of the oriental in their features. Another generation and there would be nothing left to see but anybody looking at her sister could see her father had been Chinese. Her own father, on the other hand, could have been any one of the Caucasian men working on the Gympie goldfields. She and Patricia looked nothing alike. 'Is there anything else you need me to do?'

'You can bring the washing in off the line and fetch some more wood for the stove.'

Always so much washing! The kettle heated the tank water for scrubbing dirty napkins. The never-ending pile of soiled cloths needed to be rinsed and scoured. Sometimes Lillian left Patricia's house with fingers as wrinkled as currants.

Nevertheless, she did as she was asked. After the task was done, they sat and ate bread and stew together at the table. Her sister washed the plates while Lillian dried and stacked them. It wouldn't do to leave anything lying about for long. Flies buzzed at the windowpanes and lazily dived at the meat safe. When the room was back in order, she wrapped the children against the westerly wind, ready for their outing.

Lillian carried Stephen while Patricia carried Thomas. Peter trotted beside his mother. Word about her sister's kindness had travelled the street and, as they passed by familiar fences, they were stopped so neighbours could gaze at the baby, tutting their tongues with regret over his poor mother's demise.

It was a relief to enter Musgrave Park to let the boys safely run where they liked.

Thomas did his best, his chubby legs pumping up and down to keep up with Peter's games. Stephen had nestled into the crook of Lillian's neck and dozed off. Although small, he began to weigh on her arm like a bag of dried beans. Patricia laid a blanket on the grass and side by side the sisters sat, smiling at the older children's carefree antics.

Lillian glanced across at Patricia, tracing the familiar contours of her face with her gaze. She knew it better than her own; the small mole by her ear, a half-inch childhood scar on the right side of her chin where she'd come off second best against a classmate named Bartholomew Ames. Patricia's heart had always melted at the sight of babies, whether human or animal. She would indeed have made a wonderful nurse if there had been an opportunity to train, if their mother hadn't grabbed the first lifeline thrown in her rush to protect her daughters. The Flemings had been good to them, however.

Lillian trusted her sister but what of this new plan? It troubled her. Her pound note would comfortably feed the family for three weeks in a row if she spent it on meat and vegetables. She hated second-guessing her own decisions. One moment, she thought she should have brought the abandoned baby to her sister, the next she was glad to have left it behind. It felt as though she was stuck on a seesaw with no way to hop off. Nonetheless, the mother at Dutton Park had been a stranger, not a neighbour – a neighbour with the means to pay a premium until the child returned to their fold. Would there ever be a time to unburden herself of her horrible secret?

'Will you cope on your own this week?' Lillian asked in an effort to distract herself.

'I'll manage.' Perhaps it was the relaxing warmth of the sun on Patricia's back that made her dismiss Lillian's concern with a flick of her wrist.

As the shadows began to lengthen and Stephen started to stir, they called to Peter and Thomas and gathered up the blanket to trudge back to the house. Lillian added a log to the stove before she left.

'See you next week,' Patricia called from where she sat with Stephen once more attached to her breast.

It pained Lillian to leave her, not knowing if Alfred would return, but she knew the Shaws would never forgive her absence at the dinner service so she had no choice but to retrace her steps to Rosemead.

As Lillian turned down Shafston Road, her stomach plunged. There at the gate stood Donald, still dressed in his Sunday best. He casually raised a hand above his head and waved.

CHAPTER 5

KANGAROO POINT

*W*hen Lillian spotted Donald, she was reminded again of her sister's unfortunate marriage. Alfred had caught sight of her sister outside his office building only a month after they had arrived in Brisbane. She remembered the day well. Patricia had taken particular care with her black hair, piling it above her slender nape. They were on their way to Fortitude Valley for an interview at a grand house, a reference from Mr Fleming tucked into Patricia's basket because she always took care of the important things. In spite of it, they'd been denied positions at two other houses. One surreptitious look at Patricia's almond-shaped eyes and olive skin and the ladies hadn't let them take a step inside. Lillian had been furious. How dare they be so judgemental? Her sister simply pinched her arm and told her to hush.

On their return to their boarding house, Lillian saw Alfred first. He was a law clerk, dressed immaculately in a light three-piece suit and on his way to court to deliver a last-minute document. The attorney waiting to receive it would turn out to be Fergus, representing a man accused of stabbing a storekeeper in a burglary gone wrong. Allegedly – Alfred insisted – as he tried to waylay the two of them. He'd mostly ignored Lillian and tried to impress Patricia by flippantly sharing several details of the crime.

That innocuous encounter was the first time Lillian ever questioned her sister's ironclad judgement.

Their mother – who had known so many different types of men – had spoken sternly to both her and Patricia before she died about what to look for in a husband: '*Do not be swayed by the first man who gives you a compliment. Don't pretty yourself up to ensnare the wrong one. The right man will choose you because of who you are, not what you look like, and you should do the same for him. Beware of the one that pursues you with a vengeance because they will tear you down as soon as lift you up. Choose one with integrity and a good head on his shoulders, one who is slow to anger and quick to forgive. Then you will enjoy great happiness.*'

Lillian knew the lecture by heart, yet, after being immersed too long in maudlin thoughts, Donald's unexpected appearance at the gate set her spirits soaring.

'Pleasant evening, isn't it?' He tipped his hat and winked.

'Yes.' She waited for him to say something else but instead he took a pipe and a tin of tobacco from his pocket and prepared it for use.

He lit a match to the pipe's well and puffed on the tip to get it going, squinted against the coiling smoke and relished the flavour. 'Ah, that's hit the spot.'

It had been two weeks since the magpie had forced Mary to halt at the exact same spot. In the intervening days, Donald hadn't bothered to seek Lillian out for a proper conversation once. What could he want with her now?

'Come with me.' He turned on his heel and she followed meekly behind until they reached the stable.

'Your mother will be expecting me,' she said.

'They're not here. Olivia went to a recital with her friends. Mother and Father are visiting the Ormonds.'

'Mrs Menzies will get cross...'

'Forget about that old goat. Come in.' He disarmed her with a smile and held out his hand. 'Please. There's something I need to show you.'

Lillian's breath grew shallow as she extended her fingers and let him take them.

Donald lifted the latch and slid the door across its rail. The pungent aroma of straw and fresh horse manure enveloped them. To her it was the smell of excitement and fear. The interior was yet another place where they had stolen illicit kisses under the possibility of discovery at any moment. The stakes were much higher for her, of course. Donald would suffer a reprimand at worse, while she would most certainly lose her position.

He disappeared inside. She swallowed caution and followed. The bay where the buggy was usually parked was empty. Donald's mare, Duchess, stood in the shadows of her stall, her shifting hooves rustling the straw. The mare softly chuffed as he strode over and gave her a fond scratch beneath the jaw.

'Hello, girl.'

'Should you be smoking that pipe in here?' Lillian whispered.

'I'll be careful.' Donald carefully blew a smoke ring at her and grinned impishly.

She grew impatient to know what he wanted with her. He brought her hand to his mouth, planted a gentle kiss on her knuckles then unfurled her fingers. At the touch, a familiar jolt of pleasure coursed through her. From his pocket, Donald withdrew a small box and placed it in her palm.

What on earth was he thinking, giving her a Christmas gift? She looked down at the crimson case. The velvet texture tickled her skin.

'You know I trust you, Lillian, and I thought you'd be the best person to ask.' Donald removed the pipe from between his lips with his free hand. 'Open it.'

She did as he asked to reveal a stunning gold brooch within. It was oval-shaped with two tiny rubies and a diamond set in a row along the centre.

'It's absolutely beautiful, Donald.' Even in the dim light she could tell the piece would have cost him a small fortune.

'Do you really think so?'

She nodded and smiled up at him.

He let out a deep sigh of relief. 'Good. I knew you would give me an honest answer, Lillian.'

'Of course.' She smiled coyly. 'I'm always honest with you.'

She hesitated whether to take the brooch from its box. Was there some sort of protocol about who was meant do the attaching? Perhaps she should wait for Donald to do the honours. There was no way she could wear the beautiful piece of jewellery inside the house anyhow. Mrs Shaw didn't allow her maids to wear adornments. It was one of her many finicky rules. Her son surely knew that.

Donald unwrapped his hand from hers and snatched the box back. He took one final confident look at the treasure before snapping the box shut and returning it to his pocket.

Cold realisation dawned. The brooch was never intended for her. He'd bought it for Mary.

Lillian took a few flustered steps back and stumbled over a rake jutting out beside the nearest stall. 'I have to go,' she said, dizzy with the extent of her embarrassment.

'Lillian, oh, I'm sorry. Did you think –?' Donald, the idiot, finally realised the sin he'd committed. He reached out to help her steady her jellied legs.

She yanked her arm away, enraged. 'Don't touch me!'

'Lillian, come on. Don't be like that. You know Mary and I — '

'I was a fool to think you'd ever think of me in that way. Catherine warned me.'

Donald had the audacity to laugh. 'Ah! What's that mad Scotswoman been saying about me?'

Lillian edged away until her shoulder bumped hard against the stable door. She turned with relief and sprinted, leaving Donald standing beneath dusty shafts of filtered light ruefully shaking his head.

At the back steps of the house, she dashed a sleeve across her eyes. There would be no more tears wasted over that scoundrel. She paused to pick a few strands of straw from the hem of her skirt and gather herself. Looking up again, Lillian was horrified to see Olivia had wandered up the driveway, and was now standing twelve feet away observing her. A cruel smile played at the corners of the girl's lips. It widened with delight as her brother emerged from the stable. He stopped and stared at them both, his expression a mixture of guilt and embarrassment.

Lillian panicked and hurried inside, frustrated to know that by doing so she was feeding Olivia's misplaced suspicions. She lifted her skirts and took the stairs two at a time to reach her room and slam the bedroom door shut behind her. She hurled herself across her bed and gave her pillow a thrashing with her fists. How could she have been so stupid to think Donald would ever want to marry a silly girl like her?

If Lillian had had time to wallow in her fury, she would have but it was impossible. Despite her inner turmoil, she rose after a few minutes and began to get ready for the evening meal service. She splashed some water from the washbowl on her hot cheeks, refashioned her hair into a respectable bun and tied her apron around her waist. She marched back downstairs and maintained a stoic silence while polishing the silverware to within an inch of its life and placing each piece on the tablecloth.

Catherine, watching Lillian's studious attempt at normality as she set out glassware, was having none of the façade and forced a confession. With emotions simmering barely beneath the surface, it did not take much to confess the whole sorry story.

'Och, that cheeky bastard. Fancy asking yer to approve of his tawdry trinket. Whit was that fool thinking? Dinnae he know that hell hath no fury as a woman scorned? I'll tell you whit, lass, I'm going to piss in his tea tonight.'

'You'll do no such thing! Besides, I'm the scorned woman, not you. If anyone is going to do it, it's me.'

'Aye, but yer won't, will yer?'

Lillian scowled at the truth of it. She might be mad at Donald for his callous disregard of her feelings but she couldn't turn off her feelings for him so quickly. She was nonetheless grateful for Catherine's loyal support and the offer to defend her honour in such a shocking way elicited a small smirk.

That week, whenever Lillian found herself in the presence of a Shaw, she turned her face to the wall and attempted to dissolve right into it. Mrs Shaw took note of her maid's submissiveness and gave her an approving nod. As Lillian went about her work dusting and polishing the family's heirlooms, she did her best to ignore Olivia's titters and Donald's apologetic glances. She could see the enjoyment the little witch gleaned from her heartache. At least Donald had the good sense not to approach when she had no choice but to be in the same room.

Even so, he paraded about like the cat that ate the canary. Mary evidently received his gift with much delight. Lillian found the receipt for the brooch while gathering laundry from Donald's hamper. The bauble had cost him the best part of three weeks' wages. When Mrs Shaw found out through Olivia, she was so pleased she immediately announced she would host a ladies' luncheon in the second week of January.

'Might as well start the year productively once we've got past Christmas,' she said.

Lillian discovered the carefully calculated guest list on Mrs Shaw's bedside table as she was reaching beneath the bed for the chamber pot. Given pride of place in scratchy copperplate at the top of the list were Mary and her mother, Elizabeth. She held the notepaper between her thumb and forefinger as if it were a soiled handkerchief and carried it over to the hearth to set a match to it. She watched impassively as the yellow flames licked the names away and the heat became too much for her fingers to bear. The last piece floated on to the charred logs. Using the poker, Lillian prodded the remaining evidence into the ashes.

It gave her a modicum of pleasure to hear Mrs Shaw ask first her husband, then her son and daughter, before finally turning to Catherine, Mrs Menzies and herself to see if any of them had seen the precious list. They all promised profusely they had not. Only one of them was lying. Lillian was proud of her believable performance. She took a sliver of comfort whenever she thought about Mrs Shaw worrying whether her memory was going to rack and ruin.

CHAPTER 6

THE ADVERTISEMENT

*L*illian returned to Montague Road the following Sunday. Perhaps it was her imagination but little Stephen appeared to be looking plumper. Patricia was no more tired than usual. The bruise and scratches on her face and neck had already faded. Perhaps the transition of caring for three children rather than two was negligible. Alfred had not yet returned nor bothered even to send a short telegram to reassure his wife of his whereabouts. By all accounts, life at the cottage seemed to be running more smoothly as a result.

Stephen gurgled and stared in wonder at Lillian's face as she picked him up. He absorbed each of her features as he involuntarily poked his tongue in and out between rosebud lips. She laughed at his contortions and hoped when at last he was able to return to his family he might provide them with some respite from their grief at losing poor Molly.

'Mrs Hamilton has been down to visit him twice. She seemed very pleased with his progress. He's quite settled, as you can see,' Patricia said. 'I should think they will take him back when Molly's husband, Nicholas, has had more time to get over his loss. His mother told me at her last visit he'd begun to ask after his son. Oh, before I forget –' She handed Lillian a piece of folded up paper.

'What's this?'

'I need you to place a small advertisement in the paper for me when you're next doing errands on the north side.'

Lillian unfolded it and read the contents. The message didn't make any sense. A kind person with no children would like to adopt baby; small premium. Alice. 'Who's Alice?'

Patricia glanced up. 'I am.'

'Why wouldn't you give your own name?'

'Don't be daft. I can't give my real name.'

Lillian waved the slip. 'This is a lie. You've put here you don't have any children but you do. Why would you say you don't? What do mean you want to adopt?'

Patricia waited with patient amusement. 'Lillian, it's only a white lie and it's for a good cause. There are plenty of people out there who find the idea of caring for other people's illegitimate children morally disagreeable.'

'Stephen's not illegitimate. His mother died. How can anybody object to something like that?'

'In Molly's case, yes, there was no other choice. But you of all people should know there is a demand from women who've conducted themselves questionably.'

'Why should I know? I haven't done anything like that!' Lillian found her voice rising but she couldn't help it. Her sister's tone felt condescending but it appeared she was not done yet.

Patricia fixed her with a stern look. 'For God's sake. You know how babies are made. We grew up at the back of a brothel. Mrs Carter, the one who told Mrs Hamilton to ask if I would be Stephen's wet nurse, lives over on Boundary Street. She heard how well Stephen was doing under my care and paid a visit on Thursday to see him for herself. By the way, did you know her husband ran away with another woman?'

Lillian knew very little about Mrs Carter other than she'd been very brisk and demanding while delivering Peter and Thomas safely into the world. Now she wished she knew even less. If there was one thing South Brisbane gossipmongers enjoyed, it was a scandal. She didn't have any inclination for finding out more details. Yet she did understand both married and unmarried women relied on Mrs Carter's services regularly. The midwife attended the women in their homes and sometimes an unfortunate young lady took lodgings at the house until her bastard was born and dispatched to another family. At least, that's what Lillian thought was what happened.

Patricia continued. 'It seems Mrs Carter can scarcely keep up with the demand for her services. She's the one who told me to put an advertisement in the paper. That's how she finds them. The women who can't keep their babies pay her to take care of them while they work or she finds the babies a good home instead. Mrs Carter has her oldest daughter, Nancy, looking after the babies when she has to attend a birth.' Patricia lowered her voice to a conspiratorial whisper. 'She told me she has five babies in her care at the moment.'

'Five?' Lillian couldn't hide her surprise.

'Don't you see, Lil? If Alfred doesn't come back, I've found a way to earn a living. If I take in a few more babies, I can live off the premiums and keep food in my own children's bellies. It's not like I can go back to being a housemaid, can I?' Patricia said with frustration.

Lillian took in the walls of the little kitchen with its smoky woodstove and the tiny parlour nestled on the other side of the narrow hall. There were only two small bedrooms at the front of the cramped cottage. Where would all the extra babies go?

Stephen, who had dozed off in her arms, was fortunate to have a chance of a life with privileges when his family decided to take him back. From the outside, the Hamilton home looked grand enough for Lillian to assume it had several decent-sized bedrooms within. She'd passed by many times and admired the tidy, cultivated garden. She'd also noticed a stable at the rear large enough to house a couple of horses and a carriage.

Stephen was a bonny baby, handsome and healthy and, despite his mother's tragic passing, it was obvious his grand-mother cared deeply for him. However, the idea of her sister taking Mrs Carter's advice and adopting strangers' babies made her very uneasy. Adoption was a permanent solution. Surely Patricia didn't want a house bursting at the seams with other people's unwanted mistakes?

Her sister must have sensed her confusion. 'Oh, no, Lillian. I'm not going to adopt babies to keep for ever. I'll raise them for a few months until they no longer need my milk. After that, Mrs Carter has assured me she'll help find a good family for them, well-off couples who'd love to raise a healthy child but haven't been blessed with one of their own.'

'Fine. I'll do it.' Despite her misgivings, Lillian tucked the note inside her basket and agreed to carry out Patricia's request. Her sister had obviously brightened at the prospect of being able to increase her income and Lillian couldn't argue with the fact she was certainly adept at raising healthy children, even in straitened circumstances. Perhaps if the venture prospered, Patricia might see fit to allow Lillian to keep a greater share of her own earnings?

However, Alice was their mother's name. It had been sullied enough. She wished her sister had chosen a different one.

CHAPTER 7

ERRANDS

On Tuesday, a day that broke with a promise of sweltering heat, Mrs Menzies sent Catherine and Lillian out to conduct errands in the city. She instructed them to first head into Finney, Isles and Sons on Edward Street to pick up an order of fabric for Mrs Shaw – who'd succeeded in persuading her husband to let her have a new dress made for the January luncheon. The occasion was only three weeks away.

'Then you're to take it straight to the dressmaker,' Mrs Menzies said. 'After that, you'll need to go to the butcher and get a ham hock for tonight's soup.'

An azure, cloudless sky arched overhead as the girls fastened their bonnets against the harsh blaze of the sun and carried their baskets down to the wharf to await the ferry. Catherine flashed a flirtatious smile at the ferryman as the barge pulled up. He gave her a wink.

Lillian elbowed her in the ribs. 'What are you doing?'

'Och, hen, relax. I'm only having a wee bit of fun.'

'We'll get in trouble if Mrs Menzies or Mrs Shaw find out you've been making eyes at strange men.'

'Go on wit yer! It's only Godfrey.'

'Morning ladies. Are you going anywhere special?'

'Just a wee trip into town to get a few things,' Catherine explained.

'I shall look forward to your return.' Godfrey extended his hand to help them both embark.

Lillian scowled at his suggestive tone. Catherine simply giggled and demurely cast her eyes down to the rough wooden deck. At the far side of the river, Catherine slipped her gloved hand into his once more, allowing him to assist her on to the wharf. Lillian kept her hands firmly tucked out of the way. Godfrey could keep his chivalrous assistance to himself. She'd had enough of men and their deceptive games.

Together, the girls walked briskly towards Queen Street. Lillian had decided earlier it would be much easier to fulfil her sister's request before she and Catherine found themselves laden down with Mrs Shaw's fabric and the ingredients for Mrs Menzies' soup.

She tugged on her friend's arm. 'Would you mind waiting here a moment? I need to go into the Brisbane Courier.'

Catherine stopped and gave her a querulous look. 'Whit for?'

Lillian blushed. 'Patricia needs me to place an advertisement.'

'Is she selling or buying?'

'Selling.'

'Whit's she selling?'

Did Catherine have to know everything about everything? And why did Lillian feel so guilty keeping the particulars a mystery? It shouldn't be such an ordeal to place a simple ad in the paper. Plenty of other people did it. Yet she hesitated to give an honest answer. Catherine continued to stare, waiting.

'Fine. She's selling her ability to take care of other people's children.'

'Och, yer joking. Has Alfred not found another job, then?'

Lillian and Catherine often whispered secrets into the darkness between their beds at night. At that moment she regretted admitting her many misgivings about her brother-in-law. Catherine's disdain was apparent in the way she spat out his name. Lillian blamed herself; the two didn't even know each other.

Catherine at least had the decency to notice her discomfort. 'Come on then. If yer going to do it, we'd better hurry,' she said.

Lillian entered the high-ceilinged foyer at the newspaper's offices and spoke to a well-dressed young man behind the reception desk. She handed him a penny to place Patricia's – or was that Alice's? – advertisement in that week's edition of The Queenslander before hurrying back outside to shake off her unease. It was clear Catherine's curiosity over the matter was still burning.

'How is yer sister, really?'

'What do you mean?' Lillian said, guarded.

'Yer've not been yerself lately. At first I thought yer were pining for Donald's affections but now I'm thinking it's something more than that. Yer often not happy when yer return from yer family on Sunday. Is there something else on yer mind?'

There certainly was plenty on Lillian's mind but her troubles would have to stay tucked up in there. Her sister's new enterprise skirted a fine line between benevolence and profiteering from others' misfortune. As far as Lillian was concerned, it would probably drain her sister of any remaining

skerrick of energy she had left and she didn't feel at all confident about which angle Catherine would see it from.

'No, there's nothing. Thank you for your concern but I'm
fine, really.' Lillian pulled a handkerchief from her sleeve and
wiped beads of sweat from her face.

Catherine pursed her lips, obviously unconvinced. 'You're
a dark horse sometimes, Lillian. Very well. If yer not in the
mood for confiding, I guess we'd better keep moving.'

They continued up the street side by side. However, Lillian
was acutely aware that her refusal to share the source of her
bother had cooled the usual warmth they shared. She hated
keeping secrets but didn't want to burden her friend with the
mistakes she kept making. Why indeed did Lillian feel she had
to place that advertisement for Patricia? She could have
promised and then thrown the piece of paper away when she'd
got back to Rosemead. It could have joined Mrs Shaw's list in
the fireplace ashes. But then Lillian realised Patricia would
most likely scan the newspaper's pages, wondering where
it was.

She and Catherine arrived at Finney, Isles and Sons in
awkward silence and meandered their way around several
mannequins before reaching the wide material counter.

There was something about the space, with its row upon
row of fabric bolts, that made Lillian feel wrapped in a
colourful cocoon. The sounds of horses and carts rattling down
the street were muted. She inhaled a scent of newness and
possibility. If only she could work in a store such as this.

'We're here to collect a package for Mrs Edith Shaw of
Shafston Road, Kangaroo Point, please,' said Catherine to the
poised assistant standing behind the counter.

'One moment.' The assistant headed out to the storeroom
to look for it. Lillian seized the opportunity to sidle over to a
nearby stand and admire several pairs of white gloves on

display. They were so white and pristine she scarcely dared touch.

She thought about the pound note. If there were anything of value to retrieve from the disaster that had come from following Donald into the stable, it was noticing a better hiding place for her treasures. Retrieving chamber pots, she'd spied Donald's half-full tobacco tin on his bedside table and sprinkled the expensive contents out of his bedroom windows on to the hydrangeas below before taking it. She'd taken the tin up to her room, opened it and placed the note, her bag of coins and the photograph inside. Her copy of *Pinocchio* she wrapped in the embroidered handtowel that had been hanging on the washstand. Although the volume was battered with a couple of pages ripped, Lillian kept it as a sentimental memento, to remind herself that books were both a way to escape reality and to increase one's knowledge. Both were equally desirable qualities. Later, under the ruse of taking scraps out to feed the chickens, she went outside, slipped into the stable and tucked the tin and book behind a wobbly board in the unoccupied stall. Safety assured, it gave Lillian a thrill to know she could buy a new pair of gloves any time she wanted. Although, if Catherine kept the assistant distracted a little while longer…

The powdery fabric greatly tempted her twitching fingers and she was relieved when Catherine tugged her away from the stand, steering her from the store out into the busy street.

'Dinnae yer dare get me caught up in yer pinching, Lillian Betts,' Catherine hissed in her ear.

She flinched with embarrassment. It was hard to break old habits. 'I wasn't going to.'

'Do yer think I cannae tell when yer lying?' Catherine stalked off and Lillian was forced into a jog to catch up.

'I'm sorry, Catherine. You're right. I do have a few problems at the moment. I'm not ready to talk about them yet. Can you understand?'

Catherine came to a halt and sighed. 'Aye. It's easy enough to see yer troubled. I'll be ready to listen when yer ready to talk.'

Lillian hugged her. 'Thank you for being such a good friend.'

Catherine returned the embrace and Lillian felt her friend's shoulders relax. It was a relief to know they had reached a truce.

The road at noon was crowded with trotting horses pulling their laden carts. Lillian and Catherine sidestepped several steaming piles of dung as they crossed over to the well-patronised dressmaker's shop to leave the material. Again, she found herself taken by the rolls of ribbons and lace, and jars of buttons sitting in bright rows along the shelves. The shop seemed utterly frivolous and yet several women stood about immersed in serious sounding conversations. She and Catherine left as quickly as they could after giving Mrs Shaw's instructions to the woman at the counter. Their shared distrust of opulence as well as self-consciousness about the way they stood out in their dowdy uniforms bound them together in their haste.

The last stop was several blocks farther. Looking up the street between the buildings, the road seemed to be shimmering in the high temperature. As they entered Mayne Butchery's cool interior, the smell of raw meat made Lillian hold her nose. She forced herself to step forward to the display of red flesh and request the large ham hock Mrs Menzies required for her soup. The butcher's biceps bulged as he brusquely thrust the wrapped side of meat over the counter top.

Out on the street, she struggled to carry the weight of it in her basket and walk.

Catherine, who had outpaced her, turned around and watched with amusement. 'Shall we catch a tram?'

Lillian's shoulder and forearm began to ache. She relished the opportunity to put the basket down beneath a shop awning for a moment. 'And pay for it with what?'

'I have some money.'

'You know I can't pay you back. I'm happy to walk.'

Catherine groaned. 'I've met some really stubborn people in my time, Lillian, but yer really take the cake!'

'I'm sorry.' Lillian pouted. 'I don't want to be a burden.'

'Yer'd be doing me a serious favour. I cannae bear listening to yer moaning and groaning a minute longer.' Catherine seemed to soften at the defeated look on Lillian's face. She put her own basket down and switched it for the one with the ham hock. 'Come on, yer silly sausage. My feet need a rest, too. I'm paying for yer fare and yer'll do well to keep your mouth shut about it.'

Lillian gratefully leaned against her friend's shoulder as they continued to the tram stop. 'Very well. If you insist.'

'I do!'

They clambered aboard the next tram with two seats to spare. As the horses picked up speed, Lillian watched the passing buildings begin to spread out. They continued until they were near enough to the wharf to disembark.

With time saved, she and Catherine slowly wandered along the river bank, stopping regularly to switch baskets. They stopped for a while to sit on the grass, raising their hands to shade their eyes against the sun's glare on the water as they looked across at the wharfies working at the docks. The men were unloading a recently docked sailing ship, hauling large crates on to the wharf and loading them on to carts ready to deliver to expectant businesses. The workers' muscled arms rippled beneath the heavy weights. Lillian and Catherine marvelled at their perseverance under such brutal humidity.

Lillian cast a stone into the lapping water and watched it skip three times. 'Did you know it used to be possible to wade across the Brisbane River in the old days?'

'Really?'

'When I was little, my mother told me the water was so clear you could see right down to the bottom.'

When she'd emigrated in 1863, her mother had learned about Brisbane's early history from a friendly sailor – just like the ones working on the wharf across the way. It was so difficult for Lillian to imagine her mother's long months sailing at sea as she had only ever seen her walking about on dry land, and briskly at that. There was no point in dilly-dallying with so much to do. She tried not to dwell on what it was that had to be done. She and Patricia had shared an upbringing, learning of things no child ought to know.

Lillian soothed herself. *We survived. We are here. I am here.* Those three short sentences – uttered on birthdays, each New Year dawn, or any time at all – had the desired calming effect so desperately needed. She pictured broad sails snapping at their masts and waves rushing against the hull of the ship as it coursed through the tropics on its path to this land she called home. Reaching out to pluck a blade of grass, she muttered: 'My mother died.'

'I'm sorry. I cannae believe yer never told me that before. Is that why yer and Patricia are so close? I'm nae stranger to loss myself.' Catherine stretched out on her side and rested her cheek in her hand. 'It burrows down so deeply yer fear it has wrapped around yer for good, doesn't it? I often think about my own mam and pa. The emotions toss me about, causing more harm than a ship on a high sea could ever do. Somewhere around the Equator, when I travelled over, I realised I probably wouldn't ever make the return trip home.' Catherine's face clouded with the memory. 'Even though they're not dead, I sometimes feel as though they are, being so far away. What I would give for a slice of my mam's black pudding. I dinnae know what else to do except keep 'em in my heart and take another step forward.'

Lillian nodded with agreement. Her own mother had shared many stories and taught her many lessons. One of them she held dearer than all the others. She remembered the words, if not the sound of her mother's voice and decided to share it with Catherine. She pointed at the water and wagged her finger at it. 'Mine would say: "I learned a good lesson from that brown snake of a river, Lillian. Stay true to your original course and always trust your gut. Don't be steered by others who will carelessly muddy up your plans."'

'There!' Catherine grinned. 'Didnae say yer Mam was clever?'

Lillian shuddered and remembered Madame Claudette's angry bark reaching like tentacles through the crack beneath the door. Feeling her mother flinch – a subtle twitch – the signal their time together must come to an end.

Patricia had saved them both from a similar fate. She'd promised Lillian their story would have a different ending. She owed her sister her life. Patricia used to make good decisions and Lillian always trusted her. But that was well before Alfred came along. It was nice know Catherine cared about her, too.

'What made you come to Queensland?' Lillian asked.

'At home, my parents struggled all the time. There was never enough to eat. I sought an opportunity to make a different life for myself. Melanie and Rosemary wanted to join me on my grand adventure.'

'Is it what you hoped for?'

Catherine's brow creased. 'Yer know, most of the time I'm

too busy living to give it much thought. Aye, for sure the work is hard, but we have sunshine and freedom and that's more than some have.'

'My ma had a similar idea.'

'Was she a maid like us?'

Lillian swallowed her pride. 'No. She made a poor decision.'

Catherine slowly nodded. 'I see.' She scrambled to her feet. 'Listen to the two of us gettin' so maudlin. We'd best head back. Mrs Menzies will be worried about her ham hock. It's startin' to smell in this heat.' She extended a hand and hauled Lillian up.

A deep blast from a ship's horn over at the dock startled Lillian but succeeded in blocking out the treacherous sounds inside her mind, shouts and moans that still haunted her years later. As far as she was concerned, her mother hadn't been very smart at all.

'I know yer usually go and visit Patricia, and maybe now I understand why it's so important, but will yer please consider spending next Sunday with me and my pals? The girls and I are planning on taking the train out to Sandgate for a wee picnic to celebrate Christmas early, seeing as we all have to work on the day. I'd love yer to come. Surely your sister could spare yer just the once? I've told Melanie and Rosemary so much about yer. There'll be some lads going as well. I promise they'll take yer mind right off Donald and remind yer there are others better suited,' said Catherine, looking hopeful.

For a second Lillian was sorely tempted to accept the offer – she'd never been to Sandgate before – but in truth she was too worried to leave her sister for another week without knowing how she was coping on her own. Besides, it was Christmas. She had always celebrated with her sister.

'I'm sorry. I can't.' Lillian said. 'Alfred isn't home at the moment.'

Catherine looked genuinely surprised by the admission. 'Where is he?'

'Somewhere up north looking for work.' Lillian still felt her sister was withholding the entire truth about Alfred's decision from her.

'Will they move if he finds something, do yer think?'

The thought hadn't crossed her mind. If Alfred was successful in his foolhardy jaunt, then a move was a certainly a possibility, even though Patricia had always threatened she would return to Gympie over her own dead body. Alfred would have a next to impossible time bullying her sister into changing her mind on that matter. Lillian knew one thing for sure; she would not be going with them if he was successful.

'I doubt that very much. Truth be told, Catherine, I think she'd cope far better if she let him go for good.'

'Aye.' Catherine nodded. 'I'd agree with that. Yer'll come next time, then. As long as yer promise yer refusal is definitely because of yer sister and nothing to do with still holding a candle for Donald. Because if I find our yer lying to me I shall kidnap yer on Sunday morning and nothing yer say will make me change my mind.'

Lillian poked out her tongue at Catherine's menacing glare. 'Thank you for understanding. I promise it has absolutely nothing to do with Donald. Please keep inviting me to come with you. I would love to meet your friends soon. They sound like such good fun.'

'Och, they are!'

'I find it hard enough to understand what you're saying at the best of times. What am I going to do when there's three of you all talking jibberish at once?'

''Tis true, we do enjoy a good blether. Rosemary's taken up with a lad from over the south side. Perhaps yer ken him. Matthew Hetherington's his name.'

Lillian tried to think. 'The name doesn't ring any bells, sorry.'

''Tis no matter. She's asked him to bring his friends along for the picnic. Melanie's always complaining there are no decent men in this city.'

Lillian tried not to let disappointment set in as they dawdled slowly towards the wharf but it was difficult not to feel some resentment toward her sister. Patricia was the one who had rushed into an early marriage. They had both learned a hard lesson from her mistake. Lillian wished she could be as carefree and unattached as Catherine was, with friends who reminded her of her origins and kept her spirits up during long days at work. Her own family sometimes made her feel sad and frustrated. If Patricia's little advertisement received any inter-est, she worried she would be needed at the cottage even more than ever. Lillian had a strong feeling she wouldn't have to wait long to find out.

CHAPTER 8

ENTERPRISE

hen Lillian returned to Montague Road that Sunday, still sulky at being unable to attend the festive picnic with Catherine and her friends, baby Stephen was no longer there.

She held out the small Christmas pudding Mrs Menzies had given her. 'Here, Merry Christmas,' the cook had said brusquely, leaving Lillian standing at the foot of the steps not knowing what to say, so surprised was she by the woman's unexpected kindness. Finally Mrs Menzies reverted to her usual scolding: 'Off you go and don't be late back.' Lillian had found her voice at last and thanked the cook, pleased to have something delicious to be able to present to her sister.

She peered into the dimly lit parlour. 'Where's Stephen?'

Patricia received the gift and closed her eyes as she held it to her nose and inhaled. 'Mm, this smells wonderful. How kind of your cook. Stephen's father came on Friday to retrieve him. I must say he wasn't anything like what I was expecting, rather young. He thanked me several times and handed over the final fee. It was a shame to see such a fit young man and know he was a widower. It's easy enough to see how handsome he would be if he wasn't so affected by his tragic loss.'

Lillian sat down at the table. She, too, felt sorry for the man she'd never met. 'That's a shame. I wanted to say goodbye to Stephen. He was a sweet little thing.'

Patricia sat down opposite. 'I, on the other hand, have to say I was quite pleased to see him go. He may have started off tiny but his weight soon caught up with his appetite.'

Lillian set her basket before her and fished about in the bottom of it for her wages. She shelled the coins out noisily in front of her sister.

Peter rushed inside from the yard in a blur of energy and Thomas toddled after him, struggling to climb the steps by himself. 'Aunt Lillie, we've got new babies.'

Her nephew's face flushed with happiness at having news to share.

'Babies?'

He nodded vigorously and, at the same time, Lillian's ears pricked at a small squeaking sound that swiftly grew into a distressed wail. It came from the large dresser beside the back door where Patricia kept her linen, and more recently Stephen.

Her sister rose and went to pick the baby up. She held it upright at her shoulder, rubbed its back and returned to show Lillian. 'Yes, I was just about to tell you. Thanks to your errand, word has now spread. A delivery boy knocked on my front door to deliver a telegram responding to my ad the day after it appeared in the paper. The family who sent it was desperate to find a home for their twins.'

'Already?' Lillian sucked in a breath. She had hoped the undertaking would fail, doubtful as to what kind of person would answer a newspaper ad and hand their child over to a stranger. The spectre of the mother in the park flashed across her mind.

'Yes!' Patricia obviously felt pleased with herself. 'I was surprised to get a response so quickly. Mind you, Mrs Carter warned me it wouldn't take long.'

Lillian rose to go and peer at the other tightly swaddled baby, which had been neatly tucked inside another drawer. Comparing them, it seemed the little sisters' features appeared to be identical, although one was clearly larger than the other. The smaller tot cried piteously. Lillian lifted her out and cuddled her. 'Do they have names?'

'That one's Georgina and this one's Penelope,' said Patricia, unfastening her shirt buttons. 'Rather grand names, don't you think?'

'What's wrong with Georgina?' Lillian stroked the baby's florid cheek. She seemed to be wriggling with pain.

Her sister attached the other twin to her breast. She gave Lillian a grim look. 'Georgina's got some tummy troubles. That's the fourth muslin wrap I've had to put her in already.'

'Patricia! What if she's contagious?' Despite feeling sorry for the poor mite, Lillian was more worried about her nephews' safety.

Patricia shook her head. 'I don't think so. It's probably the goat's milk. She can't seem to tolerate it.'

Lillian's heart sank. 'I thought you were going to nurse them yourself?'

'I can't very well manage to feed all three.' Patricia gently nudged Thomas away from the infant's head. He wanted to climb on his mother's lap. 'Thomas, please. Look, I really wasn't expecting to receive two at once, was I? Their grandfather – at least that's who he said he was – agreed to pay an extra eight shillings if I would take them both. I swap some of their feeds with goat's milk that Mrs Banfield agreed to donate. Sometimes I give them sugar water to top them up because mine's not going far enough. If Georgina improves tonight, I'll fill her up with a little pap in the morning. Look up on the shelf by the sink and you'll see some soothing powder. It's the bottle which says laudanum on the front.' Patricia plucked her son's fingers from Penelope's face. 'Thomas, for heaven's sake, stop touching.'

Lillian followed her sister's instructions and continued to rub Georgina's back as she grizzled. She brought the bottle and cup over to the table and set them down.

'Fill a cup with some water from the kettle,' said Patricia. 'It should be cool enough by now.'

Lillian fetched the water and watched her sister carefully measure a small amount of powder on to a teaspoon before stirring it in.

Patricia hoisted Penelope into the crook of her arm. She gently slipped the spoon between her lips. The infant choked on the concoction a little but managed to swallow most of it down.

Peter peered at her. 'Poor baby,' he cooed before deciding he'd had enough of infants who stole his mother's attention, and headed back out to the yard to play.

'Take Thomas with you,' his mother called after him then redirected her attention back to the baby and sighed. 'There, there, little one. You'll feel better soon.' Patricia hummed a lullaby as Penelope's eyelids grew heavy and she drifted off. She returned her to the makeshift crib and turned to take Georgina from Lillian.

'Don't you need to feed her first?'

'She'll only throw it back up. It's better to starve the fever.' Patricia administered a similar dose with the same spoon and soon Georgina was fast asleep again as well. She settled her alongside Penelope in the drawer. Lastly, Patricia picked up Thomas, who'd been impatiently whining and clawing at her skirt, and put him to her breast. 'You can have what's left.'

As Lillian watched her sister bustle about, she could truly see that childminding entailed a relentless juggling of needs. Patricia turned her attention to wiping Thomas's face and when Peter returned, bored, she gave him some pudding to eat. Lillian felt tired just watching her and it saddened her to know Patricia's days were so filled with duty. She stood up, took a quick look at the newborns sleeping and descended the back steps to hang some wet napkins on the line. The sunshine across her back was a welcome balm for her troubled thoughts. On her return, she saw Patricia returning the medicine bottle to the shelf. Her sister jumped and dropped the used teaspoon into the sink with a clatter. 'You gave me a fright.'

'Sorry, I didn't mean to.'

'Shall we take the boys for a quick walk by the river?' Patricia turned and asked her brightly. 'The boys could do with a stretch.'

Lillian eyed the twins. 'What about the babies? They're still asleep.'

'They'll be quite all right.' Patricia's voice sounded strained. 'We won't take too long, twenty minutes at most. I'd love some fresh air.'

Lillian sat Peter in a chair and hastily laced his boots up while Patricia did the same for Thomas. They traipsed out on to the front porch and Lillian quietly pulled the door shut. Large, grey clouds had begun to gather.

'We might get a storm,' she warned.

'Come on, stop worrying all the time. It's a way off yet.' Patricia skipped lightly down the steps and up the front path. Her sons chased after her.

Lillian took a deep breath before following. They walked a short distance before crossing the gravel road and gathering some stones for the boys to throw off the end of the wharf.

77

Patricia looked beyond the water to Milton Reach and grabbed Lillian's hand. 'Are you disappointed with me?'

'What are you talking about?'

'Don't play dumb. You've been seething with judgement since the moment I told you I was going to be a wet nurse.'

Lillian thought about the silk gloves in the department store she could have, if she wanted. She also thought of Catherine and her Scottish friends and wondered about the fun they were likely having out at Sandgate. Lastly, her mind turned to precious moments stolen with Donald. Only then did she feel ashamed.

'I'm not disappointed with you, Patricia,' she finally said. 'I'm more concerned than anything else. It's easy to see how taking care of so many children would tire a person out. There's never any time for you to have a rest.' Lillian turned and hugged her tightly. 'You're the most capable person I've ever known, so perhaps you're right. I should stop worrying because everything will turn out for the best.'

Patricia managed a wan smile. 'I will be fine. We'd better head back. I think I felt a drop of rain. Would you mind keeping an eye on the boys so I can have a little lie-down?'

The boys howled when they were told their stone-throwing time was over but, as large splats of water smacked against their faces, they reluctantly retraced their steps towards the house. Lillian saw her sister's shoulders slump as they grew closer. An infant was wailing. She had never seen her sister look so sad and defeated. It sent a chill right through her.

'I'll get her. You can still have your lie-down.'

'Thanks, Lil.'

It took a moment for their eyes to adjust to the dark interior after being outside. Penelope had escaped her wrapping and her tiny arms flailed about with distress. Patricia stood stock-still in the centre of the kitchen and stared at the dresser.

Lillian rushed over to pick up the anxious tot, and gently rubbed her back in an attempt to soothe her cries. As she rocked Penelope beside the stove, the tiny girl continued to whimper against her shoulder.

'She's hungry. What shall I give her? Patricia?'

Her sister hadn't moved. Peter, too, was standing quietly beside his mother. They were looking at Georgina, still in the drawer.

'Patricia?'

'You'd best be off now, Lillian.'

'What about your lie-down?' The rain was falling more heavily now. She hadn't caught what Patricia had said.

'I'm fine. Give Penelope to me. You mustn't be late getting back.'

'No, I –'

Patricia was fierce. 'Go!'

Indignant and worried, Lillian collected her basket.

Her sister pushed her back towards the door. 'Don't tell anyone, please.'

Lillian shrugged her off and wondered how many secrets a person could keep before there were too many and they all came bursting out. She wanted to know what was wrong with Georgina but it was true she had to get back to Rosemead. The sky had grown dark and she was as afraid of lurking dangers as Mrs Menzies' anger.

'I'll be back next week,' Lillian said. 'I promise.'

Letting herself out and hurrying through the muddy streets, she found Victoria Bridge as busy as ever. Dodging other pedestrians, she kept her head down and stayed close to the rail. Her thoughts spun as she tried to make sense of her sudden dismissal. What had happened to Georgina? Why wouldn't Patricia let her help?

Deep down, Lillian knew. There was no money to cover the cost of a proper burial and the responsibility would fall to her sister to pay for one. Could they have traced the girl's family and demanded they take responsibility? Patricia had explained what had happened at her arranged meeting at the station with the twins' grandfather. Lillian hadn't a clue who the family were and they themselves knew Patricia only as "Alice". Had the water used to mix with the soothing powder not boiled for long enough? Perhaps the laudanum needed more diluting? Lillian refused to cast suspicion on her sister's intentions but Patricia was so tired.

She felt guilt tugging. The pound note could buy proper food. Perhaps what had happened to Georgina was her fault. Lillian felt she had given her sister everything else and the thought of remaining a domestic servant for the rest of her life was even more horrifying.

The rain eased. She hurried over the bridge and failed to notice a group of men milling on the street corner before colliding straight into the back of one.

'Whoa! What do we have here, boys? Slow down, darling. What's the rush?' The man who spoke was unshaven and reeked of whisky. He eyed her greedily.

She instinctively stepped back. 'I'm sorry. It was an accident, truly.'

The man spread his hands wide and grinned at the other men. 'No need to apologise, darling. Why don't you stay and talk with us for a while?'

Lillian folded in on herself and clutched her basket to her chest. 'Please excuse me,' she said.

'Now, why would I do that?' The man's mouth twisted into

a snarl as he reached out and grabbed her arm, squeezing so tightly it hurt. His mates watched closely. 'I said stay.'

'Let me go!' She tried to wrench herself free, to no avail.

His grip tightened. She felt his coarse, chafed hands grate against her skin. Was he one of the wharfies she and Catherine had admired only a few days ago? He certainly had a vice-like grip that showed off his strength. 'No need to be rude, is there?' The other men crowded at his sides and leered at her, their breaths hot and rank. They smelled like Alfred after he'd been at the pub for a few hours. She let her body go limp and pressed up against her captor.

'That's better, my girl.' The man rubbed his unshaven face against her neck.

She stayed as still as she could.

He licked her lobe and whispered in her ear: 'How much will it cost me?'

Lillian sprang to life, stamping on the mongrel's foot and twisting her heel as hard as she could.

'Bitch!'

His momentary shock gave her time to pull away but his friends lunged in for the recapture. She didn't wait for the angry, injured man to retaliate. Instead she swung her basket upward, whacking the next closest fool on the side of his head. She'd learned to protect herself a long time ago. Lecherous men loved whores and she was damned if she was going to be confused for one.

'We've got a fighter!' A third man rounded behind, catching her about the waist and clamping on tight. She thrashed and screamed. Passers-by fearfully stepped to the side of the road and hurried away from the fracas. Why wouldn't anyone step in to help her?

A policeman appeared like a miracle. 'Oi, chaps! Let the lady go.'

Chastened by the sight of authority, the man unceremoniously dropped her to the ground and took a step back.

'Are you all right, Ma'am?' the constable asked.

'Whatever she's saying don't listen to her. We were just having a laugh,' the main instigator of her terror explained. 'No harm done, hey, Miss?'

Lillian didn't plan on hanging around to disagree. Bunching up her skirt, she ran as fast as her legs would carry her along the street, leaving her basket behind and paying no heed to the spectacle she was making of herself. She expected the officer to give chase and ask for her turn of events but evidently he was pleased to let her go. Several minutes later when she dared to check the street behind it was clear. It was not until she arrived at the wharf, catching sight of the glowing kerosene lamp perched on the incoming ferry bow, she noticed two buttons had torn from her blouse. She clasped the fabric edges together and leapt on to the docking barge.

With despair, Lillian realised she had lost her fare when she dropped her basket. The ferryman approached ready to take it and she had to explain to him what had happened. As it turned out he was the same young man who had helped Catherine to alight city-side when they'd ventured into town to do errands. Lillian hadn't been polite to him as she'd still been smarting over Donald and wasn't trusting males of any description, no matter how cordial they might seem. His name did spring to mind. Godfrey listened guardedly as she relayed her sorry plight before raising his index finger in the middle of her speech and retreating to get something out of a large wooden chest. He brought a huge wool jacket back and placed it over her shoulders.

'Sorry to hear about your troubles this evening, Miss.' She clutched the rail and gave him a relieved smile.

'Thank you very much,' she croaked.

He gave her a nod and left to retrieve fares from other alighting passengers who were stealing concerned glances in her direction. Lillian swallowed hard and clasped the jacket tightly about her torso. The ferry soon cast off and she kept her gaze firmly on the approaching shoreline and twinkling lanterns beyond, numb from such an atrocious afternoon.

'Goodness, what happened to you?' Mrs Menzies looked aghast at Lillian when she entered the kitchen, still wrapped in Godfrey's coat.

'Some disgusting men grabbed at me on my way back.'

'It's far too late to be wandering the streets on your own.' Mrs Menzies peered out the window as if to confirm it. 'You look a fright and you are unacceptably late. Go and change right this instant. You're dripping all over my clean floor. Wash your face and pin your hair up properly. Mrs Shaw will have a fit if you serve her dessert looking like that. She's been asking where you are. Good grief, what is the world coming to?'

Lillian was dismayed but not surprised that she received absolutely no sympathy from the cook. Mrs Menzies had little tolerance for any sort of shenanigans and she knew well enough she had left her departure from her sister's house more than an hour too late. Mrs Shaw would probably dock her wages.

At least Catherine showed some concern. Once Mrs Menzies had finished delivering her admonition, her friend hopped up from where she had been whipping cream and retrieved a cloth from the linen press for Lillian to wipe her streaked face.

'Come, I need yer to cut up some apple for the fruit salad.' Catherine took her by the hand and gently guided her into the pantry. Instead of reaching for the box on the bottom shelf, she reached up to the top one. In her hands was a bottle of Mrs Menzies's brandy. 'Have a sip of this. It'll calm yer nerves.'

Lillian didn't argue. She let Catherine pour her two capfuls. The liquid burned a hot trail down her gullet but within moments she began to feel its effects.

'Better? Yer cannae be too careful these days. I've seen it's getting worse out there in the evenings. There are far too many larrikins that'll wish yer nothing but harm. There, dinnae cry.' Catherine rubbed Lillian's back. 'Ye've had a nasty shock. If yer like, I'll take care of serving the wine and ye can bring the dishes through when yer hands stop shaking. The brandy'll soon take care of the rest.'

'What are you girls up to in there? Hurry up. The dessert needs to go out and Lillian still needs to tidy herself up.'

'Coming, Mrs Menzies.' Catherine rolled her eyes and scooped several apples from the box.

Lillian screwed up her face. 'That one's got spots all over it.'

'Och, it's nothing a wee peel won't fix.'

Lillian hugged Catherine. 'Did you have a nice time with your friends at Sandgate?'

'Aye, it was grand. Yer'da loved it.'

'I'm certain I would've. You can tell me all about it tonight.'

'Of course.' Catherine grinned.

Lillian was grateful for her friend's tender care. She put a candle in a candlestick and lit it with a match before carrying it up the back stairs quickly to clean up. Staring at her reflection in the looking glass, Lillian thought the flickering flame made her look ghoulish. Never had a description felt more fitting. She shrugged the greatcoat to the floor and undid the remaining buttons on her shirt, swapping it for a clean one. Apron and cap fastened, she returned to the kitchen. Soon being busy serving dessert distracted her enough to put the unpleasantness of the entire afternoon, if not entirely out of her thoughts, at least tucked away in a far corner.

There was always so much to attend to at Rosemead and for once Lillian was happy to put her head down and bury herself in the work. By night she was too exhausted to be haunted by nightmares, and yet her anguish manifested in other ways – a whittling away of weight, strange pains in her stomach.

'Goodness me, Lillian, what's the matter with you?' said Mrs Shaw later that week, not stopping for a reply. Spurred on by her newfound connections, the matriarch had begun to plan her luncheon in earnest. They would be catering to ten of the orphanage's ladies' committee members and Mrs Shaw would use the opportunity to debut her new burgundy silk dress. Of course Mrs Shaw had not forgotten Mary and Elizabeth Forsyth were at the top of her lost list, either. In the intervening days, the woman cobbled together a list of all the invitees back on a fresh sheet of paper and took to carrying it around in a beaded reticule attached to a belt around her waist. An air of thwarted suspicion clung to Lillian's employer everywhere she went. Lillian felt the woman's eyes boring into her back. If she'd known exactly how closely Mrs Shaw was watching her she would have been far more careful.

CHAPTER 9

THE LUNCHEON – KANGAROO POINT, JANUARY 1892

*L*illian took up her post in the foyer ready to receive the women's shawls and parasols. When Mary and her mother Elizabeth entered, it was impossible not to notice the brooch Donald had given her. Mary had proudly pinned it to her blouse and there it sat nestled at the base of her throat. The gems twinkled in the morning light.

Mary nodded at Lillian with vague acknowledgement, perhaps remembering it had been she who had been given the task of cleaning her soiled gloves. Lillian wondered if the snipped thread had unravelled yet. Mary was wearing a new pair but then again the girl probably had ten more to choose from. Lillian fervently hoped their reacquaintance might conjure up a memory for Mary of being stabbed in the ear by that ill-fated magpie.

Out of the corner of her eye she caught Catherine staring at her with exasperation, urging her to direct the guests into the drawing-room where Mrs Shaw had resplendently arranged herself on the ottoman in her brand new dress, ready to receive them.

Mary already knows the way, Lillian thought bitterly.

Catherine stepped forward politely to guide Mary and her mother through when it became awkwardly clear Lillian was deliberately neglecting her duties. She returned to admonish her. 'Pull yerself together, hen. I ken it cannae be easy seeing Miss Mary again but for God's sake, it's not worth receiving a scolding from Mrs Shaw for yer troubles.'

'I'm sorry. You're absolutely right, Catherine, as always.'

'Sarcasm doesn't flatter yer.'

Lillian swallowed her pride and continued to answer the door, pour the tea and hand around plates of cake and finger sandwiches. At last the ladies were settled and Mrs Shaw called the meeting to order.

From her post in the corner next to the tea trolley, ready to attend at a moment's notice, Lillian listened intently.

'Happy New Year, ladies. Shall we begin?' It was an authoritative command from Mrs Shaw rather than a question. 'I want to start by asking whether you have all had a chance to read the recent *Society for the Prevention of Cruelty* report.'

'Oh yes! You mean the one about the baby farmers, don't you? It's quite shocking.' The utterance came from Mrs Burns, whose husband owned a large department store in Queen Street. Their business had continued to thrive, despite the economic downturn. As such, her opinion held greater weight than most.

'Yes, that's the one, Tabitha,' Mrs Shaw confirmed, nodding.

Mrs Burns lifted the fan hanging from her wrist and swished it briskly back and forth in front of her pasty face. 'I simply cannot understand how any mother would simply hand their child over to these unscrupulous women. Surely alarm bells must ring?'

'Perhaps, if I may?' Mrs Sophia Arnfield hesitantly raised

her gloved hand. 'The situation is certainly dire, but the Diamantina does not have the facilities available to assist those unfortunate mothers. Surely this is now a matter for the government to consider allocating some funds towards. After all, it is not the fault of an innocent child, rather that of the father who is never called to account for his misconduct. Now that is the true root of the problem.'

Mrs Shaw raised her right eyebrow at the dissenting remark. 'Be that as it may, Sophia, it is just as much the fault of the young woman, is it not, to cast her virtue to the wind at the mere utterance of a false promise by one of these errant young men you talk about?'

Mrs Arnfield looked at the other women to garner support. Finding none brave enough to agree, she avoided making eye contact with Mrs Shaw. 'Yes, Edith, of course. But what if the poor woman is taken against her will?'

Murmurs bristled around the room.

Mrs Shaw slowly and deliberately smoothed her hands over her new skirt. 'Hmm yes, Sofia, that is another sad matter but one I am quite sure you will find is not the norm.'

Mrs Arnfield would not be subdued. 'The government's, as well as the churches', approach, continues to be strongly for encouraging both men and women to consider their Christian principles. If the unethical could be encouraged to hold their virtue in higher regard, we might find the problem of so many illegitimate children littering Brisbane streets would cease to be such a pressing issue.'

'And yet the fact of the matter is it does continue to be a problem,' Mary chimed in excitedly. She settled sheepishly back into her seat when her mother placed a calming hand on hers.

When Elizabeth Forsyth spoke, hers was a deep, measured

tone. She clearly had practice dealing with spirited discussions, Lillian thought.

'Mrs Shaw, do please tell us how the Diamantina Orphanage might best benefit from our help? Is that not, after all, why we have been summoned here this morning?'

Mrs Shaw smiled gratefully at Mrs Forsyth for directing the conversation back to its intended trajectory. 'Most certainly, and thank you for asking the question, Elizabeth. Ladies, as we all know, the Diamantina continues to provide our city with a valuable and, dare I say, a humanitarian solution to the sad situation many of our respectable families find themselves in during these difficult financial times. We cannot be wasting our attention on illegitimate babies delivered by irresponsible women, as calamitous as their fate may be.' She leaned forward and picked up her cup and saucer from the small table in front of her. 'No, we must focus our care on those whose families, through no fault of their own, simply cannot afford another mouth to feed. This extends of course to the widowers who lose their wives in childbirth. It is sadly too common an occurrence.'

Mrs Shaw raised the cup to her lips and took a long, measured sip before speaking once more. 'Unless we receive more government funding, the Diamantina will have to turn these deserving families away as well,' she said. 'I propose we proposition the governor to hold a ball at Government House and use the funds raised to refurbish the Diamantina's buildings to a more comfortable standard. Wouldn't it be wonderful if we could also employ more custodians to care for the children who deserve such care?'

The ladies nodded their approval, although Lillian noticed some appeared more enthusiastic than others.

'The government will have to do something now such a shameful report has been made public,' said Mrs Burns. 'A ball would be very suitable, I should think.'

Mrs Shaw pursued her lips. 'Yes, yes, Tabitha. The politicians can no longer turn a blind eye. The public must be reassured. Now, shall we move on to the allocation of jobs?'

'What happens to the children whose parents haven't married?' Mary interrupted, the annoying sound of her voice jarring Lillian from her angry thoughts.

'What?' Mrs Shaw turned to the younger woman and eyed her curiously. 'It's often a sorry state of affairs, Mary dear. But you are old enough to know the truth of the matter if your mother doesn't mind me explaining.' Mrs Shaw paused but Mrs Forsyth indicated she might continue. 'If a relation can't be found to take the child, the mother must find someone to foster it. The women who take them are sometimes found to be baby farmers. They ask for a premium to cover the care of the infant while its mother returns to work. Sometimes these babies are adopted into a respectable family, which we can all agree is the best outcome. Unfortunately, quite often innocent babies die. They simply cannot stomach artificial substitutes instead of their own mother's milk and this is a sad but natural conclusion. However, among these women are those who unashamedly seek to profit. Some of these dreadful women carry out the most despicable deeds. I've read about some awful cases of neglect and even murder in both the English and Queensland newspapers.'

'Oh dear!' Mary raised her hand to her mouth.

Mrs Shaw nodded sagely – or sanctimoniously, Lillian thought. 'I hope the report will encourage police to be more determined with their enquiries to ensure those people are properly regulated and held to account. I could tell the moment we met that you were an intelligent and inquiring young lady, Mary. You may be interested to read the Society's report for yourself to fully appreciate why baby farming is a becoming such a scourge on our city.'

Mary stole a thoughtful glance at her mother. 'Indeed I may.'

Lillian hoped the heat she felt rising to her cheeks was not obvious to the seated guests, not that they paid her any heed unless to summon her for a fresh pour of tea. How dare those women sit in their comfortable, well-furnished homes and cast cold judgement on those less fortunate than they were? How could they truly understand the desperation that gripped a woman into making such a necessary agreement? A mother who was quite possibly adoring of her baby forced to abandon it, or the woman who agreed to provide care in order to receive an income and keep her own starvation at bay was still worthy of their dignity.

The chatter subsided at the sound of a latecomer announcing their arrival with a long press on the doorbell.

'That'll be Cora,' said Mrs Jean Carruthers, a plump woman of about forty, sitting up with anticipation.

Lillian hurried out to receive the guest, glad for a chance get away from the self-righteous faces skirting the drawing-room. She opened the door and saw the visitor retreating down the veranda steps to scoop her baby out of a large perambulator. A blanket trailed behind as the mother lifted the baby over her shoulder.

The woman wore a fashionable pale-blue dress and a hat adorned at the hem with feathers of a similar hue. She appeared to be about twenty-five, Lillian guessed. A maid in a black uniform hovered sullenly beside the pair.

'Hello!' The mother laughed and kicked at the perambulator's front wheel. 'Could you be a dear and show Emily a good spot to store this jolly contraption. I'm afraid neither of us has quite got the hang of the blasted thing. I can make my own way inside.'

She stomped up the steps and passed Lillian in a cloud of

lavender, the tot's face bobbing with curiosity over her sleeve. There was something unrefined and refreshing about the woman, a lack of the usual airs one might expect from a lady of such pedigree. Lillian had little time to dwell on her observation, however. Mrs Shaw would be expecting her to return and continue serving immediately.

Together, she and Emily each lifted an end of the unwieldy carriage – lacquered black with cream-spoked wheels – and managed to raise it on to the veranda, where it no longer absorbed the sun's heat. She pointed to a wicker chair and asked if the young maid would like to take a seat. Emily quickly accepted.

'You're not from the south side, are you?' Lillian asked, attempting to make conversation.

Emily nodded. 'Yes, I am.'

'Perhaps I've seen you before?' Lillian racked her brain as she pushed the pram further into the shade.

'Mrs Miles lives on Grey Street. That's where I work,' Emily replied.

'I feel as if we may have crossed paths.' Lillian had to admit she felt that way about most people once she found out they were from the other side of the river. It was a sense of solidarity.

Emily scrunched up her nose in thought and shook her head. 'I'm sorry, but I don't think so.'

And yet still the sense of familiarity scratched at Lillian.

Once ensconced in the chair, the girl retrieved a ball of cream-coloured wool and knitting needles from her bag and set to clicking away industriously. The beginnings of a bootie had already started to take shape.

Lillian left the maid to her peace and quiet and reluctantly returned inside. It was clear to see the newcomers' arrival had caused an excited stir. With her free hand, the woman unfastened her bonnet and flung it like a boomerang at Catherine, who was forced to catch it mid-air. She held the baby aloft for all to admire and soon he was being passed around the women like a parcel at a child's birthday party.

'Oh, Cora, he's absolutely delightful. What did you decide to call him?' Mrs Burns asked, squeezing his fat cheeks between her thumbs and forefingers.

'Alexander Paul James, after Archie's father.'

'What a darling,' said Mrs Carruthers, reaching out for a turn. The boy settled happily on her comfortable lap.

'Thank you, my dears. Archie and I are over the moon, although I must say I haven't had an ounce of sleep since we got him. That child has a robust set of lungs and he loves nothing more than to use them after midnight.'

'Cora, he is wonderfully fortunate to have now begun his life with you and your husband,' Mrs Shaw said. She beckoned the new mother take a seat on the ottoman beside her.

Cora scrunched up her nose as Mrs Carruthers returned her son to her with a knowing look. 'Oh, dear. Mrs Shaw, I must apologise. Before I join you, it seems I will need to find a place to change him.'

'Please, let one of my girls do that for you. You've only just arrived. Lillian, come here. I believe you've changed babies before.'

'Of course, Ma'am.' She went directly to the mother, who eagerly handed over her pride and joy.

'Please be careful, he does like to wriggle. You'll find a clean napkin in the pram. Emily will be able to help.'

"Yes, Ma'am.' Lillian enjoyed the warmth of the baby's body as he nestled against her chest then winced as a pungent aroma wafted from beneath his beautifully embroidered gown and hit her nostrils. Despite the indignity of being assigned such a task, she couldn't help but be beguiled by the infant's complete trust in her.

Emily looked up from her knitting as she emerged back out on to the veranda with her charge.

'I've been told to change him.'

The maid set aside her knitting and began to rise.

'No, it's fine. I'm happy to do it if you would like to stay put,' Lillian said.

Emily reached into the perambulator to retrieve a clean napkin. Lillian took it and the maid resettled with her knitting.

Lillian carried Alexander down the hall to the laundry. There she laid a clean towel on the folding table. She lifted his gown and was rocked by a jolt of recognition. In shock, she took an involuntary step away from him.

There on his right thigh was a reddish mark. Surely this poppet wasn't the same baby? Scanning his tiny round face, it was impossible to recognise him as the same newborn she'd discovered wrapped in a shawl on the grass at Dutton Park. That baby had still been slick with vernix, his face wrinkled like a prune. This talcum-soft, peach-cheeked child was plump and vigorously pumping his freed legs into the air. Yet there he was lying there with the unique port-wine stain on his leg. He began to squirm as his mother had warned and Lillian stepped forward, placing a firm hand on his belly to prevent him from rolling off the table. She removed the soiled napkin and wiped his bottom clean with a damp rag. She was overjoyed to see him. After folding and fastening the fresh napkin with a pin, she experienced a surge of relief. This baby – Alexander – had survived after all! Not only was he alive but he would grow up to be a wealthy man like Donald, annoyingly satisfied and arrogantly ignorant to the many injustices of the world. Lillian carefully lifted the little boy so she could see him face to face. Those same soulful eyes he had used to gaze at her at the park wisely blinked back at her again.

'Hello, Alexander. I'm so glad to see you again.' Lillian smothered his face with kisses until he squealed in protest.

~

Cora seemed visibly delighted when Lillian returned him safely to her arms.

'Thank you for taking care of him.'

Lillian bobbed a curtsey and returned to her station by the wall, occasionally stealing a glance at the fortunate child. He sat contentedly in his mother's lap for a quarter of an hour as the ladies continued chatting over him before beginning to frct. She recognised the tell-tale signs of hunger and wondered whether Cora would excuse herself. Instead, the mother caught her eye and summoned her again.

'Please ask Emily to come.'

Lillian rushed outside and beckoned Emily to follow. The maid reluctantly placed her knitting down on the wicker seat and sighed.

'I knew he wouldn't last,' the girl said with resignation and followed Lillian in.

'Emily, Alexander is hungry.' Cora handed him over and immediately returned to her discussion with Mary.

Emily looked at Lillian expectantly. She led her into the hall and down to the kitchen. Mrs Menzies gave them a perfunctory look then returned to thinly slicing a cucumber.

Emily took a seat at the table and proceeded to unbutton her blouse before placing Alexander at her breast.

So Emily was a wet nurse, not a housemaid. Lillian hesitated, unsure whether she should stay. She wondered who was looking after the girl's own baby while she had the job of caring for Alexander.

'We'll be fine here, thank you. You can go back to your serving,' said Emily, staring fondly down at the little boy's downy head.

Mrs Menzies looked up. 'Yes, go on, Lillian.' She jutted her chin toward the sideboard. 'Take those cakes up with you.'

Lillian shut the door behind her and returned to the drawing-room with the plate, wondering whether the young girl she'd passed little Alexander to in Dutton Park was a relation of Cora's. Perhaps she'd been a sister? They certainly shared a similar sense of fashion. How else could Cora come to have him now? To think, he could have belonged to her and Patricia instead, if she'd kept him. What then might his future have held? Lillian felt positively ebullient at the change in his fortune. She'd made the right choice for the baby, after all.

Catherine roused her from her daydream with a pinch on her elbow. Snapping back to attention, Lillian caught Mrs Shaw glaring at her. Mrs Shaw pointed at Cora and Mary's cups, which were empty. She retrieved the teapot from the trolley and found to her dismay that it held very little tea. She quickly retreated to the kitchen once more to refill the pot with hot water and fresh leaves.

'Good heavens,' Mrs Menzies said when she saw her. 'Have they finished that one already?'

The cook was arranging a triangular sandwiches on a plate. When she entered the pantry to retrieve some more butter, Lillian refilled the teapot with boiling water from the large kettle resting on the stove. She looked over at Emily but the girl had her head down, still gazing at Alexander. In one quick motion Lillian coughed up a wad of phlegm and spat inside the teapot, swiftly replaced the lid and gave the vessel a careful swill. It was the only thing she could think of doing to truly express what she thought of the ladies' ill-informed opinions.

Mrs Menzies re-emerged. 'Tell Catherine to come and get these sandwiches before the edges dry out.'

'Yes, Mrs Menzies.'

'I shouldn't be too much longer.' Emily said, casting a strange look at Lillian. 'He's getting sleepy.'

Lillian hurried from the room with the full teapot to give Catherine Mrs Menzies' instructions. She realised she didn't even care if Emily had seen her. Back at the meeting, she struggled to keep a straight face as she poured a fresh cup for each of the visitors. She watched with fascination as they daintily lifted their little fingers and sipped away at her special brew.

Emily finally came back in to hand Alexander back to his mother and Cora contentedly held her sated baby boy. The pride the woman had for her little son was clear to see. She dismissed Emily back out to the veranda. The wet nurse seemed relieved to go. Lillian noticed Olivia sending odd glances at the mother and baby, her mouth turned down at the corners. Why was that girl so mean?

Mrs Shaw bestowed a matronly smile on Cora and Alexander and reached over to stroke the boy's fair scalp gently. 'This beautiful baby right here, ladies, is why the Diamantina needs our continued support. With such need comes opportunity, if not to adopt as Cora has, then to foster as many into the community as possible. It is the desire of Mr Horrocks, our inspector, to ensure opportunities arise for all children under his care. He feels it is even more desirable to find places for them in rural areas where they may enjoy the fresh air and learn the ways of agriculture.' She paused and gave Cora an apologetic smile. 'That's not to say little Alexander won't receive a great many opportunities right here in our city, of course. How blessed we are to have upstanding Christian women like our wonderful Cora, prepared to adopt such precious babies into their own homes.'

Lillian peeked at the new mother and spied unmistakable hurt and anger behind her carefully arranged expression. The

Diamantina preferred to receive legitimate children and she was quite certain a married woman would not have chosen to give birth behind a stand of trees in a deserted park. Had the young, finely dressed girl she had thrust Alexander at crossed the road from Dutton Park and pleaded Alexander's case for admission into the orphanage? Would Cora, so obviously a breath of fresh air among such stuffy opinions, be so generous as to adopt, as Mrs Shaw implied, if her womb was capable of producing offspring? What of her own dear Patricia? Like Emily, she too gave babies life-saving milk and, like Cora, a secure place for an infant to sleep. Sometimes, despite best intentions, such goodwill did not go far enough.

The meeting adjourned and, as far as Lillian could tell, nothing had been agreed on except that Mrs Shaw would petition the governor about holding a fundraising ball. The attendees seemed unanimously satisfied with the morning's proceedings as they prepared to leave.

Lillian helped Catherine pick up the empty crumb-scattered plates from the occasional tables dotted around the room. Hands full, they prepared to return to the kitchen. At the threshold Lillian paused, hearing voices coming from the foyer. Mrs Shaw had shut the front door behind the last of her guests and turned to address her daughter.

'I thought that went very well, don't you, dear?'

Lillian heard Olivia sniff and imagined the younger Shaw lifting her nose aloft as she uttered her reply.

'I don't see why you had to invite Cora Miles.'

'She's the child's mother. She needed to come. The women need to see a successful outcome resulting from the fruits of their labour. It encourages them.' Lillian detected a hint of exasperation in Mrs Shaw's voice.

'You know she lives on the south side, Mother. I heard her husband's family were originally convicts.'

'Olivia, sometimes I fear that school is bestowing an inflated sense of entitlement rather than a solid education upon you. I blame your father. Sometimes we must overlook such detriments to meet the greater good of our community. The Mileses have done very well for themselves and their holdings continue to grow. Don't forget your grandfather began his career in a humble forge.'

Lillian stepped into the hall in time to see Olivia roll her eyes at her mother. The girl turned on her heel and knocked the plates from her hands.

'Why are you standing there eavesdropping?' Olivia screeched. 'Get out of the way.' She stalked past in a huff.

Lillian got down on to her hands and knees and kept her eyes on the floor as she gathered up the plates. One had broken in two. Despite the low murmur, she heard Mrs Shaw clearly.

'I'll thank you for your discretion.'

Mrs Shaw had nothing to worry about. Discretion was Lillian's most useful attribute.

CHAPTER 10

MONTAGUE ROAD

*L*illian was too afraid to ask Patricia about Georgina, and Patricia wouldn't say anything more. Other strangers' babies arrived and several Sundays rolled by uneventfully, even though a heavy pall hung between the sisters. It was with even greater dismay then the afternoon Lillian turned up to find Alfred sitting on the front porch. His feet rested on the railing, one on top of the other, as he reclined on a chair pulled from the kitchen puffing away on his pipe. Despite poor Georgina's disappearance, her sister Penelope had thrived. Patricia had stopped using laudanum so often to soothe the infants to sleep. Mrs Carter had helped Patricia find a good home for the remaining twin and for that Lillian was grateful. She thought of Alexander and hoped the little girl would be as fortunate.

'Lillian!' Alfred's manner was jovial, as though he'd long forgotten their acrimonious parting. 'Your sister's expecting you.'

She strode up the steps with an air of confidence she didn't feel. Alfred made no sudden move to clip her ears to put her back in her place yet she remained on high alert.

Nestled in the new basket she had been borrowing from Mrs Menzies since her unfortunate attack on William Street were Olivia's paints, pilfered once again from her desk. She hadn't had a moment to call her own since taking that last fateful trip up Gladstone Road and she was tired of having to answer to everyone but herself. Since the morning of Mrs Shaw's Ladies' Committee luncheon, Lillian had wanted to return to Dutton Park, as if the place might reveal answers to the mysteries with which she was wrestling: who was the woman who had given birth to Alexander and who was the girl who must have surrendered him to the orphanage? If she hadn't seen the stain on his leg while changing his nappy, she could almost have fooled herself into believing what she'd witnessed was nothing more than a bad dream.

Before Lillian stepped inside, she was curious to know what Alfred had achieved while away.

'How did you enjoy your time up north?' she asked.

He shrugged. 'It was interesting enough.'

She waited for him to say more but he didn't appear to wish to share anything further. Patricia had been concerned he would find out about their old life in Gympie if he'd happened to chance upon the wrong person. Heaven forbid he'd stumbled upon that old crone, Madame Claudette. If Alfred had incriminating information, he was keeping it to himself. Lillian saw no point in persisting with questions and risk rousing his ire when he was evidently in such a good mood.

She peered down the hall and spied Patricia standing beyond the back veranda washing clothes in a large metal tub. Her sister's shoulders heaved up and down, strumming a grinding rhythm on the glass-ribbed washboard. Peter hit at stones with a stick in the sunny yard beyond. It took a moment for her eyes to adjust to the gloomy interior. When they did, a sorry sight and the smell of stale piss hit like a wall. In the children's bedroom on the left, a different baby lay cocooned in muslin in the centre of Peter's bed. In the kitchen she found Thomas sitting listlessly on the floor. He looked up at her and began to cry. She picked him up and hugged him tightly. His napkin was wet and heavy against her palms.

The dresser's top drawer had been removed and placed on the floor in the corner. Within it, two more motionless babies lay side by side, unstirred by her nephew's tears. She was about to call out to her sister to ask what was wrong with them when her attention was drawn to the parlour. On the sofa lay yet another sleeping infant, a tuft of strawberry-blonde hair peeping above the blanket.

'Patricia?'

Her sister raised her head. Defensive and defeated, Patricia looked as though she hadn't slept for several days. Her cheeks were sunken in her face.

Lillian quickly moved to the tub with Thomas still on her hip. Peter rushed over, more with relief than delight. She gently disentangled herself from their clutches and put Thomas on the ground at her feet. She reached for Patricia and pulled her into a tight embrace, horrified at her shoulder bones jutting from beneath her blouse. 'You can't keep doing this. Alfred can't approve of having so many babies around him all day. Did he manage to bring home any money?'

Patricia rested her head beneath Lillian's chin. 'He got back on Tuesday. He said he had no luck at all up north. I've been trying to keep the children out of his way so they don't upset him but it's difficult. When he first saw them he wanted to know what they were doing here. I explained everything and he cheered right up.' Patricia pulled back from Lillian's grasp and stared at her. 'It was the strangest thing. I thought he might fly into a rage. I didn't expect him to *like* the arrangement. On Wednesday he went straight out to the *Brisbane Courier* and put another ad in the paper.' Patricia lowered her voice. 'Now we have three more babies, although one of them Mrs Carter brought over yesterday. She has too many to care for herself, you see.'

Lillian helped Patricia lift and tip the large tub of dirty water over the vegetable patch. She had never liked that grumpy midwife, and now she wanted to scratch her eyes out. She followed her sister back inside. 'Why are they so quiet?'

Patricia glanced at the drawer to point at each baby. 'Alfred picked that one up from Cabbage Tree Creek Station on Friday. He sent me out to collect that one from a house at Fortitude Valley. The one sleeping on Peter's bed was colicky when Mrs Carter left. I suspect that's why she gave him to me. None of them would settle when they arrived. I didn't want to resort to sleeping powder. Not after, well, you know. But they kept us awake all night with their squalling. I was afraid Alfred might do something he'd regret. The laudanum is the only thing that works.'

'When are you going to adopt them out?'

'Alfred said we're not to let any more go as long as their families keep paying the weekly sum.'

Lillian thought back to the Ladies' Committee discussion and swallowed hard. 'It's not right, Patricia. Look at you. You're too thin.'

'What else would you have me do?'

She did not know. A helpless ache settled in the pit of her stomach.

'Here, let me finish doing that for you.' She picked up the washboard and beckoned her sister back out into the sunshine to take a seat on the bottom step. She led Thomas to the grass and removed his filthy napkin. Taking the contents to the long drop, she flicked the mess into the hole before returning and adding the soiled cloth on to the small pile beside the empty tub. She refilled the tub with hot water from the kettle. Thomas escaped half-naked and gleeful over to his brother.

'I'll get him a new one.' Patricia started to stand up.

'Leave him. He'll be perfectly fine for a little while. The air on his skin will do him some good. He has a rash.' Lillian did mean to sound accusing but it was hard not to feel annoyed about her youngest nephew's unnecessary suffering. 'You're not giving him a soothing powder as well, are you?'

Patricia shook her head and leaned back to let the sun warm her face.

Although there were merely eighteen months between them, Lillian thought her sister looked much older. The lines about her mouth and forehead seemed to have deepened.

She slid the washboard back into the tub and scrubbed the remaining napkins vigorously before wringing them out. Twisting and pounding at the material felt therapeutic, an outlet for her simmering anger. The water from the tub seeped into the earth as she tipped it out again.

Mosquitoes were already beginning to rise in the moist air and nip them.

She slapped at them as she pegged out wet laundry to flap dry on the line then began to tend to the babies inside, bringing them out one by one and wiping down their soiled bodies with a damp rag and fresh water. Their floppy limbs unnerved her. She thought of poor Georgina, probably disposed of into a watery grave. What would happen to these? What would happen to Patricia if Alfred made her continue with such lunacy?

'Why is that louse sitting on the porch smoking and relaxing like he has all the time in the world? He should be out there looking for a job, or at the very least helping you.' Lillian knew her voice was rising yet she felt powerless to stop it.

'There's nothing available right now for a man with his level of education,' Patricia said. 'So many men are looking. The competition is fierce.'

Lillian thought of her hidden pound note and was grateful she didn't have a bank account. Otherwise, she might have lodged it in one of the banks that had recently closed.

'I see. Is he still too high and mighty to get his hands dirty down at the docks? Or use his father's old connections to find something to do at one of the factories.' Her anger was in danger of boiling over. 'He could at least give you a bloody hand around the house.'

'Don't carry on, Lillian. Men don't change babies' napkins. You know that.'

'Patricia!' Alfred shouted. 'I want some tea.'

'Yes, one moment,' Patricia called back.

'Hurry up. I want to head out shortly.'

Lillian glared at Patricia. 'No need to ask where.'

Patricia rose quickly then swayed and stopped, grabbing on to the rail.

'I said hurry up!' Alfred hollered.

They heard a loud thump as his boots hit the porch's wooden boards.

Lillian hurried to ensure the babies were safely tucked into their makeshift beds and sidestepped her brother-in-law as he entered the kitchen with a face full of thunder. Retreating outside, she hurriedly turned her attention to her nephews.

Alfred's voice loudly carried. 'Jesus, Patricia. How hard is it to make your husband a simple cup of tea? You're bloody useless, you know that?'

Lillian rushed to put a fresh napkin and some patched britches – hand-me-downs from Peter – on Thomas. The children's shoes lay nestled in a row at the back door so she fetched them as well, checking inside for spiders before lacing them on to their feet.

'Come on, let's go for a little walk.' Lillian kept her voice falsely bright, not wanting to alarm them. She could do nothing more for the babies obliviously sleeping inside. As long as they continued to slumber, they would probably be all right.

Peter skipped ahead while she carried Thomas on her hip. No fancy perambulator with cream wheels for her nephew. He was far too heavy to hold for long but she had to put some distance between them and Alfred. With any luck, by the time they returned their father would have left to seek out his next drink. Lillian didn't know how he was going to pay for it. For some reason he had forgotten to ask for her wages and she preferred to be out of sight when he remembered.

She hurried around several corners before slowing to take in the finer details of their surroundings. Peter picked up a stick and flicked at stones in the dirt before turning to sniff a yellow rose protruding through a picket fence. Birchley's grocery store was up ahead. Lillian jingled the saved coins inside her pocket. The children needed to eat. She entered the store and purchased a small tin of pressed ham, some cheese wrapped in greaseproof paper and a box of crackers. On the counter sat several glass jars stocked high with bright sweets. Impulsively, Lillian requested a penny's worth and dished a couple out to each of the boys. They shut their eyes with delight as their mouths were flooded with the new sensation.

'Can I have another one?' Peter asked, as soon as they had left the shop.

Thomas reached up. 'More!'

'When we get there.'

'Where are we going?' asked Peter.

Lillian didn't have a plan. She guided them east toward

Musgrave Park where they would be able to run and play and she could rest and keep an eye on them. After half an hour she called them over for some cheese and crackers. She wondered what state her sister would be in when they returned to the house and dearly hoped Alfred had left.

Her wish was granted. Lillian found Patricia humming a tune and bustling about as she came out to greet them. Lillian glanced furtively into the bedrooms and beyond to the yard in case Alfred was still skulking somewhere. One of the babies was missing.

She turned to Patricia. 'Where is he?'

'Alfred?'

'The baby.'

Patricia swept at the floor with her boot. 'Alfred took him out for some fresh air.'

Lillian checked her sister's face but there was no apparent sign Alfred had laid a hand on her.

'Why?'

'He had an appointment with someone interested in adopting so he thought it was a good idea to take him to meet them.'

'You told me he wasn't interested in adoption as long as the families kept paying. Why are you lying for him?'

'I'm not.'

She ignored Patricia's indignation. 'You are. Anyhow, nobody's going to want a child in the state that baby was in.'

'Alfred said they're very keen.' Patricia's voice wavered.

'What about the baby's mother? Is she not paying you each week to care for him?'

'She'll be able to stop all that and carry on with her life when we tell her we've found a good family for her son, won't she?'

Patricia's brusque dismissal made Lillian wince. She

glanced into the washing up bowl and saw a solitary spoon. 'Have you taken more soothing powder? For God's sake, Patricia. Is that what happened to Georgina?'

'Please don't mention her name,' Patricia whispered, plucking the remaining baby out of the drawer. Dark eyes popped open. The infant turned her tiny face inward, squinted and opened her mouth.

'You'll have to feed her,' Lillian said, terse.

Patricia gazed despairingly as the baby squirmed. 'I can't keep doing this, Lillian. Feeding them all takes so much out of me. I'm very tired.'

She watched Patricia grow resolute. Despite her worries for the babies, there was a measure of relief. If her sister couldn't be a wet nurse any more, then surely she and Alfred would put a stop to all the nonsense. He would have to drown his pride and start looking for honest work in earnest.

Patricia handed the baby over and thrust a bottle into her hands. 'Here, give her that.'

Lillian peered at the opaque liquid swirling with granules. 'What is it?'

'Sugar water. It'll fill her up until I can pay Mrs Banfield for some more goat's milk.'

'I thought you said it was no good?'

Patricia groaned. 'Do it.'

Lillian put the teat to the baby's mouth. She latched on and took a tentative suck. Fooled by the substitute, the little girl began pulling on the rubber. When the bottle was empty, Lillian put it down on the table and held the baby upright to burp her and let her take in her surroundings. Instead, her little head lolled back against Lillian's arm as she fell back to sleep.

'You had me drug her!' Lillian was livid. Coal embers of irritation burst into hot flames.

'What else do you expect me to do? You've no idea, Lillian,

what it's like. Don't you dare judge me!' Patricia's voice rose to a shout.

'Here.' Lillian reached over to retrieve the last of the ham, cheese and crackers from the basket. 'Eat something. You're turning into a stick.'

Patricia brushed her sleeve across her eyes and shook her head.

Obstinate as ever, Lillian thought. She retrieved her wages envelope and rose to place it on the mantelpiece above the woodstove. A sense of panic mixed with her anger and clawed at her heart. Those babies would be drinking nothing but sugar water for the rest of the week if Alfred got his dirty hands on her hard-earned money. She pulled out a sixpence and placed it in Patricia's palm.

'Hide this to be safe. The babies must have some milk or formula.'

How could Patricia have got into such a fearful mess when, other than marrying Alfred, she had always been the one in charge of good decision-making? The burden of her sister's questionable enterprise sat heavily on Lillian's shoulders as well. There was no denying it. She couldn't control Patricia's stubborn nature any more than her sister could control Alfred's drinking and it was driving her wild.

A loud rapping sounded at the front door and made them both jump.

Patricia planted her palms on the table and hauled herself up to answer it. Lillian followed. A policeman waited on the veranda. Young with a stern demeanour, he removed his hat to reveal a thick crop of auburn hair, which bled into thick muttonchops that ran down the side of his face.

'Good afternoon. Constable Joffrey,' he introduced himself.

Patricia swallowed hard but managed to keep her composure. She raised her brows with curiosity as if a visit from the law was the last thing she had been expecting. It was a relief for Lillian to see the whip-smart girl from Gympie had not been lost for good. Her sister's studious appraisal of the young officer lasted long enough to elicit a nervous cough as he was the first to break his gaze.

'Hello, Constable, how may we help you?'

'I'm here to investigate reports a baby farm is being run at this address. You won't mind if I come in and take a look around?' Regaining his sense of authority, Constable Joffrey didn't wait for permission as he put a foot inside the hall.

What would Mrs Shaw say if she thought one of her maids was abetting a baby farmer? Lillian had never thought of her sister as such: Patricia had always been the first to volunteer to take care of the newborns at Madame Claudette's – so big was her heart – but in that moment Lillian's mind finally snapped into focus. That was exactly what she was and the constable was about to have his suspicions confirmed if he took three steps further.

Patricia gracefully stood aside.

Lillian couldn't bring herself to move out of the way. She held the baby in her arms tightly and rocked her. 'My little one's only just drifted off. Please try to be quiet,' she said.

The constable scowled at her impertinence. 'That's your child?'

'Of course! Who else's would it be?' She felt emboldened by lying. It was the safe cushion that had always helped her through tough circumstances. It was a relief to see he was not the same constable who had come to her rescue on the other side of Victoria Bridge when the gang of men had set upon her. Constable Joffrey cast a cursory look at the sleeping infant before noticing Peter and Thomas peering fearfully around the parlour door.

'Those two are mine,' Patricia said. 'Come here, boys.'

They rushed for their mother's skirt, wary of the stranger.

He poked his head into each of the bedrooms before making his way down to the kitchen. 'Who do the other babies belong to?'

'I care for them so their mothers can continue to work. There is nothing untoward happening here, Constable. I have to make a living, same as anyone else. There's no law against childminding, is there?'

'Indeed, no. Baby farming on the other hand...' The constable stroked his chin and wrinkled his nose. 'Who else lives at this address?'

'My husband, Alfred Hooper.' Patricia said. 'He'll be home shortly. You can speak to him yourself.'

The officer frowned at the sound of her brother-in-law's name. 'Alfred Hooper, you say?'

'That's right. Why?'

'I've heard that name before. Married, you say?'

Patricia nodded.

Constable Joffrey rearranged his hat. 'Righto, I'll be off. But rest assured, Ma'am, your activities are being monitored. I've had my orders. While you appear to be operating your service honestly, there are others known to us that are taking advantage. I'm sure you won't mind if I pay you another visit at a later date to see that everything is continuing to stay as it should.'

Patricia pursed her lips. 'If you feel you absolutely must, Constable, I can't stop you.'

He ignored her acerbic tone. 'This house needs a good air out. Open those windows. A closed space is a breeding ground for disease.'

'Open windows encourage flies. You have children, do you?'

The constable hesitated. 'Younger siblings. You'll do well not to question me further, Ma'am. Good day to you both.'

As soon as she'd pushed the door shut behind him, Patricia collapsed against it, her face drained of colour. 'Who reported me?'

Lillian shrugged. 'It was only a matter of time.' She remembered Mrs Shaw's words about the Society for the Prevention of Cruelty's report. 'The newspapers have been asking the general public to be vigilant.'

Patricia covered her face with her hands. 'I can't even trust my neighbours!'

'It could have been one of the babies' families. Perhaps Penelope and Georgi –' Lillian wondered about the twins' mother. Supposing she'd had a change of heart and wanted them back?

'As if they would say a word. Think of the shame of everybody knowing you'd given birth to a bastard! Babies die every day, Lillian. I've said it before. Dysentery, flu, consumption. It's only by the grace of God my own babies are still here. No, it could have been Mrs Carter. I've heard the women who are able to have started giving her a wide berth. She hasn't been keeping the babies in her care for very long at all. There are rumours. Perhaps that constable has already visited her. She might have mentioned my name to save her own skin.'

Lillian bit her tongue. If Patricia wanted to lie to herself about the seriousness of her predicament, she couldn't stop her. Her sister was no more virtuous than Mrs Carter. The silent admission left her torn. Patricia was the only family she had left. Her sister needed her, too, for her support as well as her wages. However, with Alfred frequenting the hotels, Lillian would be damned if her backbreaking labour would be wasted down the gullet of that soft-fingered idiot a minute more.

To an unsuspecting onlooker, Patricia had managed to curate her tenuous reputation as a respectable woman despite her unconventional heritage. Nobody, not even Alfred, knew the true nature of their parentage. Lillian had been made to swear to carry their secret to the grave and at times it had seemed far too big a burden. She shuddered as she remembered her admission to Catherine. But baby farming was the last straw – even their disreputable mother would be appalled. Undoubtedly, selling one's body was certainly preferable to profiting from the starvation and death of innocent babes.

Lillian grabbed her basket from the table.

Patricia looked at her, startled. 'Where are you going?'

'I need to clear my head. I'll be back before it gets dark.'

Lillian felt as though she was radiating sparks as she marched up Gladstone Road. Sweat trickled down her back, her shirt stuck to her shoulders, and still she strode onward through the dust to Dutton Park. A well of relief rose in her to see the iron entrance gates appear on the horizon. She came to a stop in front of the small stand of trees where Alexander had begun his life. She ducked and pushed past the brush and branches until the patch of grass where he'd been cast from his mother's body was revealed. No trace remained of the ordeal that had taken place.

She knelt and began to cry, great heaving sobs that pressed her corset up into her ribs, a suffocating and inescapable grip. At last she sat back and wiped her eyes on her sleeves. A single green woollen thread, trapped and flailing on a branch, caught her eye. Lillian rose to untangle the fibres from its twiggy prison and twirled it thoughtfully around her index finger.

She rustled through the basket. Out came the paint box, an empty jar and an assortment of brushes. Down to the water's edge she rushed to fill the jar, excited to begin painting. Fingers of sunlight filtered into the sheltered glade. Other people strolling in the park cast mildly curious glances in her direction as she set up the space, flipping the sketchbook, adding a little water to the paints. But as she touched the first slash of green to the blank page she found herself shielded from the rest of the world. No wonder the mother had selected such a spot. She was like the kangaroos who lifted their heads from their rest in the late afternoon, otherwise left undetected.

Lillian tried to record her memory of that day as faithfully as she could. She painted Alexander lying wrapped in the shawl. It was easy enough to create an exact paint match to the green woollen thread. She added details such as ants scurrying in the dirt beside Alexander, who was helpless to fend them off. An artistic liberty – his port-stained leg kicking free. In the background Lillian loosely captured his mother in pale, ephemeral strokes, a suggestion of a figure with hair flowing down her back as she retreated through the headstones, her identity a mystery. Her hand flew above the page until the picture was complete. Only then did she sit back to contemplate what she had done. It was as she recalled and for nobody else to see; she would make quite sure of that. It was enough to have the truth recorded there on paper, along with the green thread to convince her, once and for all, that her mind had not played tricks on her that day.

She was not quite finished. Tearing the painting out, Lillian laid it on the grass and placed a stone at each corner to stop it from blowing away. She tipped out the dirty water jar and went to refill it with water from the river. Returning, she began a new picture; this one depicting her sister's kitchen. Quicker strokes, darker browns. Patricia sitting at the table nursing a baby while two more slept in the dresser drawers behind her. Thomas playing with a small metal train at his mother's feet. Peter chasing skinks in the grass beyond, in a small square of light framed at the back door. Again she held her brush, dipping and tapping, resolute and refusing to stop until the last stroke was made. Lillian carefully held the book up to the light. She felt sad looking at the scene but she'd never been able to see everything so clearly. She did not know what would happen to Patricia but her sister would reach her own breaking point when she was ready, Alfred be damned. If Patricia was not so headstrong it might have happened already.

On returning tired to Montague Road, Lillian found her sister dozing in the rocking chair. Peter looked up at her expectantly. She raised a finger to her lips. For once he and his brother understood they should leave their mother sleeping. They let their aunt lead them to their bedroom. Together they curled up on Peter's bed with the sleeping baby at their centre as Lillian whispered a story about fairies and goblins and carried them in their imaginations to wonderful places far, far away from that hot, smelly little house.

A thud against the porch boards woke Lillian with a start. Had the constable returned? She felt the softness of the children's sleeping bodies pressing up against her. No further noise came so she extricated herself from their arms and legs and crept toward the window. It was a relief to find dusk had not yet settled. She peeped from behind the curtain but nobody appeared to be on the porch waiting to be welcomed.

She stole out to the front door and carefully turned the key. Counting to three and chiding herself for being spooked, she swung it open and thrust her head outside.

Alfred slumped against her skirt from where he had propped himself against the frame. She pulled her feet out from under him and stepped back with disgust.

'Lillian, I'm sorry,' he slurred, reaching for her ankle with a wavering hand.

She stayed out of reach.

'I'm a lousy husband,' he said, louder.

'Yes, you are.'

'No,' he groaned. 'You don't really mean that, do you, Lil?'

She ignored his blubbering and gave him her hand so he could heave himself up to a sitting position. He looked up at her through bleary eyes. 'You need to know that everything I do is for this family. I do my best but Patricia's impossible.' He hung his head, dejected.

Lillian could see he was too full of drink to be able to hurt her. She considered inflicting some injuries of her own while he was too inebriated to escape but decided he was too pathetic to bother with. She would not stoop to his level of worthlessness. 'Come on, you can't stay out here. It's still daylight, for God's sake.'

'You're my sister. You know that, don't you, Lillian?'

His whining was annoying but nowhere near as disgusting as the rancid breath that smothered her as he slowly lurched to his feet. Alfred clutched the doorframe for support and slurred his self-pitying words into her face. She craned her neck out as far as she could while half-carrying, half-dragging him into the kitchen, where he tripped and fell next to Patricia who was still sleeping – drugged, Lillian assumed – in the rocking chair.

'Patricia,' he said, before spewing brown liquid across the floor.

Patricia briefly stirred.

Lillian fetched Alfred a bucket, a pillow and a blanket and left him lying prostrate. He threw up again, powerful retching that made her want to gag, too. Behind her, one of the babies began to cry. She stepped over her brother-in-law, pinching her nose with her fingers at the sight of the vomit-stained pillow at his head, and carried the infant back to her sister.

'Patricia, wake up.'

'Mm?'

'I can't come home next Sunday. My friend Catherine's asked me to go on an outing. I said I would.'

Patricia was doleful as she took the baby. She saw Alfred lying on the floor at her feet and nodded permission without a word.

Lillian left the cottage with a heavy heart but she had made up her mind. She would not return until the babies were gone; adopted out or returned to where they had come from. It just wasn't right.

CHAPTER 11

SPRING HILL

*L*illian held up her ends of the double sheet and folded them over. 'Yes, I would love to come.'

Catherine dropped her hands, clapped them together and squealed with delight. 'Look what yer made me do! Do yer really mean it? Och, Lillian, we're going to have a grand time! Yer not toying with me now, are yer?'

'No, Patricia said she could manage without me for one weekend.' Lillian felt a pang at the lie. She'd lied to her sister as well. When she'd left the cottage there had been no offer from Catherine but Lillian knew it would only be a matter of time.

'The others will be so surprised. I cannae believe it.' Catherine picked her end of the sheet up from the floor and closely inspected it. 'No harm done.'

'Thank you for not giving up on asking me,' Lillian said. She meant it. It had been dreadful turning down her friend's requests so many times. Catherine would know the perfect way to take her mind off her problems.

It felt very strange to turn right the following Sunday afternoon instead of the usual left. They disembarked from the ferry, smiled at their friend Godfrey and linked arms to head up Edward Street.

'Rosemary's beau, Matthew, is bringing along a friend. None of us has met him yet but I have to warn yer, from whit she's told me we shouldnae expect too much from him. He dinnae sound like much fun at all. We think Matthew's simply taken pity on the poor fellow. He told Rosemary the lad needs cheering up. I hope he makes an effort to be bonny. We dinnae want him casting a pall over our outing.'

Lillian grinned at her friend and squeezed her. 'Nothing can ruin my day!'

She skipped along feeling euphoric as she took in Catherine's descriptions of the others they were due to meet. They wandered beneath the shop verandas on Edward Street, headed toward The Stock Exchange Hotel. She wasn't much for drinking: Alfred's appalling behaviour when he was on the grog naturally gave her little tolerance for drunken antics. She liked it well enough not to run off and join the Temperance Union. Catherine assured her the hotel was only a short stop for them to grab some lunch. Lillian was concerned she couldn't afford such a luxury and wondered how Catherine could, either; they received the same small wage packet each week.

'We'll have nought to worry about,' said Catherine. 'Yer'll see. The lads will take care of us.'

All Lillian had to do was smile, laugh at the men's jokes and listen to their yarns as if they were the best she'd ever heard.

They entered the lounge and immediately found themselves enveloped in a cloud of tobacco smoke. Through it, Lillian saw a girl of about their age standing next to a table by the back wall. The girl caught sight of them and urgently waved them over. As they arrived, she happily wrapped her arms about Catherine's neck and gave her a quick peck on the cheek. Catherine introduced Lillian to Melanie and around the table to Rosemary, Matthew, and Matthew's cousin Arthur. She paused when she reached the solemn-looking stranger.

'This is my friend, Nicholas Hamilton,' Matthew said.

Lillian tried hard not to show her surprise at the familiar-sounding name. Was he really the same person?

Nicholas flicked a cursory glance at her before reaching for his glass. He raised it to his lips and took a quick sip. She felt disappointed by his lack of interest in making her acquaintance; not even granting her a smile in greeting. She had donned her only good dress and carefully pinned her hair up to make a good first impression on Catherine's friends. She had even risked stealing a few drops of Olivia's eau de toilette to dab on her wrists and behind her ears. It had pleased Lillian no end when Donald lifted his eyes from the newspaper he was reading to gaze at her as she'd entered the dining room that morning pretending to look for something she'd misplaced.

Then again she was a stranger to Nicholas even if she did know of the misfortune that had befallen him, had cradled his baby son, Stephen, handed to Patricia for care. The man showed every sign of being in mourning for his wife. His hair was unkempt and his chin bore several days' worth of dark stubble. She longed to enquire whether his son, Stephen, was doing well but kept her tongue in check. It would be dreadful to create an atmosphere of awkwardness among everybody and her question would only raise several more.

'Don't mind him,' Matthew said. 'This is the first time he's been out since his wife died.'

Even the unflappable Catherine drew in her breath at Matthew's lack of diplomacy. Rosemary elbowed him in the ribs. 'That's sad, Nicholas. I'm sure we're all very sorry for yer recent loss.'

Nicholas stared up at Rosemary and gave her a wry grin. 'I don't need any more sympathy, thank you. I'm absolutely drowning in it. Matthew, another ale will do.'

'Coming right up, mate!'

Arthur stood up and patted Matthew's shoulder. 'I'll go. It's my round. Ladies, please have a seat. Does anyone else fancy a drink?'

Catherine wedged herself on to the padded bench behind the table, ordered an ale and nudged Lillian.

She sat down on a wooden chair Arthur had pulled over from a vacant table. 'A shandy please, Arthur.'

'Right you are,' he said and left for the bar.

He soon returned with a tray and handed them their beverages. Lillian sipped at her shandy and stole another glance at Nicholas. In spite of his melancholic demeanour, she could see Patricia's account of him was right. He was young and handsome. His dark hair, although not brushed, had soft curls that licked at his clean collar. His large tanned hands absently caressed the side of his beer glass and he tilted his head occasionally, determined to follow along with the merry conversation while not adding anything of value himself. She noticed the amused glint in his hazel eyes when Melanie took to entertaining them all with impersonations of her employers. The small crack in his austerity assured Lillian he was a man who hadn't entirely given up on life.

She found Melanie's mimicry of Mrs Arnfield uncanny. The thick Glaswegian accent dissolved into upper-crust elocution with alarming accuracy and even the saddest onlooker would be hard-pressed not to laugh. Lillian giggled until tears rolled down her face and clung to Catherine at times in order to stay on her chair. The shandy had gone straight to her head.

Nicholas, at last, directed a bemused stare in her direction as she tried with difficulty to regain her composure. Lillian didn't care what he thought of her. She couldn't remember the last time she had felt so happy.

Matthew went back to the bar and ordered several plates of potato and roast beef. When the steaming food arrived from the kitchen he urged them to help themselves and they did.

Lillian lost any sense of guilt she felt about taking advantage of his generosity after Catherine whispered in her ear to explain Matthew was a teller at one of the remaining banks still open. His salary quadrupled theirs.

After lunch, they decided to wander up to the Windmill on Wickham Terrace and take in the city panorama. Matthew pointed out the Royal Bank of Queensland as they strolled along and indicated the window where he sat to work. Lillian could see how fond Rosemary was of him. The feeling appeared to be mutual. The two often walked on ahead with hands locked together. The sight made her long for Donald despite her better judgement. Catherine had linked her arm through Melanie's to follow closely behind the couple. The girls laughed uproariously from time to time at something one had said to the other. Arthur lagged, seeming relaxed and content now that he had a belly full of food and beer. Lillian smiled as she watched him throw regular glances at Catherine whenever her head was turned. That left Nicholas, trudging quietly beside her. To Lillian's delight, he finally turned and asked where she was from.

'Kangaroo Point,' she replied. 'Catherine and I are housemaids at the Shaws'. Mr Shaw is a solicitor.'

He shook his head. 'I mean your family. Were you born and raised in Brisbane?'

She raised her arm and pointed across the water. From their vantage point it was easy to pick out the tiny pitched roof of Patricia's cottage on Montague Road. A wave of sadness knocked the breath out of her. She waited a moment to take stock before speaking. 'My sister lives over there so I guess that's where I'm from, too. Usually I go and visit her on Sunday but she's been very busy lately. Catherine's been pestering me for a very long time to come out with her and her friends and I finally said yes.'

'Indeed. I understand what you mean.' Nick's eyes flicked towards Matthew. 'I wondered if I recognised you. My family and I live on Vulture Street. I'm sure I've seen you somewhere before.'

Lillian was intrigued by his admission. Here she was thinking he had no interest in her. Of course, if they both lived on the south side, chances were high their paths might have crossed at some point. She remembered wondering the same thing about Cora Miles's maid.

Nicholas frowned as he pondered the connection. 'I can't quite put my finger on where or how, though. It's bothering me.'

She shrugged and bit her bottom lip. If she admitted she'd helped her sister to care for Stephen after Molly's death it wouldn't help their budding conversation along one bit. She decided to change the subject. 'You wouldn't be related to the same Hamilton family who owns the tailor shop on Stanley Street by any chance, would you?'

He brightened. 'Yes, I am. My father runs the store. I work there. We all do.'

'Perhaps you've seen me walking past. I know my brother-in-law has bought a suit from your store. It always seems to have a lot of customers.'

At last he rewarded her with a genuine smile. 'You must be right. It's a busy street.'

They caught up with the others, who had stopped by the

windmill. Lillian felt puffed after scaling the incline as the midday sun beat down but the view made the walk worthwhile. She looked at the large properties bordering the street and wondered if one of them belonged to the Forsyths. Hadn't Mary said she was from Spring Hill? Lillian pushed the thought from her mind. She would not let Mary or Donald impinge on her happiness that day. The group entered Wickham Park to find some shade.

Lillian had decided on a whim to pack her sketchbook. Once seated, she pulled it from her basket, along with a lead pencil she'd taken from Mr Shaw's desk in his library. She made a quick sketch of the others as they rested in various states of repose on the grass. It was an afternoon worth remembering.

Melanie peered over her shoulder to watch as she made the finishing touches. 'That's quite a good likeness of us, you know. Well done.'

'Thank you.' Lillian blushed at the praise. She was not used to having an audience for her work.

'Look, everybody, come and see what Lillian's drawn.'

She hoped the extra minutes she had spent attending to Nicholas's profile were not obvious.

'You have quite the talent, Lillian,' was all he said as he surveyed the picture. 'Have you any others in there?'

She flipped the cover over and slid the book back into the basket. 'No.'

He gave her a strange look but she could not show him the scene of the infant and its abandoning mother, nor her sister and the babies. She should have hidden them in the stable along with the promissory note, photograph and books. It was a disappointing end to an otherwise wonderful afternoon. Their conversation withered and, as the light began to fade, she and Catherine regretfully bade their farewells.

'Yer know,' said Catherine as they headed back to Shafston Road, 'it seemed that every time I saw Nicholas, he was looking at you.'

'Don't be ridiculous.' Lillian said and smirked. 'Besides, it's Arthur you should be worried about. He spent so much time with his eyes on you he almost tripped when we were walking up to the Windmill.'

'Really? Are yer sure?'

Lillian laughed at her friend's hopeful face. 'Definitely. As for Nicholas, I knew who he was as soon as Matthew introduced us.'

'Yer did?' Catherine was intrigued. 'Why didnae yer say?'

'I couldn't bring myself to tell him. The truth is the Hamiltons live not far from Patricia's.' Lillian paused. Catherine had been so kind to bring her along to meet all her friends. The outing had been such a soothing balm for her worries. It was too late anyway: she'd already said too much. 'Catherine, Nicholas has a son. His wife died from childbirth fever. His mother learned from our local midwife, Mrs Carter, that Patricia was still nursing Thomas. Mrs Carter also probably knew about Alfred not having a job. My sister agreed to be the baby's wet nurse until Nicholas could stand to be under the same roof with him. You see, the boy made his grieving worse.'

'Dear me, that's tragic. Yer sister's a saint. I ken why ye always want to go home on Sundays.'

'It was a paid arrangement,' Lillian said unkindly.

'Even so, to take a stranger's baby into yer house and care for it when ye have yer own baby to feed is a very kind deed. Do yer and her look alike? Perhaps that's why he thought yer were familiar? Sometimes sisters do look very similar.'

Lillian shook her head. She and Patricia looked nothing

alike but that was yet another secret to keep. 'I don't think Nicholas will be ready to start courting again for a long time. Even if he was, why would he be interested in a maid like me? I'm sure he could do much better.'

'Och, yer have more to offer than yer ken, sweet Lillian.' Catherine squeezed her hand. 'We'd better walk faster. Yer ken what Mrs Menzies is like.'

Lillian rolled her eyes and they both laughed.

That evening, Lillian lifted her head and whispered across their dark attic room. 'What do you fancy doing next weekend?'

'What about Patricia?' Catherine whispered back.

'What about her?'

'Och, it would seem our Lillian has begun to show a wee bit of gumption at last. Perhaps we can go visit the museum or the zoo? There's lots we could do. You should come to the Exhibition this year, but that's not until August, though.'

'I don't care! I'm definitely coming.' Lillian lay her head back on her pillow and smiled. She thought with enthusiasm of rides, exhibits and tasty food. Thousands of people went each year and yet she never had. After the wonderful afternoon she and Catherine had spent, Lillian was reminded that life was happening beyond the walls of Rosemead and her sister's cottage. It was a life a girl could enjoy, if she could find enough courage to stand up for herself. When she thought of her conversation with Nicholas, warmth flooded her insides. If what Catherine said had been true – that he'd had his eye on her or, heaven forbid, wanted to court her – she'd have to be careful not to let slip that his wife's death had plunged her own family into chaos as well. It was a risk she was prepared to take.

CHAPTER 12

AUGUST, 1892

*S*pring was threatening to arrive behind a flurry of westerly wind. The riotous birdcall and fresh buds on branches filled Lillian with optimism. Catherine had happily included her on every outing over the last few months wherever their time off coincided. The Glaswegian introduced Lillian to so many new experiences such as croquet in the Botanic Gardens and lunch at various tearooms with Melanie and Rosemary, she felt as though she had been reborn.

With Matthew and Arthur in tow, they attended the annual Exhibition; a carnival of noise and colour where the scent of cattle and straw combined with the sickly-sweet taste of jam tarts. The place was crammed with people from all walks of-life. Lillian loved every minute.

She squealed with delight when Catherine came off the merry-go-round and told her Arthur had asked if they might be allowed to court. Lillian tried not to let envy stain their friendship. More often than not, Catherine and Arthur were hardly separate from the wider group at all. Lillian was content to make conversation with Melanie when the couple had eyes only for each other.

At the same time, Rosemary and Matthew considered calling a halt to their courtship because he wanted to put the feelers out for work in New South Wales. Rosemary hysterically declared right next to the sheep pens she could never move past the river and if Matthew had any sense he would stay put. The ultimatum proved fruitful because Matthew acknowledged the error of his thinking immediately. He dropped to his knee in the dirty walkway and proposed to Rosemary. Everybody cheered with delight except Rosemary, who told him to stop being so silly, as if she would accept a proposal that had livestock as witnesses. It did not take her long to go back on her stance and accept when Matthew pulled a diamond ring from his pocket and slid it on her finger.

There was much excitement as their wedding approached. Melanie was naturally required to be her sister's maid of honour and Catherine was included in the party.

Sadly, for Lillian, Mrs Shaw decided she couldn't possibly be without two maids on a Wednesday so she was denied permission to attend the joyous occasion at the courthouse. Mrs Shaw berated her for her long face and sulky movements but Lillian could not shake off her despair at being excluded from such an exciting event. It was agony waiting for Catherine to return and tell her all about the ceremony and wedding breakfast. Her friend did not disappoint and enthusiastically regaled her with all the details.

Despite their many months living in close quarters, due to the sherry Catherine had consumed at the breakfast, her Glaswegian tongue made the retelling almost impossible to decipher. It was clear by her tone, however, the event had been a success. Lillian was very happy for Matthew and Rosemary. They were a handsome match. However, one thing Catherine said did stand out immediately.

'Nicholas asked where yer were.'

'Nicholas?' Lillian had tried to forget their brief encounter that day they had walked up to the Windmill as he had not returned with Matthew on any of the other outings. Lillian had assumed with some remorse he must have been content to dwell on his loss rather than have everybody rub their carefree antics in his face. Perhaps it was her secrecy regarding the sketchbook that had soured him?

'Aye, he looked very dapper in his morning suit and top hat. I think I even saw him smile. For a split second I could see why yer liked him.'

'I beg your pardon?'

'Dinnae play coy with me, hen. Ye've not mentioned Donald once since the day you met Nicholas.'

Lillian reflected on the truth of the remark. It was true that Donald's hold over her had weakened. He'd tried to catch her hand once as she wandered past him on the landing after fetching his father a ceramic water-bottle to warm his bed. She'd been surprised and then annoyed at his presumption. The spark that had never failed to travel the length of her body at his lightest touch had been well and truly doused.

However, Catherine's observation was not entirely correct. Neither were Lillian's waking moments consumed by thoughts of Nicholas. She'd decided she did not want to link herself with a man who carried such a heavy load of baggage, even if he was handsome. She was barely twenty years old and, if she wasn't careful, her love life might end up mirroring that of her sister, whom she had refused to go and visit for the past four months. Lillian absolutely did not wish for more drama in her life. She had only just escaped it. Mothering another woman's child was not something she cared to be doing either, not after seeing the mess Patricia had made for herself. At any rate, Catherine soon scuppered any further thought on the matter.

''Tis a shame he's leaving next week. His father's sending him to England to buy new material for their store. He'll be gone six months at least.'

Lillian was only mildly disappointed. She believed her newfound sense of calm and contentment came from being able to sample the city's array of entertainments. When each Sunday rolled around, she had continued to make the decision not to visit the cottage on Montague Road. It was the longest the sisters had ever been apart and she felt regretful about the separation but she simply could not stomach another minute helping Patricia run her baby farm and Alfred stealing her money.

As the weeks passed, the treachery had become easier to stomach and her spirit felt lighter for it. When Catherine wasn't available to go on an outing, she continued to borrow Olivia's paintbox and took pleasure in finding a quiet space hidden in the sweeping Botanical Gardens. Her favourite spot was close to the river bank where she could capture the passing barques and schooners making their way up to the docks. Through experimenting, Lillian had begun to develop some mastery in her portrayal of the muddy waters that eddied about the ships' sterns.

The river demarked the line between her old life and new. Patricia had sent a telegram two weeks after Lillian's final visit, which a delivery boy had brought directly to Rosemead. The message enquired as to her whereabouts. Lillian took the time to send back a reply: Has business ceased question mark stop. To this question, she'd received no further correspondence.

While half-expecting Patricia to turn up at the back

doorstep with the children in tow, Lillian knew her sister had far too much stubborn pride to come and beg her to return. The Shaws owed nothing to Alfred now that he was no longer in their employ so she stopped worrying about losing her position. Indeed, Mrs Menzies had recently and begrudgingly admitted Lillian was becoming quite adept at her chores. Which is what made it more shocking when one day, after returning from a short errand to deliver a cake down the street to Mrs Carruthers, she entered the kitchen only to have Mrs Menzies immediately rush up wearing an even more formidably sour expression than usual. Catherine, busy shelling a bowl of peas, kept her eyes downcast.

'Mrs Shaw said you're to report to her immediately,' Mrs Menzies instructed, giving Lillian a shove between her shoulder blades down the hall.

Filled with foreboding, she dragged her heels along the carpet runner and turned left into the drawing room, where Mrs Shaw sat in her favourite burgundy armchair beside the tapestry curtains.

Mrs Shaw removed the pince-nez from her nose and coolly stared at her. 'Lillian, you have worked for us for more than a year, is that correct?'

'Yes, Mrs Shaw, almost a year and a half.' She clasped her hands behind her back to keep from fidgeting.

'And in that time I have found your service to be fairly satisfactory. However,' Mrs Shaw continued after a pause, 'Olivia tells me an important item belonging to her has been going missing and miraculously returning on a regular basis. As you can imagine, my daughter is most upset by the discovery that somebody might be using her belongings without permission.' Lillian nodded, trying to appear concerned but, more importantly, innocent.

'Do you have anything to say about this matter, Lillian?'

She forced herself to meet her employer's shrewd gaze. 'I'm sorry to hear of it, Mrs Shaw. Perhaps if I knew what the item was, I could be more helpful.'

Mrs Shaw pursed her lips. 'I was hoping you might be just the person to enlighten me.'

'Me? I haven't a clue.'

Mrs Shaw's voice held a hard edge. 'Lillian, I do not believe you. I summoned you in the hope you might confess your transgressions but it appears you are more interested in maintaining a deceitful lie. I know you took the paint box from Olivia's room on more than one occasion. We conducted a search of the servants' quarters and to my sad surprise found this...' Mrs Shaw reached behind her chair and then held up the incriminating paint box. 'Beneath your bed.'

Lillian felt her cheeks betray her with their rising heat. Her usual reliance on wit to save herself failed and all she could offer Mrs Shaw was a wide-eyed expression of denial as she vehemently shook her head side-to-side. Finally, mind reeling, she found her voice.

'Olivia wasn't using her paints. I only borrowed them.'

'You mean you stole them,' Mrs Shaw said sharply. 'This makes me wonder what else you may have taken from my home without asking.'

Lillian swallowed. 'I haven't taken anything else.'

'When I questioned Catherine earlier, she said she had no knowledge at all of how this paint box might have ended up in your room. She swore neither of you had put it there but then again I'm not surprised she would stick up for you. You're as thick as thieves.'

Lillian shook her head vigorously. 'Catherine had nothing to do with any of it, I swear.'

'I'll be the judge of that.' Mrs Shaw picked up a small bell off the occasional table beside her chair and rang it. In a moment, the familiar sound of Catherine's footsteps came hurrying up the hall. Lillian watched her friend pause at the door, eyebrows raised with expectation.

'Come in, Catherine,' Mrs Shaw said, beckoning.

Catherine stood beside Lillian and waited. Lillian dug her nails into her palms and fought an overwhelming urge to run.

'Lillian tells me she was the one who hid Olivia's paints under her own bed.'

Catherine kept her eyes trained on the carpet. 'Oh, she did? There must be a mistake.'

'You told me neither of you knew how they had got there.' Mrs Shaw swept her gaze back and forth between them. 'Tell me the truth. Did you lie to me to cover for Lillian?'

Lillian felt numb. She should have been more careful. It was foolish to think Olivia wouldn't go skulking around in their room. She kept her gaze fixed on the coalscuttle sitting on the hearth and willed Catherine to protest her innocence.

'I–,' Catherine stuttered before the full force of her fury erupted. 'Mrs Shaw, yer ken as well as I that yer daughter wouldnae use those paints again. Why cannae Lillian use them? She does the most beautiful drawings. Yer should see them. Wait here.' Catherine ran from the room, leaving Lillian to stand before Mrs Shaw's frosty disdain.

She was not gone long. Lillian's mouth dropped when she saw what Catherine held in her hands. It was her sketchbook. Catherine thrust the pages at Mrs Shaw and stood back with her hands on her hips. How had she found her hiding place? After Nicholas's interest in seeing more pictures, Lillian had carefully slotted the sketchbook down behind the boards in the stable alongside her other treasures.

'Catherine, that's enough! How dare you question my authority?' Mrs Shaw pursed her lips as tightly as if she'd sucked on a lemon and flipped the book shut. 'What on earth am I meant to do with the both of you now? Finding good help is next to impossible. I trusted you girls.'

'Mrs Shaw, please!' Catherine implored.

'You were willing to cover up for Lillian by lying for her. I find that just as distasteful as stealing. Catherine, if you mind your tongue and finish out the week, I will be gracious and provide you with a reference for your next position. Lillian, I will not be extending the same courtesy to you. Now go pack your things and leave me in peace.' Mrs Shaw picked up her pince-nez and returned them to her nose.

Catherine stormed out and Lillian followed meekly behind. She hadn't dared to ask for her sketchbook back. Up in their room she watched her assemble her meagre belongings.

'I'll be damned if I'm going to work another day for that despicable woman.'

'I'm so sorry, Catherine. This is all my fault.'

'Och, Lillian, I dinnae blame yer. Yer've done nothing wrong. Olivia Shaw is a spoilt cow with nought better to do with her time than get maids in trouble. I've had enough of this place.'

'At least stay until the end of the week. Mrs Shaw will change her mind about your job once I'm out of her sight. She'd be lost without you. She's angry, that's all.' Lillian began to pace. 'That little witch, Olivia, has always looked down her nose at me. I don't think it was even about the paints. She saw me come out of the stable with Donald and has been waiting for her moment to get rid of me.'

Catherine collapsed on the bed next to her belongings in defeat. 'I'll miss yer, I really will. Yer did a foolish thing. I tried to warn yer months ago to take better care. At least yer can stay with yer sister. What'll I do?'

Lillian flew down the double flight of stairs and headed for the stable, hurrying to the empty stall to retrieve the tobacco tin. She half-expected it to be empty. If Catherine knew about the hiding place then probably Olivia did, too. Tearing the lid off, she saw with relief that the promissory note, bag of coins and her photograph still lay inside. She ran back to the room shared with Catherine for so long and thrust her hand out.

'Whit is it?' Catherine stuffed a blouse into her carpetbag, on top of her brothers' portrait.

'It's yours if you want it. I have a little saved as well.'

Catherine picked up the tin and poked at the note and coins. Unimpressed, she threw it back. The tin bounced on the quilt and fell to the floor, scattering the contents.

'Please take it, Catherine, all of it, and stay. Mrs Shaw will forgive you. It's me she doesn't like.'

'I don't want yer bloody money, Lillian. We're friends. Don't yer understand? Yer cannae buy my forgiveness. It's not for sale. I only did what yer would have done for me.' Catherine picked up her hairbrush and nightgown.

Lillian began to cry. She carefully picked up the note and coins and began gathering her own belongings into her old carpetbag, one she'd inherited from her mother. She would miss sharing this humid, cramped space with Catherine. She had become her best friend. What awfulness would be awaiting her at her sister's? Would Patricia even take her in?

She snapped the catch shut. 'I can't believe this is happening.'

Catherine rose and wrapped her arms around her shoulders. 'I cannae either, hen. We'll meet again soon. Promise yer'll write.'

Lillian wiped her eyes on her sleeve and wandered gingerly down the narrow passage to the top of the stairs. Looking out the window at the end of the landing she could see the afternoon was already beginning to fade into pastel colours.

At the bottom of the stairs, Mrs Menzies put her hands on

her hips and glared at her as she descended. 'Does Mrs Shaw expect me to get all the work done around here myself? You've got us all into a right mess, you have.'

'Goodbye, Mrs Menzies.' Lillian staggered past her and struggled down the driveway.

Donald rounded the gate sitting high in the buggy, Duchess tugging at the bit. He was dressed from head to toe in his cricket whites.

'Hello.' He doffed his cap and squinted down. 'Are you going on a holiday?'

She shook her head, dropped her bag on the gravel and pulled out her hanky to wipe away more tears.

He pulled on the reins to bring his mare to a complete stop. 'What is it, Lillian?'

'Please don't ask, Donald. I have to leave Rosemead. Your sister...' It was impossible to finish the sentence.

'What's that girl done now?'

Lillian couldn't trust herself to speak. She retrieved her bag and hurried past before he could descend and try to offer some comfort. She heard him call out her name as she continued down Shafston Road, heading for the wharf. He would know the truth of the matter as soon as he went inside and spoke to his mother and she did not want to be anywhere near to see the look of disappointment on his face.

If Lillian had hoped to expect an ounce of sympathy from her sister, she was to be sorely disappointed.

Patricia was livid at her return. 'Have you forgotten why people ended up in this mosquito-infested hell-hole in the first place?'

Lillian knew Patricia would be hurt by her prolonged

absence but her sister's appearance shocked her. Patricia had always been thin but never wasted. Her frayed, patched dress hung off her emaciated frame.

'I was only borrowing the paints. Olivia never used them so I didn't think she'd notice. I started to forget to put them back where they belonged because I was using them so often.'

'I was so afraid this day would come. You and your stealing! Don't even try to say it wasn't your fault. I know you'll be more likely to swear to the truth on your precious copy of *Pinocchio* than you would on the Holy Bible.' Patricia paced across the floorboards. 'How could you be so stupid?"

'That's what Catherine asked.' Lillian dropped her belongings down and slumped, dejected, against the wall. In her haste, she hadn't gone back to the stable to fetch the book. Why hadn't she taken them with her when she got the note? Donald had appeared and made her forget.

'If you're going to stay here you'll have to share a bed with Peter. It's not ideal.'

'It won't be for long, Patricia. I'll sort out something else.'

'With no reference? Good luck with that.'

She took her bag and retreated to the children's room. The photograph. She would show it to her sister, remind her of their bond. Lillian pulled her belongings out and opened the tobacco tin. The picture had vanished. She sat down, stunned to realise it must have slipped under her bed in the attic when Catherine tossed the tin back. A fresh torrent of tears began to fall.

Alfred took no pleasure in her return at all. 'What the hell are we meant to do with you? We can scarcely afford to feed ourselves.'

'Alfred, please.' Patricia placed a palm on his chest to calm him. He roughly brushed her off and stomped outside.

Lillian kept herself busy and let Patricia order her about until her irritation at having a prodigal sister return abated. Truth be told, she knew her presence was begrudgingly appreciated. As she'd feared, Alfred had not allowed Patricia to stop accepting new babies. Mrs Carter had brought around another only the evening before, as the woman kept running out of room at her own house. Lillian's extra pair of hands made the constant cleaning and feeding of the poor little souls slightly more manageable. She assuaged Alfred by handing her last wage packet over before he even asked for it. When he had set out for The Ship Inn to spend it, she handed the bulk of her savings to Patricia to hide in a safe place. Despite having more freedom during the months not visiting, Lillian had found it difficult to ignore a lifetime habit of not spending. The generous peace token broke the last of Patricia's resolve against her.

She swiftly became adept at recognising when the babies were stirring – a sigh and a wriggle – and had their bottles ready before they began to cry. In turn, Patricia did not seek to dose them with soothing powder quite so often.

When their little charges were sleeping, Lillian busied herself with laundry and gathered wood from where she could find it to stoke up the stove. Sometimes she took Peter and Thomas for a walk to the park so they could run about in the fresh air. Her nephews had grown during her absence from the cottage. Peter would be attending school the following year. Returning from one such outing, Patricia met them halfway up the street, excitedly waving a telegram above her head. By the time she reached them, she was quite out of breath.

'Lillian, I need you to take the train to Bundaberg tomorrow morning to meet someone for me.'

'Bundaberg?' Lillian frowned. 'But that's such a long way to go.'

'Alfred's found another baby for us and they're offering to pay fifteen shillings!' Patricia snatched Peter's hand and hurried off with him back home before Lillian could argue further.

Fifteen shillings was a higher sum than usual. It sounded as though Alfred was putting his negotiating skills to good use. The family must be very comfortable if they were willing to pay almost double the usual premium. Even so, it saddened her to think that the price of getting rid of an unwanted baby was less than the cost of a china dinner set.

CHAPTER 13

NORTH COAST RAILWAY LINE BRISBANE TO BUNDABERG

*L*illian held on to her ticket tightly and stepped aboard the carriage. Struggling down the aisle with her basket, she found a seat and slid across it to the window. The new interior smell of varnish pleased the senses and she felt relief at the prospect of not having to spend long hours rocked about in an uncomfortable coach. She had brought along a cushion to put down on the wooden slats.

A horn let out a long blast and the train jolted before edging out of Melbourne Street Station. Before long, Lillian found herself rattling across Albert Bridge at Indooroopilly and rolling on through the outer suburbs, an array of cottages whisking by. The last time she'd forged this route was in the opposite direction the day Patricia had brought them both from Gympie aboard a Cobb & Co coach to begin their new life. The Flemings had been sad to see them go but had written them references and wished them well. Today the same feeling of butterflies taunted her stomach and she wished she had been able to eat more for breakfast.

Six years ago, Patricia had been full of excitement, her eyes shining as she spoke about all the possibilities awaiting them in the city. The jobs they'd get and the people they'd meet; respectable people. As a thirteen-year-old, Lillian had believed every word, such was her unshakeable belief in Patricia's judgement. She'd taken her most precious possession and gazed at it with hope; a formal photographic portrait taken of herself at three sitting on her mother's lap with Patricia standing beside them. Now, looking out the window at the vaguely familiar passing scenery, it was hard not to feel disappointed.

Three hours later Lillian touched the cool windowpane as the locomotive pulled into her birthplace. Even the cushion beneath her did little to relieve the discomfort from sitting still so long. Familiar memories of old friends long since forgotten flooded her thoughts and, beyond the station walls, a mere fifty yards along the street, she could make out the corrugated iron peaked roof of Madame Claudette's. She wondered if, after all this time, the old woman might welcome her back, despite Patricia's final act of disrespect. How simple it would be to return and leave Brisbane behind for good. To hell with respectability. If only her sister hadn't spat in the woman's face when, at their mother's funeral, an offer to work for her had been made.

There was no time to disembark. The steam engine spewed forth a sooty cloud and set off once more, weaving through cane fields. The towering grass rose about the carriage, obscuring the last sight of the town. Lillian took out a copy of Charles Harpur's poetry – borrowed from Mr Shaw's study before her expulsion from Rosemead – and tried to distract herself with the imagery of the verse. It was not her first choice, as she would have much preferred a novel, but Mr Shaw's taste in literature leant toward Australian writing and non-fiction. She had had to make do with what had been available during a small window of opportunity. As the train rolled along, Lillian interspersed her reading with listening to the clackety-clack rhythm of the turning wheels. After another short stop at Maryborough the train continued on through the countryside until at last pulling in at Bundaberg.

The trip had been tedious and stiflingly hot and left Lillian feeling tired and frustrated. Why had Alfred insisted on collecting a baby from so far away? She supposed it was no bother to her brother-in-law as he wasn't the one having to retrieve it.

Lillian alighted on the small platform and stepped into the waiting room as Alfred had instructed. It was a relief to be able to stand up and stretch her legs. He'd described the building in enough detail she could tell he'd been there before. Had he come this far north when he'd left Patricia alone to fend for herself last November? The baby she'd been bid to retrieve was a boy, she knew that much.

Lillian stood back nervously as the stationmaster barrelled past, shouting down the platform as a rear carriage was uncoupled. A gang of Kanakas loaded heavy sacks of grain into an empty rail car. She pulled the sandwich Patricia had made her that morning from the basket and watched the men work as she ate. Their chocolate-coloured skin glistened with sweat. She felt a stirring at the sight of their muscular bodies, similar to the way Donald used to make her feel. Before too long, a tall gentleman wearing a bowler hat and a pale yellow handkerchief inserted into his breast pocket approached and stood beside her. He did not look at her. In his arms, he held a healthy-looking infant. Lillian guessed the child to be at least one month old. How had the family managed to keep him a secret?

'Alice?'

She nodded, her heart hammering at the sound of her mother's name.

The man fumbled inside his trouser pocket and withdrew a white envelope. He handed it to her. 'Here's the premium.'

She discreetly received the offering and peered inside to confirm the amount was correct.

Seeing all appeared to be in order, she slid the envelope inside the basket.

The man took one final dispassionate glance at his grandchild before thrusting him into her arms.

'Good day, Madam.' He tilted his hat and left as quickly as he'd arrived.

He hadn't even told her the baby's name or provided a bottle of milk for the journey back. Lillian despaired at the idea of re-embarking on another long ride in a stuffy carriage with the tiny stranger. She wondered what had happened to his mother. Had she had any say in her child's fate?

Patricia had at least been kind enough to lend Lillian her wedding band. Lillian used her thumb to toy with it beneath the weight of the baby. She reasoned fellow passengers should think her a respectable mother off to visit relations in Brisbane.

The little boy gazed up at her with alert blue eyes. He appeared to be content. Still, Lillian fingered the small glass bottle of soothing powder hidden inside her pocket. Six hours without any milk would give rise to a furious objection eventually. At the first sign of agitation, Patricia had instructed her on the amount of laudanum he would require for sedation. She was to wash it down with the bottle of sugar water stored in the basket.

The very thought of tranquilising the baby filled Lillian with dread. She had not been able to erase the frightening memory of poor little Georgina from her mind. Still, this one appeared to be strong and healthy and she wondered if his mother had nursed him. Perhaps being a little older he would be better able to handle the drug's effects?

She vowed the trip would be the last favour she would carry out for Alfred and Patricia. As soon as she returned home, she was going to begin searching in earnest for a new position. Lillian would not allow herself to be party to their sordid enterprise a moment longer. The whole practice had filled her with distaste from the beginning, despite her sister's assurances they were doing a good deed for unfortunate unwed mothers.

'What a dear little chap.' An old woman with a missing front tooth advanced up the aisle and admired the boy. 'You must be very proud of him, dear. What's his name?' The woman put her hand out to stroke the baby's cheek and Lillian did her best not to flinch.

Lillian scrambled to think of one. 'His name is... John.'

'Ah, yes. John is a fine name.' The spinster poked the baby's cheeks with her crooked finger. 'Sensible. How far are you travelling?'

'I'm heading to Brisbane.' Lillian shifted uncomfortably in her seat.

The woman tutted and shook her head. 'Such a long way.'

'I'm going to visit my sister.'

The woman fixed her milky eyes on Lillian. 'I hope he doesn't cause you too much trouble on the journey.'

To Lillian's relief, the stranger continued to the other end of the carriage and settled in a seat by the exit.

She looked down. 'Well, John, if you don't make a fuss I'm sure we will get along wonderfully.'

The baby boy blinked then turned his head to take in the rush of the luminous sugar cane. His eyelids began to grow heavy and soon he was sound asleep.

At the third hour he woke and began to fret and Lillian recoiled with fear. He turned his little face toward her and opened his mouth like a fish gulping out of water. With no milk forthcoming, his cries grew more urgent. She jigged him up and down to distract him from his hunger but that did not work for long. Other passengers in the carriage began to pass disapproving glances. There was no other choice but to use the soothing powder.

Lillian placed John on the seat, clamping one hand on his chest to stop him from rolling to the floor, and discreetly retrieved the medicine bottle from her pocket and the bottle of sugar water from the basket. She unscrewed the lid and the teat and tapped a small measure of powder into the water.

Shaking it vigorously, she reached for John and resettled him on her lap to administer the dose, pressing the teat to his lips. He let out a squeal of protest at the indignity of the foul-smelling rubber and clamped his lips shut in disgust. Lillian nervously tried again. It was obvious he was used to being fed the natural way. Who had been the last to feed him? Was his mother pining and engorged?

She squeezed some of the mixture on to her little finger and gently rubbed it on his lips. His tongue flicked out like a snake's. She repeated the action and he opened his mouth for more. As she slid the teat on to his tongue, he tentatively began to suck. It was not until he set a steady rhythm going that she released a long sigh of relief.

He drank a good half of the bottle before the laudanum began to take effect and he sank into a still sleep. Lillian spent the final hours of the trip intently watching his chest rise and fall, terrified in case it stopped moving.

At last the train pulled back into Melbourne Street Station. She disembarked and hurried back past closed shop fronts. One had a sign in the window that briefly caught her eye. John was getting heavy so she didn't stop for a closer look. The interminably long trip had exhausted her and she was glad to see a flickering candle behind the front window of the house. Patricia had waited up. It did not surprise Lillian to hear

Alfred's steady snoring coming from the bedroom he shared with her sister as she entered the house.

Her sister pulled back the blanket. 'Oh he's a fat one. Here, give him to me. I've prepared some milk for him. Did you run into any trouble?'

'No, but please don't make me do that trip again. I worried the whole way back.'

'You did the right thing by us and this baby.'

'I called him John.'

'Is that his name?'

'His grandfather didn't say. When another passenger stopped to admire him, I had to make one up.'

'It'll be easier next time. I like John. It's no-nonsense. You made a good choice.'

Lillian glared at Patricia. 'Tomorrow I'm going to start looking for a new position. You know how I feel about all this.'

Patricia carried John over to one of the dresser-drawer cribs. 'I wish you well in your search but please remember it was a poor decision you made that returned you to this house.'

Lillian turned and retreated to the children's bedroom feeling dejected. As she bunked down with Peter snuggled into her side, she considered trying to return to domestic work. With no reference from Mrs Shaw and a four-year-old one from Mr Fleming, it was going to be tough to present herself in a favourable light. How wonderful it would be to learn a new skill instead. She didn't know how she would bear to remain inside these four walls waiting for John inevitably to lose his lovely little roly-poly body.

A germ of an idea began to sprout, a tendril of possibility growing from spying that simple sign stuck in a window. It excited her so much that sleep became an illusion.

CHAPTER 14

OPPORTUNITY

*I*n the morning, Lillian thought about her idea as she examined a bright yellow button nestled in her palm.

Patricia peered at the button too. 'You know, Madame Claudette often paid Mama with gold picked straight from the miners' pans.'

They were sorting through an upended jar together at the table, trying to find a match for one Peter had accidentally torn from his shirt. He'd been climbing up the balustrade on the front porch.

Lillian shuddered. 'I don't want to think about it. Can we please change the subject?'

Madame Claudette hadn't been the woman's real name; Lillian and Patricia knew that. Hell, the whole of Gympie knew that. How could it be when the woman had the acquired nasal drawl of a second-generation colonist? Madame Claudette thought such a pseudonym gave her establishment an air of European class but none of the men seemed to pay it any heed. What did they care about monikers? They came for what they needed – some with alarming regularity – before leaving to resume their backbreaking work.

Lillian felt a guilty pang. She hadn't been entirely without her charms, their mother's employer. After all, Madame Claudette's benevolence did allow the ladies under her care to take turns caring for their children. In the past, that included Lillian. Some might even have said Madame Claudette was kindness personified but she and Patricia knew the woman had a shrewd business sense; she was investing in future employees.

If there was an ounce of goodness to come from the arrangement, Lillian had learned that to feel secure in such an unpredictable life, a person had to be prepared to work hard. She would not, however, stoop so low as to follow in her mother's footsteps. In fact, she was sure she would rather starve to death. Feeling buoyed by her overnight plotting, perhaps such a drastic measure might never be necessary?

Lillian put the yellow button back and picked up a red one. She held it out. 'Will this one do?'

Patricia squinted and clucked her tongue. 'Too small.'

She dropped the glass piece into the jar to keep searching. Maybe they wouldn't find a match and the search would be in vain? It occurred to Lillian her mother had done the same while she was alive; kept searching for a good reason her life had turned out the way it had. What had an educated woman been doing living in a bawdy house as someone she wasn't ever destined to become? Thank God Patricia had been given the opportunity to go and work at the Flemings' house. Soon after, it had been Lillian's turn to leave their mother and her misery behind. In the same way a lost button ruined a shirt, a poor decision had ruined Mama's life. Lillian wasn't prepared to make any more mistakes. She had to start thinking more wisely if she was going to ever get out of her sister's cottage and start living the life she felt destined for.

Patricia sighed and scooped the remaining buttons back into the jar. 'I give up. You'll have to go to Hamilton's and buy one for me. I think I've got a penny somewhere.'

This was the permission Lillian had been waiting for. She washed her face, pinned up her hair and set out for Stanley Street. Passing a number of familiar shops, she stopped outside the tailor's and remembered Nicholas. Catherine had told her he had been sent to England. Lillian hadn't known whether to feel relieved or dismayed. The window display was full of long bolts of cloth. In the corner, a piece of white card had been wedged bearing a discreet announcement in neat block letters: *Seamstress Apprentice Required. Apply Within.*

A bell tinkled overhead as she entered the store and a young woman standing behind the counter appraised her. 'How may I help you?'

Lillian balled her hands into fists to keep them steady and approached her. 'Good morning. My name is Miss Lillian Betts. I'd like to buy a button, please.'

The girl pointed to a selection of long thin glass containers on the wall. 'Which colour would you like?'

Lillian peered at several different sizes of red ones. She tapped on a jar. 'I think one of these will do.'

She watched the young assistant expertly tip the jar upside down to catch a single button before sliding it into a small paper packet and handing it over.

'That'll be a ha'penny, please.'

Lillian gave her the coin.

'Will that be all?' The girl pressed her finger on the till and the drawer flew open. She deposited the coin inside.

Lillian crumpled the packet in her palm and took a deep breath. 'Actually,' she said, 'I'd like to apply for your seamstress apprenticeship.' She pointed at the sign in the window.

The girl seemed doubtful and Lillian felt even more self-conscious.

'Wait here a moment, please.' She retreated into a back room and returned with an older lady.

'Hello,' the woman said, removing her glasses and polishing them on her apron. 'This is a welcome surprise. I only put the sign up last night before closing. Tell me, what experience do you have with dressmaking?'

Lillian swallowed her nerves. 'I confess I have none but I am a quick student and willing to follow all instructions.'

The older woman's expression matched the younger's; friendly yet quizzical. 'Have you brought any references with you?'

She felt a flash of anger towards the spiteful Mrs Shaw and handed over the one written by Mr Fleming four years ago. 'I have this one.'

The woman opened up the letter and frowned. 'This is four years old. I'm not sure whether you would really be suitable. Our apprentices are usually younger. How old are you?'

'Almost twenty,' Lillian said. 'I've been helping my sister care for her children. Her husband was gone for quite a long time for work. She lives only a few streets away. Would it help if she wrote a note to vouch for my character?'

The woman considered the offer then asked, 'Who is your sister?'

'Mrs Patricia Hooper. She lives on Montague Road.'

The older woman clutched the string of pearls at her throat. 'Patricia Hooper, you say?' Lillian nodded. It had been a risk to say anything at all.

The assistant's eyes widened.

'Very well. I'll have to check with my husband but in this case I'm sure he will be prepared to give you a trial. Be here tomorrow at nine sharp.'

'Thank you, Ma'am. I will be.'

'You may call me Mrs Hamilton. This is my daughter, Florence.'

Lillian almost stumbled over her boots as she left the store. She was too excited to return home and so decided to continue up the street. She still had some change in her pocket and knew exactly what she wished to use it for.

The postmaster looked up as Lillian entered the post office. She strode to the long counter and dropped her coin on the top.

'I'd like to send a telegram, please.'

'Certainly, ma'am. What is your message?'

Lillian told him and watched intently as he recorded each letter. Satisfied, she wandered outside and hoped Catherine would receive it. She missed her dear friend and hoped to find out whether Catherine had decided to stay on at Rosemead. Would Mrs Shaw bother to forward the letter to the appropriate new address if she hadn't?

CHAPTER 15

SOUTH BRISBANE – JANUARY 1893

*U*nder Mrs Hamilton's steady tutelage, Lillian began to feel proficient in her new trade in only a matter of months. She soon grew used to wielding the large dressmaking scissors to cut patterns carefully from the cloth. She stood close and handed pins to her employer as the latter knelt at a lady's skirt to hem it to the correct length. Before long, she was trusted enough to stitch fabric pieces together on one of the Singer sewing machines in the workroom. It was fascinating to watch a bolt of material being transformed into a dashing creation that showed off a woman's figure to perfection. She tried not to envy Florence's wonderful embroidery skills. The younger girl had had years of practice. With a tailor for a father and a dressmaker for a mother, it was her birthright.

Despite her excitement for her new job, each evening she still had to return to her sister's cottage. And, each time, she was disappointed to discover there was no telegram waiting for her from Catherine. There'd been a time Lillian had wished she didn't have to climb the attic stairs to the room they shared because it meant she had to descend them the next day to start working again. What she would give now to talk to her friend and be allowed to sleep in a bed in a room above the Hamiltons' store. Patricia and Alfred often fought and then he stormed off to the hotel with Lillian's wages. The amount she earned was even less than Mrs Shaw had paid. Would she never be free from their strife? She had sent another couple of telegrams but all had gone unanswered. Where could Catherine be?

To add to her feeling of confinement, in the last few weeks the rain hadn't let up. It pounded down through the night, occasionally interspersed with a storm full of lightning flashes and thunderclaps. The only upside was the scent of the bushfire that had permeated the air dissipated. Every street became a boggy quagmire. More often than not Lillian was the one given the job of scrubbing and sweeping customers' messy bootprints from the showroom floor to prevent anybody slipping and hurting themselves.

Her ears pricked up when Mr and Mrs Hamilton entered the shop together on Saturday afternoon. They'd taken the delivery cart over to the council depot to load up with sandbags. Several men from surrounding businesses braved the rain and were now busy unloading and stacking them on the front steps of the store. The couple stepped inside shaking off their wet umbrellas and wiping their feet on the welcome mat.

Mr Hamilton was an excellent tailor and his wife a talented dressmaker. Consistent demand for both their services had continued throughout the previous year and it was clear they appreciated the extra pair of hands Lillian offered to the business. She often gave herself a pinch now and then over her good fortune but, to be fair, she worked diligently. They treated her well enough and were never cruel. Mrs Hamilton had even told Lillian she had a flair for design when she had hesitantly showed the woman a couple of her drawings. While having to return each evening to Montague Road was unpleasant, at least she was well on the way to procuring a skill she felt sure would set her up for a successful future.

Mrs Hamilton's words to her husband as she hung up her hat in the workroom sent a shiver of anticipation through Lillian as she sat hemming a pair of trousers.

'Wasn't it lovely to get Nicholas's letter yesterday? The trip seems to have done him a world of good. I never dreamed he'd stay away so long. What day do you think he'll arrive, dear?'

'Another month, I reckon. Remember, he did mention he was going to organise a short trip across to Paris before embarking on the *Avoca* back in London.'

'Yes, you did mention that. I hope Stephen doesn't get too much of a fright when he sees his papa again. It's been such a long time. Nicholas won't believe how much he's grown.'

Before her employment at the Hamilton's store, Lillian had often wondered what had become of the first little boy Patricia had taken into her care. It soon became clear from Mrs Hamilton and Florence's chatter in the workroom that he had not accompanied his father on the voyage to London. Mrs Hamilton had procured a nanny who took care of him at their house on Vulture Street. Lillian could easily understand why she hadn't let Patricia keep him.

She'd tried not to think of Nicholas too often and the idea of his imminent return filled her with a combination of dread and excitement. How was he going to react when he found her there at the shop? What if he knew she had been fired from the Shaw's for stealing? Perhaps Matthew and Rosemary had taken the time to write and tell him what had happened? Surely Catherine would have told them?

Although she'd made a friendship of sorts with Florence, she missed her old friend's irreverent sense of humour, which had carried her through many days of hard work and the heartache she'd experienced over her infatuation with Donald.

It pained her to think Catherine might be putting distance between them even though she had assured Lillian of her friendship before they had parted. Lillian worried she had changed her mind and then realised she'd never told her friend exactly where Patricia lived.

Florence was a different sort of person. She had grown up surrounded by the finer things while Lillian had to disguise her bad habits to be able to fit into her new surroundings.

Today, though, Florence appeared extra cheerful as she greeted customers and went about her tasks.

'Do you think Nicky will bring us gifts, Mama?'

Mrs Hamilton rolled her eyes. 'I shall be grateful if he brings himself back in one piece. That will be enough of a gift for me.'

'I hope he brings me a trinket from London – a belated Christmas present. I'd love to go and visit the city myself one day,' Florence said wistfully.

'All in good time, dear. Pay attention to what you're doing. Look, that seam is crooked! Take a break for a minute. Go and get me the green velvet from the shelf. I must try to finish this jacket order today.'

Lillian found the exchange between Mrs Hamilton and Florence amusing. In many ways they reminded her of her relationship with Patricia, the way they bickered and reconciled so often. She sat down behind her sewing machine and concentrated on threading the needle. She was about to begin stitching the two sides of a skirt together when the bell jangled above the entrance. The store had been fairly quiet due to the inclement weather and all of them were anxiously listening to the reports about the rising river from those brave enough to pop in for their orders.

Florence came rushing into the storeroom and stood in front of Lillian's sewing machine looking flustered. 'Your sister's here. She says she needs to see you immediately. Lillian, I have to warn you she doesn't look well at all.'

Lillian glanced at the clock hanging on the wall with irritation. There were still three hours left before closing. What was her sister doing there? She reluctantly took her foot off the treadle and stood up to follow Florence to the counter.

Her sister stood drenched to the skin and dripping water all over the floor, her lip swollen and bleeding. Mrs Hamilton would not be pleased to see her in there in such a state.

'What's the matter?'

'You must come home.'

'I can't leave yet. Mrs Hamilton won't give me permission when the store's still open.'

'You have to ask, and hurry. I've left the children alone.'

It had struck Lillian as very odd to see her sister unaccompanied but she had not stopped to consider what pressing matter could warrant such circumstances. A look passed between them, a reminder of what had happened last time.

'Very well. I'll ask.' Lillian swallowed her fear about what trouble might await at the cottage. She found Mrs Hamilton trying to reach a bolt of linen cloth from a shelf above her head.

'Be a dear, Lillian, and fetch that down for me, will you?'

She retrieved the unwieldy material with difficulty, handed it over and cleared her throat. 'Mrs Hamilton, I wouldn't ordinarily dare ask this of you but my sister is requesting I go home with her immediately.'

Mrs Hamilton frowned. 'Is there a problem?'

Lillian looked back towards the showroom counter then faced Mrs Hamilton again. 'I think so. I don't know. She didn't say.'

'With the rain carrying on the way it is I expect Mr Hamilton will want to close up early anyway. He's concerned the river may break its banks if there is no respite. We'll have a repeat of the disaster three years ago if it does. I suppose as long as you don't make a habit of asking, I will make an exception this time. You can make up the lost hours next week.'

'Thank you, Mrs Hamilton. Of course.'

Mrs Hamilton held up a jar and peered inside. 'You'd better go and find out what the matter is. Do take care. Take one of the umbrellas, otherwise you'll get drenched.'

Lillian bunched up her skirt and petticoat and set off down the swampy street behind Patricia. The rain sluiced the umbrella she held in her other hand with such force it was quickly rendered inoperable. Patricia seemed to be immune to the deluge and continued to rush as quickly as her mud-logged boots would let her. It wasn't until they were able to get under the cottage's bull-nose porch roof that Lillian was able to ask her what had happened.

'It's Alfred.' Her sister put her fists at her hips as she bent over double and gasped for air. 'He's been arrested.'

Lillian could hear babies crying inside. 'Arrested?'

Patricia stood up and looked at her wildly. 'Yes!'

Lillian's mind whirled with several reasons why such a thing could have happened. 'What's the charge?'

'Child endangerment,' Patricia whispered.

It was difficult for Lillian to hear her sister's voice above the deafening din on the corrugated iron above their heads. She wrenched the pins from her hair and squeezed the water out of it. 'Is everyone else all right?'

'I was so scared I had to come and get you immediately. What will happen if he tells the police about all the babies? They'll come for me as well. That nosy constable has already been back for another inspection.'

'When?'

'A few days ago. I didn't want to worry you. He won't leave us be. You'll look after the children if I have to go to gaol, won't you, Lillian?' Patricia's face was pale and her hand shook as she took out her key and unlocked the door.

Thomas rushed for his mother with tears streaming down his face.

'There, there, Mama's home. I wasn't gone for very long. Look, Peter was with you the whole time.' Patricia led her son down to the kitchen and reached for the bottle of soothing powder on the shelf. She took a glass that had been sitting next to it and tapped a generous amount into the bottom before filling it with water from the kettle on the stove. Carefully swirling it around, she took a large gulp.

'What are you doing?' Lillian asked, astonished.

'I don't know what's going to happen.'

For a moment, Lillian was riveted to the spot. If her dependable sister didn't know what to do, then what hope did she have? 'Drinking laudanum isn't going to help.'

'Lillian, Alf was the worst he's ever been. We had a rotten fight. He knows about Gympie. He met a man at a hotel in Bundaberg when he was up north. While they were yarning he found out all about us, the brothel, Ma, everything. Do you remember that rat Bartholomew Ames? The boy at school I used to fight with because he called me rude names. It was him!' Patricia took another swig from the glass. 'Alfred told me he was so hurt I'd lied to him about my history that he took a girl to his bed that same night! She'd come to Bundaberg with her family to work on a station and was barely eighteen. How could he do that to me?'

Lillian shook her head. She wouldn't put anything past Alfred.

'John is his baby, Lillian. He made you go all the way to Bundaberg to retrieve his bastard child.'

Lillian had known deep down there was more to the trip north than Alfred had let on. He'd been quieter since his return but insistent the baby needed to be collected. Now everything made sense.

Patricia waved her hands frantically. 'I told him he'd need to find a new family to look after John because I wasn't going to do it any more. He tried to say the girl hadn't meant anything to him. He wasn't going to do it but Bartholomew had egged him on. I told him to get out. He didn't go willingly, oh no. He called me the most dreadful things, Lillian. He told me he didn't love me any more and then he snatched John right out of the dresser while he was sleeping and stormed out in an appalling temper.' Patricia's words began to slur. 'Mrs Carter knocked on the door twenty minutes later to say she'd seen him getting carted off by the police. Somebody had reported him wading into the water by the wharf holding a baby. He's a monster, he truly is. I know he'll give me up. He might tell on you, too.'

Lillian looked at the dresser that had been serving as a crib for so many months. She'd tried not to feel hopeful when she saw only two babies were remaining that week. Not counting the missing John, the bottom drawer held one last pathetic inmate; a little girl Mrs Carter had brought over two evenings ago.

'How many, Patricia?'

'Babies?' She paused to count them up in her head. 'I've cared for nineteen, I think. Perhaps twenty.'

'No.' Lillian repeated the question. 'How many?'

Patricia struggled to look her in the eye. 'Four, including Georgina.'

Lillian bristled at the mention of the poor soul's name. 'Where?'

Patricia blinked heavily. 'Alfred took them away. He didn't say where and I didn't ask. The river, probably.'

'Didn't any of the families want to know what had happened to them?'

'One did. I wrote them to say we had found a family for their baby, and they were glad to pay the final premium.' Tears began to seep from Patricia's eyes. 'She wrote back to say she was grateful.'

Beyond the window, the downpour got stronger. Great torrents carved up the road. The rain beat like thunder on the corrugated iron roof. Lillian returned to the front porch to escape Patricia's panicky rambling. Rising above the cacophony, she heard shouting. A man appeared through the teeming curtain pulling a woman along behind him. Others quickly followed.

'Get out, get out! The river's broken its banks.'

She turned at the sound of a chair clattering to the floor and caught sight of Patricia staggering. One look at her sister's face and it was clear to see the medicine had truly begun to take effect.

Lillian hurried back to her. 'How much have you taken today?'

Patricia struggled to focus.

Lillian gripped her shoulders and gave her a hard shake. 'How much soothing powder have you taken today?'

Patricia's head dropped. 'I don't know. Half the bottle, perhaps a bit more. Oh, Lil, I need to go and have a lie-down.'

'Patricia, you can't! We have to go right now. The street's flooding.' She gazed into Peter's startled brown eyes, so much like his mother's. Next, Lillian grabbed a muslin cloth from the dresser and fashioned a sling across her hip and shoulder for carrying the baby. Another quick look out the window showed her the trickle of neighbouring families had become a torrent, sweeping up the road as surely as if the river had been carrying them itself. She lifted the baby into the sling and pushed Thomas towards his mother. Patricia had just enough wits left to gather him into her arms. Lillian watched her frail frame struggle with his bulk and considered that it would have been better to take him herself and give Patricia the lighter load. Unfortunately, there was no time to make the switch. She grabbed Peter's hand and pulled him along the hall.

As they all huddled together on the front porch, Lillian realised they were already too late. A creeping barrage of flood-water swirling with sticks and debris had already begun to engulf the lower end of Montague Road. They watched in horror as the mass steadily surged toward them. It reached the steps in under a minute.

'We're going to die,' Patricia screamed, burying her face into Thomas's hair.

'No we're not!' Lillian wanted to slap her for giving in to hysteria. The children needed to be kept calm if they were to have any chance.

The rising torrent swallowed the steps one at a time. If they didn't immediately start climbing, it would be seconds before the water swept right through the house. Lillian wrestled beneath the weight of the baby to undo the buttons at the waist of her sodden skirt and stepped out of it.

'Lillian.' Patricia's jaw dropped.

'It'll weigh me down. I suggest you do the same.'

Her sister obeyed and almost fell over as she struggled out of her skirt.

'Here, Peter. Good boy. Let's go back up the hall. Quickly now.' Lillian herded the little party back through the house, splashing through the kitchen to the back step. The water

161

swirled around them and pushed against their knees. Something hard floated beneath the surface and bumped into her ankles. 'You can let go now,' she said, lifting Peter up so he could rest his feet on the handrail.

Patricia anxiously grabbed at his legs to help him stay upright against the surge.

'Now, Peter, We're going to play a game and pretend we are real monkeys just like the ones in the picture book I read to you, remember? You're going to shimmy up the water pipe first and I'll be right behind you,' said Lillian.

Peter looked equal parts excited and doubtful. He'd been told by his mother all his short life to never climb on the roof and now here was his aunt telling him to. It was too much for the small boy to take in.

'It's all right, Peter. I won't scold,' Lillian assured him.

Needing no further encouragement, he scampered nimbly up the pipe and crouched atop the water tank, peering back at her.

'Stay away from the hole at the top. Can you reach over the drain and climb up on to the roof now? That's it. Good boy.'

Lillian watched him navigate himself to safety then began climbing up with considerable difficulty owing to the baby pressing against her middle. The poor poppet cried out with discomfort. Lillian had no choice but to ignore her as she hoisted herself up on to the balustrade and stood up to reach the drainpipe, not even sure if she would be able to pull herself up over the drain. Carefully removing the sling over her head, she held the baby up and slid her on to the roof. The infant howled even louder as the rain pelted her little body but Lillian had no choice other than to ignore the sounds of distress. Better to be soaking wet and alive than floating down the river, dead.

Clawing along the iron a couple of rivets appeared beneath her fingers and she grasped at them desperately, gaining enough grip to be able to swing her leg up over the rim. The metal was slippery but she managed to haul herself up and collapsed for a couple of seconds next to Peter and the baby.

Lying flat, she quickly twisted around to reach down to help Thomas and Patricia up. The water was up to her sister's waist. Patricia had anchored herself by locking her arm around the post. Thomas clung to her hip with terror.

'Patricia, look at me,' Lillian shouted over the roaring torrent.

The floodwater created ominous sounds. Creaks and bangs deafened them as logs and furniture pillaged from abandoned houses farther down the street came bobbing like wooden icebergs dangerously submerged beneath the maelstrom.

'I'm scared,' Peter whimpered at her shoulder.

Lillian turned to look at him. 'Get back, Peter. Go and sit with the baby.'

She reached back to reassure him and his little hands clasped hers. 'You have to let go. You can do it.'

Water and blood mixed and flowed down her forearm from where her elbow had caught against the curved metal edge. She could do nothing to fix the wound. Thomas and Patricia still needed her help. At last Peter relinquished his grip and scuttled back up the roof. A short scream sounded below and startled her.

Peering back over the edge, Lillian failed to comprehend what she saw. Instead of her sister and nephew's faces looking up, the river surged menacingly at the gutter. She looked across and saw nothing except an abyss of water and triangle rooftop islands, some of which appeared to be moving along on the current. There was no trace of them.

'Patricia!' she screamed. Lillian plunged her arms into the water and felt beneath the surface for hair, an arm, anything that would let her know it wasn't too late. 'Patricia!'

Lillian called out across the black river until her throat felt as if it had been torn by razor blades and still could not believe her sister wouldn't call back.

Death pounded in her ears and blackened her vision at the edges. If the water rose two more feet, she, Peter and the baby would be swept away, too. Lillian scrambled on the slick surface and wrapped her arms around them in a tight embrace as the rain continued to lash down unforgivingly.

Peter stared up at her, his eyes huge. 'Where's Mama?'

'Shh, don't worry.' Lillian kissed the top of his plastered head to comfort him. Tears poured down her cheeks but her nephew couldn't see them on account of the rain and for that she was grateful. Peter's heart would break the same as her own, but for now she needed to keep him calm, even though she felt so desperate.

The baby continued to scream and Peter put his hands over his ears to block out the noise.

'Are we going to die?' he shouted.

'No, we're not. Somebody will come and rescue us,' Lillian shouted back.

He looked on fearfully as a large branch slammed against the iron roof. She squeezed him even closer as a vision of Thomas tossing and turning helplessly in the murderous water shook her to her core. Her whole body shuddered with the hopelessness of their predicament and, if the children weren't with her, Lillian was sure she would have given up and thrown herself in as well.

Time seemed to stand interminably still. They were stuck on their prison with the water lapping only inches below her feet. And there it seemed to stay. They sat marooned under a layer of steel-grey cloud that shrouded the stars. The only light Lillian could see was the lantern-illuminated windows of houses safely perched on rises in the distance. She had never felt more desperate or alone. Peter kept calling out for his mother and brother, their names stabbing Lillian every time.

The little boy tried to keep his eyes open but was struggling against his exhaustion. The baby took comfort sucking on the tip of Lillian's finger. She wanted to resent the little stranger when the river had so ruthlessly claimed her own darling Thomas and Patricia. She hadn't even bothered to ask her sister the baby's name. After so many months, they'd all begun to look the same. But the gentle, fruitless tugging at her finger produced a flood of warmth towards her small charge. The baby was depending on her.

Several more hours passed until a voice called through the dark. Lillian blinked through the gloom and made out a shadowy figure approaching in a small dinghy. She screamed: 'We're here! Please help us.'

'Ahoy there!' the man yelled back, waving an arm in greeting. 'I'll take you to higher ground.'

As he neared, Lillian recognised him as the ferryman from the wharf at Kangaroo Point. His eyes widened with astonishment as he neared, to see her surrounded by small children.

'Godfrey, thank God,' she said and wept with relief.

'Give me the boy first,' he instructed.

Peter clung fearfully to Lillian's undergarments, distrustful of the strange figure balancing in the boat.

'It's all right, my darling. He's come to rescue us. I'll be right behind you,' she whispered in his ear.

Peter sniffed and shivered but gave the ferryman his hand. Godfrey hoisted the small boy into the boat and planted him on the centre bench. He huddled there like a bedraggled kitten.

Lillian's turn came. She stood up shakily and made sure her

JOANNA BERESFORD

younger charge lay secured in the sling. Unhindered by skirts but now feeling very aware of her drawers clinging to her skin, it was simple enough to hop into the boat assisted by the ferryman's strong hand. She took her place beside Peter and blushed with embarrassment. He kindly handed her a wide piece of canvas and she covered her legs with it.

'Right you are, love. Hold tight to the children. There's a lot of debris floating around out there. We'll have to take it slow.'

She reached out to place a firm hand on Peter.

'Are they both yours?'

'Yes... they are.' She shut her eyes at the weight of the words.

'Is there somewhere in particular I can take you? I haven't seen you in a while. Are you still over at Kangaroo Point?'

Lillian sadly shook her head. Where could he take her? She pondered the question for a moment before answering. 'Take me as close to Vulture Street as you can, please.'

Godfrey nodded and began to pull on his oars.

It felt surreal to drift past the second storeys of buildings. The water looked like ink and appeared to stretch on for a mile in every direction. There appeared to be something wrong with Victoria Bridge but Lillian couldn't quite work out what it was as they were headed in the opposite direction.

'You're the fourth rescue I've done tonight. You're lucky to be alive,' Godfrey said.

Lillian hung her head and didn't reply.

'Are you feeling sick? I can slow down if you need me to.'

'No. I'll be fine.' She turned in her seat to look up ahead. 'Please keep going as quick as you can.'

At last the dinghy glided to a stop on a slope in the middle of Cordelia Street. Godfrey assisted her out of the boat and carefully handed the children over one at a time. The baby wriggled with discomfort in the crude sling.

'Will you be all right from here?' He gazed at her with concern. 'I'd like to get back out in case there are others.'

'Yes, quite. Thank you for everything. I've never felt so relieved to set foot back on land. I can manage from here.'

'Look after those children.' Godfrey stepped ankle-deep in the water to launch the skiff before jumping nimbly back in.

'Thank you again.'

He doffed his cap and grinned. 'Anyone in my position would do the same.'

Godfrey pulled on an oar and began to row off in the direction they'd come from.

Lillian suddenly called out. 'Godfrey?'

He lifted his oars and waited.

'Have you seen Catherine lately?'

Godfrey called back: 'I haven't seen her for a few months. I heard she got a new job somewhere.'

She nodded in understanding and watched him until he disappeared around the corner of a building. She didn't wish to dawdle another minute. Peter was almost asleep on his feet but she encouraged him to start walking. They continued past Musgrave Park and around the corner until the Hamiltons' sprawling Queenslander appeared on the rise ahead. Lillian had a worrying thought. What if the family had been trapped at the store? What a state it would be in.

As she turned up the front path and climbed the wide steps to stand beneath the veranda awning, the baby stirred against her chest. She had no name for the foundling and the Hamiltons would be expecting one. The tiny face held two dark eyes, which stared up at her transfixed. Lillian felt a fiercely protective jolt course through her body.

'You're mine now, little one. I'll think I'll call you Alice Patricia.' It was the only name that would do.

PART II

Had there been in Shakespeare's time such a being as an Australian girl, he might have found in her some type of lovely and loveable womanhood. I know then, past and present Antipodean maidens, true as Cordelia, fearless as Portia, brilliant as Beatrice, and patient as Hermione...

— *FROM A LETTER TO THE EDITOR OF THE BRISBANE COURIER, JANUARY 1893*

CHAPTER 16

VULTURE STREET

*A*s soon as Florence's concerned face peered through the pane of stained-glass beside the front door, Lillian collapsed.

'Mama, come quickly.' Florence swung open the door. She had spied the baby wrapped in the crudely fashioned sling around their apprentice.

Footsteps came hurrying up the hall. 'Who is it?'

'Lillian. She has children with her.'

Lifting Lillian's arm over a shoulder each, Florence and her mother gathered her up and half-carried, half-dragged her through to the drawing-room, where they carefully deposited her onto a sofa.

Mr Hamilton got up from his armchair, his face etched with concern. 'What in the Lord's name has happened to you?'

The strength that had pulled Lillian through the past hours of fear and grief evaporated. All she could do was rest her head against the back of the seat as her body was racked with sobs.

Mrs Hamilton immediately set about putting things in

order. 'Jonathan, for heaven's sake get the girl some brandy. Florence, there are clean towels in the linen press, and go and find something dry for her to change into.'

Mr Hamilton rose hurriedly to fetch a decanter and glass from the sideboard. He poured a generous nip and brought it over. Lillian hadn't the will to refuse and so accepted the offering. The liquor burned her throat but she drank it down.

He took note of Peter huddled at her feet. 'Is that your sister's boy?'

'Yes.' Lillian glanced down at the baby still pressed against her front and tried to wrestle with the binding knot but it had pulled too tight. Mrs Hamilton stepped in to take over and gently worked away at the ends until Lillian was free of her precious load. The older woman took Alice from her and gently rocked her beside the mantelpiece. Lillian watched anxiously.

She felt vulnerable without the child nestled against her.

Mrs Hamilton looked up. 'Who is this little one?'

Lillian forced herself to meet the older woman's gaze. 'Her name is Alice.'

'Well, aren't you a pretty thing?' Mrs Hamilton cooed. 'Let's get you all dry and warmed up.'

Lillian was grateful not to be pressed with further questions.

Florence soon returned with towels and a clean robe. Her mother reached out and took a towel from the pile, stripped Alice's soaking clothes and napkin from her tiny body, and vigorously dried her. Alice was too exhausted to object to the brisk treatment. Mrs Hamilton left the room with her and returned two minutes later with the baby snugly bundled up in a grey cotton shawl. The collar of a small white gown encircled her soft cheeks like a cherubic halo and Lillian briefly wondered if the garment had belonged to Nicholas's son,

Stephen. Mrs Hamilton propped Alice on her husband's lap and prepared to mete out the same attention to Peter.

'What's happened to their mother?' she asked.

Lillian shuddered and began to cry again.

Mrs Hamilton rubbed her back in a futile attempt to offer some comfort. 'I see. There'll be time to tell us soon enough. Let's get you out of those wet clothes. Florence has found something warm and dry for you to wear. You've had a dreadful shock, dear. Go with her and she'll show you where you can change.'

Lillian followed Florence down the hall. Though numb and shivering, she took in the pretty paper and paintings adorning the walls.

Florence directed Lillian into her bedroom. 'That's a nasty cut you have on your arm,' she pointed out. 'It might need stitches.'

Lillian twisted her elbow around for a better look. Now she was safe, the wound had begun to sting. The girl's bedroom reminded her of Olivia's, though not to the same scale. A floral quilt covered the bed. There was even a small writing desk beneath the window.

'I'll get a dressing. You can have some privacy,' Florence said and left.

In the silence, having shed her soaking blouse and drawers, Lillian tried to gather her thoughts. She had made the right decision to come to the Hamiltons for help. They were kind people who would not set her out on the street. She'd had her doubts the day Patricia fetched Stephen to care for him so Nicholas wouldn't have to set eyes on his own child. It wasn't fair to hold a baby responsible for his mother's death. Yet, if Thomas hadn't needed carrying, Patricia would have been able to climb out of harm's way. If baby Alice had never been surrendered to their house, Lillian could have carried Thomas instead. It was easy to tell Mrs Hamilton had never intended to give up her grandson for good. She had simply recognised her son needed space to grieve. Lillian had Peter and Alice to care for and she knew she would do everything in her power to protect them.

'I was worried you might have all been caught in the flood, too,' she said when Florence returned.

'Thankfully, Papa insisted we close up shortly after you left. We'd all heard the talk, hadn't we, about a repeat of the 1890 flood if the rain kept up? After the boys finished sandbagging and you'd left, we tried to pack as much stock on to the highest shelves we could. There wasn't enough time to get everything done. We only had minutes.' Florence dabbed some iodine on Lillian's cut and wrapped a clean bandage around her arm. 'Papa's heard all the shops on Stanley Street are flooded right up to the second storey. Looks like our efforts were a waste of time after all.'

Lillian nodded with the truth of it. 'I'm sorry to say he's right. A ferryman I know was out searching for people stranded on their roof. That's how the children and I were saved. He rowed us right up Melbourne and Cordelia Street. Most of the shops were under. I saw houses floating away.'

Florence hesitated and then reached over and hugged her. 'I'm very sorry, Lillian. Papa's going to be upset about the store but you've suffered much worse.'

Lillian sat stiffly. 'Thank you, Florence.'

Florence let her go. 'Mama tried to tell him to find a better location for the store after the last one but he insisted on staying in the same street. "How will my customers find me?" he said. You'll have to tell him what you saw.'

Lillian towelled her hair dry and borrowed Florence's comb and some hairpins to draw it back in a loose bun before they returned to the drawing-room. Sitting back down on the sofa, she was heartened to watch Florence lead Peter to the kitchen to find something to eat. She noted the Hamiltons' home was filled with many fine things. Mr and Mrs Hamilton sat in their chairs quietly watching her. She owed them some sort of explanation about the events that had led her to their doorstep.

'Patricia's gone. Thomas, too. We had no time. I made Peter climb on to the roof and pushed Alice up after him. I climbed up next. When I turned back to help Patricia and Thomas, the water was up to the guttering. I couldn't see them anywhere.' Her face contorted with anguish as her voice rose and cracked. 'They've been swept away. I didn't know what to do, we were completely stranded. A ferryman – Godfrey is his name – found us and asked me where I wanted to go. I don't have any other family in Australia and you were the first people I thought of.' She buried her face in her hands. 'They've gone!'

Mrs Hamilton wrapped her arms around Lillian. 'How dreadful for you. We're so sorry. Perhaps she was able to grab on to a branch or something? You mustn't lose hope. They may have been saved.'

Lillian shook her head vehemently. 'You weren't there, Mrs Hamilton. You didn't see the water. It was everywhere.'

Mrs Hamilton cupped Lillian's face in her hands. 'Your sister once did us an incredible kindness in our own time of need.' She exchanged a look with her husband. 'It is time for us to repay the favour. We are extremely pleased you've come to us. Do not despair.'

'Thank you very much, Mrs Hamilton.'

'I think under the circumstances you may call us Jonathan and Dorothy.'

Lillian sniffed. 'I couldn't.'

'Yes, you must. I insist,' Dorothy said.

'Thank you... Dorothy.' The intimacy of using her employer's first name brought on a fresh flood of tears.

Florence returned with Peter, who was holding a biscuit in his hand. He clambered on to the sofa next to Lillian. Alice had fallen asleep, nestled in Jonathan's lap.

As Florence went back to the kitchen to retrieve a pot of tea, Lillian noticed a toddler peeking coyly out from behind the door leading to the hall. Stephen had grown into a beautiful child with dark curls that matched his father's and the same light blue eyes she had seen on his mother. At the sight of him, she held out her hand and beckoned. He edged closer on unsteady feet until he was in front of her, raising his small hand and using his index finger to prod at her wet cheeks. Peter lifted his head from her shoulder to watch him. Stephen brought up his other hand to reveal a toy cart nestled in his palm. The older boy drew closer to inspect its bright-red paintwork.

Stephen gave Peter a turn. Her nephew spent a moment spinning the wheels and rolling it along the arm of the chair. After a few moments, Stephen snatched it from his hand and wobbled back behind the door. He poked his head out and giggled, disappearing once more. Peter slowly stood up and wandered towards the little boy's hiding place. When Stephen re-emerged, Peter pounced and tickled him, drawing forth a gale of laughter. Soon they retreated from the room. Before long the sound of little feet pattering up and down behind the wall was heard, accompanied by happy shrieking.

'Stephen will enjoy having somebody to play with,' Dorothy said.

How strange Peter could slough off his grief to grab a

moment's joy. Lillian could not imagine how to navigate a strange new world that no longer held her sister. She wished she had drowned instead. Why hadn't she insisted Patricia climb up first? If her sister and nephew had drowned, as she suspected, it would be all her fault.

Lillian felt she owed her hosts some information as a thank you. Haltingly, she told Jonathan what she'd seen during her rescue. After her description, he was keen to go and have a look at the damage himself. He put on his coat and hat and stole out into the rain to walk down to the water's edge, planning to hail a passing dinghy if he could. Lillian waited impatiently with Dorothy and Florence for his return to hear exactly how much the store had suffered. When he came back to the house an hour later, his face was drawn and his clothes drenched.

'How bad is it, dear?' asked Dorothy.

Jonathan removed his hat and pulled at his beard. 'Lillian was right. The whole street's gone under. Our stock's going to be ruined.'

Dorothy reached out to take his hand. 'Nicky will be home soon. He'll help us get everything back in order.'

Jonathan nodded and sighed. 'We've done it before. I didn't think it would be so soon we'd have to do it again. I should have listened to you, Dorothy.'

'Now, there'll be no more talk like that. What's done is done,' his wife replied, patting his back.

Lillian thought of the bolts of fabric and expensive machinery lying completely submerged in the muddy water. There were unfinished orders that would have to be started afresh, not to mention the mammoth job of scrubbing down walls and floors when the river receded.

≈

That evening, the street outside was eerily dark. There was no gas to be had to light the streetlamps and they surmised the river must have damaged the pipes. Dorothy tried to distract Lillian from her grief by handing her a needle threaded with lemon-coloured cotton and a square of linen. Her hand shook as she made the first stitch. What was the point of such a meaningless activity when her world had turned so grey?

'Keep going,' Dorothy coaxed, until Lillian's fingers began to fly into a steady rhythm. Before long, with the rescued baby in mind, she had fashioned a tiny pair of baby booties in one corner.

'That's sweet. Next time pull your stitch a little tighter,' said Dorothy. 'It'll come along soon enough. We'll have you adding embroidery to the gowns in no time.'

Florence joined them at the table where her mother had set a candelabra to shed light as they worked. The three of them continued sewing until Lillian was so tired, the thread began to blur in front of her eyes. The children had drifted off to sleep an hour ago, safely tucked into the four-poster bed in the spare bedroom.

She stifled a yawn. 'Please excuse me. I'm struggling to keep my eyes open.'

'A good night's sleep will do you a world of good.' Mrs Hamilton began to gather the threads. 'I think I might do the same shortly.'

Florence lifted one of the candles from the candelabra and set it into a smaller holder. 'Here, take this to guide you.'

Lillian took it and gratefully bid her hosts good night. She crept towards the bedroom, the orb of light chasing the shadows down the hall ahead of her. In the dark, she closed the door and changed into a cotton shift, another item borrowed from Florence. At the foot of the bed, Alice lay nestled in a small crib emitting a reassuring snuffle every now and then. The baby's sleep was natural. Lillian gazed at her peaceful expression and silently promised not another drop of soothing powder would ever pass her innocent lips. Alice was meant to survive and Lillian longed to hear her strong lungs prove it, loud and clear and full of life. Earlier that evening, Dorothy had boiled some of their own nanny goat's milk for Alice, who had hungrily gulped it down. Lillian was proud of the baby's appetite. Dorothy had said she would purchase some formula when the chemist reopened in the morning.

Slipping in next to Peter, she hugged him close and inhaled the scent of his clean hair.

His black eyes blinked up at her.

'Aunt Lillie?'

'Shush. Go back to sleep.'

'I miss Mama and Thomas,' he whispered.

'I know you do, darling. I miss them, too.'

She let go of him, rolled on to her back away from her nephew's despairing gaze, hoping for merciful sleep to release her from the misery, but the relief of being tucked up in a warm bed in a safe place gave way to more tormented thoughts that left her smothering screams into her pillow.

As the hours ticked by and further sleep eluded, Lillian peered into the darkness trying to make out the shapes of the room's furniture. A large wardrobe loomed in the corner.

Occupying the space would only be a temporary measure. How could it be otherwise? Florence had explained to her earlier the room belonged to Nicholas. The family expected his arrival any day and, after so long at sea, he would be looking forward to his old comforts. What was he going to think when he found her here with nowhere else to go?

A dark square sat silhouetted on the wall. It was a portrait of Molly Hamilton; Lillian had noticed it earlier. Dead like Patricia and Thomas. Dead like her mother. What was the point of survival when you had to carry a broken heart through the days? As dawn broke and the first magpie warbled, Lillian drifted off to restless sleep for an hour before Alice's hungry cries woke her. As her eyes snapped open, Lillian was instantly reminded her life had become a terrifying nightmare. *I am still here. Patricia and Thomas are not.* Awake, there was no respite from her devastation.

CHAPTER 17

SOUTH BRISBANE

*L*illian hugged a shawl around her shoulders and sipped a strong cup of tea at the dining room table. The Hamilton's housemaid and nanny, Lucy, brought a poached egg and two slices of toast and set them down. After being a servant for so long it was a strange feeling to be served and Lillian had no appetite for the food before her. She said, 'Thank you,' anyhow before the slight girl of about fifteen returned to the kitchen. By rights, Lillian herself was still only an apprentice and didn't truly deserve to be sitting there alongside the rest of the family. The Hamiltons had been very kind, yet she worried how long the welcome would last. Did Peter and Alice's presence in their home rekindle unpleasant memories for them about Molly's demise? Perhaps somewhere in Stephen's young memory he recalled Peter from spending his early days at Patricia's cottage? It was a silly thought, of course.

If her presence upset the family, they showed no sign of it. Dorothy had carefully taken Alice from Lillian's arms when she'd carried her into the kitchen at a loss about what to give her. Alice appeared to tolerate the contents of the bottle Dorothy had told Lucy to prepare for her. Peter sat quietly at the table alongside her. He picked at the porridge Lucy had put before them.

'Doesn't he like oats?' Florence asked curiously.

'Yes, usually. I'm afraid he's lost his appetite.' Lillian left her chair and crouched in front of Peter.

He pouted and looked down at the floor. 'Where're Mama and Thomas?'

'I don't know yet. We have to be very brave.' Lillian felt anxious about Peter's stoic refusal to cry.

As the morning wore on, Dorothy seemed to enjoy nurturing Alice. Florence entertained the two young boys while Lillian passed the hours staring out of the rain-streaked window into the cloudy skies. Dorothy gave Alice back to her when the little girl fell asleep and she trudged back to the bedroom and laid her in the crib. She gazed at the baby's little face, so peaceful and calm and felt hot, angry tears for her sister and Thomas begin to fall again.

When Stephen went down for his afternoon nap, Peter slept again that afternoon, tired from his changed surroundings. Lillian sought permission from Dorothy to go and see the city's carnage for herself in the harsh light of day. Despite everything, a paperboy had still managed to deliver the morning paper. The front page held a picture showing the destruction of Victoria Bridge and ships marooned in the Botanic Gardens. The accompanying article relayed how the river had carried many houses downstream, where they had been dashed like matchwood against the bridge's piles until the structure itself had been cut away, severing the north side of the city from the south.

She headed down Melbourne Street until the way was blocked by washed-up debris and stagnating floodwater. A disgusting stench of raw sewage rose up from the steaming mud. A couple of youths paddled by and called out to see if she would like to catch a ride to travel further along. Lillian accepted gratefully and once safely seated directed them to take her to Stanley Street, where she could see for herself the damage done to the bridge and the Hamiltons' store.

The young boys eagerly obliged, thrilled to be paddling over roads normally traversed by horses and carts. As the boat reached the junction, Lillian looked beyond the People's Cash Store to where the tailor's stood, jutting like an iceberg out of the dirty river. Mr Hamilton – Jonathan – had not been exaggerating. She was filled with despair at the state of it. Water was still lapping at the second-storey windows.

Turning her gaze towards the bridge she had crossed countless times before, Lillian was stunned to see it rising like a sundial from the river for some hundred yards before coming to an abrupt stop. A broken finger, it pointed across to crowds of people lining the north bank staring back to the south. It was impossible from such a distance to see the expressions on their faces but she had no doubt they wore the same look of disbelief as she did.

Lillian retrieved the handkerchief she'd embroidered the night before and used it to wipe away the tears falling again for Patricia and Thomas. The young boys shifted uncomfortably in their seats.

'I'm sorry,' she said. 'It's hard to take in, that's all.'

They nodded in agreement and navigated the boat back in the direction they'd just come, pulling on the oars until Lillian found herself returned to the same spot they'd picked her up from.

'Thank you so much for your help.' She waved goodbye, glad she hadn't asked to be taken further to Montague Road. It would be fruitless to return until the river retreated – dangerous, too – and she wasn't ready to see the state of her sister's home.

Lillian traipsed back up Vulture Street to the Hamiltons' passing clusters of dishevelled people along the way. Some clutched cases or carpet bags; all looked lost and numb. Perhaps she could take the children to the municipal buildings when Nicholas returned? How would the Hamiltons be able to continue to employ her when they had lost so much themselves? It was too overwhelming to think about but think about her future she must.

As the hours turned into a day and then two, relentlessly indifferent to the trauma the little family had suffered, baby Alice continued to rally. Despite the thrashing by the rain and earlier hunger, her cheeks grew rosy and her eyes locked resolutely on to the face of every person who held her. Though Lillian tried to remain indifferent, a seed of affection began to grow a tendril, replacing the initial resentment over her survival.

Still, even gazing on innocent babies couldn't lessen the blow when a familiar constable appeared at the residence. Lillian spied him coming up the front path and watched warily as Dorothy answered the door, certain he had found her refuge and come to escort her to join Alfred at the watch house.

In the newspaper that very morning, she had seen the announcement: *Mr A Hooper of Montague Road appeared before the Magistrate's Court on charges of child endangerment.* What had he done with poor John? To think it could have been baby Alice. Lillian's chest constricted. She would be lost without the baby girl she rescued from the waters and now loved as her own.

'I'm looking for a Miss Lillian Betts and I understand she is currently lodging at this address?'

Mrs Hamilton glanced over her shoulder with concern. 'Yes, Constable, she is.'

'Could I have a few words, please?'

Lillian stepped out from behind Dorothy and on to the bright veranda, doing her best not to betray the fear swelling inside her.

'Miss Betts. A body has washed ashore at Sandgate that matches a description lodged of your sister, Mrs Patricia Hooper. I need you to accompany me to the morgue to identify the body.'

Jonathan or Dorothy must have put out some inquiries. She swallowed and nodded. 'Of course.'

Lillian stood inside the Department of Agriculture and Stock building and stared at the row of sheet-covered bodies. The constable spoke to one of the staff who walked briskly up the line and pointed to one.

She didn't want to pull back the sheet and yet she did, too. Perhaps the constable was mistaken? The corpse beneath wouldn't belong to her sister and she could return to the Hamiltons to resume her wait. Taking a deep breath, Lilian nodded and the worker pulled the sheet back. It took her a moment to be sure. The water had done appalling things to her sister. It had pulled at her black hair and torn out chunks of it, swollen her face and dragged the wretched clothes from her body. Lillian's eyes travelled down the pale, scratched hands and there she stopped. Patricia's wedding ring hung on a finger wrinkled like a prune. Lillian nodded, unable to turn away from the sight. She retched and covered her mouth.

'The smell is... hard to take,' said the constable.

Lillian shook her head – that wasn't it, although indeed the air inside the cool room hung heavily with the taint of decomposition. The finality of her sister's demise was macabrely set before her and she had already cried herself dry.

'Come, I'll take you out.' The constable made to lead her up the stairs.

'No! Where is he?' Lillian twisted away, wild. 'Where is he? Where's Thomas?' She almost tripped in her haste as she scoured the row of covered bodies. 'Which one is he?'

'Who? Who is it that you want?' The constable followed her with a furrowed brow.

'My nephew. He can't be left alone. He's only a little boy.' Lillian fell to her knees on the cement floor. 'He needs his mother.'

The constable's strong hand on her shoulder brought Lillian to her senses. She stared up at him with helpless rage. 'My nephew, Thomas. He was with his mother when they were swept away. Did you find him?'

The constable's pursed lips of regret gave her the answer before he began to shake his head. 'I'm sorry. He's not here.'

She staggered to her feet and buried her face in her hands. 'What am I going to do?'

'You're going to bury your sister. It's the only thing you can do.' The constable's matter-of-factness cut through her anguish.

Lillian watched him re-cover Patricia's face with the sheet. There was little choice but to keep moving, even though it hurt like hell. The sea might have given up her sister and stolen Thomas but it appeared Alfred had not yet done the same to her.

CHAPTER 18

REUNION

'*N*icholas! Oh!' Florence scattered spools of thread across the table as she scrambled to stand up and hug her older brother. 'Welcome home.'

'Thank you, Flo. I'd like to say it is good to be back but I wish the circumstances were different. Is Mama here?'

'No. She's gone with Papa to the store to see about the clean-up. She'll be so cross to have missed you. Come and sit down. Let me put the kettle on.'

Lillian stood listening in the hall just beyond the door. She'd come inside to fetch a jug of water and some cups for the children who were happily playing in the garden. At the sound of his voice she'd frozen, feeling guilty for eavesdropping on the unaware siblings' reunion. As she waited indecisively, Florence continued to ask her brother about his travels but Nicholas seemed far more concerned to find out what damage the store had suffered.

Florence gave up, exasperated. 'Come, you'll at least be wanting to see Stephen. He's running about with Peter somewhere.'

'Peter?'

'Yes. Our apprentice is staying with us for a little while, the poor thing. She lost absolutely everything, Nicky, including her sister and younger nephew. It's quite the tale. She managed to climb on to the roof of their cottage with the elder child, Peter, and the baby just as the flood washed right through. We all feel so sorry for her. To make matters worse, a constable came around yesterday and took her down to the morgue to identify her sister. Sadly, it was her. The poor girl's absolutely bereft.' Florence lowered her voice. 'There's no money to pay for a proper burial. The little boy still hasn't been found.'

Lillian heard Nicholas cough. 'That's horrible. There still seem to be an awful lot of people wandering around the streets looking lost. I bet there are others in the same situation. I guess we've been lucky, after all. I wasn't aware Mama had acquired a new apprentice. She never mentioned anything in her letters.'

'Yes, Lillian's a few years older than the last one but we've all been getting along nicely. She'll be outside with the children if you'd like to say hello.'

'Lillian? Very well, please lead me to meet this unfortunate new apprentice and, more importantly, my son. I'm afraid he won't remember me after so long apart.'

At the sound of chair legs scraping against the wooden floor, Lillian panicked. She took a deep breath, stepped into the kitchen and came face to face with Nicholas.

He stared at her with confusion.

Florence smiled. 'Lillian, I was just telling my brother you were staying with us at the moment. We were just coming out to the garden to see you.'

'You're the apprentice?' Nicholas raised his eyebrows.

She straightened and tucked a loose strand of hair behind her ear. 'Yes.'

'Do you know each other?' Florence asked, flicking a glance between them.

'No, not really,' Lillian said. 'We met only the once, on an outing with friends.' She could have sworn a look of hurt flashed across Nicholas's face.

'I see.' Florence crossed her arms, unconvinced.

'I thought you were a maid,' said Nicholas.

'It's true, I was, but everything... changed.' Lillian watched Nicholas for any sign he knew why. If he did he was making a very good impression of being ignorant. Perhaps he hadn't corresponded with Matthew, after all? When they'd met all those months ago, he had far more important matters on his mind, namely his wife's recent death. She softened. 'Your mother – indeed your entire family – have been very kind to me. I've learned a great deal about dressmaking. At least I was until the flood happened.'

'Yes, my sister has explained the circumstances that have led to you staying. I am very sorry to hear about your losses.'

At his unexpected kindness, Lillian looked away and blinked back the tears threatening to spill. She was grateful they had returned. He seemed genuinely perturbed by her situation. 'Thank you, Nicholas. Now you have safely returned, the time has come for me to return to my sister's cottage to see if it is salvageable. You will need your room back.'

'I hadn't realised it was occupied.'

Florence stepped between them. 'Mama thought it best to lodge Lillian and the children in there as it's the biggest.'

'Yes, of course. Don't make other arrangements on my account. I can sleep in the drawing room for the time being.'

Lillian held up her hands to protest. 'No, I couldn't let you do that. If the cottage is ruined, there's space at the municipal buildings for people with nowhere else to go. I'll manage, somehow.'

Nicholas ran his left hand through his hair. 'Why don't we go take a look at your sister's house together and you can make your decision then? I'll not have a lady and her children sleeping in a less suitable place on my account.'

From Jonathan's latest report, Lillian had learned the Brisbane River had receded behind its banks and yet she was fearful of what she might discover at Montague Road, now the path was clear to investigate. With Florence kindly offering to watch the children for a couple of hours and Nicholas waiting expectantly, she felt she had little choice but to take up his offer. She managed to stave off the excursion for a few minutes by leading him through to the garden where Stephen and Peter were playing. Alice slept soundly in Stephen's old pram in the shade of an overhanging jacaranda. The children froze like statues and stared at the unfamiliar man.

Florence strode over to Stephen and scooped him up. 'Come and see your Papa.'

The little boy buried his face into her shoulder but it was not long before curiosity got the better of him. It was a sweet sight to see Nicholas pat the little boy's head and pinch his cheek. Nevertheless, his sister could tell he was impatient to head away.

'Oh, go on then. There'll be plenty of time to hear about your travels this evening.' Florence sighed and pointed to the stable. 'You'll find Skylark where you left him. I've been riding him while you've been away.'

When Lillian and Nicholas reached the leaning fence in front of the cottage at Montague Road, Lillian quickly descended from the carriage, picked up the hem of her skirt and trudged through the drying mire of mud where the garden path should have been. To her relief, she could see the building was still on its stumps, although silt had left the front door wedged ajar. She did not expect to see much in the way of contents as the place had been open to looting by opportunistic thieves.

Nicholas stopped at the gate. 'This is your sister's house?'

'Yes.'

He shot her a shrewd look. 'I met her once.'

'I know.'

She heard him suck in a breath and waited for a barrage of accusations to follow. Instead, Nicholas followed her to the porch and pushed on the door. It scraped open a couple of inches.

'After you,' he said.

Lillian squeezed past the door, which creaked on rusted hinges. As her eyes adjusted to the dim interior, her fears proved correct. Further up the dark hall the kitchen had indeed been stripped of its meagre wares, whether by light fingers or floodwaters it was impossible to tell. Only the heavy furniture remained; Patricia's rocking chair, the table and dresser, all displaced from their usual positions. The table had slammed hard up against the wall, its corner leaving several dents in the wet wood. Her sister's rocking chair lay forlornly on its side, one of the arms splintered in half. A vision of Patricia rocking back and forth so tired froze Lillian to the spot. It had been less than a week ago. Turning slowly to take in the rest of the room, she noticed several inches of slimy mud coating the floor and the wallpaper hanging in loose, stained strips. In the muddy corner a familiar small tin lay. She picked it up and brushed it off. Opening the lid, she drew in a breath. The promissory note and coins were still there. Lillian clasped it to her chest.

Like the door through which she'd entered, the back one had warped and was stuck in its frame. Lillian edged forward and hardly dared to peer through the grimy window beside it.

Outside, the yard's grass had pressed flat in an easterly direction, a tell-tale sign of the flood's deadly path. It was the scene where her sister and nephew had been torn from her life for ever. The vegetable garden's scattered rock border brought a large lump to Lillian's throat. She swallowed painfully, it still hurt after so much screaming, and turned to Nicholas who was picking his way up the hall.

'It's hopeless, isn't it?'

'If it's the mess that's worrying you then don't. We'll have the place cleaned up in no time.' Nicholas looked up. 'Please don't consider leaving our house because I've returned. Besides, knowing my mother, she simply won't have it.'

Lillian tried to remember the man she'd met all those months ago on that wonderful Sunday outing. Apart from the concern he appeared to feel for her, he seemed a different person from the sad, serious fellow she'd met previously. She was grateful for the change.

It was as though he had read her thoughts. 'I wasn't very good company last time we met, Lillian. My wife's death hit me very hard and I have no doubt you understand what that kind of loss feels like. I remember your willingness to walk beside me and your talent for drawing. I hope in time you will find comfort returning to this house with all its memories. If I'd known then who your sister was, I'd have –'

Lillian raised her hands. 'Stop. Nicholas, I didn't tell you because I was worried about how you'd react. It wasn't the right time. I wondered if we would have another opportunity to meet but you stopped coming out with Matthew and the others. Then I...'

'Left Rosemead,' said Nicholas.

Lillian's eyes flew open. 'Exactly.'

'I did go to the wedding but you weren't there.'

'Mrs Shaw wouldn't let me go. Catherine told me she saw you.'

Nicholas retraced his steps to poke his head inside the two bedrooms. 'It'll take some work but it can be done. I don't want to rush you but when you're ready to leave, would you mind if we make a short stop at the store before we head home? I'd like to surprise my parents.'

She was just about to tell him that of course they should when the thumping of boots mounting the porch steps raised the hairs on the back of her neck. The next lousy thief who dared to stick their head inside her sister's cottage was going to get a kick in the groin. She wasn't afraid to be the one to do it.

Nicholas raised a finger to his lips and motioned her to stand behind him. A large figure shoulder-barged their way through the front door. The surprise on the intruder's face matched their own.

'Who the hell are you?' Alfred asked, leaning proprietarily against the doorframe.

'I'm Nicholas Hamilton. I brought Lillian down to check on the state of her sister's cottage.'

And you are?'

'Alfred Hooper and I think you mean my cottage.'

Nicholas glanced back at her for confirmation. Lillian nodded with defeat.

Alfred muscled past them and continued into the kitchen. 'Where's Patricia?'

'I thought you were – '

'What, Lillian? In gaol? Lucky for me I've got friends in high places.' Alfred whistled. 'Come on through, gentlemen.'

Lillian blanched as Fergus entered the house but a small squawk slipped from her lips at the sight of Donald appearing behind him.

His gaze swung between Nicholas and her. 'Hello, Lillian.'

The two men eyed each other with distrust.

'Where did she take the children then?' Alfred stooped to pick up a broken bowl off the floor and turned it over in his hands. 'What a bloody mess.'

'She's not here,' Nicholas said.

Alfred scowled. 'I can jolly well see that.'

'I thought someone would have told you,' Lillian murmured.

Alfred looked up. 'Told me what?'

'She's...' She couldn't – didn't want to – finish the sentence.

Nicholas stepped forward. 'I'm sorry to have to be the one to tell you, Alfred, but your wife and younger son drowned in the flood. Your wife is in the morgue awaiting burial. Unfortunately, the boy has not yet been found.'

Alfred stared at Nicholas. 'What about Peter?'

'Lillian saved him. They climbed up on the roof. He's safe and well. My sister's watching him.'

Alfred raked his fingers down both sides of his jaw.

'Jesus, I'm sorry, Alf.' Fergus reached out to put a consoling hand on his friend's shoulder but Alfred roughly shrugged it off and heaved the broken bowl at the wall, where it smashed to pieces.

Lillian flinched at the sound but, by the amazed looks on the other men's faces, she appeared to be the only one unsurprised by his violence.

To see her brother-in-law react with anger drew forth little compassion from her. He had been too cruel for too long. His sorrow for Patricia would never run as deep as her own. Her sister was her blood, her life. Without her, Lillian was an anchorless buoy tossing about in a relentless storm. Peter and Alice had become the only reason she drew enough strength to rise from her bed each morning. She agonised over the wasted time spent gallivanting around the city with Catherine when she should have been here helping her sister.

'We'd best be going, Lillian,' Nicholas said.

Fergus and Donald stood aside in the narrow space to let them past. Donald's eyes were on her as her sleeve brushed against his but she refused to acknowledge him. She felt shame rise over his knowing she'd been fired for stealing from Olivia. Perhaps he thought she was trying to steal Alfred's house as well?

She and Nicholas were halfway down the front steps before Alfred charged outside and grabbed her by the wrist, wrenching it back. 'You're not innocent, either, Lillian. Just you remember that,' he hissed.

Lillian remained outwardly calm despite the searing pain. 'Let go of me.'

He didn't move.

Nicholas was half a head taller than Alfred and his expression grew fierce. 'She said let go.'

Fergus appeared beside Alfred and whispered in his ear.

Alfred roughly dropped her hand and launched a gob of spit insultingly close to Nicholas's boot. 'This is my bloody house, Lillian. Don't go thinking you've got any claim to it. I'll thank you to bring my son back to me.'

'I won't!' She couldn't bear such a thought. He wasn't fit to care for a dog.

He sneered. 'Patricia told me what you did. I wouldn't trust you with anyone's child let alone my own. Peter belongs at home with his papa.'

'You'll not get another thing from me, you disgusting excuse for a father. Patricia and Thomas's funeral is at St Andrew's, tomorrow at ten o'clock. The Hamiltons have kindly forwarded me my wages in order to pay for it. You can attend, or not. It makes absolutely no difference to me.' She turned on her heel and stalked off. If Alfred wanted to lay chase and hurl more abuse, he could easily catch up but she wouldn't dignify a look back to check.

Nicholas caught up with her in the carriage, pulling hard on the reins to bring Skylark to a halt. The beast gently snickered before reaching down to yank out a tuft of dirty grass battling its way up through the mud. Lillian was bent double struggling to catch her breath, embarrassed by her sweaty face and the events that had transpired in front of him. Nicholas leapt down from the carriage and waited quietly until she had regained enough composure to stand up straight again.

'I'm sorry you had to witness that,' she said.

'He's quite the gentleman, your brother-in-law, isn't he?'

'I can't begin to tell you how neglectful he was of Patricia,' she cried.

'Judging from what I've seen, it's easy enough to make an accurate assumption. How's your wrist?'

She carefully balled her fist up and rolled it in a circular motion. 'It hurts but I think it will be fine. Nothing broken.'

'I should have knocked his block off.'

'There's no point sinking to his level.' Nonetheless, she felt a quick thud in her chest at his chivalrous offer.

'I have some money set aside if you will accept a donation to help with your sister's funeral.'

Lillian blushed. She held up the dirty tin and gave it a rattle. 'I will manage, thank you. If you want to attend you are very welcome. However,' she added, looking at him through lowered lashes, 'I understand if you don't.'

Nicholas studied her. 'I will come. Save your money, too.'

She recognised in his expression the same deep sadness

that had burrowed deep within her soul. Molly Hamilton was not yet dead a year.

'Would you prefer to return to go straight back to Vulture Street?' Nicholas asked.

Lillian's eyes widened. 'Absolutely not. We need to get you to the store. Your mother and father have been talking about your return ever since they received your letter. I will not be held responsible for delaying your reunion a moment more.' She hesitated. 'Also, I want to say I'm sorry. I should have told you about Alfred. I didn't know he would be back so soon. He had a... run-in with the law. I thought I had enough time to sort out what to do next.'

'Try to put him out of your mind.' Nicholas offered his arm and she accepted his help back into the carriage. The bottom of her skirt was covered in mud.

As they neared the junction, Lillian began to fret over what Dorothy might think of her son and apprentice appearing together unchaperoned. On top of this, despite Nicholas not asking questions, the fact remained he had overheard Alfred's threats. She was afraid.

Her first concern was unwarranted. Only joy lit up Jonathan and Dorothy's tired and worried faces when they saw the carriage pull up on Stanley Street. When they alighted and entered the store, Lillian was upset to see the state of the interior. Filthy bolts of fabric lay stacked against the shelves. As at the cottage, watermarks streaked the wallpaper right up to the ceiling, yet the clean-up was well under way. An army of helpers – employees and volunteers –was busy throwing ruined goods out on to the street while still others swept muck from the floorboards.

Dorothy threw down her broom and embraced Nicholas as soon as he crossed the threshold.

'Welcome home, Nicky! How was the voyage?'

'We weathered a storm while crossing the Equator but otherwise it was fair.' Nicholas gazed around the shop and grimaced.

'Now don't fret,' Dorothy said, patting her son's arm lightly. 'We'll be all right. At least, thanks to you, there'll be exciting new stock to put out on display. That'll bring the customers back in. Insurance shall cover the rest.' Dorothy took a step back and scrutinized her son. 'I see you've met our apprentice, Lillian.'

'Yes.' Nicholas gave his mother a wry grin. 'For the second time, actually.'

'Really?' His mother raised her eyebrows. 'Lillian, you never told us you knew our Nicky?'

Lillian squirmed uncomfortably but Nicholas interrupted before she could offer an explanation.

'We've been over to Montague Road to have a look at her sister's house. It's still standing but it'll need a lot of work to make it liveable again. Her brother-in-law turned up.' Nicholas's lip curled as he glanced at Lillian. 'I assured her she and the children could continue to use my room for as long as it is needed. I'll ask Lucy to make up a bed for me in the drawing-room.'

'Yes.' Jonathan stroked his beard. 'I'm sure you'll manage in there just fine for the time being.'

'There, it's settled.' Nicholas smiled and it occurred to Lillian, standing there with his family, she was seeing yet another side of his character. She didn't doubt he still greatly missed his wife, yet the cloud of sadness that had cloaked him the last time they had met appeared to have lifted. Here was a man at ease in his own skin. For an unsettling moment, he reminded her of Donald. She had been too stunned at the sight of her old flame standing in Patricia's ruined house to enquire whether the flood had spared Rosemead. She had also been pleased to watch Donald eyeing Nicholas with a spark of envy.

Only here, surrounded by people who had shown her nothing but care and respect, did Lillian stop to wonder why the Shaw brothers had accompanied Alfred in the first place. What was her brother-in-law doing out of gaol? She had no doubt he'd called on Fergus to defend him from the charge. It was the only answer that sprang to mind.

Despite his penchant for drinking Alfred could be charming when he wanted to be. He had fooled Patricia into marrying him, after all. Whatever the reason might be, standing there with the Hamiltons, Lillian felt fortified enough to face what she must the following day – her sister's and Thomas's final farewell.

CHAPTER 19

MINSTRELS

*I*n the end, Alfred's brooding presence at the funeral had rattled Lillian but he'd been sober enough not to make a scene in front of the Hamiltons. Indeed, his demeanour had been somewhat cowed and Lillian wondered if the realisation his wife and son were truly gone for ever contributed to his circumspection. Peter had approached his father with caution until the moment Alfred knelt to shake his hand. Alfred had looked over his son's head to Lillian and stared open-mouthed at the sight of Alice cradled in her arms. A current of uneasy understanding passed between them.

She'd hesitated to have Thomas included in the minister's eulogy without his body having been recovered but, in the end, as the words flowed around the small gathering, it had felt like the right thing to do. Looking on as her sister's simple coffin was lowered into its grave, Lillian felt completely bereft but, as she raised her eyes, she was warmed by the sight of several young women – strangers to her – standing with their heads bowed in deep respect. They made her understand her sister had provided some hope in a moment of their own darkness. Her life had counted, she had done something good with it and she'd been loved.

The days passing after the funeral did little to dull Lillian's sadness. A grey pall hung over her thoughts and she began to wonder if her grief would ever lift.

Lillian turned listlessly in front of Florence's looking glass. The pale pink brocade dress was the finest thing she had ever worn in her life. With Nicholas's return from London and Alfred's unexpected release, she had been concerned as to what might become of her. She could scarcely afford a room of her own with her apprentice's wage and, with two young children in tow, everything seemed impossible. Florence was the one who had graciously come up with the best solution. She had announced at dinner that she absolutely must share her room with Lillian. Together they set up the enclosed back porch as a makeshift nursery for the children.

Although he never said so, Nicholas appeared happy to be restored to his room.

While the arrangement was certainly unconventional and neighbours might have whispered, Lillian couldn't afford to let them bother her. She doubted Florence would ever understand what her kindness meant. Besides, the flood had upended social norms for the time being. She was one of the hundreds who had experienced a devastating loss. People found themselves billeted from the municipal buildings to strangers and friends alike. There was nothing like a disaster for the city's inhabitants to band together enthusiastically. It was what colonists did best. Yet Nicholas's invitation to the theatre that evening had still come as a surprise.

She assumed Nicholas's offer to take her to the theatre was out of pity and she'd been nervous about accepting, confined as they were under the same roof. But, as both Dorothy and

Jonathan had also decided to attend – thus chaperoning– it seemed the only thing left to do was say yes.

Nicholas continued to be an enigma. He didn't press about how she had managed to become his mother's dressmaking apprentice. Perhaps he'd asked his parents when she wasn't about? Lillian's heart sank whenever she dwelt on the possibility he might not care enough to bother about the particulars – until he'd invited her to accompany him to the theatre.

Florence was never far from her brother since his return. She continued to implore him to regale her with all the details of his travels. The moment Lillian had told Florence about her brother's invitation, the girl had flown to her wardrobe and selected three dresses for her to try on. Again, Lillian was hesitant to accept well-meaning charity. However, Florence kept insisting a choice be made until reluctantly she pointed at a pale pink gown which was cinched in at the waist and had puffed sleeves.

'You look absolutely splendid,' Florence said once she had finished buttoning the dress up Lillian's back. She turned her around to face the looking-glass. 'All the other ladies will fade into the background when you make your entrance.'

That was the last thing Lillian wanted. She'd never attended an evening theatre performance before and anxiously wondered whether her lack of graces would show and embarrass them all. How could she pretend to enjoy herself with her sister not a week buried in her grave? Still, she'd existed alongside the Shaw family for a good year and a half before her fall from favour; if she mimicked their airs and graces well enough, she might just pass.

'Aren't you a pretty picture?' Dorothy clasped her by the hand as she entered the drawing room.

Nicholas rose from his seat and cleared his throat. 'You do look very nice, Lillian.'

She blushed at the compliments, in spite of her inner turmoil.

Jonathan placed his brandy glass on the small table beside his chair and grunted as he stood.

'Yes, charming indeed. Righto, the horses are harnessed. Shall we?'

Lillian thought Jonathan seemed tired that evening but it was understandable he should be. He'd been down at the store with Nicholas for long hours each day salvaging what he could and coordinating the clean up. After the first salvage, Dorothy preferred to spend her time back at the house cataloguing the new shipment of fabric Nicholas had brought home from Paris and London. The bolts of cloth were taking up half the drawing-room, nestled behind the sofa and stacked against the bookcase. Dorothy had set Lillian and Florence to cutting out new patterns and pinning them to the fabric whenever the demands of caring for Alice, Stephen and Peter allowed. Lillian lived in fear of the children leaving sticky finger marks on the expensive material and chased Peter and Stephen from the room every time their games became too boisterous. She knew the tasks were Dorothy's way of trying to keep her mind off her losses and for that she was grateful.

The horses, Skylark and Saffron, chuffed softly as the party climbed into the carriage. Jonathan picked up the reins and clicked his tongue and they were soon headed down Vulture Street towards the wharf. The ferry was now the only way to cross the river. Lillian looked out across the water. She was pleased to see the water calm that evening, small ripples dancing across its surface. The dangerous surging force of before had steadily abated. How could it be the same river? The horses calmly embarked on to the ferry and they were taken across without incident. They disembarked on the north side and continued through the streets to arrive at the Gaiety

Theatre on Albert Street, where they joined the line of carriages waiting for an usher to come and assist their passengers' descent.

Despite her grief, Lillian was intrigued at the prospect of watching the Empire Minstrels perform. Aboard the ferry, Jonathan explained they would be watching an hour of comedy filled with an assortment of dance, song and acts. His description reminded Lillian of her brief time spent with Catherine frequenting some of the entertainments Brisbane had to offer. It seemed so long ago, she'd forgotten the fun they'd had.

The foyer's interior gleamed as they entered, with lamplight reflecting off tiles and jewels glittering in ladies' décolletages. Lillian fingered the string of glass beads at her neck and was thankful Florence had persuaded her to wear them. She pulled back her shoulders and tried to appear relaxed.

To her dismay, two familiar figures advanced through the throng. She caught an awkward look pass between the couple. Regardless, Matthew was evidently thrilled to see his dear friend returned from Europe.

As they drew closer he called out. 'Nicky boy! How good to see you. I didn't know you were back from London?'

Rosemary stood beside her new husband with pinched lips. Was she mad at her? Lillian thought again of the unanswered telegram she'd sent to Catherine. Perhaps her old friend had decided not to forgive her for the trouble she'd caused them both after all? The growing crowd was pressing in on all sides. Lillian felt claustrophobic and depressed.

'Only a few weeks,' Nicholas replied, seemingly oblivious to the underlying tension. 'There hasn't been much time to pay anyone a visit, I'm afraid. Our store went under.'

'That's a shame, mate. Sorry to hear it,' said Matthew.

Rosemary fixed her gaze on Matthew and an awkward silence descended on the four of them.

Mercifully, a bell began to ring signalling it was time to enter the theatre.

'Right you are then.' Nicholas tipped his hat. 'Enjoy the show. We'll catch up soon.'

'You too. Let's catch up soon,' said Matthew.

Rosemary pulled her husband away through the crowd and Lillian quickly lost sight of them.

'Shall we go in?' asked Nicholas, smiling down at her.

'Please.'

She took her seat, acutely aware of Dorothy and Jonathan seated on the other side of Nicholas. His jacket shoulder brushed against her sleeve and sent a thrill coursing through her. With so many people in the audience, the air was heavy with dust and lingering clouds of perfume. Lillian sat up a little straighter and tried to read the program. However, the lamps soon dimmed and the curtain rose to reveal the company of performers who immediately burst forth with an enthusiastic song for the opening act. Lillian soon found herself swept up by their energy and settled back into her chair to try to glean some enjoyment from the show.

By the time two couples on stage had finished their dance routine to Ta-ra-ra-boom-ta-ray, she had almost forgotten the awkward earlier encounter with Rosemary and Matthew. It was heartening to see even the usually serious Nicholas throw back his head and give a barrelling laugh at the on-stage antics. Lost in the merriment of jokes and tumbling, she casually swept a look over the upper balcony and came to an immediate halt at the sight of Olivia Shaw sitting ramrod straight in a high box to the right. Her old nemesis was staring down at her, a scowl on her silly face.

Lillian's breath caught beneath her stays.

Nicholas leaned in. 'Are you feeling all right?'

She didn't want to worry him. All she could do was nod her head and try to focus on the closing burlesque performance, *Margherita.*

The lamps went up. Lillian felt clammy despite the press of bodies as the audience exited down the aisles and out into the foyer. The laughs and excited recounting of favourite parts of the show reverberated around her from the other patrons. She wished she could grab Nicholas by the hand and hastily pull him outside. They caught up with Jonathan and Dorothy next to the refreshment stand. The older couple had spied some friends and Lillian smiled politely at the introductions and impatiently hoped they would soon move on. At long last the four of them were able to head towards the entrance. A welcome draft of warm evening air blew across her skin.

As they reached the top step a sudden sharp stab in Lillian's side pulled her up short. She turned angrily to see who had been so careless and found herself face-to-face with Olivia.

'Oh dear, did I hurt you?' The girl mismatched her apology with a sly smile.

Lillian kept her arms at her sides despite the throbbing pain pulsing beneath her ribs. 'Not at all,' she returned sweetly.

Olivia leaned in close. 'What are you doing here, Lillian? I wouldn't have thought the theatre to be a place for someone like you.' She twirled her decorative parasol in her hand with the pointy end still facing out. Her expression changed from one of false concern to outright haughtiness.

Lillian thought if the girl held her nose any higher she would fail to see where she was going.

Olivia hung on the arm of an older man Lillian did not recognize. His presence didn't stop her taking a parting shot.

'What a shame Donald wasn't here to see you. He and Mary had other plans.'

Lillian cocked her head to the side. 'Never mind. I saw him only last week. Please pass on my regards, though.' She took a step back, eager to distance herself, and promptly bumped into Jonathan.

'Watch your step, dear.'

'Yes, I'm sorry. I –'

Olivia interrupted. 'Oh, Lillian, you always were the clumsy one, weren't you?'

Jonathan peered at Olivia through his monocle and frowned. 'And who might you be?'

Olivia extended her glove. 'Miss Olivia Shaw.'

Jonathan ignored her offered hand. 'If you'll excuse us, Miss Shaw, our carriage has been brought round. Lillian, follow me. Dorothy and Nicholas are waiting.'

She did as he asked, thrilled to leave Olivia agog. It was clear to see where Nicholas's gruffness came from but at that moment she felt a deep affinity for his father. He was as shrewd as businessmen were wont to be. He'd seen straight through Olivia's false pleasantness and protected Lillian's dignity in one fell sweep. She'd never before enjoyed the benefits a father offered; Jonathan's chivalry threatened to make her lose all sense of decorum, such was her desire to wrap her arms around him with gratitude. She warmed even further as Nicholas, standing by the carriage waiting, placed his broad hand on the small of her back to assist her up on to her seat.

Once ensconced, Dorothy leaned over. 'Who was that appalling young lady, Lillian? Nicholas was busy with the usher and the horses but I saw how she poked you with her parasol. How disgraceful.'

Lillian reddened but felt released from her need to protect herself with a lie, however uncomfortable the admission might be. She had grown tired of her secrets. Jonathan had shown her the truth was always clear enough to see. 'That was Olivia Shaw,' she said with a sigh. 'The daughter of the family I used to work for.'

Dorothy narrowed her eyes. 'Before you returned home to help your sister, you mean?'

She shook her head. 'They have a large home at Kangaroo Point called Rosemead. Mr Shaw is a solicitor. There was... an incident. They had to let me go.'

'Ah, well, don't worry yourself about it.' Jonathan said. 'You can't trust a lawyer as far as you can throw a stick at them, a wily lot. If the family were all as rude to you as that young lady then you're better off being well away from them.'

Lillian giggled at their outrage on her behalf. Nicholas reached over and briefly clasped her hand. Jonathan and Dorothy turned their heads away to watch the passing scenery. Lillian struggled with deep emotion. She stole a glance at Nicholas and found him staring back. There was no mistake. His eyes were dark with desire.

CHAPTER 20

MONTAGUE ROAD

*L*illian rapped on the door and at the sound of footsteps coming wondered if she had made a mistake. She squeezed Peter's hand. He stood beside her and waited expectantly without a clue for what was in store. She was grateful Florence had offered to take care of Alice for an hour.

The door swung open.

'Hello, Alfred.'

'What do you want?'

'I've brought Peter.' Lillian disentangled her fingers from the child's tight grasp and gave him a little push forward.

Peter took a hesitant step before glancing back at her with confusion.

Alfred reached out and patted his head.

'I'll be off, then,' said Lillian.

'What?'

'You said you wanted your son back so I have returned him.'

Alfred looked at her with alarm. 'The house isn't ready.'

Lillian peered inside. Indeed, the interior seemed little different from her last visit with Nicholas. The floor had been washed, that was all.

'You said you didn't trust me to take care of him, that you knew what I had done.' She gestured at the bewildered boy. 'This is what you said you wanted. He's been asking why he hasn't seen you.' She knelt before her nephew and planted a kiss on his cheek. 'Be good for your papa.'

Peter stared back at her, uncomprehending. Lillian nodded at him resolutely, confirming his fears, before rising and heading back down the path. Each step was harder to take than the one before it. She reached the spot where the front gate had once hung and clung to the leaning post. It was clear Alfred was calling her bluff. She had no choice but to draw a deep breath and continue walking as Peter's gut-wrenching wails followed. She hoped he would forgive her.

As she reached the crossroad, a whistle pierced the air and drew her to a halt.

'Hang on!' Alfred shouted down the street.

Lillian turned to see him hurrying towards her, the boy watching them both from the porch. She kept her expression neutral.

Alfred was panting as he caught up. 'Think of your sister, Lillian.'

She thought of nothing else.

'She'd think you were being selfish.'

Lillian clenched her hands into fists and held them at her sides. How dare he call her selfish?

Alfred began to pace, flinging his hands in the air as his frustration grew. 'You can't bloody well show up unannounced and dump Peter on me. I have to go to work.'

Lillian folded her arms. 'I didn't know you'd found a job.'

Alfred had the good grace to look sheepish. 'Fergus found something for me.'

She was genuinely confused at his admission. Why did Fergus persist in having anything to do with Alfred? They had nothing in common. 'I didn't think the Shaws would want anything more to do with ours,' she said. 'What's he got you doing?'

Alfred scuffed his boot at a pebble on the ground. 'Labouring, mainly. His father's extending the stable at Rosemead.'

'Congratulations.' She didn't bother to hide her sarcasm. Any last vestige of fear she had felt towards him, the one who had usurped her sister's freedom, had disappeared the night of the flood. He should have been at home to save Patricia and Thomas. 'What does Mrs Shaw think?'

Alfred picked at his face and looked worriedly back over his shoulder at Peter. 'I haven't seen her.'

'You're lucky, then. If you need me I'm still staying at the Hamiltons' over on Vulture Street.' She turned around and continued walking.

'Lillian, don't be ridiculous,' Alfred implored. 'You have to take Peter with you.'

She stopped and swung around to glare at him. 'Why did you say you wanted him back if you didn't mean it?'

'I was angry, in shock. That bloke you were with had just told me Patricia and Thomas were dead.'

Lillian tried not to let herself be pulled in by Alfred's self-pity. She would not let him get under her skin. 'What happened to baby John?'

He hung his head. 'The police took him to the hospital. I don't know what happened after that. Perhaps they took him to the orphanage?'

'I know he was yours. How could you do that to Patricia?' Lillian wanted to slap him. 'The police would have come for her as well if the flood hadn't. I'm still trying to decide which fate would have been worse.'

'She wouldn't have gone to gaol. Fergus got me out. They couldn't prove I meant to harm that baby.'

'Your baby.'

Alfred turned his face to the sky and groaned. 'Fine, yes, my baby.'

'Did you?'

'I wasn't thinking straight, Lillian. No, I didn't want to hurt the boy.'

It was so infuriating to know he believed the story he was telling, the wicked, self-serving drunkard. If only she could completely cut him from her life then perhaps she and Peter could begin to heal and start anew.

'All right.' Lillian pretended to consider her choices. 'I'll take care of him on one condition.'

Alfred frowned. 'What is it?'

She looked steadily towards the cottage, taking in the bedraggled yard and dried mud encrusted halfway up the weatherboards. 'Let me live in the house.'

'With me?'

Alfred's confusion amused her. She laughed bitterly. 'No, absolutely not with you. With Peter and Alice. I can't rely on the Hamiltons to keep a roof over my head for ever.'

His face turned an ugly shade of red. 'That's absurd. Why would you think I'd move out and let you stay here instead? Where do you expect me to go?'

Lillian tried hard not to scowl at him. If she lost her composure, she would threaten her own plan. 'Ask Fergus, since he seems to be so keen to help you. Perhaps you can stay in the Shaw's stable? I've been inside. There's a loft that looks comfortable enough.'

There was no need to tell him she had visited that space

with Donald not so long ago. She watched Alfred's usual anger begin to rise. A lashing was the least of her fears. His face contorted and she felt a pang of fear for the children if he decided to refuse her risky request.

He spat on the dirt. 'I need some time to think about this. Can't say I'm happy about it. I saw you with that baby at Patricia's funeral. You're going to bring more in, aren't you?'

Lillian fixed him with a withering look. 'Absolutely not. You did a terrible thing making Patricia look after all those poor, innocent babies. You put your own comfort ahead of their wellbeing. I'll never forgive you for any of it.'

Alfred appeared incensed by her accusations. 'You're a bloody bitch, you know that? If Peter weren't on the porch, I'd give you a hiding.'

Lillian didn't budge. 'You have until the end of the week.' She looked past him and beckoned her nephew with her finger. 'Peter, come with me. Your papa has to go to work.'

The child hurried off the porch and glanced anxiously up at his father for confirmation.

He nodded sourly. 'Go with Aunt Lillian.'

Lillian and Peter hurried back to Vulture Street. The boy was pensive and she knew she had some explaining to do. Not telling him beforehand had been unfortunate yet necessary. She couldn't risk him spoiling everything by blurting out the plan. A small spark of happiness ignited within her. She recalled her mother's old lesson on love, which had been whispered under their bedcovers on many dark nights. The words easily sprang to mind and Lillian recited them under her breath as the Hamiltons' house appeared over the horizon. '*Some say love is like fools' gold – shiny, glittering and exciting – but a*

chunk of iron pyrite is disappointing and useless. You want the type of love you find to be soft and malleable like real gold. That kind of love will never lose its glitter. It pays to be careful about telling others what you've discovered because if you make a mistake they'll laugh and shake their head at your disappointment.'

Lillian picked up her skirt and began to skip, revelling in the warmth of Peter's small hand in hers. Nobody would replace her sister but maybe she still had enough love surrounding her to be able to continue living? The Hamiltons had been so kind. Peter and Alice needed her to be their mother. A husband would be a luxury.

CHAPTER 21

TWIST OF FATE

Florence came running outside. Lillian was sitting on a loveseat beneath a flowering purple bougainvillea arbour, whispering childhood tales in Alice's ear while the boys played. The little girl had grown strong enough to be able to sit stoutly upon her knee. Lillian thought she was adorable.

'Lillian! Someone is here to see you.'

'Is it Alfred?' She was not looking forward to returning to Montague Road to find out his decision.

Florence seemed flustered. 'No, it's not. He says his name is Mr Shaw and he has a delivery for you.'

It was Fergus then. She'd begun to lose hope. The week of no news had been difficult to take. Perhaps he would be the bearer of the news and she wouldn't have to wait any longer?

Florence reached out to take Alice. 'You'd better hurry. He seems impatient.'

Lillian gently handed the baby over, uncurling pudgy fingers caught in her hair. Entering the house, she glanced at the small clock on the sideboard. The hands showed half past four. Her stomach flipped. Nicholas would be home soon. She didn't want him to come across Fergus.

However, it was Donald who stood up as she entered the drawing-room. She stopped short.

'Hello, Lillian.'

'Oh!' The sight of him brought an unwelcome and familiar jolt of affection despite herself. 'It's you.'

He looked at her hopefully. 'I know you weren't expecting me.'

'Florence said Mr Shaw was here. I thought she meant your brother.' Lillian was annoyed to hear her voice sounding so breathy. 'I suspected he might have had a message from Alfred for me.' She swallowed hard, sat herself in Jonathan's comfortable armchair and gestured toward the chaise. 'Please, do sit down. I didn't think you would be the one delivering the news.'

'How are you keeping?' Donald took a seat and took in the surroundings before letting his gaze settle on her. 'I'm so sorry about your sister and nephew. I know how close you two were.'

She looked at him steadily. He would not know how much his condolence pained her. 'We were. I'm doing as well as can be expected.'

'My mother – '

Lillian held up her hands. 'It doesn't matter, Donald. There's no point in bringing up the past. I've made my peace with it.'

Donald looked down at the whorls on the carpet. 'I didn't believe her. I know you wouldn't have stolen anything.'

Lillian rolled her eyes. 'Perhaps you don't know me very well, after all.'

His head snapped up with surprise. 'So you did?'

'What did you expect? I earned a pittance and every penny went towards supporting my family.'

Donald was silent for a moment. 'Olivia said she saw you at the theatre.'

She pressed her lips together. There was no point telling him his sister had viciously poked her in the ribs with a parasol. She merely nodded and changed the subject. 'How is Miss Forsyth?'

Donald reddened and struggled to meet her eye. He reminded Lillian of the simpering young woman who had been unable to take her eyes off the carpet the first day they had met. He and Mary were obviously cut from the same cloth. 'Very well. Actually, I wanted to be the first to tell you. Mary and I are engaged to be married.'

'Congratulations.'

'Lillian.' He reached for his pocket watch and fumbled with it. 'I'm sorry for... the way I treated you.'

She tried to hide her disdain at his unexpected apology. 'Please, there's no need.' The clock on the sideboard chimed and made her squirm. She felt overcome with tiredness. 'Why have you come?'

Donald reached into his trouser pocket and retrieved a key. 'Alfred has decided to let you stay in the house for Peter's sake.'

'And where will he be staying?'

'There is room at our house while he's helping with the building. Papa said it made sense to have him close by.'

'And your mother?'

'Fergus talked to her.'

Lillian gazed at him coolly. 'Why are you helping him?'

'Alfred?'

'Who else?'

'Fergus is the one feeling sorry for him. He feels guilty for the way Alfred lost his job.' Donald paused for a moment. 'You see, it wasn't Alfred's fault.'

'It wasn't?'

'No.'

Lillian waited, curious and strangely agitated about hearing what he might say. Nicholas would surely be arriving home soon. Donald looked uncomfortable but he wouldn't elaborate. It occurred to her he felt as protective of his brother as she had about her sister.

At last, he held out his hand. 'Here. This is for you.'

She hid a smirk as she took the key from him. Mary's brooch was the last thing he'd offered her. She stood up. 'Thank you, Donald. You really didn't have to come. You could have posted it.'

'Fergus was going to but I said I would personally deliver it. The truth is I wanted to see you.'

'You did?' She clutched the little key tightly and felt an unwelcome little thrill. Donald rose from his seat, reached out and stroked a wisp of hair from her cheek.

'I miss you,' he said, taking a step closer.

Lillian felt her throat tighten. She thought she had put her feelings for him behind her.

'What's happening in here?'

She gasped and retreated. Nicholas stood in the doorway, looking angry.

She held up the key. 'Don... Mr Shaw was bringing the key to Patricia's cottage. Alfred has given permission for me to stay there and care for the children.'

'And how do you intend to continue with your apprentice-ship if you do that?' Nicholas growled.

Lillian swallowed. She had not fully worked out the details. All she knew was that she wasn't going to give Peter and Alice up. Alfred would never take Alice to care for as his own, even if he were able to be trusted. She had hoped to pay someone to watch them while she continued learning from Dorothy, though on her apprentice wage it would be difficult.

'Perhaps it is for the best.' Nicholas glared at her. 'If you'll please excuse me.' He headed straight for his room.

Flustered, Lillian turned back to Donald. 'Thank you again for bringing the key. It was good to see you.' She found that she meant it. 'Let me show you out.'

He looked confused. 'Did I do something wrong?'

'Donald,' Lillian exclaimed, laughing with exasperation. 'I forgive you, but for the love of everything good in my life, you must go.'

She ushered him out the front door and watched him mount his mare to be sure he was really going to leave.

He gazed down at her. 'Goodbye. Lillian. I fear this may be the last time I say it.'

'It is for the best.' Lillian released a deep breath as he rode off and strode back inside.

'Nicholas? Could I have a word?'

He opened his bedroom door wearing an inscrutable expression.

'I owe you an explanation,' Lillian said.

'No, you don't.'

'I do, and you are jolly well going to listen to it.' She was sick of being dismissed.

Taken aback at her assertiveness, Nicholas stayed quiet.

'You know I used to work for Donald's family. He used to, well,' she began hesitantly, blushing, unsure how to continue, 'toy with me.'

Nicholas folded his arms.

'I thought Donald liked me but I was a silly little fool.' There, she'd said it.

'From what I could see, it appears he still does.'

'No, he doesn't. He's engaged to Miss Mary Forsyth.'

'Then why was he taking the liberty of touching your cheek? I saw the way he was looking at you. You're lucky it was me and not my father who walked in.'

Lillian nodded at the truth of what he said. She was indeed extremely grateful although still embarrassed.

'Donald was mistaken.'

'Was he?'

'Definitely!'

Nicholas cocked his head. 'Are you sure?'

'Of course I'm sure. He made me very unhappy once. I'll not put up with anyone who doesn't respect me ever again.' She felt quite indignant he wasn't believing her.

'Did he ever..?'

Her eyes widened at the suggestion. 'No! I can assure you it never came to that. I wouldn't allow him.'

Nicholas relaxed his shoulders and unfolded his arms. 'I was hoping you would say so. I will have to take your word, I suppose.'

'I'm telling the truth!'

'Lillian Betts, you think I don't know you're a thief and a liar?'

She was concerned to understand he'd seen through her, after all. 'I am not!'

'Yes you are. Don't take me for a fool. Matthew told me what happened. Rosemary heard from Catherine how you stole from the Shaw's yet both of you ended up dismissed. That's why she was looking sour at the theatre. I don't think she's been able to forgive you for what happened. She's not as even-keeled as Catherine. Did you think I wouldn't find out? I've been waiting patiently for you to confess and you never have. Do I think it was a coincidence you happened to walk into my parents' store and ask for an apprenticeship? No, of course not!'

Lillian felt helpless under his onslaught.

His eyes flashed as he continued. 'I thought you might have said something at your sister's house. I'd figured it out and you knew it but still you said nothing. You knew my little boy before I did. You knew how in debt we were to your sister and you took full advantage of that knowledge to wheedle your way into my family.'

Shame filled her and she covered her face with her hands, defeated. 'Do you hate me, Nicholas?'

'Hate you?' He strode over to his dresser to pull open the top drawer and retrieve something before returning. 'It would be easier if that were so. Since I returned home from England and saw you standing in our kitchen, I have been unable to think of anything or anyone else. For God's sake, I thought of you when I was in London and Paris when I should have been still been grieving for my wife. And now I see I shall have to hurry before somebody else comes along to snatch you up.'

Lillian watched in astonishment as Nicholas lowered himself on to one knee and revealed a small box nestled in his palm.

He released the catch to reveal a diamond ring. 'Lillian Betts, will you marry me?'

She stared at the precious stone shaped like a teardrop and set in rose gold. It was exquisite. Donald's brooch for Mary paled in comparison. She stooped and flung her arms around Nicholas's neck. 'Yes, I will. Of course I will. I want you more than anything in this world.'

He slid the ring on to her finger and rose to take her in his arms.

She pulled back and held up the key. 'What am I meant to do with this?'

'Keep it for a while. Alfred doesn't need to know just yet. He can suffer for a while longer.'

Before closing her eyes to meet his lips, Lillian caught sight of Molly's portrait hanging on the wall staring down at them. She hoped the ghosts she and Nicholas shared would some day release their hold and allow them a future of happiness together.

CHAPTER 22

CELEBRATION

They were married on the Hamiltons' back lawn beneath the arch laden with bougainvillea. Mercifully, Alice slept in Dorothy's arms throughout the whole ceremony. Peter and Stephen took up their duties as pageboys, standing by Nicholas in front of a large group of gathered witnesses. The Hamiltons had many friends and all were pleased to be celebrating after the difficult time they'd had cleaning up after the flood. Florence eagerly embraced her position as maid of honour and Lillian tried extremely hard not to resent Nicholas's caring and sensitive sister for not being Patricia. She, herself, wore a gown of ivory silk, which Dorothy and Florence had made for her. It was the most beautiful thing she had ever seen in her life.

She had been doubtful that all would go as intended until the very moment Nicholas slid the gold band on to her finger. There was much to cause her worry. Fears of Alfred changing his mind about letting her be Peter's guardian kept Lillian awake most nights. It was usually Peter who woke her early each morning hungry for his breakfast. He peered across the bed with almond-shaped eyes like his mother's and gave her the courage to get up. Alfred's threat, thrown out in a fit of rage not so long ago to confess Lillian's own part in their baby-farming enterprise, kept her checking over her shoulder every time she ventured into the streets in case a policeman should be about to tap her on the shoulder. After all, her brother-in-law had never given her any reason to trust him.

On their wedding day, Lillian shared none of those anxieties with Nicholas. It seemed the baby farm was one secret he hadn't discovered. Since she'd accepted his proposal, the solemn pall of intense mourning had quietly been replaced by excitement.

On their wedding night, she moved back into Nicholas's bedroom. As she sat waiting expectantly, he reached beneath the bed and withdrew a wrapped gift box.

He carefully placed it on her lap. 'This is for you.'

Lillian ran her hands over the floral paper.

'Open it,' he said.

She carefully undid the ribbon and pulled away the wrapping to reveal a polished cherrywood box. Nicholas reached over and unfastened the catch. She lifted the lid and her breath caught. There inside was an array of brand-new watercolours and brushes. Beneath the box, her husband had added a new sketch book.

'They're beautiful!' She couldn't bring herself to look up. 'I didn't get you anything.'

He pulled her into his chest. 'Lillian, you reminded me that life was worth living. That has been the greatest gift you could ever give me. You have a talent and it is a shame you have never been given the pleasure of owning your own set.'

She buried her face into his neck to hide her embarrassment and thought of her original sketchbook. What had Mrs

Shaw done with it? She supposed the spiteful woman had burned it in the drawing-room fireplace.

Nicholas lazily dragged a finger across the nape of her neck. 'Come here, my beautiful wife.'

She delighted in his light touch and waited as he loosened the ribbon on her nightgown. He pulled the shift over her head and she sat before him naked as he appreciated her pert breasts and gently curving belly.

'May I continue?'

She bit her lip to disguise her mirth. Some things about her past she was determined to keep close to her chest – even from her husband. Demurely, she looked up from beneath her lashes into his sweet face as he gently laid her down upon the fresh sheet. As he stretched out beside her she twisted and straddled him, excited to see the wonder in his eyes. Perhaps she would guard her origins by never speaking of them but there were other ways to honour the past. Her keen observations had stood her in good stead while learning in the classroom, but her education extended much farther than that. She was a harlot's daughter and, that night, her husband would receive some lessons to make him forget he had bedded a respectable woman.

CHAPTER 23

HONEYMOON

*L*illian saw Florence suppress an amused giggle as she and Nicholas entered the dining room the following morning. She had felt a tinge of regret while packing up her things and moving next door; sharing a room had kept her nightmares at bay. Florence had tried her best to gently rouse her when the fear threatened to take over and hugged her when it did.

As a common wall separated the two rooms it was not difficult to figure out why Nicholas's sister was squirming in her seat. Her husband's groan of spent pleasure had loudly filled their bedroom. Afterwards he had slept soundly while she lay awake, pleased with herself for so clearly satisfying him. While their lovemaking had been painful at first, she knew she would grow to enjoy it immensely.

Nicholas had woken her with a wounded expression in the morning. She had to promise him of her virginity for a second time, explaining her knowledge had come from reading clandestine books in the libraries of the houses in which she had worked. It was hard to tell if he'd been convinced of the physiological truth but her conscience in that matter was clear and she would strongly defend it. The depth of feeling she held for her husband made her dalliances with Donald pale into insignificance. It felt suspiciously like true and trustworthy love.

They were a ready-made family of five but, unlike her sister's marriage, sharing the care of the children with Lucy, Dorothy and Florence gave Lillian enough time for some leisure. Her apprenticeship was no longer required but she asked Dorothy if she could continue with her tutelage. Lillian was determined to become an expert at designing and sewing fashionable gowns.

Despite the economic depression continuing to sour the lives of many in the suburb and the broken bridge restricting crossings to the ferries alone, there was no shortage of well-to-do customers placing orders at the Hamiltons' newly refurbished store. Nicholas and Jonathan had successfully restocked the showroom with the bolts of fabric Dorothy had fastidiously catalogued. Florence returned to the store to serve customers while Lillian fit her sewing around caring for the children when Lucy had other chores to attend to.

Despite her good fortune, she felt increasingly restricted living under the same roof as her in-laws and longed for a place for her and Nicholas to call their own. Given the opportunity, she preferred to head out to find a park to use her new paints and sketchbook in peace and capture something of the natural environment she found so soothing.

As the weeks passed it was clear Dorothy had begun to monitor her appearance each morning at the breakfast table, waiting for tell-tale signs of nausea. Her mother-in-law would be sorely disappointed if she thought she was going to receive another grandchild any time soon. Like the tricks Lillian performed in her marital bed, her life lessons included wisdom for preventing conception. Although Nicholas had since removed Molly's photo from the wall and replaced it with one from their own wedding day, the spectre of her predecessor weighed heavily on her mind.

Each night she soaked a little sponge she had obtained from Mrs Carter in vinegar and inserted it before Nicholas came to bed. She intended to use the method for as long as was possible to get away with. Even Alfred and Patricia had enjoyed some early days of bliss within their marriage before the relentlessness of babies took up all her sister's attention. There were already enough children in her and Nicholas's life. Uninterrupted time with her husband was precious.

Lillian considered the agreement she had made with Alfred to stay at the cottage with Peter, and by default, Alice, in order to provide a familiar setting and hopefully alleviate the little boy's grief. That had been before Nicholas's proposal. She didn't want to live in the Montague Road cottage anymore. Alfred would be snatching it back as soon as he found out about the wedding. She would have to talk with Nicholas and see if they could find somewhere else to set up the home she so desperately desired. First, she needed to find out why Alfred had sent her a telegram telling her to meet him at Rosemead.

Lillian asked Lucy to watch the children while Nicholas was at work. She didn't want to worry her husband. Going the long way, heading east along Vulture Street before turning north into Main Street, it felt strange to find herself navigating the familiar streets at Kangaroo Point again. As she neared Shafston Road each step on the road drummed a rhythm on the footpath: turn back, turn back. Lillian pushed on with determination until the long picket fence rose into view. The sound of hammering and sawing echoed about as she strolled up the driveway and stood in front of the stable.

Although it was probably a waste of time, Lillian had continued to mull over her lost sketchbook. She wished there was some way to be sure it had been destroyed and, if it hadn't, she wanted it back. There was also another pressing reason for her visit. She had decided to give Alfred the key back to his cottage before he could ask for it. She wasn't going to let him think he had any control over her ever again.

She hardly dared to cast a look around in case Mrs Shaw or Olivia caught sight of her or, worse yet, Donald. Alfred stood astride two rafters high up in the frame of the new extension. As far as Lillian could tell there was no indication that either the stable or the house had been affected by the flood at all. The garden lay in full bloom and the heady scent of frangipani brought back conflicting feelings. The surroundings reminded Lillian of Catherine and she acknowledged missing her old friend. Florence had been so kind as to share her room but she was still young and naïve, without the worldly wisdom Catherine had once shared with her in the dark space between their beds. She risked a look up at the house and found the small window. The curtains were closed.

Lillian knew Alfred had seen her but he took his time hammering a row of nails into the timber before raising a hand in greeting. She felt on edge as he descended the ladder. Surely he understood she would rather not linger there any longer than necessary. Perhaps that was exactly why he dawdled? Perspiration dripped down his face and soaked into his shirt collar.

He wiped his sleeve across his face. 'You got my telegram, then?'

Lillian screened her eyes against the midday glare and nodded.

'How's my boy?'

She knew she had to keep civil. 'Peter is fine. You're welcome to visit.'

Alfred scratched his chin and nodded. 'Perhaps next week. Have you come to give me my house back?'

Lillian held up the key. 'Yes, in fact I have. The house is yours, after all, and you should live there.'

Alfred blinked with surprise yet answered with sarcasm. 'What about you?'

Lillian stood as straight as she could. 'Nicholas Hamilton and I were married last week. I would like Peter to stay with us.'

'Well, well. I suppose you expect me to offer my congratulations, Lillian. You've certainly come up in this world.'

She would not rise to the bait. 'Why did you want to see me, Alfred? Surely you didn't have me come all the way over here simply to ask after Peter?'

Alfred studied her. 'I found some things that belong to you.'

Lillian tried not to sound hopeful. 'What are they?'

'A couple of books.'

He was standing uncomfortably close. She pressed her lips together against the whiff of whisky on his breath.

'How did you know they were mine?'

'I have my ways.'

'Where are they?'

'In your special hiding place.' Alfred smirked and jutted his jaw towards the stable door. 'Go and get them yourself. It's what you were hoping for, isn't it? I saw how you always wanted to be off somewhere painting rather than helping your sister. Waste of bloody time, if you ask me. I knew you wouldn't be able to resist coming all the way over here if there was a possibility I knew where they were.' Alfred scoffed and spat on the ground. 'I can read you like a book, Lillian.'

She might have been busy painting but there was no point reminding him he'd been off drinking at the hotel. What good would it do now? She peered through the open stable door.

'The other bloke's gone to get some more nails and lining so you'd better hurry up before he gets back and I have to explain what the hell you're doing here.' Alfred put his boot on the ladder's lowest rung.

Lillian glanced back at the house again.

He drew his mouth into a sneer. 'Donald's not home. None of them are. Mrs Shaw and her stuck-up-bitch of a daughter could be back soon, though. They've already been gone a couple of hours to some fancy luncheon or other. I reckon I could guarantee you're not at the top of their list for visitors and I'd like to keep my job, thanks very much. So get on with whatever you have to do. I've got to get back up on the roof.'

Lillian didn't waste another second. As Alfred clambered up the ladder, she slid the heavy door aside and crept inside. The familiar scent of straw and manure filled her nostrils as she hurried over to the back stall. Everything seemed to be more or less in the same place as the day Donald had led her inside and revealed the brooch intended for Mary. She snuck over to the stall with the loose board and tugged at the one in the middle at the sound of Alfred resuming his hammering. Reaching into the void, she felt, there beneath her fingers, the sketchbook wrapped in a piece of calico. The last time she'd seen it, Mrs Shaw had been poring through the pages with disgust. That fortune kept favouring her was unsettling. Perhaps penance had been paid the day she buried her sister? Her book, *Pinocchio*, was still there as well and she pulled it out.

There was no sign of her photograph and she hadn't expected it to be there. If only she could have a memory of her mother and sister to hold on to. Had Catherine found it and chosen to take it with her? She knew how important the picture was to Lillian.

A curse rang out, followed by an alarmed shout. A series of thumps escalated down the unfinished roof and an almighty crash sounded just behind the stable wall. Lillian rushed outside and heard Alfred moaning somewhere in the shrubbery.

'Alfred!'

She found him lying prostrate on the ground noisily trying to suck in gulps of air. His right leg was splayed at a painfully unnatural angle.

Despite her hatred, instinct caused Lillian to spring into action. 'Stay still. I'll go get help.' She raced to the back door and pounded on it hoping to find Mrs Menzies working in the kitchen. There was no answer to her distressed calls. She rushed back to Alfred and saw rivulets of blood had begun to trickle from his ears and nostrils.

Lillian carefully clasped his hand and considered what else could be done. If she raced to the hospital one of the doctors might be entreated to come and help him. Or she could wait until the other labourer returned, which Alfred had said could be any minute.

During her frantic mental deliberations, Alfred's eyes closed. He was hyperventilating as he tried to form words with his lips. Lillian put her ear to his mouth in an effort to decipher them. Two syllables reverberated and she sat up, startled.

'Fer-gus... at the cottage...bag...'

'I don't understand. Fergus? What bag?'

Alfred winced. The effort of speaking was taking its toll. 'Just tell him, you little bitch,' he spat.

Tears of pain slid down the sides of his face and mingled with his blood.

Lillian picked the sketchbook and her copy of *Pinocchio* up off the gravel before giving her brother-in-law a final, regretful look. Like the Shaws, her husband and the rest of his family would soon be getting home.

'Don't move, Alfred. I'm going to get some help.' She had to hurry if she was going to get to the hospital and then get home. Nicholas and Florence would be wondering where she'd got to. She didn't intend to leave her name with a doctor; it was better that way. It was time to leave Rosemead, that deliverer of rogue justice. The place had done nothing but taint everything good in her life and she was glad to say goodbye. Even though she felt nothing but anger toward Alfred, she refused to sink to his level.

CHAPTER 24

SOUTH BRISBANE

'*D*orothy, there's something I've been thinking about and I'd like to tell you about it,' Lillian said, as she stitched up a hem.

Nicholas's mother lifted her foot from the sewing machine pedal and looked at her. 'What is it, dear?'

'I have an idea about what to do with Patricia and Alfred's house.'

Dorothy peered at the new row of stitches she had sewn. 'I imagine that place holds a great many memories for you.'

Lillian nodded carefully.

'How does it look now it's been cleaned up?'

'It still needs new wallpaper hung and there were only a few pieces of furniture worth saving. The problem is there's still a mortgage to pay, which Alfred was taking care of until he had his accident.'

'Yes, wasn't that dreadful? I suppose the children were fortunate not to lose him entirely. What a thing to happen, falling off the roof like that.'

Lillian looked up and found Dorothy staring at her, a glint

in her eye. Exactly how much did she know about Alfred and Patricia? What passed between them did not need saying aloud. Her mother-in-law had obviously noticed Patricia's bruised face the day she'd come to collect baby Stephen. Lillian pondered whether that was the reason why Dorothy hadn't insisted she and the children return into Alfred's care after the flood had receded and his release from the watch house had been secured. Mrs Hamilton was a charitable woman indeed. She put the contemptuous Mrs Shaw to shame.

Before leaving Alfred, Lillian had found the key in his pocket and run to the hospital. She'd run right up to the entrance and found a nurse to tell her about his fall and where he could be found. An ambulance was quickly dispatched and, as the horse and cart turned up the road, she melted into the grounds and headed at the last minute to Montague Road; there was nothing more she could do.

Donald had been the one to turn up at the Hamiltons' house bringing the news of Alfred's accident only two hours after she had returned from her outing. Not long back from work, Nicholas had opened the door at the knock and she'd watched the two men warily eye each other up. Lillian didn't have to try too hard to look distressed. She had seen Alfred's injuries, after all.

Donald told them he'd arrived home and found an ambulance parked in the driveway and a doctor and a nurse attending to Alfred. He told Lillian and Nicholas he'd come straight to them the moment the doctor had assured him Alfred would pull through, but not without the real possibility of a brain injury. Fergus had come home shortly after and was still at Alfred's side.

Lillian had felt quite shaken after the retelling of events. Nicholas had thanked Donald and then led her to the couch to recover. Alfred had survived. As the weeks passed and Alfred regained his senses, it became clear he had no memory of the accident at all. Traumatic amnesia, the doctors had explained. Lillian had risked a visit to the hospital to see the patient for herself and only after probing him with questions was she convinced her secret would remain safe. Each time she felt her conscience pricked about being at the Shaws' in the first place she took out her old sketchbook and looked at her early paintings. It had been the right thing to do.

The next time she heard from Donald was via a short telegram alerting her to Alfred's transfer to Dunwich Benevolent Asylum. With his broken leg and brain and still ever-reliant on his whisky, it was the safest place for Alfred to stay. She no longer had to worry whether he would change his mind about taking the children. Patients admitted to the Stradbroke Island sanatorium rarely returned to the mainland.

The next day Lillian had penned a letter asking for the name on the mortgage to be transferred into her name. The serious head injury Alfred had suffered from falling ensured he would not be troubling either her or Peter again. Dunwich Asylum on Stradbroke Island was the best place for him. It had been no trouble to forge Alfred's signature and have the correspondence delivered to Fergus at his office. In it, she explained Alfred had confessed to her the true nature of their relationship, one she hoped she had rightly guessed as criminal. What sort of racketeering, it was impossible to know for sure. She thought the white lie would ensure a prompt carrying out of the rest of the letter's instructions and she'd been proven right. She had sent Alfred some money, both to attend to his needs on the island and alleviate her guilt.

'Do you intend to sell it?' Dorothy asked.

'No, but I do need to think of a way for the place to pay for itself.' A small smile played at her lips. 'I was thinking of turning it into a shop.'

'A shop? What will you be selling?'

'A dress shop, of course. A showcase for all our dresses!' Lillian squealed.

'A real shop?'

'Yes. What do you think?'

'Oh my. Have you told Nicholas?'

'Not yet. I wanted to see what you thought before I broached the subject with him. You know how cautious he can be about new ideas. You've been so kind teaching me new skills so I didn't have to go back to being a housemaid, then welcoming me as Nicholas's wife. A little shop would be something you and I could run together, if you wanted to, that is.'

The older woman reached out and patted Lillian's knee. 'I've really got my hands rather full, dear. Would you consider Florence, perhaps? I'm afraid she's become rather bored in the store lately, keeps talking about wanting to travel abroad. This idea of yours might be the perfect solution, an exciting new business you could build together. Well! Fancy that. A real dress shop.'

Lillian understood what Dorothy meant. Florence continued to pester Nicholas with questions about London. Her head turned at anybody who happened to mention they were sailing off to Europe. She could understand Dorothy's fear of losing her daughter to another continent. Florence would be very useful in the shop. She was industrious and an accomplished seamstress, more so than Lillian herself, due to the extra years of tutelage. It would give Lillian time to do what she wanted, which was designing.

'Will you manage without us?'

Dorothy smiled. 'I'll advertise for another apprentice if I need to.'

Lillian leapt up from her seat. 'I want to show you something.'

Rushing to the bedroom she shared with Nicholas, she retrieved the sketchbook he had given her on their wedding night. She hurried back to the drawing-room and dropped it on to Dorothy's lap.

The older woman looked up with surprise. 'What's all this?'

'I've been working on the layout.' She flipped through the pages then stopped to reveal a floorplan. 'Look, there. We could use one of the front rooms as a display area and the other for a fitting room. If we remove the wall between the kitchen and the parlour, we could have a workshop at the back.' Now that Lillian had shared her idea with Dorothy, she felt even more excited. She had been worried earlier her mother-in-law might think the whole concept ludicrous. Her interested expression said otherwise.

~

While Dorothy had been enthusiastic about the idea for the dress shop, Nicholas, as expected, was more circumspect.

'Are you sure? Won't that be difficult returning to work at the house after everything you've been through?'

Lillian shook her head emphatically. 'Darling, you know I miss my sister every day. And yes, it was truly shocking Alfred had that fall so soon after –'

Nicholas scoffed. 'Ha! I'm sure you're devastated. I still can't work out how you managed to get the house signed over into your name.'

She swatted at his shoulder. 'He agreed to do it to secure Peter's future and so the government wouldn't take it to fund his keep at Dunwich. Won't you at least think about my idea?'

'Who'll look after our three children if you're out working all day?'

'We'll be able to hire a governess.'

'I hate to tell you, Lillian, but we're hardly members of the upper class. Just because some other women have decided to fancy themselves with a little shop to pass the time, it doesn't mean you must.'

She found it hard not to take offence at his dismissiveness. 'Your mother hired one for Stephen.'

Nicholas frowned. 'That was different. His mother died.'

'Please, Nicholas, let me at least show you my drawings? Your mother thought it was a good idea.'

'Oh, ho. Now the truth comes out. So you've already discussed it with her before you thought to check with your husband?'

Lillian rushed to their room to grab the sketchbook he had given her and quickly brought it back. She knew he was softening. Nicholas thumbed through the pages filled with watercolours of the latest dresses she and Florence would be able to whip up in no time.

'I can see you've been putting your wedding gift to good use.' He carefully closed the book. 'Very well. I can see you've put a lot of thought into your plans. You'll need some good shelving installed.'

'And a workbench, and mannequins and a sign to hang out the front!'

'Yes, there's quite a lot to think about.'

'So can we?' Lillian pressed her palms together as if in prayer. 'Please?'

Nicholas laughed. 'Very well. Let's give it six months and see how it goes. If the shop ends up running at a loss, then will you promise to consider selling the cottage? We could certainly use the money to reduce our mortgage.'

She crossed her arms. 'I won't need to because it's going to be the best dress shop in South Brisbane. Florence is going to help.'

'My sister has been plotting against me as well?' Nicholas threw up his hands. 'I give up.'

Lillian grabbed his waistcoat and pulled him close to kiss him. 'I love you, dear husband.'

Nicholas agreed to pay for an extra governess to assist Lucy in looking after the children while she and Florence spent four days with their sleeves rolled up to their elbows and petticoats tucked into their drawers, scrubbing the last traces of silt from the walls and furniture. They agreed the kitchen table should stay to serve as a workbench. When their orders grew, they would invest in a new one. Lillian was secretly pleased to keep it. It reminded her of the conversations she and Patricia used to have sitting at it drinking tea. In one small way at least, her sister was still with her. She hoped Patricia would be proud of what she was setting out to do. She missed her terribly.

They decided to paint the tongue-and-groove walls rather than repapering and selected a cheery lemon yellow for the purpose. The result lightened the previously dark rooms and lent an air of spaciousness to the place. Nicholas sawed out a wide gap between the kitchen and parlour and lined the walls with pine shelving to hold jars of thread, buttons and hooks.

Jonathan appeared in the carriage one afternoon carrying two mannequins from his own store. They dressed the first with a waist-shirt and navy bell skirt and covered both garments with a royal-blue frock coat. The second they adorned with a deep-purple velvet dress and hoped the contrasting styles would appeal to both younger and more mature customers.

'We'll call the blue gown the 'Georgina' and the purple one the 'Penelope',' said Lillian. She folded her arms, resolute.

'That's a lovely idea!' Florence exclaimed with a grin. 'Each design shall have its own name. I wish I'd thought of it myself.'

Lillian secretly stitched tiny baby booties emblems into the bodice of each dress.

When everything had been done, Lillian stood on the front porch and took a big breath before entering. As she took in the surroundings, it became clear her sister's spirit did not dwell within those walls. She'd experienced the same feeling when her mother had passed away, when she and Patricia had come to clear away the last of her things to vacate the room for another woman. The place they'd so closely associated with their mother all their life and couldn't imagine belonging to anyone else had in fact become an empty husk. Like that single room, the hollowed-out cottage had released her sister. In its place, Lillian saw potential for her dream to arise – a way to ensure her future. She gazed at the shop's beautiful interior and, for the first time since the death of Patricia and Thomas, sweet calm descended.

When the bell above the entrance tinkled several weeks after opening, Lillian was sitting at the workbench embroidering a cuff. A beautifully dressed woman stepped inside and investigated the clothed mannequins with interest, reaching out and touching the blue frock coat.

Lillian stood to greet her, gulping with dread. Standing before her was Cora Miles, the guest who'd arrived late to Mrs Shaw's luncheon and bearing the very same baby Lillian had abandoned in Dutton Park. 'May I help you?'

The woman's fingers fluttered at her chest. 'Oh, yes! Gosh,

you gave me a fright. I didn't see you there. Ahem. I would like a new gown. My friend, Mrs Susannah Hayes, ordered a dress from your establishment and debuted it at the theatre last night. She was quite the centre of attention and I had to beg her to tell me where she had bought it.'

'That's wonderful to hear.' Lillian struggled to maintain eye contact with the woman. Despite the many months that had passed, she had not forgotten the familiar face. 'Why don't you let me get Miss Hamilton for you? She was the one who made Mrs Hayes's dress.'

Lillian quickly retreated out back where Florence had taken a chair out into the yard to sit and drink her tea on her break. 'We have a customer.'

Florence was nonplussed. 'Why don't you take care of her?'

'She mentioned Mrs Hayes's dress. I thought it best she speak with you.'

'Fine.' Florence put down her cup. 'I'll be right in.'

Lillian felt a stab of guilt for cutting short Florence's break but she needed some time to gather her composure. What if Cora remembered her?

Florence breezed in. 'Hello, Mrs...?'

'Mrs Cora Miles.'

'A pleasure to meet you. My sister-in-law tells me you're a friend of Mrs Hayes?'

'That's correct,' Cora said and laughed. 'If Susannah thought she'd be able to keep her wondrous new dressmaker a secret from me... I wasn't going to let her leave last night until I had a name. I must say, your attention to detail is extraordinary.'

'Thank you very much.' Florence glowed at the praise.

'Susannah's dress fitted her so perfectly, I knew I simply had to come to see for myself.' Cora leant in conspiratorially. 'Between you and me it's nothing short of miraculous the way you were able to minimise her backside and maximise her bust.'

If Florence was amused by such an accurate observation she kept it to herself. 'A good design will bring out the best features of any woman,' she said. 'Whatever you would like, you shall have.'

Cora broke into a smile. 'That's exactly why I'm here.'

'I will need to take your measurements first. Please step over to the mirror.'

Lillian edged in and watched Florence remove her ever-present tape measure from about her neck and expertly take measurements from Cora's slender waist, hips and bust line while she obediently stood still.

Next, Florence retrieved several bolts of new-season fabric from the rows of shelving along the wall. 'What do you think of this silk poplin? No? How about the taffeta with broad stripes? You could have a velvet jacket in the magenta. The colour suits your complexion.'

Cora twisted this way and that in front of the looking glass as Florence draped one fabric after the other around her shoulders.

'Oh yes, I do like that. The sleeves must be puffed. The bigger the better.'

'Yes, of course.'

Florence placed the taffeta and velvet fabric bolts on the counter. 'You know, a lace frill about the neck and cuffs would really give it something extra.'

Cora clapped excitedly. 'I do love lace.'

'Come and see our selection.' Florence led her to the glass display cabinet.

Lillian had to admire her sister-in-law's entrepreneurship. While a talented seamstress, Florence never missed an opportunity to squeeze every last shilling from their customers.

'Lillian, could you please assist me at the register?'
Florence's voice held a tinge of reproach.

Lillian quickly tallied the final amount on the till and
handed Cora Miles her invoice.

'If you'd like to leave your address I'll have Lillian here
deliver your new dress to you personally and take care of any
last-minute adjustments that may need to be made,' Florence
offered.

Cora's eyes widened. 'Would you really? That would be
very convenient.'

A thread of curiosity wove its way through Lillian's mind.
Despite her fear of being recognised by Cora as the once-lowly
housemaid who had changed her son's soiled napkin, there lay
her opportunity to catch a glimpse of Alexander again.

Cora released the catch on her reticule and retrieved some
money for payment as well as a calling card. She placed them
on the counter.

Lillian placed the notes in the till and held the card
nonchalantly between her thumb and forefinger. 'Thank you,
Mrs Miles.'

'No. Thank you, ladies, for your help. I can't wait to see my
new dress!'

As soon as Cora had left the shop, Florence and Lillian
bent their heads over the card to read the inscription. Grey
Street! The fancy address belonged to exactly the type of
customer they were hoping to attract, ones with plenty of
money.

'Why did you say I'd pay her a house call? We don't offer
that service,' Lillian couldn't help muttering.

Florence turned to her and grinned. 'We do now.'

While their shop was in an unlikely location, Lillian had
hoped it might help them to become known as one of Brisbane's
best-kept secrets, letting the society ladies pass on knowledge of

its existence by exclusive word of mouth. First Susannah Hayes and now Cora Miles. Her plan seemed to be paying off already.

Lillian wished there was a way to disguise who she'd once been. She'd taken great pains to change her appearance since marrying Nicholas, piling her hair fashionably high and powdering her face to conceal her freckles. Equipped with the ability to turn her designs into reality, Lillian wore only beautiful clothes and always remembered to keep her shoulders back for elegant deportment. When she saw herself in the looking glass, she sometimes almost didn't recognise the stranger staring back. Perhaps it was no wonder Cora Miles hadn't batted an eyelid. She looked nothing like the drab housemaid who used to slink against the walls and stay in the shadows.

As long as Olivia Shaw didn't come knocking, everything would be fine.

CHAPTER 25

GREY STREET

*L*illian traipsed up Cora's front path, which was bordered by a decorative low hedge, carrying the carefully wrapped dress firmly tucked beneath her arm.

She pressed the bell and heard a tinkling melody ring out inside the house. Through the pane of glass she watched a silhouette approach and heard a squeal from a young child. When Cora's housemaid opened the door, Lillian took a quick step back in shock. She stumbled on a small lawn ornament and almost dropped the package. The servant in question appeared equally taken aback. As Lillian tried to regain her dignity a furious war of emotions fought across the other woman's face. At her side, a small boy clutched her hand and looked on wide-eyed.

The housemaid stared up and down at Lillian's fawn-coloured linen dress with disbelief.

Lillian spoke first. 'What happened to Emily?'

'Forget about Emily. Whit happened to yer?'

Lillian blinked, confused. 'I wrote you three telegrams. You never replied.'

'Och, I never got them. I left Rosemead the very next week. Mrs Shaw wrote me a reference and told me to come here to the Miles's house.' Catherine took stock of Lillian. 'Did yer not get the telegram I sent you? I found your sister's address at the post office. It took me a wee while to send it, what with the flood and everything.'

Lillian shook her head. 'No. I didn't get yours, either. My sister's cottage went under in the flood.'

'Aren't we a funny wee pair?' Catherine pulled her in for a hug. 'Certainly looks like yer've certainly done all right for yerself.'

Lillian struggled to hold back her tears. She'd missed her friend so badly.

'Who is it, Catherine?' Cora called out from inside.

'Lillian Betts, Ma'am.'

'Betts?' Cora popped her head into the hall, looking confused.

Lillian hurriedly swiped at her eyes. 'Good morning, Mrs Miles. Betts was my maiden name. I am Mrs Hamilton now.'

Catherine's eyebrows shot up. 'Och, yer don't say?'

Cora smiled happily. 'That's what I thought. It is funny how often that happens, isn't it? I still have old friends calling out my maiden name whenever they see me despite my being married four years now.' Her gaze flicked between the two women. 'How do you two know each other?'

Lillian shot a scared look at Catherine. She would be undone if the truth be known.

'I once worked at a large house where Miss Betts – I'm sorry – Mrs Hamilton grew up,' Catherine fibbed.

'Gosh, it's a small world. Please show dear Mrs Hamilton through to the drawing-room while I go and ask Cook to prepare us some tea. It must be lovely for you to see each other again.'

Cora sauntered toward the kitchen while Catherine briskly ushered her inside and bade her sit in one of a pair of floral armchairs. The room wasn't large but it had been beautifully appointed.

'Thank you.'

Catherine grinned at her. She turned her head. 'Alexander, please come here.'

'No!' His chubby face was resolute.

'You must. Mama has a visitor. Sorry, Lillian. As much as I wish we had time to talk, if we're going to keep up the charade, I'd best be getting on with my work. Yer'll be wanting yer tea, won't yer?' With that, she and the little boy headed up the hall.

Cora returned and settled into the other armchair. 'Has Miss Hamilton really finished my dress already?' She gazed at the wrapping with expectation. 'May I?'

'Yes, of course.' Lillian handed her the parcel. She couldn't help but feel proud as Cora untied the twine, pulled back the paper and gasped with delight. She brushed her fingers over the velvet jacket before carefully placing it to one side to reveal the taffeta gown beneath. She held it up for a better look at the detailed embroidery and then stood to drape the design against her svelte figure. Even in the room's soft light, the fabric revealed its glorious hues.

'Oh, it's absolutely perfect.' Cora turned to Lillian. 'Will you excuse me a moment? I simply must try it on immediately!' She rushed from the room with her purchase.

With Catherine in the kitchen probably cursing her name and Cora busily trying on the new dress to check whether further alterations needed to be made, Lillian found herself alone until the child, whom Catherine had shuffled off into the recesses of the house, toddled back bolder than before.

'Train,' he said, raising his toy for her to inspect.

She was reminded of the night she, Peter and Alice had

arrived at the Hamiltons' home and Stephen had similarly greeted them; shy but hopeful. Her little family, which now included Stephen, had exhausted and blessed her every day since. She wanted the dress shop to be a success for them, a legacy. 'That's a fine-looking locomotive, Alexander.' She whispered his name. He had grown into a handsome boy and looked cherubic in his sailor's shirt collar and little knickerbockers, seeming not at all concerned that she, a stranger, already knew his name.

'Your turn?' he asked.

'Yes, please.' Lillian took the proffered toy and pretended to be amazed at its weight and colour, and the way its wheels were able to turn.

Catherine reappeared. 'Och, wee Alex, leave Mrs Hamilton alone.' She held out her hand to the child.

'I don't mind,' Lillian said, summoning a shaky smile.

'Of course you don't. Look at you in your fancy clothes,' Catherine whispered conspiratorially. 'It's easy to see why Mrs Miles doesn't recognize you. You must tell me how you did it.'

A swishing of taffeta and Cora reappeared, taking a twirl in the centre of the room.

Even Catherine had to admire the immaculately tailored outfit. 'You look beautiful, Mrs Miles.'

'Thank you, Catherine. Mrs Hamilton, I adore it. Would you help me with the jacket?'

'Of course.' Lillian took the jacket from the table and stood to help Cora put her arms into the sleeves.

'Catherine, please pour the tea.' Cora turned her attention to the covered buttons running the length of her bodice.

'Miss Hamilton thought there might need to be some minor adjustments but it appears to fit you perfectly,' said Lillian.

'It does. It really does. I cannot wait to wear it out. Olivia

Shaw is getting married to Christopher Burns in two weeks' time. It will be the perfect occasion.'

At the sound of Olivia's name, Lillian felt her stomach swoop. Her fingers twitched at the memory of secretly borrowed paints. Her dismissal and that of her dear friend Catherine still stung. She lowered herself back into the armchair as Catherine began to pour her a cup, her face set like stone. It was embarrassing to have to accept it and she thought of what she had done to the Shaws' teapot last time she'd seen Cora and Alex together. At the time, Catherine had promised to piss in Donald's tea to defend her honour. She couldn't wait to tell her friend what had happened since they'd last seen each other. It had been far too long and the idea of waiting until they had a chance to be alone was excruciating.

'Do you know her?' Cora asked.

Lillian took a tentative sip and replaced the cup to its saucer. 'Who?'

'Olivia Shaw.'

Was a housemaid really so inconspicuous in a grand home, as Catherine said, that Cora's memory hadn't been triggered? Would Catherine share the truth when Lillian left? It could put an end to her new business. Lillian wouldn't blame her but how would she explain to Florence what had happened? She hated to think Nicholas would believe himself proved right. She didn't want to sell Patricia's cottage. She remembered how Catherine had protected her so many times and tried to relax.

Lillian sipped at her tea and nodded in response to Cora's question. 'I have seen her a few times.' She tried to ignore Catherine's amused smirk.

'I have Olivia and her mother to thank for referring Catherine on to me, actually,' explained Cora. 'Unfortunately, they simply didn't have room at Rosemead for another maid any more. They never said why exactly, and I hate to assume, but,' Cora added, leaning forward and gazing at Lillian, 'the slump has made everything so difficult for many people. I'm so lucky. Catherine's been such a wonderful help to me. Alexander adores her.' She twirled again in the dress. 'He's such a lively baby. When Emily went and got married, I was left quite in the lurch.'

Olivia was no friend of Cora's after all, Lillian thought, sending her the disloyal and discarded help.

Cora stopped and bestowed a happy smile on her house-maid at the memory. 'I personally got to know the Shaws through my aunt, Sophia Arnfield. Of course, Olivia is quite a number of years younger than me so we don't see each other all that often. However, I was given an invitation and so I will attend. Don't you just love the wedding season? I'll have to tell all my friends about your lovely shop. They'll all want a dress when they see me in this one. I hope Olivia doesn't feel that I'm trying to outshine her.'

'Thank you, Mrs Miles. Your compliments mean a great deal to me,' Lillian said.

'Us south-siders have to stick together and make a good impression. I think it's marvellous you've decided to have a shop of your very own, and so close and convenient to me. How did you talk your husband into it? I don't think mine would ever let me.'

Lillian felt a swelling of pride. 'I am enjoying the challenge. My husband was dubious to begin with but his sister and I are proving his fears unfounded. I do hope we'll see you again soon.'

'Yes, you most certainly will.' Cora glanced at the clock perched atop the fireplace mantle. 'I'm afraid I'm going to seem rude but I do have a suffragist meeting to attend at one o'clock. That is unless you'd like to come?'

'Oh, thank you but I must return to the shop. The tea was

lovely. I'm so glad you are pleased with the dress.' Lillian replaced her cup and saucer on the table beside her chair. It was the same type of furniture piece she'd spent hours dusting and wiping down many times at Rosemead, that Catherine was still polishing. The irony was not lost on her.

'Thank you again for personally delivering my dress. What a lovely touch. Catherine, please show Mrs Hamilton to the door, and then be a dear and hang my new outfit in my wardrobe.' Cora looked around the room. 'Alexander, where are you? It is time to get ready for our outing.'

The little boy giggled behind the curtain and Cora ran over to tickle his round tummy.

Lillian watched them as they left the room, Alexander squirming in his mother's arms.

As she reached the veranda, she turned to Catherine. 'How's Arthur?'

Catherine nodded. 'Good. He wants me to marry him but I'm sure I prefer to stay independent.'

'You'd be a beautiful bride.' Lillian hesitated before reaching for Catherine's hand. 'I've missed you so much.'

'Och, yer'll have no time for a wee housemaid like me now yer've married into the fine Hamilton family. Did yer forget it was me who said Nicholas had his eye on yer that day we walked up to the Windmill?'

Lillian smiled. 'How could I? When shall we meet again?'

'Judging by the look of Mrs Miles's face when she put that dress on, I'd say less than a month. You've done well for yerself, whether by hard work or by deception I shall reserve my judgement.' Catherine winked.

'I'm so glad to see you,' Lillian said.

'Ah, hen, and I am to see yer, too.'

Lillian returned to the shop on Montague Road feeling light and happy at finding Catherine safe and sound. Her mood dampened at the sound of hammering coming from behind the cottage. She skirted down the side and found Nicholas crouched in the backyard with a stack of wooden stakes, knocking them into the ground one at a time.

She put her hands on her hips. 'What are you doing?'

'Mama said you'd discussed a need to extend the workshop. I've organised the draftsman to come and draw up the plans. There are no shortage of builders looking for work. We should have it done in no time.'

Lillian raised her eyebrows. 'For someone who was feeling sceptical over whether the business would prosper, you're being awfully helpful.'

'My darling, there's no need for sarcasm. Besides, Florence told me the society ladies have found the shop.' Nicholas picked up another stake and positioned it. 'At this rate, I'll be able to retire soon.' He raised the hammer.

'Go on with you. Why are you sticking stakes in the ground?'

Nicholas brought the hammer down on the stake and sat back on his haunches to survey his handiwork. 'I'm trying to map out the space you'll need.'

'I see.' She turned without offering further objection and trudged up the back steps. Better to leave him to get on with his tinkering. It was true the shop was attracting quite a few customers but she worried in these straitened times whether pouring more money into an expansion was wise. It was enough to know Nicholas supported her dream. Of more immediate importance were the two skirt orders that needed to have the cloth cut out.

Florence greeted her in the workshop. 'Well?'

'Well what?'

'What did Cora Miles think of the dress and jacket?'

'She adored them.'

'Really?' Florence's face lit up.

'Yes.' Lillian sat down heavily in one of the chairs and propped her elbows on the table. 'She tried it on and twirled around her drawing-room.'

Florence laughed. 'She did not.'

'She did.'

'No alterations needed?'

'Not one. You did a perfect job.' Lillian glanced back out the door, feeling nervous as Nicholas hammered in yet another stake.

'Thank goodness.'

Lillian reached over to her sister-in-law and gave her arm a squeeze. She enjoyed the enthusiasm Florence had for their business. Dorothy had been right; Florence was bored with being an assistant in her parents' store. She had needed to extend herself. For now, at least, her thirst for travelling appeared to have been subdued.

Lillian reached across the workbench to retrieve a swathe of lavender-coloured silk that had a paper pattern pinned to it. She carefully began to cut the material with a pair of shears but stopped at hearing the mewling sound of a newborn baby.

She straightened as a cold sweat erupted all over her body. It would not pay to extend the property at all. Lillian needed only to think of how quickly things went wrong for Alfred and Patricia to see how fortunes could so quickly change. No. They would not dig. The shop must stay the same. She dropped the material and called out: 'Nicholas, come here, please. I need your help.'

Florence looked up from her own work with concern. 'What's the matter?'

'I need Nicholas now!' Lillian felt frantic.

Her husband appeared at the back door wiping his hands on an old towel to remove the dirt.

'What is it?'

She blinked and wondered what to say. 'I need you to hold this cloth steady,' was the first thing out of her mouth.

'Look at me, I'm filthy. Why wouldn't you ask Florence?' He stared at her, confused.

'Yes, I can help you, Lillian,' Florence said, picking up the material Lillian had been cutting out.

Lillian snatched it from her. 'No!'

'Hey, what's got into you?' asked Nicholas.

'Nothing.' She quietened down. 'I don't feel very well. Would you take me home?'

He sighed and wistfully looked at the backyard. 'Very well. Of course I will.'

Lillian stood, feeling shaky. 'Florence, I'm sorry to do this to you but I have a pain in my stomach. Will you be all right if Nicholas takes me home to rest?'

Florence nodded. 'What do you think it could be?'

Lillian felt guilty for worrying her but the walls were pressing in and she had to get away. 'I'm sure it's nothing serious.'

'Go and put your feet up. I'll be all right to close up later.'

'Thank you.' Lillian gave her a pained smile. She snatched her sketchbook of designs from the table, made her way out to the front steps and descended to the carriage.

Nicholas handed her up and took his seat beside her. He whipped the reins and Skylark started with a trot into the street.

Abruptly, he turned to look at his wife. 'You don't look sick to me.'

Lillian frowned. 'What are you talking about?'

He shook his head. 'I know you well enough, my dear. What's troubling you?'

'It-it's just the very idea of making a change to Patricia's home.'

'You didn't mind when we removed the wall to widen the display area.'

Lillian reddened. 'No, that's true, I didn't. Only, don't you think we should wait until we've got more orders coming in? I don't want to get into further debt.'

'First you say you don't want a change and then you say you don't want more debt. Which one is it?'

'Both.'

Nicholas slowed Skylark to a walk.

'Why are you slowing down?' Panic rose in her throat.

'You worry too much. I've looked at the projections. The building work won't set us back too far. You and Florence are making a name for yourselves. You have to have more faith. You know I'm sorry about your sister and Thomas. I truly am. But the house is yours now. You have every right to do what you like with it.'

Her panic flipped into anger. 'Very well. Build the damn room if you must.'

'Lillian!'

'Well, obviously that's what you want. You've ignored everything I've said about the matter. Why should my objections get in the way of your plans?'

'You're being quite unreasonable.' Nicholas slapped the reins and the stallion sped back up to a trot.

Lillian crossed her arms, turned her face away and refused to say another word. In truth her mind was full of possibilities for the new space. She knew they needed it for the business to be able to grow. Continuing orders were cramping the space around the work table but how could she be sure that builders wouldn't unearth any secrets? Patricia had said Alfred took babies to the river. Could she really believe that was all?

When Nicholas reached their new home she hopped down.

'Will you be all right?' he asked tersely.

'Yes, don't fuss. I'll have a little lie down and be right as rain.'

'Very well. I need to get back to finish what I was doing.'

She sighed. 'Must you?'

'Yes, I must.' He clicked his tongue and turned Skylark and the carriage back in the direction they'd come.

Lillian watched him head down the street until he'd turned the corner. Hurrying inside, she listened for the familiar noises of the children playing but instead was greeted by silence. They had employed a governess who came early in the morning to take care of Stephen and Alice and deliver Peter to school now that he had begun attending. Lillian had carefully vetted the applicants and followed up on their references to ensure only the most reputable woman received the position of caring for her precious children. She remembered the young woman, Jemima, asking if she might be able to take Alice and Stephen for a stroll to Musgrave Park for some exercise before picking up Peter in the afternoon.

Lillian was grateful to find the house empty. She went straight to her wardrobe and dug around in the back of it until she found her old sketchbook that she had retrieved from the Shaws' stable. She noticed a brown smudge on the calico still wrapped around it. Lillian shuddered to recognise the stain as a drop of Alfred's blood.

She unwrapped the sketchbook and turned the pages to study the paintings she once thought she'd lost. The scene at Dutton Park was as she remembered but staring at the picture of her sister in her kitchen triggered a welling of sadness. She flipped to the next page and withdrew the portrait of Donald to tear it in half. As an afterthought, she took the painting of the day at the Windmill out as well. There sat Nicholas, looking so sombre, and Catherine in the background with the Scottish sisters and the other men. That day seemed an eternity ago. She'd been angry with Patricia as she'd pointed out the cottage across the river for Nicholas. It had been too far away for him to note the exact place her finger had been aiming. None of that mattered. She would never get to be angry or excited or sad with her sister again and the pain hit her as suddenly as the moment the flood had swept her away. Lillian bent over the book and sobbed until her head pounded and her tears ran dry.

Sick of her grief, Lillian rose unsteadily to her feet and studied the room. Perhaps she would take the Windmill picture to the framers and hang it in their bedroom as a surprise for Nicholas to make amends for her tantrum?

She considered how much there was to lose if any secrets lurking in the soil at Montague Road were uncovered. Like the dress shop, the Hamiltons' store on Stanley Street was doing well in the wake of the flood. Customers adored the European fabrics Nicholas had brought back. Enough so that Jonathan and Dorothy had helped her and Nicholas scrape together a deposit on a three-bedroom cottage on Whynot Street. They'd moved in only a few weeks earlier and Lillian still couldn't quite believe she had a house to call her own. The only marring of an otherwise perfect setting was the crack of the mounted troopers' stock whips as the men drove what they would call the blackfellows, gins, and piccaninnies beyond Boundary Street late in the afternoon.

She had always been used to seeing Aboriginal people walking along Montague Road and fishing down at the river. Sometimes they ignored her and sometimes they lifted a hand in greeting. She did not understand their ways but she had not felt afraid. On Whynot Street, however, situated so close to the city boundary, the savage insistence on policing and on banishment after dark frightened her children and made her feel uneasy. Some members of the mob, emboldened by the drink they'd been given in exchange for a day's labour, were defiant enough to shout insults in their own tongue at the uniformed constables herding them along. Lillian couldn't say she blamed them. Despite not being sure of the meaning of their words, the despairing indignation over their treatment resounded clearly. West End – Kurilpa, they called it – belonged to them, not the white fella.

Nicholas, on the other hand, was matter-of-fact about the round-up. 'The security of businesses is paramount, dear. We can't have them wandering around looking for an opportunity to loot.'

She had not known about this uncaring streak in her husband, nor his insistence on upholding the official reason for needing to clear the streets. Patricia had been teased many times for her exotic looks and, rightly or wrongly, Lillian would never embrace her husband's opinion on the matter. When she went to bed at night, she slept soundly and didn't worry about her business sitting on the other side of the mandated line. Yet, despite the unpleasant nightly interruption, she delighted in her home. It smelt so new. The hardwood floors were coated with a high varnish and the swirling blue pattern of the wallpaper was cheerful. She and Nicholas had the largest bedroom. Peter and Stephen shared the next and the last one was for Alice.

Lillian looked back at her sketchbook and attempted to wipe tear blotches from the Dutton Park picture before giving up and tearing that page out as well. She folded it in half twice and tucked it into the back cover of the new one she'd brought back from the workshop with her. Its pages were steadily filling up with new designs for the next season and she wanted to do some more work on them that afternoon. It worried her to think Nicholas might come across the old sketchbook should he be looking for something in the wardrobe. Donald's old tobacco tin still hid the valuable note. It would be the perfect place to hide the folded watercolour as well. She had secreted the tin behind a row of button-filled jars on the very day the dress shop opened. It had seemed an auspicious thing to do.

CHAPTER 26

'What is it?' Lillian eyed the envelope with suspicion.

'Only an invitation to the biggest event of the season.' Cora suppressed an excited giggle. 'Olivia Shaw wanted to know all about my new dress on account of the many compliments I received at her wedding. If I didn't know better, I'd say she was a tad jealous. I didn't feel at all guilty because I truly felt beautiful. It was glorious. Olivia said she simply must meet you. I suggested to her that you and your husband might appreciate an invitation to the orphanage fundraiser ball that's taken for ever to organise and she agreed that was a good idea.'

Lillian went pale. She remembered the first meeting held in the Shaw's dining room. Indeed, it had taken the ladies a long time to organise the event and still Cora did not seem to recognise her as the maid who had taken her baby and changed his soiled napkin.

'Why would you do such a thing?' she asked.

Cora's face fell. 'Are we not friends? I thought you would be pleased. Most people would be thrilled to receive one.'

Lillian tried to summon a smile. 'I am glad to call you a friend, Mrs Miles.'

'Please, you know I prefer Cora.'

'Cora.'

It was true their acquaintance had overstepped professional boundaries. The first time it happened, Cora had come to the shop to place her third order. Lillian was beginning to wonder if there was any room left in the woman's wardrobe for storing all her dresses. Cora loved poring over the drawings as she selected her next design. 'This one is my favourite, Lillian,' she would say, carefully lifting one of the page corners before flicking over to the next. 'Actually, no, I think this one. Gosh, oh dear, I can't decide.'

It occurred to Lillian the woman might be lonely. She knew Cora's husband, Archibald, was fourteen years older than his wife. He'd made his fortune in the building industry. With the ongoing depression, he had wisely made full use of his lumber yards to mill and export timber to better-paying economies. At least that was how Cora explained it. Cora also lamented that the Gentlemen's Club saw more of him than she did. It didn't take a genius to understand why other women in her social circle questioned the sincerity of her marriage.

Cora also came from a large Irish family and was an enthusiastic suffragist. As such, she was bound to ruffle a few feathers.

However, it was easy enough to see Cora held genuine affection for her husband, in the way that she expressed her admiration of him. The reason Lillian was doubly sure was because she and Catherine had finally managed to snatch a few hours together at Musgrave Park, catching up on all they had been doing since the sorry incident at Rosemead that had led to their expulsion. The time had passed too quickly, sitting beneath the Moreton Bay figs, and Lillian was looking forward to another catch-up when time allowed. Catherine had sworn not to tell Cora. It would only lead to more questions and Lillian was glad Catherine understood how important her shop, and indeed her marriage, was to her. It was not fair, she knew, to keep asking her old friend to hold secrets but there did not seem to be any other way.

Catherine had told her Cora was not the gold-digger others thought her to be. She also loved her adopted son, Alexander, very much. Lillian had agreed to sew several outfits for him as well.

'Cora, do you have time for a cup of tea before you head off?' Lillian offered, trying to salvage their exchange.

'Yes, that would be lovely.'

Florence raised an eyebrow from where she sat at her sewing machine as Lillian set the kettle on the stove to boil. 'Are we adding hospitality to our services now?' she whispered.

'Shush, or I won't make one for you. Besides, you started it with home deliveries.'

Nicholas entered the workroom through the back door. 'I'll have one, thanks.'

Lillian sighed. 'Careful, dear. You're bringing dirt inside.'

Nicholas looked down at his feet and sheepishly edged out on to the back step to untie his laces. To her bitter dismay, he had hired a builder and was continuing to supervise the laying of the extension foundations rather than keep himself busy at the Stanley Street store. She saw Cora standing in the doorway between the shop and the workroom, watching Nicholas as he hunched over to untie his laces.

'Nicholas, this is Mrs Cora Miles, our best customer.'

He finished yanking off his boots and straightened.

Cora smiled and held out her hand.

Nicholas took it and apologised for his dirty state. 'A pleasure to meet you, Mrs Miles.'

'And you, Mr Hamilton. I do hope you will convince your wife to attend the orphanage's fundraising ball. It's going to be held at Government House. My husband could introduce you to Sir Henry Norman, if you like.'

'The Governor? Well, that would be an honour. A ball sounds just the ticket, don't you think, Lillian? I know I could use a good night out.'

'Indeed. I hope I shall see you both there.'

Lillian cleared a bolt of cloth off the workbench and offered Cora a seat. She poured the tea and Florence and Nicholas joined them. Joy flowed through her as they chatted and drank around Patricia's old kitchen table.

Cora drained her cup and set it back on its saucer. 'Thank you very much, Lillian. If you'll excuse me, I must be heading off to see what trouble Alexander is getting up to with Catherine.' At Nicholas's quizzical look she explained: 'My three-year-old son and my long-suffering housemaid. It was lovely to get to know you better, Florence. You and Lillian make a formidable pair of businesswomen. See you at the ball, Nicholas. I can't wait to see the fabulous creation you'll be wearing, Lillian.'

'I see you have made a new friend, my dear,' Nicholas said when Cora had rushed off.

Florence looked forlorn. 'Why didn't she offer me an invitation?'

'If I could give you mine, I would,' Lillian grumbled, and headed into the shopfront to select some fabric. If she was going to come face to face with Olivia Shaw at the ball, she had better make sure she looked fabulous. There were only two weeks to prepare.

CHAPTER 27

SEEKING A REUNION

'May I help you?' Lillian asked.

The young woman, her hair sharply pulled back from her face, looked nervously around the display area. By her plain dated-looking dress, Lillian assumed she was lost but then she suddenly recognised her. What was the girl doing here of all places?

'Yes, I'm looking for Alice. Is she here?'

Hearing the familiar name gave Lillian a fright, until recalling Patricia had chosen it as an alias – their mother's name – for her baby-fostering enterprise. Her pulse ticked against her temple. Go away, she wanted to say.

'Although...' the familiar girl touched the mannequin. 'I'm not sure I've come to the right place. I was sure this was it.' She leaned in close and sniffed the fabric. 'Didn't this use to be a house? A woman named Alice lived here. Mrs Carter brought me here and said Alice would take care of my baby. I got married last week so I've come to take her back.'

Lillian knew who the girl was really asking for. 'Pat... Alice died in the flood. The water rose right up to the roof.'

The young mother froze. 'Died? What about the baby, my daughter?'

'I'm so sorry to be the one to have to tell you this but I'm afraid your baby died as well.'

The girl let out a despairing groan. 'You're wrong!'

Lillian shook her head sadly. 'I wish I were. The lady you ask for was my sister. I'm as sorry as you are.'

The girl stared at Lillian, confused. 'We've met.'

Lillian blanched and lied. 'No, I don't think so.'

'Yes, you used to be a maid. I remember. You were helpful.'

'I'm sorry. You must be mistaking me for someone else.'

'I don't think so. I've got a good memory for faces. You say Alice was your sister?'

Lillian swallowed. 'I think it best if you leave now.'

The young mother looked wildly around the room and began to sob. 'My baby died?' She grabbed the mannequin for support but it buckled beneath the weight of her and toppled to the floor. 'Oh, I'm so sorry.'

'Leave it.' Lillian stooped over and picked the mannequin back up.

The girl lurched from the shop and stumbled down the road crying.

Lillian's heart pounded. Part of her wanted to give chase and demand to know why the silly girl had evidently kept having babies if she couldn't keep them, but she held back. She adored Alice, and indeed Stephen, as much as she loved Peter. They were her family and no one would be allowed to try and tear them apart.

The doorbell jangled as Florence entered the shop, back from a fitting. She frowned. 'Who was that?'

Lillian watched through the window as the unwelcome visitor paused at the corner to look back in their direction before continuing out of sight. 'Someone who tried to steal something from us.'

Florence came to stand beside her, worried. 'Should we call the police?'

Lillian stepped back inside. 'No. That won't be necessary,' she said. 'I took care of it.' An icy finger of fear traced its way up her spine. Lillian hoped the girl would not return. It was time to go home and get ready for the ball.

CHAPTER 28

THE GOVERNOR'S BALL

*L*illian knew she had succeeded in creating a gown to be the envy of every other lady when she descended the staircase and found Nicholas rendered speechless. She had chosen a tulip-bell skirt in deep-red velvet. The leg-of-mutton sleeves were enormous and she had selected the most unforgivingly tight corset and a stiff crinoline petticoat to accentuate her waist. She already felt light-headed but was determined not to let Cora or Florence and their shop down.

'Remarkable,' Nicholas said at last.

'Do you like it?' She twirled slowly before her husband.

'You are breathtaking, my dear.'

She kissed him. 'You look very handsome in your tails and top hat, too.'

'Why thank you. Shall we go?'

Lillian placed her hand in the crook of Nicholas's arm and let him escort her outside to the waiting carriage. She glanced back at the house and saw the children silhouetted in the upstairs window with their governess, Jemima, standing behind them. The governess had agreed to come and watch them for the evening. The children were waving excitedly and she raised her gloved hand to wave back. The unwelcome memory of washing Mary Forsyth's bloodstained glove in the Shaws' laundry flashed before her. Would she have to contend with Donald and his new wife at the ball, too?

She and Nicholas headed for the river and waited to board the Garden Ferry. As the vessel drew in to dock, Lillian could scarcely believe her eyes.

'Godfrey, is that you?' She waved excitedly at the ferryman as he looped a thick piece of rope around a post, and felt Nicholas's quizzical gaze boring into her.

'The one and the same, Ma'am. May I ask how you know my name?' The man removed the cap from his head and peered up at her.

'Nicholas, please help me down. Hurry!'

Nicholas hopped down and gave her his hand without protest.

Stiffly she slipped from the carriage and marched up to the man.

'Don't you remember me?'

'Can't say I do. But it is a pleasure to make your acquaintance this evening. Are you heading to the Governor's Ball?'

'Yes, we are.'

'I thought so. You're the fifth carriage I've brought across already.'

'Godfrey, it's me, Lillian. You rescued me and my children from the roof of my sister's cottage during the flood.'

'I don't believe it.' The ferryman's eyes flew wide open. 'You were half-drowned, if I remember correctly. How are the little ones?'

Lillian smiled and tears sprang to her eyes. 'They're doing very well, thank you. Please, let me introduce you to my husband, Nicholas Hamilton.'

Nicholas came around the front of Skylark to shake Godfrey's hand. 'A pleasure.'

Godfrey appraised them both. 'You both look splendid tonight. I'm glad to see you doing so well, Ma'am.'

'Yes, I am,' Lillian replied. 'I found Catherine, too. She's working on the south side.'

Godfrey began to untie the ropes mooring the ferry to the wharf. 'I'm glad to hear it. You'll have to excuse me, Lillian. I'd better get this ferry over to the other side so you can get to your ball. I hope you have a pleasant evening.'

Nicholas helped Lillian back into the carriage. The encounter had buoyed her with confidence. She began to feel excited for the night ahead.

They drew up beside the sandstone portico at Government House. Every lamp along the colonnaded veranda shone a circle of light on to the immaculately raked driveway. An usher came to greet them and, once more, Lillian had to try to descend gracefully from the carriage. With Nicholas at her side, she took a deep breath and stepped into the foyer, marvelling at the glorious chandelier as they passed beneath it. They moved into the hall where the band was playing a lively waltz.

'Archie, they're here!'

Lillian scanned the room's perimeter at the sound of her friend's voice. Cora and her husband were standing next to a marble mantelpiece with champagne flutes in hand. Others in the vicinity glanced over with disapproval at the outburst.

If Cora cared, she didn't show it. 'Lillian!' she called out just as loudly.

Archibald Miles tilted his head in greeting as Lillian and Nicholas navigated through the assembled crowd.

'You'll notice my wife has had enough champagne already,' he said with a good-natured grin as they drew close.

'Stop it, Archie!' Cora slapped his sleeve lightly. 'This is my first glass. Lillian, Mr Hamilton, I'm so glad you decided to come.'

'I'd prefer if you called me Nicholas, Cora.'

'Very well. Nicholas, Lillian, this is Archibald.'

'Archie will do. A pleasure.' Cora's husband stuck out his meaty hand and Nicholas accepted the hearty handshake. 'And you must be the talented dressmaker who is taking all my money.'

Lillian blushed.

'Hush.' Cora batted her husband again. 'He doesn't mean it, Lillian. Tell me, have you been to Government House before? Isn't it grand?'

Lillian shook her head. 'It's beautiful but no, I haven't.'

'I have, once,' said Nicholas.

Lillian turned with surprise at his admission but found her husband's expression hooded. He'd probably attended a soirée there with Molly. Would her shadow ever stop following them around? The Shaws had certainly been many times before, she thought with bitterness. She'd pressed many a silk gown in readiness during her time at Rosemead.

A waiter sharply dressed in a black suit presented a tray in front of her. She thanked him and took a flute, nervously sipping as the delicious bubbles popped and fizzed about her nose.

Where was Olivia?

'Lillian, I see you have outdone yourself for tonight,' Cora commented, pouting. 'I didn't see this dress in your book.'

'No, it's an original design. I mixed and matched a few ideas,' she replied, distracted.

'Well it's not fair. Now I want one just like it.'

'You have enough dresses, my darling,' said Archie.

'Never!' Cora set her champagne down on the mantel. 'I do hope the dancing will start soon.'

'There is still dinner to eat beforehand. Perhaps hors d'oeuvres might be in order.' Archie signalled a different waiter who obligingly brought over a tray laden with appetizers.

'Thank you, kind sir. Don't mind if I do.' Archie grinned and selected a delicacy, popping it straight in his mouth. He reached for two more and held one aloft in each hand. 'Delicious.'

'Archie, don't be boorish. Honestly, I can't take him anywhere,' said Cora.

Archie ignored his wife's scolding and turned to Nicholas. 'Cora tells me you're a cloth merchant for your father's business. I've brought several suits from Hamilton's. Always found them to be very good quality.'

Nicholas nodded graciously. 'Yes, that's right. I was in London and Paris at the beginning of the year to find some new stock. I docked back in Brisbane just a week after the flood came through. The river caused a lot of damage to the store.'

Archie tutted. 'Yes, I can imagine it would have. I lost a fair amount of timber down the river as well; swept it clear out to sea. A dreadful business.'

Cora's mouth had turned down at the edges as the men spoke. 'Oh pish! Let's not talk about such serious things. Tonight is about having fun. Come, Lillian, let's leave the men to their talk. We shall go and meet some interesting people.' She grabbed Lillian by the elbow and began to steer her away before suddenly turning around. 'Archie, don't forget to introduce Nicholas properly to Sir Henry. A handshake at the door doesn't count. I promised you would.'

Archie tapped the side of his nose with his finger. 'Yes, darling.'

Cora theatrically rolled her eyes at her husband and pulled Lillian like a prize bull at the Exhibition toward a group of ladies in a nearby corner.

'Hello, my dears. This is one of the people responsible for all the beautiful dresses I've been wearing lately,' Cora announced.

At first mention of Lillian's skills the other ladies sniffed with derision. What was a mere dressmaker doing rubbing shoulders with the upper echelon, no matter how clever her work?

Although Lillian was ready to slink away, Cora headed off their snobbery. 'Mrs Hamilton is a businesswoman, with her own dress shop and employees,' she said.

Lillian raised an eyebrow at the lie. She was quite sure Florence wouldn't be pleased to be thought of as an employee. They were equal partners, even if Cora had neglected to extend another invite. She suspected it had more to do with Florence's status as an unmarried woman than anything else. As she looked about the grand room, she saw everybody appeared to be paired off. Also, unless she was mistaken, there was only one of Florence. Who were the other employees Cora had conjured up? But to her dismay, she found her friend hadn't finished speaking.

'Not only that,' Cora continued, 'she is married to Nicholas Hamilton, of the famous Hamilton's on Stanley Street.'

At this, the ladies' interest piqued. They had all noticed the handsome man talking to Archibald Miles. Many of their husbands' wardrobes had at least one suit from Hamilton's hanging on their rails.

One of them, a pretty girl roughly the same age as Lillian, with blonde hair piled high and free tendrils curling about her neck, nodded politely at her. Expensive diamonds caught the light and sparkled at her earlobes. 'How lovely to meet you,

Mrs Hamilton. I don't suppose you've brought any calling cards with you?'

Lillian opened her satin beaded reticule and handed her one. Several others around the group extended their hands as well. After a few minutes of cordial chatter, she and Cora extricated themselves under the pretence of seeing an acquaintance across the room. Lillian tried to ignore Cora's wink.

'I'm starting to think you are quite incorrigible,' Lillian whispered.

Cora lifted her nose into the air. 'Oh, I wouldn't have it any other way, my dear. Those women may think we're beneath them but we'll have the last laugh when they start spending their pounds in your lovely shop.'

'You spend your pounds in my lovely shop.'

'That's because I already know how marvellous you are.' Cora linked an arm through hers.

As their husbands caught up with them next to the grand piano, the announcement for dinner was made. They headed through to the dining room and found their place cards on the damask tablecloth in a row down the right side of the table. Lillian took her seat, admiring the cut-crystal glasses and the array of polished cutlery set out before her. A waiter asked if he could place her napkin on her lap and she nodded her permission.

Nicholas sat down at her right and squeezed her hand beneath the tablecloth. Lillian could see his eyes were shining.

'I've just met Sir Henry,' he said.

'Isn't this all exquisite?' she whispered back.

'Yes quite!' someone interjected.

Lillian whipped her head up at the sharp tone as the interloper haughtily continued:

'It's certainly superior to the service we've had in the past in our own home. We had one girl who could never quite get rid of spots on the knives. It's so hard to get good help these days, don't you think?' added Olivia, dressed in a sea-green gown adorned with lace, as she took a seat directly opposite them.

Lillian breathed in as deeply as her corset would allow, which wasn't much at all. She kept her expression serene. 'I'm afraid I simply must disagree with you. My Jemima is an exceptional governess and maid.'

Olivia studied her carefully. 'Only the one?'

Before Lillian could summon a suitably tart response, Cora interrupted.

'Olivia, how nice to see you. Here is the wonderful new friend I was telling you about, Lillian Hamilton. She made both the dress I'm wearing and her own. Isn't she clever?'

'She is certainly a very creative woman,' Olivia replied, feigning innocence. She nodded at Lillian, seemingly content for now to keep up the pretence of being a stranger. 'A pleasure to make your acquaintance, Mrs Hamilton.' She eyed Nicholas. 'And is this your husband?'

Lillian nodded and picked up her water glass, already filled by yet another efficient waiter. She took an overly large gulp and struggled not to splutter as Olivia proffered her hand and Nicholas gave it a cordial shake.

'This is Nicholas,' she said, managing to swallow her mouthful without choking.

'I'm so glad you decided to join the party,' Olivia gushed. 'Cora insisted I invite you.'

'Thank you very much. We're having a wonderful evening,' replied Nicholas, his tone cool. He had not forgotten her despicable deed at the theatre, even if she didn't know he'd seen it.

'Indeed.' Olivia picked up her bread knife and dipped it into a pat of butter sitting on the table between them. 'My Christopher is down in Sydney on business. Such a shame I couldn't introduce him to you.' She slowly buttered her bun and cut it into dainty portions.

'Another time perhaps.' Nicholas gave her a stiff smile and resumed his conversation with Archie at his left. As Cora fussed about with the placement of her napkin, Olivia raised the piece of bread to her lips and stared at Lillian. Her eyes burned like two pieces of coal.

Lillian felt Jemima really had hooked her corset far too tightly. She struggled to taste her food. A procession of soup, entrée, mains and dessert passed before her barely touched. She continued to take small sips of wine as the waiter returned to refill her glass.

By the time the dinner service was complete and the carpets had been rolled up for the dancing, Lillian felt intoxicated. She gripped Nicholas as he led her in a lively two-step around the hall.

'That Archie Miles is a fine fellow. He's offered to cut me a deal on timber for the extension. I shall have to organise him a new suit,' said Nicholas. 'At first, I'll admit, I wondered what a pretty lady like Cora was doing with such a portly man. He's much older than her, isn't he? I thought she might have married him for his money, but after spending some time with Archie this evening I think he probably charmed her into marrying him. If he hadn't got in first, I might have asked her myself.'

'Mm, Cora said you'd like him,' Lillian mumbled into his lapel.

Nicholas stopped mid-step and pulled back to take a look at her. 'Did you hear what I said? I knew you weren't listening to me! What's the matter with you?'

'What do you mean?'

'You've hardly said a word since we sat down to dinner. I rather think you've had too much to drink.'

'I'm fine. Keep dancing.'

'Very well, but warn me if I need to take you outside to be sick.'

Lillian feigned shock. 'I'm a lady.'

'Not like any I've ever known. Besides, I am your husband and therefore duty bound to watch you puke on my shoes, should the occasion call for it.'

'You're so silly, you know that?' Lillian tweaked his pocket kerchief.

Nicholas kissed her forehead. 'And that's precisely why you married me.'

She giggled and laid her head back on his broad shoulder. He smelt wonderful. Despite the effects of the wine it was delightful to have her husband all to herself without the distraction of small children running about their feet. If she closed her eyes and trusted his lead, the room didn't spin so much. What was Olivia up to? Lillian didn't trust the girl any further than she could throw a shoe.

The band finished playing their tune and she excused herself from Nicholas to find the ladies' room. 'I'll be back soon. Could you find me a glass of water?'

Nicholas smiled. 'Of course.'

Lillian headed to the courtyard and found the restroom. Re-emerging, she took a moment to enjoy the view of the expansive garden, cut by the dark line of the river as it snaked past. The stars twinkled above and she enjoyed the feel of a soft breeze against her flushed cheeks. She had often stopped to admire the grand building of Government House while working over at Kangaroo Point. Tonight the blight of the sawmill opposite was reduced to a hulking shadow.

'It's pleasant out here, isn't it?'

Lillian spun around and inwardly groaned. 'Miss Shaw.'

Olivia stared out across the lawn. 'I see you haven't forgotten your place. For a moment I was quite sure you were about to call me by my first name. You're wrong anyway. I'm Mrs Burns now, remember?'

Lillian vowed to stay civil. 'Mrs Burns. Thank you again for the invitation.'

'Yes, of course.' Olivia took a silver cigarette holder, a packet of cigarettes and some matches from her reticule. 'Would you like one?'

She shook her head. 'No, thank you.'

'Very well.' Olivia placed a cigarette in the holder and held a match she had lit to it, taking small puffs to set the tip aglow. 'You know, Donald was the one who taught me how to smoke. Mother finds it all very distasteful. I thought he might have shown you as well.' Olivia gave Lillian a sideways glance and flicked the ash away. 'He was rather fond of you, you know.'

'Please don't tease me, Olivia. That is all in the past now. I am happily married, too, as you saw.'

'Does your new husband know about your penchant for stealing? No? I didn't think so. Does he even know how far down he married?'

'Nicholas knows I used to be a maid, actually. He also knows why I was forced to leave Rosemead.'

Even in the shadows Lillian could see Olivia pull her mouth into a sneer.

'Well, isn't that good of him to overlook such a glaring deficit.'

It might have been the wine emboldening her but suddenly Lillian didn't have time to waste standing there listening to Olivia. 'What do you want?' she asked, sharply.

Olivia sucked on the tip of her cigarette and blew smoke at her. 'You do have a natural flair for dressmaking, I will admit it. Perhaps you can make one for me?'

'If you'd like.'

Olivia turned and hissed: 'No, I would not like! You think

I'd ever wear one of your tawdry creations? Cora might settle for second class, but then again she would. The Irish have no taste at all.'

'Cora has only ever spoken about you in glowing terms, Olivia,' Lillian angrily spat back. 'She would be hurt to find out you thought about her so. She thinks you're her friend.'

'She won't find out, otherwise I'll tell her what you're really like.' Olivia reopened her purse and withdrew a small square of paper.

Lillian froze at the sight of it. 'Where did you get that?'

'I found it in the attic after Catherine left. You know, I did ask your brother-in-law to return it to you. After all, Mama gave him your ridiculous sketchbook. Alfred was a strange man even before that fall dented his head, wasn't he? I guess though, he thought if he did me a favour I might do one for him. Of course, I was never going to let a lowlife like him anywhere near me. I never understood why Fergus did so much for him. I guess old school ties are hard to break. I think my brother felt sorry for him. Alfred didn't like you very much, Lillian, did he? At least we had that in common. Alfred told me you were as useless as your stupid sister and your slut of a mother. After that, I decided to keep your photograph in case I ever saw you again... and here you are.'

Something deep inside Lillian broke. She slapped Olivia hard across the face, sending her sprawling on the freshly cut lawn.

'How dare you!' Olivia clasped her hand to her face and began to scramble for her cigarette holder, which still held the smouldering cigarette. She held up the scrap of paper and brought the cigarette towards its corner.

'Stop!' Lillian cried. 'Please. I'll do what ever you want. Don't burn the photograph.'

'What the devil is going on down there?'

They both turned their heads to see a small crowd forming by the open double doors that lead out to the garden.

'Mrs Burns, are you all right? Have you fallen?'

Olivia climbed back to her feet. 'A little stumble. I'm quite fine,' she called back.

Several of the men drew closer.

Olivia brought her face up close to Lillian's. 'I want you to say you're a thief and a liar, nothing more than a stupid maid who thought you could seduce my brother and failed.'

'I am,' Lillian said helplessly. 'I'm a thief and a liar. And yes, I tried to seduce your brother.'

As the onlookers reached them, she gulped. Her husband was among them. 'Nicholas, I –'

His expression was stern. 'That's quite enough, Lillian. You're drunk and have made a fool of yourself. It is time to go home.' He grabbed her by the arm and began to drag her away.

She pulled away. 'No! Olivia has something precious that belongs to me.'

Olivia laughed. 'Like you had something precious that belonged to me?'

'You didn't even use those paints. You didn't like them,' Lillian shouted.

'It is as I said. A thief and a liar.'

Lillian felt another figure close in at her side. It was Archie Miles. What would Cora think of her now she had made a spectacle in front of her husband and friends?

'That's enough, ladies,' he said in a booming voice.

Olivia smoothed her skirt. 'Very well. I was merely trying to return something Mrs Hamilton had left at my house a while ago. Here.'

To Lillian's amazement, Olivia handed over the photograph. She quickly snatched it, tucking it safely into her reticule and breathing a deep sigh of relief.

Appeased, Archie and the other men began to wander back up the slope, although Nicholas stayed close and warily watched them.

'You thought you could come here and hand out your little cards to drum up some business for your shop,' Olivia murmured. 'You're ruined, Lillian Betts. I'll tell all the other ladies what a usurper you really are.'

'Before you do, Olivia, there's something you should know.' Lillian leaned in close. 'If you ever threaten me or my family, I'll come to your house and cut out your tongue. I'm from the south side. We do things differently over there.'

Olivia's mouth dropped. 'You wouldn't dare!'

'Would you want to risk it? Let me tell you something, Olivia. Every year I am here I learn something new about myself and one thing is for sure; I'll never ever let a bully beat me again.'

Lillian left her nemesis standing on the grass and hurried to catch up with Nicholas but he turned on his heel and marched two steps ahead.

They rode home together in furious silence.

CHAPTER 29

TRIAL

*L*illian and Nicholas dropped in to Vulture Street with the children for their usual extended family Sunday roast dinner. Nicholas was still cross with her, making the barest effort to conceal his chagrin from the rest of his family. Still, for that she was grateful, if not ashamed.

'How awful!' Florence seemed shocked. She held the morning paper up, her wide eyes and raised eyebrows peeking above the newsprint. 'Listen to this. A man was hanged in Sydney yesterday for murdering fifteen babies and burying them in his own backyard. His name was John Makin. His wife, Sarah, received life imprisonment.' She lowered the paper. 'Why would anyone do something so despicable? I can't even begin to comprehend such evil.'

Lillian put her fork back on her plate. Her stomach had already been churning.

Florence continued: 'Says right here they were baby farmers. They took the babies in, pretending to look after them in exchange for payment. Some were murdered the very same day they were received.'

'Barbaric.' Jonathan shook his head with disgust. 'I read about that case when they found them back in March. Good job, I say.'

'Are you all right, dear?'

Lillian looked up to see Dorothy studying her with concern. 'You've gone quite pale.'

She forced herself to take another bite of meat. 'I'm fine, really.'

'Are you sure?'

Lillian winced. 'Yes, I am very well. There is no need for alarm or excitement. I simply had too much champagne last night.' It was easy to interpret her mother-in-law's hopeful expression. Dorothy wanted another grandchild. She threw a guilty look at her brooding husband.

'It's that unpleasant article, said Dorothy. 'Really, Florence. Must you read about atrocities at the table while we're trying to eat?'

Florence reluctantly folded up the pages and sighed. 'I wish I could be a policeman. Wouldn't it be exciting to run about solving crimes all day?'

'They're called policemen for a reason, dear sister,' said Nicholas. 'Men, not women.'

'The way those suffragists carry on, if they ever get their way we'll end up with a female prime minister!' Jonathan commented derisively. 'Why women want to bother themselves with politics, I'll never know.'

Florence picked up her plate and flounced off to the kitchen in protest.

'Stop teasing her,' Dorothy said. 'You know she's been attending those meetings.'

Lillian wished she could reach over and squeeze Nicholas's hand the way he had hers only last night. She, too, at Cora's insistence, had become interested in joining the movement.

'That girl will be the death of us,' Jonathan said. 'Thank goodness you have the shop now, Lillian. You've single-handedly managed to channel her energy into productive enterprise. I do hope the arrangement will last, at least until she finds herself a suitable husband.'

Lillian had to smile at that. Jonathan and Nicholas had both been cautious about the shop opening. With their heads for business, they had felt a store run by women was steering into dangerously uncharted waters. Still, their reaction to the Makin story did little to quell her old fears about discovery. She had enough work on her hands to keep the intrusive worries at bay, yet little reminders threatened to send waves through her newfound sense of contentment, recent arguments with Olivia aside.

She helped the maid, Lucy, gather the children's things and called out to Florence, who was still sulking in the kitchen, that they were leaving. Her sister-in-law came out and gave them all a kiss goodbye.

'You'll have to tell me all about the ball as soon as we get to the shop tomorrow, even though I don't want to hear about it because I'm so jealous.'

'I'm very sorry you weren't invited, Florence. I'm sure Cora didn't mean to be rude,' Lillian said, and squeezed Florence's hand. 'I promise I won't spare a single detail.'

'You might spare one or two,' Nicholas huffed beside her.

'What does that mean?' Florence asked.

Lillian rolled her eyes and shot Nicholas a warning look. 'I'll tell you tomorrow.'

She decided to wander over to Cora's that afternoon to offer an apology but was not looking forward to it. Mulling her argument with Olivia over and over wasn't helping and she felt she had to do something. Of course Cora would have been embarrassed by the spectacle. Lillian decided at the last minute to grab her sketchbook to take with her. Perhaps her friend would be more easily placated if she offered to make her a new gown free of charge? She could only hope Catherine had taken Sunday afternoon off. It would save her further mortification.

CHAPTER 30

FORGIVENESS

*A*rchie swung the door open before Lillian even had a chance to knock. He gazed down at her solemnly before his face creased into a smile. 'Ah, the prizefighter shows her face. Do I need to duck?'

She reddened and shuffled from foot to foot. 'Archie, I've come to apologise to you and Cora for my appalling behaviour last night.'

He threw back his head with laughter and slapped his thighs with his palms as if her contrition was the funniest thing he'd ever heard. 'Don't bother! Who hasn't had too many drinks and made a fool of themselves at least once in their life? You'll find my wife in the drawing-room. I'm off to Tattersall's. Cheerio.' He doffed his hat and strode past her, still chuckling. She didn't know whether to be cross or not.

'Is that you, Lillian?' Cora called out. 'Come through. Catherine's taken Alexander for a walk. They'll be back shortly. I'll have her make us some tea when she does.'

Lillian breathed out a sigh of relief and stepped around the corner. 'I thought she might have a half day's leave.'

'No, she tells me she prefers Saturdays. More to do about town, you know?' Cora waved her in to the drawing-room. 'You brought your book! You know, Lillian, you've really got to stop showing me your designs.' Cora pointed at a chair and sat opposite, snatching the book from Lillian's hands. She began flicking through the pages. 'Oh dear. Now I shall have to order another three dresses before all the other ladies get in front of me! Archie will probably get annoyed but, oh well.' Cora's tinkly laughter filled the room. 'Wasn't it a wonderful evening? You certainly were the belle of the ball.'

If she was feeling angry at Lillian's transgressions, she showed no sign of it. The questions kept barrelling on without waiting for answers. 'Which ones will show off my waist best, do you think? I've taken up cycling. Can you see a difference?'

Lillian held up her hands to put a halt to the onslaught. 'Cora, aren't you mad at me?'

Her friend paused. 'Mad? No, darling. The whole thing was hilarious. You really gave Olivia something to think about, didn't you? I fear the poor girl might have a black eye to complement her serpent tongue. Whatever did she say to make you so angry?'

Lillian relaxed into her seat, grateful another disaster had been averted. 'I wasn't completely honest when you asked me if I knew Olivia. She and I actually go a long way back. She is not my greatest admirer and she makes no secret of it.'

Cora ran an admiring finger lightly over one of the pictures. 'Oh dear, I didn't realise. You should have warned me. No wonder you were reluctant to accept my invitation. I'm the one who should be apologising to you.'

'No, that won't be necessary. I think Olivia and I were able to put our differences aside and call a truce. At least, I hope so.'

Cora gazed at her expectantly and Lillian reluctantly

realised her friend would not give up so easily. 'Were you school chums?'

'No, I'm three years older than she is.'

'I hadn't considered that.' Cora frowned. 'Then how?'

Lillian leaned forward and flicked a page over in the sketch-book. 'I'd really rather not talk about that nasty girl any more, except to say I can't believe her mother let her leave school to get married. She's scarcely eighteen. Now then, I brought my designs because I was hoping I could make you a dress to apologise for embarrassing you at the ball.'

'I thought you just said you'd called a truce with Olivia,' Cora said. She resumed poring over the illustrations.

Smiling with amusement, Lillian watched her before letting her gaze wander to the view of the garden that beckoned through the window. 'Doesn't mean I have to like her.'

Somewhere in the bowels of the house, a door banged shut and the sound of a child giggling travelled up the wide hallway.

Cora lifted her head and called out, 'Catherine and Alexander, is that you? Lillian's here.' Hurried footsteps sounded along the floorboards until the drawing-room door flew open and Catherine stood before them, her cheeks flushed from exertion.

Cora smiled. 'Oh good, I'm glad you're back. Could you please make us a pot of tea?' She returned to her perusal of the sketchbook while Lillian glanced up at her old, dear friend, embarrassed. Catherine merely shrugged with acceptance of the request and retreated to where she had come from. Lillian heard her bark an order at Alexander to pick up his boots and put them away. How she wished she could follow her old friend to spend an hour in the kitchen sharing stories and laughing at the expectations employers had. She hoped Jemima, her own employee, had only good things to say about her. She tried her best to be as reasonable as possible.

In the meantime, Cora had reached the end of the book. 'This looks interesting. Why do you have one folded up and tucked away inside the cover?'

Lillian frowned and turned to see what Cora was talking about. She dropped her cup to its saucer with a clatter. Her friend had unfolded the picture and was closely scrutinising it. She'd forgotten to take it out of the sketchbook and hide it in the tobacco tin at the shop. She hadn't been thinking straight at the time but it was no excuse. How could she have been so stupid?

'I don't understand. But that's uncanny.' Cora raised her head, her finger hovering over the tiny figure on the grass. 'Is that a baby?'

Lillian hadn't looked at the picture since she'd folded it up. A corner must have been poking out. She watched as Cora peered again at the infant, his legs kicking in the air, the port-wine stain clearly visible. At the time of painting, Lillian had done her best to remember the correct shape to capture it as perfectly as possible.

'Why, my Alexander has one exactly the same!' Cora looked up at Lillian with confusion.

As if he'd magically heard his name, Alexander appeared at the door. 'Mummy! We saw turtles in the lake.'

Catherine re-entered and caught him up in her arms. 'I'm sorry, Ma'am. I didn't mean for him to rush in.'

Cora dismissed the apology with a distracted wave of her hand. She was still staring straight at Lillian. 'When did you draw this?' she demanded.

Catherine stood puzzled with her hand in Alexander's and craned her neck to see what Cora was pointing at. Lillian heard her breathe out heavily and felt utter dismay. Her paintings had got them both into trouble before and now it seemed misfortune had resurfaced again.

'Is that –?' Catherine asked.

Lillian nodded, feeling dismal. She saw Catherine's teeth clench, with fury or fear it was impossible to decipher.

'You haven't answered my question,' Cora insisted.

'I painted it a long time ago,' she said quietly, watching Cora's every move as she slowly folded up the picture and replaced it inside the folio cover.

Lillian flinched when Cora set it down on the table and abruptly shoved it away. Her carefree, enthusiastic friend now sat before her like a maiden carved from ice, hands clasped tightly in her lap.

'How do you know?' Cora demanded.

Lillian's mouth was dry. 'It's hard to explain.'

'It's not. How do you happen to know the circumstances in which he was born?'

Lillian fiddled with her glove and looked up at Catherine for reassurance but there wasn't any. Realisation appeared to be dawning on Catherine's face as she pieced together a long-forgotten admission Lillian had made. *I've done a terrible thing.*

Lillian could have admitted to being the maid who'd taken newborn Alexander at the Shaw's to change his napkin, however humiliating the admission would be, but that would not explain the wistful scene she had painted. She took a deep breath. 'I was in Dutton Park the day Alexander was born.' Admitting the words out loud lifted a heavy stone from her chest.

'You were?' Cora unconsciously reached for her son. He pulled himself from Catherine's grasp and ran to his mother. The chilly tone that had descended between the women was making him anxious.

Lillian continued. 'Yes. I was minding my own business painting and enjoying some peace and quiet. I heard a strange noise and looked up to see a woman almost fully hidden behind some trees. I didn't know what to do so I waited for a long time, until she got up and left. I went to the spot where she had been lying and found him.'

'But you weren't the one who brought him to the Diamantina, were you? The custodians told me it was two women, a mother and a daughter, who brought him in. Apparently he was in a terrible state, covered in ant bites. The daughter said Alexander's birth mother had thrown him at her and fled.'

Lillian quivered. 'We couldn't afford another mouth to feed and my sister's husband would never allow –'

'You could have taken him there yourself, or to a church, or even knocked on the door of any house close by to ask for help,' Cora shouted.

'No. You obviously don't understand, Cora. I couldn't.'

'You need to leave.'

'Fine!'

'I think I can finally see why Olivia doesn't like you.' Cora's face had turned white and her teeth clenched. 'Catherine, show Mrs Hamilton out. I pity your poor husband and his family when they get wind of this.'

Lillian gasped. 'I beg you not to tell them.'

'Why shouldn't I?' Cora turned her head away.

Lillian felt panicked. She stood and clutched her sketchbook under her arm. Why wouldn't the little boy stop staring at her? Catherine remained silent.

'You have to understand something, Cora,' she pleaded. 'He's not mine.'

'I know,' Cora snapped.

'You do?' It was Lillian's turn to be confused.

'That doesn't make what you did any more excusable.'

In the face of Cora's disgust there was nothing left to do except rush toward the front door and leave. At the threshold she turned back one last time and called out. 'I had no other choice.'

Cora appeared in the hallway, wrapped her arms around her son and buried her face in his soft hair. She wouldn't say another word.

CHAPTER 31

DESPAIR

*L*illian grasped wildly at Catherine's sleeve as she was led beyond the front gate. 'Catherine, I –'

'Calm down, hen. I'll have a word when she settles down. Yer cannae expect her to understand whit it was like. Yer've come up in this world, Lillian, but the past will always be there waiting to trip yer up.'

Lillian used her handkerchief to wipe her eyes and sniffed with self pity. 'You don't think I'm despicable? I know I think it about myself. I've held on to that secret for so long. Now that it's out, I'll probably lose everything.'

Catherine clutched Lillian's shoulders and forced her to look up. 'Why dinnae yer tell me about it the day it happened? I think I remember the one. Yer said ye'd done something terrible and I teased yer. I thought yer were joking.' Catherine shook her head and glanced back at the house. Her expression softened. 'Yer've done some dubious things, Lillian Betts, that's for sure. It's taken me a long time to forgive yer. Yer've not had it easy. I remember the stories yer told me about Alfred and

Patricia.' She frowned. 'Yer were telling me the truth about them, weren't yer?'

Lillian nodded furiously. 'Yes!'

'Very well. I believe yer. Under the circumstances I wouldnae have wanted to bring a wee bairn back into that argumentative house either. We both know yer could scarcely have brought him to Rosemead. Where would we have put him? In a basket under our beds? Despite Mrs Shaw running her holier-than-thou Ladies' Committee, I thoroughly doubt she'd want to be responsible for bringing up someone else's bastard. Not when she's had three perfectly healthy, spoiled children of her own.'

'I should have taken him to the orphanage, like Cora said.' A fresh flood of tears erupted.

Catherine shrugged. 'Well, yer panicked and yer didnae. Everything is as it should be now. Wee Alexander is precisely where he was always meant to be, with a mother who loves him very much. Give Cora time and she'll come around to seeing it as we do. She's no fool.'

Lillian looked fearfully up at the wintry apparition staring down from the drawing-room window. 'She's going to tell Dorothy all about it. Nicholas will hate me and then what shall I do?'

Catherine chuckled.

'What's so funny?'

'Cora Miles loves new dresses almost as much as she loves that child. I'll be willing to bet she says nothing at all. Nobody else seems able to compliment her figure in quite the way yer and Florence do.'

Cora slid the sash window up, her face stormy. 'Catherine, come inside.'

Catherine gave Lillian's hand a quick pat. 'I'd best do as I'm told. I've not got the patience for losing another job. Take care for now.'

Lillian watched her go inside to soothe her employer's temper. There was nothing left to do but walk home in defeat.

CHAPTER 32

WHYNOT STREET

*L*illian returned from Cora's and went straight to her bed. There she lay for two days, feeling completely bereft. The pain she felt over Cora's rejection released a fresh surge of longing for Patricia. Nicholas's frosty silence turned to concern when Jemima returned to the kitchen with a plate of untouched dinner. He climbed the stairs and entered the room, stopping abruptly at the end of the bed.

'Fine, Lillian, look. You mustn't continue to sulk. What's done is done. Today's gossip is tomorrow's chip paper. All you need to do is wait until the next drama erupts and your little outburst at the ball will be forgotten.' He folded his arms across his chest as if sure his wisdom would make her rise and tell him that of course, how silly she was being, after all.

She did not have enough strength to argue. He didn't know about Cora's dismissal of her and she couldn't bear to tell him.

Nicholas crouched beside the bed and gently stroked her hair back from her face. 'What is it, dear, troubling you so badly? Surely nothing is so irreparable that we can't work it out?'

'Oh, it is. It is!' She began to wail and turned to stifle her cries in the pillow.

'For heaven's sake, Lillian.' Nicholas's voice rose with frustration. 'I can't help you if you won't tell me what it is!'

Her words were muffled by the pillow. 'My sketchbook.'

'What about the sketchbook?'

But that was all. He could not get another word from her.

Later, Lillian overheard him in the foyer talking with Florence in hushed tones.

'I came over to see if Lillian was here. She hasn't come to the shop,' said Florence.

'You'd better come in,' Nicholas replied.

'Is everything all right?'

'I'm stumped. She's melancholic. Said something about her sketchbook but I've flipped through it and there's nothing in there except pages full of dress designs. I can't see why those would cause her such distress. Perhaps you could try talking to her.'

So he hadn't checked inside the cover? Lillian sighed at the sound of the stairs creaking. She didn't want to see anybody, especially Florence and her gentle, caring face. Why wouldn't they leave her alone?

There was a light tapping at the door. 'Lillian, it's me. May I come in?'

Lillian's temple pounded. She didn't care if she didn't see anybody ever again.

Florence peered into the gloom and wrinkled her nose. With a shut window and curtains drawn, the air had turned stale. 'Oh dear.' She picked her way through a trail of discarded clothes and boots until she reached the bed.

Lillian felt a gentle press on her shoulder. She rolled over and stared dolefully at her sister-in-law. 'My life is over, Flo.'

Florence perched on the edge of the bed stared balefully down at her. 'Are you thinking about your sister and nephew again?'

Lillian began to nod then changed her mind and shook her head.

'Nicholas told me you'd been involved in an argument at the party. Is that what you're worried about? Did that woman hurt you in some way?' She lowered her voice. 'Are you embarrassed?'

Again, she shook her head.

Florence spoke a little more firmly. 'Please tell me what's happened to cause you such distress. You know the old saying; a problem shared is a problem halved.'

Lillian turned to burrow her face back into her pillow before resurfacing to take a deep breath. 'I mustn't burden you. You'll hate me for ever, the same as Cora does. I'm a terrible person and you'll all be better off without me. I destroy everything and lose everyone.' Her body was racked with sobs that frightened Florence back to standing. 'Nicholas will throw me out when he discovers what I did.'

Filled with self-pity, Lillian knew she didn't deserve Florence's sympathy but it took a moment to realise her sister-in-law had stopped offering soothing words to console her. She looked up to see Florence had begun to pace across the room from the door to the bed, as though undecided whether to stay or flee.

Suddenly Florence stopped and whispered in a voice so quiet Lillian wasn't sure she was hearing correctly: 'I think I know what it might be.'

Lillian stiffened.

'There's something I've been wanting to ask you for so long

but I've not dared,' Florence continued. 'I have often wondered if I should have asked when you first came to work for us except it never seemed the right time. You were so nervous about making mistakes but you proved to be such a hard worker. Now, you're so talented and we're doing very well with our shop. You know I love working with you.' She looked down and picked off a stray hair that had fallen from her bun on to her jacket. 'Seeing you lying here though, so disturbed by your troubles, I think the time has come.'

Lillian replied with a monotone she didn't bother to keep low. 'What is it you think you know?'

Florence pulled the folded picture from her belt. 'I found your painting. The scene is very familiar. I recognised it as Dutton Park as soon as I saw it because Mama and I go up there to visit Molly's grave sometimes. We went one Sunday to visit Molly's grave very soon after she died. Nicholas refused to come. You see, his grief had overwhelmed him.'

Lillian stared at the ceiling, motionless. Had he lain in a darkened room without hope in the same way she was?

Florence became more confident about telling her story. 'Mama said someone had to take fresh flowers to lay on the burial plot since Molly's own family lived so far away in England. The responsibility fell to Mama and me to honour her memory. We arrived at the cemetery and Mama began to pull out the weeds that had already begun to crop up. She wanted to stay and reflect for a while so I asked her if I could take a little walk.' Florence's voice grew wistful and she returned to sit beside Lillian as she continued. 'She said I could, as long as I didn't stray too far...' Florence turned and stared at Lillian. 'And that's when I saw someone crouching in front of a wrapped-up bundle on the ground. She saw me, too, and came running at me so fast I was frozen to the spot. I'd never been so terrified in my life. She threw a baby into my arms.'

Lillian shivered against the sheets.

'I didn't see her face,' Florence said. 'She'd covered herself up. I thought the girl must be his mother but she ran away so quickly, even though I screamed at her to stop. I didn't think it would be possible to run so fast after having given birth.'

'What did you do with him?' Lillian murmured.

'I was worried he might already be dead but then an ant wriggled out of his blanket and scuttled right up inside his nostril and he sneezed. The poor mite had bites all over his face. I cuddled him for a moment and then I took him straight back to Mama,' said Florence. She scratched at the skin on her wrist, lost in the memory.

Lillian watched her closely, not daring to interrupt.

Florence blinked. 'Mama checked him over to make sure he wasn't hurt. We decided to take him home and wash him up. I thought we should keep him but Mama said we couldn't. You see, we had Stephen newly born as well and he wasn't doing very well without his mother's milk. How could we possibly take in another? Papa told us to take the baby back up to the Diamantina so we did. The matron had little choice but to accept him once we told her what had happened. Mama made enquiries about a week later because I kept asking her if she thought he would be all right. The matron told us a married couple had adopted him two days later. It was such a relief to hear the news.' Florence bit her lip. 'The thing is, it's been so many months and that woman at the park could have been anyone. Forgive me if I'm wrong, Lillian, but I've thought for so long she looked exactly like you.'

Lillian's mind churned. She was so tired of keeping secrets. Her body ached with them. 'You were right. It was me,' she admitted.

Florence nodded. She seemed relieved. 'Lillian... was he your baby?'

Lillian sat up. 'No! I've never had a baby. Like you, I was in the park that day minding my own business, painting a scene of the river. I saw a woman hiding behind the trees and could tell she was in labour. I didn't know what to do. I'm not as brave as you, Florence. I shouldn't have left you with him but I couldn't take the baby home with me. Alfred, he –'

Florence placed a gentle hand on Lillian's arm. 'It's all right. Nicholas has told me a little.'

Lillian nodded. 'We'd become poor. My sister already had her own children to look after and I was only a housemaid. The woman I argued with at the ball at the weekend was Olivia Shaw, my employers' daughter and a more spiteful girl I've yet to encounter.' Lillian sat up and grabbed Florence. 'I've always regretted my decision. I prayed you would know what to do. You had some money. I could tell by the clothes you were wearing. Do you think me a terrible person?'

Florence smiled, leaned in and kissed her cheek. 'I think you are a sister to me, Lillian.'

'Why are you so good to me? I'm so afraid Nicholas won't feel the same.'

Florence gave her a stern look. 'Then you don't know my brother. He loves you dearly. Anybody can tell.'

Lillian let out a deep breath and pulled Florence into a hug. The girl had given her hope.

'I know who has the baby,' she said.

'You do?' Florence pulled back to stare at her with wonder.

'Yes. Cora is the one who adopted him. His name is Alexander.'

'No!' Florence gasped.

Lillian grinned, despite herself. 'It's true.'

'Well then, isn't he the luckiest boy in the world?' Florence smiled back.

Florence was right. It was time for Lillian to shrug off her despair, rise and get dressed for work. If Cora couldn't forgive her, it was something she would simply have to learn to accept. Fortune had definitely favoured the child.

CHAPTER 33

NEW DISCOVERIES

'*O*i, come and have a look at this!'

Lillian and Florence took their feet off their sewing machine pedals at the sound of the man's shout.

'What do you think that's about?' Florence asked, staring at the back door.

Lillian rushed outside to see. One of the builders was crouched beside a hole he'd been digging, his shovel flung on the ground beside him. Nicholas hovered above, trying to peer in and see what the man was pointing at.

'What do you reckon it could be?' The man lifted a corner of the mud-clogged fabric.

Florence appeared at Lillian's shoulder. She seemed excited. 'Buried treasure! What is it?'

Lillian raised her hands to her throat. All the saliva had completely dried up.

'Let me have a look.' Nicholas knelt beside the hole. With his hands he reached inside and dug around the bundle of decaying cloth to lift it out and place it on the ground. He, too, partially lifted the covering.

Lillian's saw black pinpoints at the periphery of her vision. Her husband had forgiven her for what she had done at Dutton Park as Florence said he would, when she had felt brave enough to share the story with him. The small package in his hands was another matter entirely.

'What is it?' The builder asked.

'It's...' Nicholas dropped the edge of the fabric and scooped the bundle up. 'I'll sort it out. You carry on with the job.'

'Righto, if you're sure?' The builder wiped his brow with his sleeve.

'Of course.' Nicholas struggled from where he had been kneeling to stand, holding the large bundle at arm's length. Lillian watched him closely as he turned, bewildered, and faced her.

'What is it?' Florence asked.

Nicholas snapped back to attention. 'Something that certainly doesn't belong here.'

Lillian pushed Florence out of her path and bolted for the front door. Her lungs seared as she raced down the road towards the wharf. Sunlight danced on the rippled water as she approached.

Nicholas shouted at her to stop running but she would not. That look of horror in his eyes!

She stumbled down the bank and scrambled desperately about for some rocks, enough to fill her pockets and blouse. She tripped under the weight of them, scraping her palms on dead branches protruding like limbs from the mud, clutching and tugging at her. She managed to pull herself back up the slope and stagger out on to the wharf.

'Lillian, please wait.'

She turned back to see Nicholas had almost caught up. He slipped on the grass in his haste but managed to keep his footing.

'Don't come any closer! Please,' she sobbed, stepping towards the edge.

'What are you doing?' Nicholas raised his palms above his head and spun around with frustration.

Lillian took another step back. 'It's all my fault. Everything is my fault. I'm sorry. I wish I could have told you everything.'

'Darling, there's no need for this. Come here.'

Lillian groaned with shame.

'You're my wife and I love you.'

Lillian took another step toward the edge of the wharf and peered into the water. 'Alfred and Patricia. What you found. They ran a baby farm...'

'Listen. I don't know what's going through your mind.' Nicholas spoke with urgency. 'When Catherine brought you to the hotel that first time we met, I couldn't believe my luck. You gave me something else to think about during my trip to London. I wondered what you were doing all the time. You've been let down by the very people who should have loved you the most. Lillian, I want to love you the way you deserve to be loved.'

She swayed with indecision. The stones in her pockets were very heavy.

'Stay there, don't move. I'll come and get you.' Nicholas called out. He edged closer, set a foot on the wharf.

Panic made her dizzy. She wanted so badly to believe him. He was almost close enough to reach out and grab hold of her.

'Please, Lillian, take my hand.'

He frightened her with a sudden lunge. Lillian stepped back but her boot met with nothing but air. The water when she hit it felt shockingly cold and knocked the breath from her lungs. The rocks dragged her under. Screaming for oxygen, she struggled fruitlessly to break the surface.

It was over. She ached for her sister and Thomas. Her

mother, too, as the sun threw fingers of light in the silty water above her head. As consciousness faded, Lillian felt an overwhelming sense of peace envelope her.

Sharp pain distracted her as strong hands tugged at her floating hair. She gasped in a lungful of air as Nicholas roughly hoisted her from the water. He clawed at her blouse and pockets, ripping buttons off and hurling rocks away. 'I've got you, Lillian.'

She sprawled across the wooden boards of the wharf and coughed up water. It kept coming, threatened to choke her anew until at last there was no more.

Nicholas laid down alongside and hugged her tightly. 'You can't leave, Lillian. Please don't leave.'

To her shock, she realised he was crying into her soaking collar, and then she understood. He'd already lost one wife. Their first meeting came into sharp focus; he'd had the despair of a man who'd lost everything. It had taken so much of his effort to contribute to the conversation. Had she really been about to put him through so much misery all over again?

'I'm so sorry, Nicholas. I didn't want anything to do with it. Patricia thought she could make some money caring for other people's babies. Stephen did so well, but Alfred made her take on too many more. I tried to get away. The apprenticeship at your parents' store was my ticket out. I thought it would be all right to turn the cottage into a dress shop and make good memories to get rid of the bad ones.' She pushed her wet hair from her face and opened up to Nicholas about all the time spent with her laudanum-reliant sister, the train trip up to Bundaberg, all the silent, sleeping babies, some of whom had died. She took another deep breath and told him about leaving Georgina's tiny body for her sister to take care of. Lastly, she told him about Alice's real identity and the woman who had only a few days ago come looking for her.

Nicholas listened intently and didn't interrupt until she had finished.

'Will I be hanged?' she gasped.

'What? No!'

'But the bag you found...'

Nicholas glowered at the water, which had so nearly claimed her. He bunched his fist and banged it over and over into the soft mud. Finally he peered at her. 'I think I have a solution, Lillian, but I fear you will not be able to stand it.'

Lillian gulped but forced herself to meet his gaze. 'What is it?'

'There's a woman somewhere in this city who has lost as much as you through no fault of her own except falling in love with the wrong man. You have the one thing in the world that is most precious to her.'

Lillian's eyes widened. 'Stop it. I don't want to hear any more.'

Nicholas was sombre. 'It will break my heart as much as yours but Alice is the price to pay. It is the right thing to do.'

'I can't lose her, Nicholas.' Lillian clutched at him, aghast. 'Alice is mine. I love her.'

'I love her, too, but that young woman is her real mother and she is mourning a daughter who is alive and well. Alice is so young she won't remember if you do it now. If what that mother said to you in the shop is true, then it is the only thing we can to do to find forgiveness for the past.'

Lillian clung to Nicholas and sobbed. 'I can't lose her.'

Nicholas hugged her. 'I'll be right there with you.'

She was so full of fear. 'What about the bones you found?'

Nicholas levelled his gaze at her. 'There aren't any bones. The bag is full of opals and gold nuggets.'

Lillian blinked. 'It is? Alfred mentioned the cottage and a bag when he... never mind. Is this what he meant?'

'Looks like Alfred was racketeering,' suggested Nicholas. 'That scoundrel Fergus was probably in on it for a lark.'

'How could he do such a thing and leave his own family at risk of starving?'

'He's at the Dunwich Asylum for good. What punishment can the law give him to exceed what has already been dished out?' Nicholas held her to his chest. 'I'm not prepared to lose you, Lillian. We are partners. I'll take the goods to the police and be done with it.'

Lillian looked beyond the wharf to the murky water flowing past. Those babies, her sister and nephew had been living, breathing beings as worthy of somebody's love as she was. She was free to atone for the past.

CHAPTER 34

ATONEMENT

*F*rom her hiding place behind the curtain, Lillian saw Emily hesitate at the gate before continuing up the path. Some days earlier, she had waited until she knew Catherine would be shopping at the market and had met her there to ask her if she knew where Cora's last house-maid was. Catherine, sighing with eternal patience, had told her. She had also said Cora was still smarting. Lillian told her Florence had been the one she had seen at the park that day and she, with her mother, had taken Alexander to the orphanage. Catherine promised to pass the information on to Cora, for whatever worth it might be. There was one bright moment to glean from their conversation. Catherine told Lillian she had finally agreed to marry Arthur. Relieved to hear some happy news, Lillian had headed straight to the post office, too determined to set the wheels of her ghastly task in motion to waste any time worrying about Cora. She sent a telegram to Emily asking her to pay her and Nicholas a visit.

Lillian didn't blame the girl for being suspicious. As she

opened the front door, Emily flinched with immediate recognition.

'It's you.'

'Yes, it's me,' Lillian replied. 'Please, won't you come in?'

Emily's eyes darted back to the street. 'Why did you ask me to come?'

'Actually, there is something I wish to do for you.'

'But you said at the dress shop on Montague Road you didn't know me.'

'I know. It was wrong. I was afraid.'

'Afraid?'

'Please won't you come in?'

Her curiosity piqued, Emily gingerly stepped over the threshold, still mistrustful, and followed Lillian into the parlour. She stopped at the sight of Nicholas standing in the middle of the room holding a little girl in his arms. Her eyes riveted on to Alice before flashing back to Lillian. 'Well, out with it, then.'

Lillian didn't blame her for being so blunt. 'The day you came to my shop...' She paused and looked to her husband for support. Nicholas nodded, willing her to stay brave. She swallowed and continued. 'I wasn't honest with you and for that I would like to apologise.'

Emily frowned. 'What do you mean?'

'I'm very sorry but I told you that your baby died in the flood with my sister.'

Emily gaze returned to Alice as though she was examining a foreign specimen. 'Is she..?'

A wave of terror engulfed Lillian at the enormity of what she had to do. All she could do was nod with humiliation.

Nicholas ventured forward and held Alice out. She could see he was in pain.

Emily lifted her arms instinctively to receive the child. She paused as Alice looked back at Nicholas with bewilderment, before giving in to relief as she pressed her nose into her daughter's hair and inhaled the sacred scent of her. 'My baby! I knew you were alive. I knew it.'

'We love her,' Nicholas said, wrapping a protective arm around Lillian, 'but she belongs with you.'

Lillian blanched as Emily approached. 'Do you despise me?'

Emily shook her head.

Alice reached for the only mother she had ever known and grizzled when Lillian made no move to take her back.

Emily clutched the squirming child tightly.

Lillian finally reached out to sweep one of Alice's curls behind her sweet little ear. 'Goodbye, my darling Alice. Never forget how much I love you.' She placed her lips on her baby's soft cheek and gently squeezed her hand.

Emily faltered.

Nicholas stepped forward and guided her to the door.

Emily took a last look back at Lillian. 'Thank you,' she mouthed and left with her precious bundle.

Nicholas led Lillian upstairs to their bedroom and helped her lie down on their quilt. He stroked her hair as she soaked her pillow with a torrent of tears. Beyond the grief, the shame she'd been carrying for so long began to unfurl. Why did the price of freedom have to be so dear?

CHAPTER 35

RESTORATION

*T*he bell jangled above the entrance and Lillian looked up, holding several pins between her lips. Cora Miles stood silhouetted against the bright daylight. Dropping her work and removing the pins to stick them in their cushion, Lillian reluctantly stood to greet her and braced for what she felt was surely going to be another admonition. Her soul had been scoured. She didn't know if she would be able to care.

Cora crossed the floor in four strides and wrapped her arms around Lillian in a tight embrace. Lillian stood paralysed with confusion. Cora squeezed her tighter so she lifted her arms to return the hug. Finally Lillian was released as Cora took a step back to gaze at her.

'You did an incredible deed yesterday, Lillian Hamilton. I'm so sorry for your loss. Emily paid me a visit and explained everything. I cannot tell you what it means.'

Lillian felt lightheaded. 'She did? Did she want to take Alexander as well?'

Cora grabbed her hand. 'Come, sit down.'

Lillian let her friend lead her to a chair beside the workbench.

Florence looked up from her work. 'Shall I leave?'

'No. Please stay, Florence. Catherine told me what you did for Alexander. You are one of the people I have to thank for giving me my son,' Cora said and took a deep breath. 'Lillian, Alexander is mine. Archie and I formally adopted him. Emily understands I am not giving him back.'

Lillian nodded, her shoulders slumping with relief.

'I treated you too harshly the other day. Do you think you are the only one with a difficult past? My grandparents lost everything in the potato famine. They came to Australia with nothing. My mother was a maid before she met my father.'

Lillian blinked with surprise.

Cora continued. 'Why do you think the likes of Olivia and Mary treat us the way they do? They think they're better than us for all the wrong reasons. They might have been born with silver spoons in their mouths but we're the smart ones, Lillian, the fighters. We worked hard and we married well to get to where we are. We've earned every good thing that has ever happened to us.'

Lillian nodded with the truth of it.

'I hope you will forgive me for reacting so badly when I saw your painting. Catherine has told me what it was like working for the Shaws.' Cora scowled. 'She told me about Donald... and Fergus.'

'Catherine obviously cannot hold her tongue.'

'Yes, perhaps you're right. But she told me you were one of the best friends she'd ever had in her life.'

'She did?'

'And after I came down off my high horse, I had to agree with her.'

Lillian bowed her head with relief.

'I'd like to tell you both more about Alexander,' said Cora.

Florence intuitively strode to the door, turned the sign over to read "closed" and returned to the table.

'You see, when I saw your painting, it was exactly the way I had imagined everything. Emily used to be one of my house-maids, apprenticed from the Diamantina. It took me a while to notice what was happening to her, several months, in fact. She did her best to hide her condition from me but eventually it was impossible not to notice. I'll admit I was jealous when I under-stood. I'd wanted a baby for three years and had not been blessed. Here was a girl who had the one thing I hoped for but instead hers was a source of shame. I could have thrown her out. She wouldn't tell me who the father was. She never gave him up but I wasn't stupid. I knew my husband had become infatuated with her.'

'You think Archie is Alexander's father?'

'How can he not be? You've seen the child. My husband loves me, Lillian. I know he does. I will not divorce him.' Cora raised her hands helplessly and let them drop in her lap. 'When Emily was almost at full term she returned from her Sunday afternoon off and seemed changed. It took another two days for me to be sure: such is the nature of a woman's belly after birth. When I realised she had indeed delivered, I confronted her on the baby's whereabouts and she confessed she had gone to the park to have him.'

'Oh!' Florence gasped.

'I'll admit it's not the easiest story to hear,' said Cora. 'Emily told me she had stolen a pound note from my purse in the hope somebody would take him home and buy him some milk. As soon as she had finished speaking, I called for the buggy and made her go with me to the park. When we got to the spot she had described, the baby was no longer there. I was extremely worried. We searched that whole park looking for him before we crossed over to the orphanage, hoping someone might have taken him there. When I enquired with the matron, there he was; a baby with a birthmark, just as Emily had described. They let me take him home and I made her feed him. She was grateful to be able to hold her child and keep her job.'

'You have a heart of gold,' said Florence.

'But I don't, you see.' Cora gave a wry smile. 'I didn't do any of it for Emily. She did a foolish thing leaving him in the park and taking my money but she was young and afraid. How could I let her throw away something I so dearly wanted? I searched for that baby so I could be the one to keep him.' She glanced at Lillian. 'It's time I told you the truth. I knew who you were as soon as I stepped into this store. I remembered you as a maid at Edith Shaw's ladies' luncheon.'

Lillian flinched. 'Why didn't you say?'

'And embarrass you? It was clear you had been working hard to better yourself. I let your workmanship speak for itself. Besides, do you think I enjoyed sitting in the Shaw drawing-room listening to simpering Edith any more than you did? No! I did it for the babies and children at the Diamantina. You see, Archie stayed with me. I got everything I wanted. When Alexander was old enough to survive without his mother's milk, I wrote Emily a reference and let her go. I worried she would make a fuss about leaving Alexander behind but I think she understood he had a better chance at life with Archie and me. I was annoyed when I heard she'd got herself into the same condition all over again. But then again, she is a very pretty girl. At least Archie wasn't the father the second time. She eventually married the father and he's an honest wharfie.'

Lillian sighed. 'I miss Alice so much I feel as though I can't breathe.'

Cora patted her hand consolingly. 'I know you do, dear

friend. We need to take your mind off this tragic matter somehow. Please, show me your new designs again. I've come to
spend my husband's money on at least three new dresses.
Summer is right around the corner. You and I, and Florence
too, if you like, have plenty of soirées ahead of us to enjoy.'

Lillian stood, went to a nearby shelf and pushed several jars
aside. She returned with her battered tin and opened it. The
bank note sprang up. 'Cora, this belongs to Alexander.'

'It does?'

'I took it that day I found Alexander at the park. I wanted
to buy something nice for myself because I had nothing. I've
wanted to throw it in the fire many times since but it wasn't
mine to get rid of.'

Cora closed her hands around Lillian's. 'Keep it. He
already has plenty. You shall buy something nice for yourself to
celebrate our friendship: a gift from me. Speaking of gifts, there
is something special I would like you to make.'

Lillian put the lid back on the tin and returned it to the
shelf. As she listened to Cora's plan an idea popped into her
mind. She knew exactly what she was going to use the
money for.

CHAPTER 36

CELEBRATION

*L*illian smiled broadly at Catherine when she answered the door.

Catherine grinned back, bemused. 'Come in, hen. Mrs Miles is expecting yer.'

'I imagine she is.'

Catherine eyed the parcel. 'Goodness. When will that woman stop? She's outdone herself this time.'

'Is that Lillian?' Cora called out. 'Oh good! Catherine, bring her through.'

Cora grabbed the package as soon as Lillian entered the drawing-room, wasting no time unwrapping it and lifting up the first two garments to admire. 'They're gorgeous. Catherine, please come here for a moment.'

'Tea, ma'am?'

'Not yet. Quickly now.'

Lillian raised her gloved hand to her lips to suppress a smile as Catherine obliged the urgent request.

'What do you think of this one?' Cora held up the last dress in the pile. The deep blue linen was lined with a silver thread that picked up the light. It was the latest fashion.

Catherine nodded. 'It's bonny, Mrs Miles.'

Cora dashed a quick grin at Lillian before returning her attention to her maid.

'Do you really like it?'

'Aye, of course. Yer have excellent taste. Yer'll make the other ladies jealous with that one.'

'Wonderful, dear Catherine. That is just what I wanted to hear. In this instance, though, it is you who will be making the ladies jealous. This one is for you.'

'Me?'

Lillian stepped forward. 'Yes, you. Cora and I want to thank you.'

Catherine's usually cynical eyes filled up with tears and she brushed them away with embarrassment. Her face shone with delight. 'Och, no, yer cannae be!'

'Yes!' Cora said with glee. 'You're about to be married. A bride should feel special on her wedding day and your Arthur is a very lucky man. I'm going to miss having you in my house, Catherine, but I truly hope you will continue to count me as a friend.'

Lillian left her friends to try on their new gowns. She felt warm inside and happy, too. Arriving home, she found Nicholas with their two boys sitting in the parlour beneath her framed picture of the special day at the Windmill. They were reading the battered copy of her favourite childhood story, *Pinocchio*. Stephen and Peter loved it as much as she had when her mother had read it to her and Patricia. Lillian wandered in and lightly caressed the newest adornment placed on the mantelpiece, pleased with her decision. It had been worth paying for it with Cora's pound note. The silver frame held one of her most prized possessions: a small photo of Patricia, their mother, Alice, and herself. Peter giggled as she squashed on to the sofa beside him and picked up her needle-work. Deep inside her abdomen, a moth batted its wings. She craned her neck to plant a kiss on her husband's cheek then began to stitch. Before long, the outline of a little bootie took shape.

There she was with a new secret, a good one – one ready to share soon enough.

Dear reader,

We hope you enjoyed reading *Every Year I Am Here*. Please take a moment to leave a review, even if it's a short one. Your opinion is important to us.

Discover more books by Joanna Beresford at https://www.nextchapter.pub/authors/joanna-beresford

Want to know when one of our books is free or discounted? Join the newsletter at http://eepurl.com/bqqB3H

Best regards,

Joanna Beresford and the Next Chapter Team

ACKNOWLEDGMENTS

Thank you to the very helpful librarian at State Library of Queensland. When I whispered I was going to write a historical novel, you looked delighted and went out of your way to track down a rich variety of sources for me.

Anna Kanowski, Emily Halloran and Alex Clark, your enthusiasm for reading my draft and sharing constructive criticism provided invaluable assistance. Janice Barrie, here's to many more moments of hilarity as you continue to educate me on the finer points of the noble Glaswegian accent. Glynis Scrivens and Terry Hughes, thank you, too, for whipping my words into shape with your superior attention to detail.

Helen Goltz, your down-to-earth approach, generosity and willingness to take a chance with this story has made this whole endeavour a wonderful experience and I thank you very much. Miika Hannila, I am indebted to you for publishing this second edition in order to take this story to new heights.

Ben, Katelyn, Luke and Cameron, you share your life with a wife and mother whose head resides mostly in the clouds. I couldn't be more grateful.

ABOUT THE AUTHOR

Award-winning author, Joanna Beresford, holds a BA in English Literature and a Graduate Diploma of Secondary Teaching.

Currently studying a Masters by Research in Creative Arts at CQ University, Joanna loves spending time with her family, travelling, and writing up a storm.

She is the author of the non-fiction title *The Last Link*, and her prize-winning short stories have been published in local and international publications. *Every Year I Am Here* is Joanna's first fiction title.

Read Joanna's blog and connect with her at:
Website: http://www.joannaberesford.com/
Facebook: https://www.facebook.com/theenglishnut/
Instagram: https://www.instagram.com/theenglishnut1/
Twitter @TheEnglishNut1

Printed in Great Britain
by Amazon

73950151R00196